Praise for the Work of Richard A. Knaak

"an accomplished author"
—Fantasy Faction

"Richard Knaak's fiction has the magic touch of making obviously fantastic characters and places come alive, seem real, and matter to the reader. That's the essential magic of all storytelling, and Richard does deftly, making his stories always engaging and worth picking up and reading. And then re-reading.
—Ed Greenwood, creator of the Forgotten Realms®

"Full of energy.... Great world building [and] memorable characters... It's easy to see why Richard has enjoyed so much success!"
—New York Times Bestselling author R.A. Salvatore

"Richard's novels are well-written, adventure-filled, action-packed!"
—New York Times bestselling author Margaret Weis

"Endlessly inventive. Knaak's ideas just keep on coming!"
—Glen Cook, author of Chronicles of the Black Company

"a writer of vast imagination and great skill, such that readers should make themselves familiar with his work"
—SFRevu

Diablo

Legacy of Blood
Kingdom of Shadow
Moon of the Spider

The Sin War:

Vol. I – Birthright
Vol. II – Scales of the Serpent
Vol. III – The Veiled Prophet

Dragonlance

The Legend of Huma
Kaz the Minotaur
Land of the Minotaurs
Reavers of the Blood Sea
The Citadel

The Minotaur Wars:
Vol. I – Night of Blood
Vol. II – Tides of Blood
Vol. III – Empire of Blood

The Ogre Titans:
Vol. I – The Black Talon
Vol. II – The Fire Rose
Vol. III – The Gargoyle King

The Age of Conan

Vol. I – The God in the Moon
Vol. II – The Eye of Charon
Vol. III – The Silent Enemy

The Knight in Shadow

Dragon Mound

Individual Titles

The Janus Mask
Frostwing
King of the Grey
Dutchman
Shattered Light: Ruby Flames
Beastmaster: Myth

DRAGON MOUND

(The Knight in Shadow)

by

Richard A. Knaak

Porta Nigra Press

DRAGON MOUND

Published by Porta Nigra Press
First Printing August, 2015

Originally Published by Sea Lion Books

Cover Design by Anna Katherina Spanier

Photograph © Norma Cornes / 123RF

For Roger Zelazny, Andre Norton, and Edgar Rice Burroughs

I

THE FOREST

The bloody ghosts of battle warred in his head, their cries forever locked in his memory. Warrior split warrior. A rain of hissing arrows presaged full-scale slaughter. Knights on horseback bore down on hapless foes on foot, and pikemen did their best to unseat knights, skewering them like pigs for the spit.

A fire-black dragon whose wings blotted out the sky—a leviathan even by his own kind's standards—soared overhead, belching flame upon those not marked as his master's servants. A bearded knight in gleaming crimson sat atop him, his lance smeared with blood, his expression more monstrous than that of the beast.

Death had ruled the land, then . . .

The rider's mind snapped back to the present, the grisly sounds of war replaced by birdcalls and the buzzing of insects. *That time is long gone,* he knew. He let out a breath and regarded the quiet autumn forest surrounding him. This interminable quest, which had been thrust upon him, had become a constant reminder that the war and its consequences would forever haunt him.

The cool autumn wind soothed him as he urged the pale steed forward over the winding earth. Evan had removed his helmet, allowing his shoulder-length, silvering brown hair to flow free. The weathered mail shirt and tarnished breastplate he had left on, a habit of precaution learned from a lifetime of struggle. A dusky-brown travel cloak obscured much of what he wore, but no one sighting him would mistake him for anything other than a knight, albeit one who had seen better days.

How strange the passage of time . . . he thought, gazing at the

1

trees standing tall and proud. In this forest it appeared as if the war had never happened. Only someone as familiar with the carnage as he was could identify a mound here and there as old fortifications, possibly even the burial places of long-forgotten dead.

Was the rest of Rundin like this? Evan had avoided the towns and villages for the most part, but those stops he had made so far had indicated that the kingdom was and had been for some time at peace. In the Far West, where he had spent so many years since the war, Evan Wytherling had heard little about the conditions in the East. He wondered what changes had occurred in the capital, Coramas. It had always been a progressive city; was it still?

What do I care? the knight asked himself bitterly. Peace or war, he had to continue the search. The shadow of Paulo Centuros still hung over him and would continue to do so until he had fulfilled his mission.

The occasional clink of metal against metal punctuated the relative quiet of the forest and its softly rustling branches, the trills, clicks, and hums of its many animal denizens. The land around him was still except for an occasional bird flitting by overhead or a squirrel darting to safety in one of the trees. Evan wondered if the forest and its creatures still recalled the armies, the dragons, the sorcerers.

I will have to visit him. He may know. He of all people might know of Novaris . . . This close to the old battle site, Evan could not shun a confrontation. If he ever hoped to be free, the knight could not avoid the one source of information he had. He would have to visit Valentin.

A shudder coursed through him. Evan Wytherling tightened his grip on the reins; the horse snorted in annoyance. The bone-pale beast turned his head to the side, one glittering black orb almost but not quite focusing on the rider. Evan immediately loosened the reins, desiring no difficulty from the animal.

Seemingly satisfied with the knight's submission, the great horse looked ahead again. Evan returned his attention to the countryside, awed by its resilience. Even the hills in the distance were covered with life, the very same hills where Grimyr had scorched the earth, bathing forest and man alike in a sea of blistering flame.

The sun, a misty, round shield, was sinking behind the hills. Evan debated making camp rather than meeting Valentin in the dead of night. But the sooner he learned what Valentin knew, the sooner he could be away.

"Away . . . to what?" the knight murmured, briefly shattering the quiet. He rubbed his chin lightly with the back of one gauntleted hand, recalling some of the stops on his long journey. He had sailed seas, crossed deserts, climbed mountains, and wended his way through more forests than he could count, but Evan Wytherling had nothing to show for all his efforts. Still the end to his quest remained ever beyond his tired reach.

Ahead, a small stream cut across his intended path. Driven by thirst, Evan dared the horse's wrath and tugged lightly on the reins. After the animal halted beside the stream, the knight dismounted and collected the near-empty water skin that dangled from the side of the saddle.

Evan could easily make out his reflection in the water despite its gentle current. Though some others recoiled at the sight of his gaunt face and weathered gray skin, the knight was unmoved. He scarcely remembered how he had looked before Paulo Centuros had claimed him for this madness. Not much different, he supposed, save that his narrow hazel eyes now held a weariness that only a journey as long and harrowing as his could have produced.

The image dispersed as he thrust the water skin into the stream and let the bag fill, his gaze rising to view the land ahead. Another hour, perhaps two, and he would reach Valentin. Once that confrontation was over, he could be away from this place of cursed memories.

The fluttering of wings overhead startled him, but when Evan looked up he saw nothing. He cursed himself for his foolishness. Sealing the skin, he rose from the stream and returned to the fearsome steed. The animal snorted at him as he mounted, but this time Evan refused to acknowledge the foul beast's annoyance. They were companions of necessity, nothing more. Magic had brought them together and only death could separate them.

The pale animal moved without urging from Evan. The knight resumed his study of the landscape, signs of the war still evident, such as the great depression to his far left. True, foliage covered much of one side of it, but those who inspected it with the eyes of a warrior might notice its perfect roundness. Evan felt a tingle; even now traces of sorcery remained, but only one sensitive to such power would be able to feel the faint emanations.

Who had died there? The spellcasters on both sides had wielded their powers with deadly precision, Centuros and his counterpart, the sorcerer-king Novaris, inflicting the most casualties between them. Nothing would remain of the victims, of course, such sorcery being monstrously thorough, but at least the depression gave them a monument of sorts that so many of the other fallen had failed to receive.

Renewed fluttering stirred him from his dark thoughts. This time he searched the treetops more thoroughly, but Evan could not see the source of the noise. Something about the fluttering disturbed his senses, but what it was Evan could not say.

Deal with Valentin. That is all that matters . . .

The horse suddenly stilled. Evan Wytherling blinked, puzzled by the animal's behavior until he caught sight of the figure in the distance.

There should have been no one else in the forest, his forest. The legacy of the war should have guaranteed that, but there she was, seated on a small mound, reading from a tiny book. Her golden hair, fastened in a braid, was of stark contrast to the forest, as was her white woolen cloak. What Evan could see of her features revealed that she was young, possibly still a maiden. She had a slightly rounded face with a full mouth, a delicate nose, and almond-shaped eyes that even from a distance revealed a more fiery soul than her gentle appearance indicated. Little more could

4

the knight tell about her save that beneath her cloak the clothing she wore was of good make and dusky blue in general coloring. Nearby, her transport, a brown mare tethered to a tree, munched on some leaves from a low bush.

A non-peasant woman sitting in the midst of an empty forest? Evan Wytherling's eyes narrowed. Something was dreadfully amiss. Why would she be out here, traveling unconcerned in the middle of nowhere? Why pause, with the sun already sinking, to read?

"No," he finally whispered, a possible, terrible answer occurring to him. "No . . . they would not have . . ."

Evan had to know. It changed everything . . . perhaps. Certainly it changed his plans.

She looked up. The knight tugged on the reins, urging the horse out of sight. Now was the time to watch. Now was the time to learn.

Now was the time to pray he was wrong.

Mardi Sinclair looked up from the thin volume she had been reading, certain that other eyes watched her. She turned her gaze to the west and from the edge of her vision caught sight of an image like none she had ever witnessed.

A knight. A paladin atop a moon-silver stallion. He wore no helmet, which enabled the young woman to see the man's determined eyes, his slightly aquiline nose, and his defiant, well-formed chin. Silver streaks cut through dark-brown hair that flowed to his shoulders. A sword with a jeweled hilt hung from a scabbard at his side.

The gleam from the breastplate beneath his travel cloak forced her to blink, and when Mardi finally focused again the magnificent rider was no longer there. Man and horse had disappeared as if they had never been.

Never been . . . Of course they had never been. Mardi

Sinclair uttered an oath under her breath that her uncle Yoniff would have found reprehensible from not only the niece of an established money lender but also a woman educated in the best schools in Coramas. Of late, he had found her attitude increasingly offensive, especially her reluctance to marry any of the landowners' or merchants' sons to whom he had presented her.

"I've tried to raise you well, Mardina." Yoniff had ever refused to use the casual, shorter version of her name that she preferred. "Given you all the things my sister would've tried to give you if the plague hadn't taken her that terrible winter along with your father and your little sister, Drucinda. You are the daughter I never had, girl, and up until recently I've felt nothing but pride. Now, however, you've grown so obstinate I'm beginning to wonder what to do with you. If you were a boy, the answer would be easy. If you'd been a boy, you'd have been a soldier, mark me. But you're . . . Aah, what can I do?"

Such conversations between the two had become common, with no end in sight. That was one reason Mardi had sought solitude so often, riding off long distances to find restful spots to read the few books she could get her hands on.

The books were her treasures, the gates to a different world that not only she but also the children she taught to read could pass through. Teaching was the one thing Mardi did that her uncle still respected. Yoniff believed educated children offered a better future to the kingdom. He did not always care for her choice of books, however; heroic adventures, tales of knights and dragons. The works about and by the nearly mythic Paulo Centuros, quite the rage in Coramas these days despite having been written so long ago, especially incensed the conservative and fiscal-minded man. Better to teach the young ones to be useful to their king and the upper class than fill their heads with the romantic, heroic verses of an age that, to most, had no meaning in these busy days. Mardi always found contradictions in such thinking but never voiced them to the man. Uncle Yoniff would not have listened.

Now she wondered whether he had been correct after all

6

about her choice of reading material. Of late Mardi had found herself too caught up in her stories, so much so that now and then she was troubled by vivid dreams of warring armies, desperate knights on horseback, and even savage dragons. This latest incident was certainly the worst. Never before had her daydreams conjured so real an image.

With a sigh, she snapped shut the tan leather-bound book and rose. Returning the thin tome to a pouch on her belt, the golden-haired woman took one last look around. No heroic knight. No magnificent stallion. Of course not.

Mounting, Mardi Sinclair urged her brown mare east. Her uncle would be wondering where she was. Caught up in her reading and her dreams, the young woman had forgotten the time. Even in a place as quiet and uneventful as this, it was never good to take chances.

What's there to fear here, though? What's there ever been to fear?

A bird fluttered overhead, landing in a treetop just ahead of her. A crow. Mardi gave the avian no more thought; in the forest blackbirds were as common as squirrels. She wished it had at least been a tiny wyvern, but such fantastic creatures were now found only in Tepis or in the far western kingdoms, not in Rundin. Likely they found it as wearisome a place as Mardi did.

Not wearisome, she corrected. *Soulless. We are losing our soul, our spark.* If only someone would listen to her. Rundin cared about little besides its ever-demanding coffers. Her uncle was a prime example of what she most feared her nation had become. The only cause he ever showed interest in was the cause of finance.

Mardi tried to focus on the journey. The trek was not a terrible one, although it did require her to keep a tight rein on the mare at times. The forest was filled with strange hill formations and sudden depressions that some of the older folk said were actually the buried remnants of some great battle. Mardi doubted those tales, though. Likely nothing greater than a few road bandits had ever threatened this area.

No sooner had she thought that than Mardi heard the rustling of brush to the side. At first she thought nothing of it; with squirrels, raccoons, and the occasional draco rat the most dominant forms of life in the forest, Mardi Sinclair felt little fear. On a rare occasion a lone wolf found its way to the region, but the last one had been sighted some two seasons before.

The brush rustled again. If a raccoon, it was a large one. Mardi urged the mare on. Home was not much farther.

A different sound, the distinctive clink of metal on metal—or so Mardi identified it—made her pause. She twisted in the saddle, searching for the source of the new noise. Her thoughts returned to the paladin, but almost immediately she quelled such dreams. He had not been real. Such heroes no longer existed; the only ones to be found in these peaceful days were the products of storytellers. Besides, had he been real, what would such a knight find to interest him here?

Neither sound repeated itself, and after a moment of hesitation, Mardi resumed her journey, feeling more disappointed than anything else. Soon she would be home, safe from the nonexistent threats of the forest. Safe from everything except the explosive wrath of her uncle.

The previous evening she had informed him of her intention to move into the small house that doubled as the school. Her parents' money had bought her that, money that should have been saved for dowry, but for which she had at last found better use. Unfortunately, Yoniff still had legal control of those funds, and before they parted ways this morning he had vowed to save her from her headstrong ways. Mardi feared that he intended to bring her up officially before the magistrate, miserly Drulane. It would be just the sort of lesson her uncle would teach her.

A bell rang out, announcing the coming night. A few moments later, Mardi caught sight of the upper tip of the church tower, the tallest structure in the town of Pretor's Hill.

"Home," she muttered. Her hand briefly stroked the pouch

containing the book of verses supposedly written by Centuros himself. It was her favorite, the one she read over and over. The nearness comforted her a little, but not enough to erase her anxiety concerning Yoniff's threat. "Dear, sweet home . . ."

A sense of foreboding had stirred within Evan Wytherling as he followed the young woman. Beyond the girl's obvious lack of concern for both her surroundings and the coming night, the knight had begun to notice subtle changes in the darkening woods. Any sense of calm faded with the diminishing sunlight. The ghosts of battle began to flock to him in greater force, stronger, more demanding than ever before.

Monstrous Grimyr circling above, roaring in amusement. The heavyset wizard Paulo Centuros, hands splayed, turning a simple, innocent stream into a river of death. Shadowy, snow-eyed General Haggad cutting down a hapless foot soldier with his toothed sword. His opposite, the bearded General Pretor—a gentle, sad giant— turning a rout into yet a stronger assault on the forces of the sorcerer-king Novaris.

Something—not a ghost—darted through the woods just to his left.

Evan reined the horse to a halt, trying to keep the woman in the distance in sight while also seeking a better view of his new companion. One hand slipped to the jeweled hilt of the blade at his side.

A black form flew at him from his right, shrieking and seeking his face. The blade met it swiftly, cutting through just before talons would have gouged scarlet tracks in the knight's cheek. Blood spattered the breastplate as the two neatly severed halves of his attacker flopped to the ground.

Snorting, the pale stallion brought one hoof down on the nearest of the halves, crushing it into an unidentifiable mess. Evan leapt off the animal, seeking the other bloody portion. When he did

9

find it, it took him a moment to identify what sort of creature it had been, so thoroughly had the sharp-edged sword done its murderous work.

A crow. One of the largest, most baleful blackbirds that Evan had seen in many a year. It had a look to it that reminded him well of another time, a time after the battle had long ended and all that remained had been the dead and dying. That was when the scavengers feasted, the scaly draco rats, the wild, voracious dogs, and the mocking carrion crows. They came to the battlefields by the hundreds, swarming over the rotting bodies even as a few hardy men tried to do what they could to cleanse the land of the carnage.

A carrion crow. Evan stared at what remained of the bird. This creature had the look of carrion, the smell of it. Even now, the scent of decay drifted from its mangled corpse.

No! All in your mind, Evan Wytherling. There has been no battle here since the great one; since Novaris, Centuros, Haggad, Pretor, and Valentin crossed this ravaged land! There has been nothing here that would feed such monsters. This is a simple blackbird, a stalker of field mice and squirrels, not a scavenger of men's dark ambitions . . .

Yet, even if that were so, it still left the question of why the crow had sought his face. Evan glared at the disemboweled avian, seeking from it an answer he knew it could not give him.

The horse snorted. Evan suddenly recalled the young woman, already out of sight. The bird would tell him nothing, but the woman might still provide him with some desperately needed answers. Wiping clean the blade, he returned it to its scabbard, then quickly remounted.

As Evan rode, he noted yet more winged furies darting among the trees. With the encroaching night, the forest seemed alive with blackbirds, all of them as large and evil in appearance as the one he had cut in two. Again the knight was reminded of the battle and the devastation, of the friends and foes lying dead by the hundreds wherever he looked.

There is no greater wonder, no more heart-wresting spectacle in all of humanity's history than the battlefield, Paulo Centuros had once said to him. *It is the essence of life and death all laid out at once for us to view for our pleasure or our pain . . .*

Again Evan Wytherling shuddered. He had to be wrong. The woman would show him the truth.

A great bell rang in the distance.

The sound jarred both horse and rider. Evan fought with the pale phantom beneath him, at last winning enough control to force the beast forward. With great trepidation, the pair followed the sound.

The knight caught sight of the source of the ringing a moment later; a church tower whose point poked out above the nearest trees. As he rode closer, more of the structure became visible, as did a number of other buildings surrounding the church. There was a stable, at least two inns of some quality, a market, and at least two dozen other buildings within the immediate area that he could not identify, but that were clearly places where people congregated often. Light from within many of the buildings illuminated much of the view before him, revealing a sprawling settlement with roots at least three or four generations strong from the looks of it.

Far ahead, he vaguely noted the woman as she rode into what was clearly her home. Someone greeted her. Several more people wandered past his view, going about their business. Even with the coming of night, the place remained active. What stood before him was not the forest he had hoped he would find, but a burgeoning town, a picturesque community clearly in the throes of a long, healthy peace.

Evan's anxiety continued to grow. His gaze shifted back to the church. He stared at it, wondering why it of all places in the town should bother him so. More than once he had received respite from a church or monastery, albeit often under precarious circumstances. He considered them places of comfort, not unease. Why should this holy place be different?

"No . . ." With a start, the wary knight realized that it was not the church itself but rather the location that disturbed him. How could they have been so ignorant, so foolish, to have built the structure on so damned a spot? Then again, the townsfolk could not have known about the place they had set the church upon. They had not been there during the war. They had not witnessed what Evan Wytherling had witnessed.

"Valentin . . ." he whispered, his lip curling in both disgust and growing fear. "Valentin, what have you done?"

II

PRETOR'S HILL

The last glimmer of daylight had already vanished before Mardi reached the tall, narrow, stone house that served as both her uncle's home and his place of business. She slowed the mare as she approached, hoping Yoniff would not hear the horse's hooves as they clopped on the cobblestones. If she could avoid him tonight, so much the better.

Although an oil lantern still illuminated the outside entrance, no lights shone from within, a promising sign. Her uncle's apartment lay behind his storefront, her own on the second story, a fairly expansive place all things considered; but living with Yoniff gave it a rather claustrophobic aura. Mardi always felt trapped, a prisoner. The living quarters in the school were barely more than half the size and yet they provided her with a sense of comfort, of being her own person.

"So, the woods again, was it?"

The deprecating voice of her uncle greeted Mardi as she dismounted. She turned and looked up at the gangly figure with the crown of ice-white hair and the flat, nearly nonexistent nose. In contrast to the ring of hair, his jacketed evening suit was a dour black, giving him the appearance of a bodiless head floating before her. That her mother and this man had been siblings ever amazed the young woman. Mardi's mother had been a round, pleasant woman who had always gone out of her way to help the less fortunate. It was that attribute, in fact, that had inadvertently led to her death. No one had recognized the symptoms of the ill neighbor she had tended to as plague until the Sinclair family had been too long exposed.

13

Yoniff Casperin had, as usual, been away on business. Mardi had survived only through sheer will, and her uncle, upon his return, took her in—with reluctance, Mardi had always been certain. No one knew where the neighbor had contracted the plague; the last known recorded case was some thirty years before.

"Yes, Uncle, I was, but there was no need to worry—"

The moneylender snorted, stepping out beyond the doorway. For a lanky figure, he moved with the grace and stealth of a cat on the hunt. His elegant leather shoes, perfectly matched to his ebony garments, touched the cobblestones without the slightest sound. "Girl, there's ever need to worry when you're not about! Have you forgotten we were to dine with Magistrate Drulane this eve?"

She had forgotten neither the appointment nor the true reason behind it. The magistrate, an old crony of her uncle's, was also a widower these past two years, and had not only an eye for Mardi but also the money she might inherit after Yoniff passed away. The moneylender being himself, he had never married nor fathered a child. Therefore, Yoniff saw such a marriage as a method by which he would garner more favor from Drulane, while assuring that his only niece did not squander his hard-earned savings on such things as poetry books, radical causes, and, of course, schoolhouses. Sometimes Mardi wondered why he did not just make the magistrate his heir instead and save all three of them unnecessary trouble.

"It must have slipped my mind." She reached for her belongings, being careful to obscure from her uncle's view the tome she had been reading.

"As it did when Master Bellowes, one of our leading merchants, brought his youngest by or when Lady Akima invited us to sup with her and her brother Edmund?" Yoniff's tapering hand slipped past her arm and darted into her pack, pulling from it Mardi's precious book. "As I suspected! The cursed trash those *friends* of yours sent you from Coramas! What are the young of Rundin coming to, constantly fantasizing when there's hard work to be done and lessons to learn?"

14

"Give me that!" She could not reach the book, Yoniff the scarecrow easily rendering it unobtainable. "You've no right to take my property!"

"What have we this time?" Her uncle held the thin tome to the open flame of the lamp. *"The Further Writings of Paulo Centuros: Reflections of a Lesson Lost.* Gads, girl, not him again! The man was a charlatan exiled from Rundin well more than a hundred years past, a romantic fool who'd preached fairy tales, not facts!" Yoniff held the book closer to the lamp, but not with the intention of reading some of Centuros's soul-touching verse.

A peculiar sensation overtook Mardi Sinclair, a cold fury such as none she had ever felt. In a tone not at all like her, she quietly said, "If you even singe the cover of that book, Uncle, I'll make sure that your hand is next."

The moment she had finished, Mardi blanched, unable to believe the words were her own. Yoniff, likewise, at first stood still in amazement. Then he slowly lowered the book to safety, at last thrusting it into her waiting hands. "A lot of drivel. If I were the Factor of Education in the capital, I'd have ousted any student who took up such trash. What do you see in it, girl?"

Recovered from her outburst, she retorted, "More than I see when I look around at Rundin, especially here in Pretor's Hill. All you concern yourself with is your business, with making even more profit. All anyone seems to care about is what they can do to gain an advantage over everyone else."

"And so hard work is to be looked down upon by you and your dilettante friends, is that it? That hard work enables most of you to go about preaching, girl, or don't you realize that?"

He never understood. Mardi could never make anyone here understand. Perhaps she simply did not have the flair for words that Paulo Centuros had once had. "It's not hard work, Uncle Yoniff. You miss the point entirely! It's the fact that our lives have become so bound to the task that we no longer look at the beauty of the world, no longer look at the soul of it!"

A harsh noise erupted nearby. Mardi turned, expecting some

violence at the inn just down the street, but the source proved to be only an overzealous worker who had lost his grip on a pair of small, empty wooden crates he had been carrying. The young teacher found herself oddly disappointed that it had not been something more exciting.

"I'll not argue fruitlessly with you out here where any may listen," Uncle Yoniff snapped, "and I won't bother inside, either!" He stared at her set expression, then, his tone softening, added, "I only want what's best for you, girl. There's no family left but you and I."

As if embarrassed by this admission of familial concern, Yoniff turned and vanished inside. Mardi remained where she was, trying to gather herself. While she believed her uncle's parting words, she also believed he would stay true to his earlier threats to keep her from permanently moving to the school.

Mardi clenched her hands, then realized she had nearly crushed her book. It still amazed her that she had spoken up to her uncle so forcefully. From where had such fury arisen? She could have never followed through on such a vicious threat . . . could she?

It affects me as well. This soulless life, this hunger that eats away at the core of Rundin. It affects me as well. If she was not careful, Mardi would find herself taking over her uncle's business, no doubt becoming an even more miserly, unseeing, and unimaginative person than he was. No longer would she dream, hope, or believe . . . in anything. All she would care about was the profit to be made and from whom to make it.

No, that's absurd! Mardi Sinclair had been educated in the finest schools. She had met many others, mostly students, who recognized the emotional and spiritual decay of their land. Although those friends were all far away now, the young woman knew they were with her in soul.

She pressed the tome against her chest, taking comfort from it. Paulo Centuros had shown them the way. He had warned them and given them hope. Mankind had always been in danger of losing its spirit to the struggles of life, but there were ever those, like her, who would help win the day.

Sometimes she wished she had been born a hero in the age of chivalry, when spirit and soul had been paramount, when imagination had reached its peak and people had had worthy causes and beliefs they could follow for their entire lives. In those days, in the days of Centuros, one person could change the world.

All she wanted to do was to change Pretor's Hill for the better.

The lamp flickered off in Yoniff's apartment. Sighing, Mardi took the reins of her horse and led her to the tiny stable behind the house. Best to first win her own small battles, beginning with her move to the school. That would be difficult enough a quest.

With her back to the direction of the inn, Mardi did not see the rider just arriving . . . but even in the dark she might have recognized—if not him—the pale, baleful steed he rode.

There appeared nothing at first glance to substantiate Evan Wytherling's fears for this town that had no right to be here. The people spoke to one another in tones of friendship, the buildings were all clean and well maintained, and the air itself was fresh, with no scent of decay, no scent of blood. It was as picturesque a place as the knight had come across in many a season.

But appearances meant little to Evan. No matter how peaceful this place was now, there had to be a hidden dread. Valentin would know where the darkness lay.

If things had changed so much here, how different indeed the rest of Rundin must have become. Despite his earlier lackluster interest, he now genuinely wondered what Coramas looked like. His one time there had been brief and not at all pleasant, but the tall, spiraled towers and elegant, patterned brick houses it had been known for surely remained among its highlights.

The scabbard and the breastplate he had worn for so long

hung from the saddle alongside the helmet. The mail shirt now lay hidden beneath his threadbare travel cloak. Anyone with a good eye might recognize him as an instrument of war, but they would no doubt simply think him a veteran campaigner and not a threat in their midst. So Evan at least hoped.

Townsfolk paused to look up at him as he rode toward the nearest inn. The young woman had passed this way, and without thought he had followed the same course. She had vanished now, but the inn seemed a likely spot to rest. To stay out of town would have been to invite too many questions. And then there was the issue of Valentin.

Once more his gaze drifted surreptitiously to the church, but he quickly looked away as the priest stepped outside. Evan had a vague image of a middle-aged man with thinning hair, but that was all. The scant glimpse proved sufficient enough to answer one question, however. He knew at least that the priest was what he appeared to be.

At the inn, the pale horse stopped. Evan dismounted, feeling the eyes of at least a dozen folk on him. Only two he marked as any possible threat, a young, groomed man and his slightly older companion—both tall and well clad in the manner of those whose families were wealthy in land —who stood near the doors. His arrival had compelled them to pause before entering, but when he turned his gaze their direction they continued inside as if not at all interested in this dark stranger.

Evan did not bother to tie the reins to a post; the horse would make up his own mind whether he stayed or not. The knight started to retrieve his sword but decided against it. Few of the townsfolk appeared armed in any manner, the deadliest weapon he had spotted so far being a belt dagger sheathed on the waist of the haughty young man who had just entered. Most carried nothing at all. Truly a town at peace.

Valentin must laugh at their trust. Evan would stay a night or two at the inn before the confrontation. Observation would tell him much of what he needed. Valentin would fill in the rest.

He entered the inn—a well lit and well scrubbed space—to see all of the dozen or so faces turn toward him, marking him as something different from what they generally expected. Most had the good sense or manners to return to their own business, but a few, especially the younger and the very eldest, continued to watch as if Evan put on some sort of minstrel entertainment. The young man and his companion, both already seated at one of the wide oak booths to the right, measured each movement he made and did not bother to hide their interest when this time he met their gazes directly.

The first sign? Possibly . . . or perhaps the pair just took the measure of every newcomer as young fools with no concept of true violence were wont to do when they had too much energy. Would they seek to prove themselves against him? It would not be the first time. He hoped they had more sense; Evan had grown too tired to waste time on such frivolity.

He sat at a sturdy-albeit-worn table located as far from the fireplace as possible, a shadowed corner that gave him a view of everyone but obscured his own visage enough. A round, graying woman in a crisp white apron who seemed to be constantly wringing her hands finally approached him. Her simple beige blouse and thick, matching skirt were also freshly cleaned, another sign of the establishment's prosperity. The almost ankle-length skirt rustled as she walked.

"Good eve, sir. I'm so sorry, so sorry! Didn't see you there immediately! Are you hungry?"

She had seen him, but it had taken her this long to build up the nerve to approach. Evan knew he must be a sight to them, but he did not care. If their sheltered peace could not stand his simple presence, then the taint had already spread far too wide. The town was lost.

Enough of that. It proved too easy of late to slip into a fog, to give up on all things, not that the damned wizard would allow him such respite. Sinking into a malaise served only to make Evan's task more daunting. *And would not Valentin love to see me thus?*

He ordered ale and whatever cooked in the huge pot in the stone-slatted fireplace, then asked for a room. The woman, still wringing her hands, turned to glance at the short, burly man clad in a gray cloth shirt and pants standing near a back doorway. The man, also wearing an apron, tugged on his impressive brown beard but otherwise did not respond to the entreaty in her eyes.

"I'll have to be checking on the room," she finally managed. "You'll hear when I bring your food and drink."

Evan suspected the answer would not be the one he sought if he left matters where they stood. He reached into a soft deerskin pouch at his belt and removed a few coins, dropping them softly on the table. Even from where he stood, the proprietor would be able to tell they were large and, more important, gold.

Sure enough, when the woman returned, a tray in her hands, her expression appeared more relieved. Before him she placed a steaming bowl of meat and potato stew, some coarse wheat bread, and a mug of brown, murky ale. "There's a room up in the back that you can have for a good price. Comes with an oil lamp and blankets, too."

Not good enough. "I want a room with a view of the front. I prefer to see where I stay."

Her relief began to fade, but then she looked close at the coin with which Evan presently played. Gold, indeed, and twice as large as any she had no doubt seen in some time. "I'll ask my husband if there's another."

The room would be his and with it the view he required. Evan knew the proprietor's ilk. He would give Evan his room even if he had to move someone else from it. The coin the man would charge would be outrageous, but money meant little to the weary knight. Centuros had seen to it that he had an inexhaustible source, provided Evan Wytherling did not seek to spend it too freely.

His coins had attracted the attention of others, including the pair most interested in him. The veteran fighter pretended to ignore them, but as he positioned himself, Evan's left hand casually swept past his dagger, jeweled like his sword. No one could fail to notice how even so near the shadows the wicked blade gleamed and the gems glittered like malevolent orbs. Interested eyes once more turned away.

The stew tasted too much of salt, but it was hot and edible and full of tender meat and a variety of soft vegetables. The ale turned out to be more tolerable. He ordered a second from a much younger, pale girl who, as thin as she was, could never have been the daughter of the innkeepers. The older woman returned to him just as he used a bit of the remaining bread to clean out the remains of the stew. As she spoke her hands hung at her sides, although her voice was still tense.

"My husband, he's come up with a room that should be to your liking. I can show you it as soon as you're ready."

"Let me retrieve my things." As he rose, Evan swept all but the smallest of the coins from the table. Even that was a goodly sum for what he had eaten, but he wanted the innkeepers' good will. In the days and nights ahead, they might find him an unnerving and undesirable guest.

The damnable steed glared at him as he returned, glittering black eyes condemning the man for having taken so long. Evan ignored the glare, going straight to his equipment. He stripped what he could from the saddle, leaving the scabbard and its contents among those items that would wait for his next trip, then ventured back inside with his belongings.

The woman was gone. In her place stood her husband, arms crossed, beard tufted out. The knight supposed he was to be more impressed by this sight. Unfortunately, the innkeeper came up only to his chest, which erased much of the potential.

"It's back up this way," the husband rumbled, making no offer to aid the traveler. "I'll show you."

Again Evan became the object of interest, but he pretended ignorance as he followed the man upstairs. The railed stairway wound to one side of the building and proved very narrow. At the top of the steps, his host guided him a few feet to the right, then pushed open the only door. "This is it."

Plain but functional. A much-used frame bed, with blankets the color of the innkeeper's shirt, a small stand near the bed on which stood a single brass oil lamp, and a table and chair next to the lone window. The window faced into town and gave him an excellent view of the church. Evan accepted without hesitation.

He paid a price less than what the innkeeper desired and more than what the room should have been worth. Alone at last, Evan Wytherling deposited his belongings, including the breastplate and helmet, then stepped to the window. Yes, it would do. The knight could see the area surrounding the church for quite some distance around.

His lips pursed as he imagined his coming reunion. "Soon, Valentin, soon—"

A scream, a man's scream, broke the peace.

Evan did not hesitate, bounding out of the room and down the stairs with a swiftness borne from the knowledge that he might very well be responsible for the injury, even the death, of whoever had cried out. The dagger stood ready in his hand, although he had no idea what good it might do. If his fears proved true, the blade would little serve him.

"He bit me! The monster bit me!"

The knight paused just outside of the inn's entrance, assessing the situation. Several people had gathered to see what the commotion was all about. Blood stained the right hand of one of the young, well-to-do men who had been watching him earlier. He clutched it in pain while his friend stood back, possibly more concerned about ruining his own clothes—a finely crafted dark-blue suit with twin tails hanging from the back of the short jacket—than seeing if his friend had lost any fingers. Some of those gathered whispered and pointed at the source of the man's wound, Evan's baleful stallion. The beast eyed not his victim but rather the knight, as if this were somehow the latter's fault.

Evan stepped forward, filling the injured man's view. "Give me your hand."

The man blinked in confusion, then obeyed. He had clearly

been fortunate. A quick inspection by Evan proved that the horse had been surprisingly gentle. None of the fingers were missing, although two would require splints. The blood came from a bite in the meaty part of the hand. Evan glanced at his mount, but the inhuman eyes revealed nothing.

"This animal has been trained for war. For battle," he informed the bleeding man and all else around them. The innkeeper's wife hurried over with a bandage, which the knight neatly applied to the wound. "Old habits die hard. You should be wary of getting too close to such an animal." He finished his work. "This will do until you can get someone to look at it."

No gratitude shone in the face of the man. "That monster should be put to death!"

"He would not have bitten if you had not tried to touch the saddle."

The young landowner began to speak, but his friend put a hand on his shoulder, silencing him. For the first time, Evan studied the man close. Clean-shaven, blond hair well combed, no doubt handsome to women who admired patrician features softened by just a little too much baby fat—especially under the chin—and taller even than the knight. His clothes, obviously not made locally, marked him as someone with enough money not to care about what happened to others unless it served him.

"Easy, Jak. Maybe you've had a bit too much. I did warn you that the steed looked ready to attack."

"But Danny—"

"Come on, Jak. Your father's going to skin you alive if you don't get that hand checked quick." Danny steered his companion away, a look of the sincerest apology draped across his elegant face. The knight was not at all fooled by the mask. "That's quite a horse you've got there, sir. Quite a horse."

Without replying, Evan watched them depart. The other townsfolk had begun to drift away. The knight turned, saw the innkeeper standing by the door to his establishment. "Where is your stable?"

"I'll not be having that creature among my own," snarled the bearded man. "Not for any money. You want a place for it, go down your left a ways and ask at the blacksmith's."

There seemed no profit in arguing with the innkeeper on this point. Whether in this stable or the one farther away, the fearsome steed would still be near enough if Evan needed him.

He took the reins in hand and headed in the direction the innkeeper had mentioned. Evan knew why the horse had attacked the man. Jak had been trying to reach the jeweled sword, either to steal it or simply to study its unusual design. Evan blamed himself for enabling the incident to occur and knew very well that the horse likewise held him accountable. Still, no one had ordered Jak to risk himself . . . unless Danny knew more than he had said.

"You could have simply snapped at him," he muttered.

The moon-pale animal snorted.

"We'll be pariahs in this town soon enough."

This time, the beast did nothing. Evan shook his head. Trouble enough to deal with Valentin in this place of all places without his damnable mount also causing him grief.

The blacksmith, a trollish man without a single hair on his head and who wore an ever-present and yet entirely honest smile, proved more amiable to the veteran soldier's needs. He studied Evan's horse up and down, remarking on the creature as if the beast were the most exquisite work of art the blacksmith had ever laid eyes on.

"Now me, I ain't seen one like this ever! Oh, the king's man, Steppenwald, he's got himself a magnificent animal, a Neulander Spotted as nearly as many hands as yours, but it still ain't as grand!" The smith—Arno, he called himself—had the audacity to approach the frustrating animal, who had the even greater audacity to pretend he enjoyed the human's petting. "I've got a prize spot for this one; I know his type ain't good to have around some of the others. Seen quite a bit of killing, has he?"

The ghosts of war stirred. "Too much."

"You must've come far, you have. No fighting in Rundin in

years. Out West?"

"Far West."

Seeing he would get no further clarification, Arno turned to another subject. "Benjamin send you here?"

Evan had never gotten the innkeeper's name, had not even desired to know it. "I stay at the inn nearest to your smithy."

"That would be Benjamin Jakes, all right. A good, decent man is Benjamin." Arno leaned forward, as if welcoming the knight to some dark conspiracy. "But untrusting until he knows you. Don't be letting his snarling get to you, sir."

Arno's notion of price proved much more reasonable than that of his good friend Benjamin Jakes. Evan suspected that the blacksmith was too kind a man if he thought the innkeeper so decent.

The damnable steed seemed content to stay. Evan retrieved his scabbard and attached it to his belt, drawing out the jeweled blade just enough to inspect the handle.

"Fine craftsmanship, sir," Arno remarked. "I've never seen steel like that. Reminds me of the kind of stuff my grandpa says they used to make. Says the steel in those days was the finest, hardest thing other than a dragon's scale." He chuckled. "See that leathery-looking piece up on the wall over the entrance? That's supposed to be scale, though I've never looked close myself. Grandpa mounted it up there for good luck, he said . . ."

Evan paid the talkative Arno's words little mind as he continued his inspection. The blade itself was not steel, but Evan let the smith believe what he saw. To explain what the blade was made of, much less how it had been forged, would have left friendly Arno as distrusting of him as the innkeeper. At the very least, the huge man would have thought Evan mad or, if he believed the knight's tale, a monster from the darkest pits. Evan silently reprimanded himself for leaving such a dangerous weapon with only the horse to guard it. Granted, it had been safe, but to even let anyone be tempted to try to seize it . . .

"I've . . . had it long," the knight finally replied the moment

25

he noticed the smith had ceased talking.

"You keep it well, sir, but if it should need some work, there ain't a better man for a week's ride than me to do it. You just ask anybody."

Arno's continued pleasantry disturbed Evan. If things were as bad as they were, surely the smith would not be so amiable. Benjamin Jakes's attitude and that of the two young men, on the other hand, were prime examples of what Evan had expected to encounter.

Perhaps it is not too late. Perhaps I've come in time. Yet there had been the carrion crow and the mysterious girl . . .

Evan parted the smith's company. The sooner he returned to his room, the better. He needed to know who came and went to the church and when.

In the distance, a crow cawed.

Mardi had just begun to pack when she heard the scream. She quickly rushed to the window and looked out, trying to see what had happened. The cry had come from the direction of Master Jakes's establishment.

The illumination from the inn aided some in identifying people, but it still took the young woman a moment to recognize Jak, Master Garn Bellowes's second oldest, as the man stumbling around in pain. He clutched his hand as if he feared it would fall off, and even from where she watched Mardi could see that it was bloody. The crowd gathering around him appeared to be no help at all, most simply staring. Mardi Sinclair had no use for the merchant's son but had never been the sort to leave any injured beast or man to suffer, and since Jak Bellowes was a bit of both, he doubly needed the aid.

She started to turn from the window and that was when the knight reappeared.

All thought of Jak's agony vanished the instant she saw the

noble figure step out of the inn doors. The dark hair with its almost luminous silver streaks surrounded his face like a lion's mane, and the expression set in those weathered features added to that leonine appearance. His travel cloak fluttered about him as if more wings than cloth.

She desperately wanted to rush outside to see him up close. Mardi abandoned her work and apartment and headed down.

"Where do you go now?"

Mardi gasped as the murky form of her uncle materialized out of the darkness at the bottom of the stairs. Surely he had heard the cries, but unlike his niece the moneylender evidently cared little enough about his fellow man to go investigate.

"I heard a scream and wanted to see if I could be of help."

"What goes on out there is no concern of yours, girl." Yoniff wore a long, draping robe that in the dark made him more ghostly than ever. "Go back to your rooms."

"I believe Jak Bellowes might've been injured, Uncle. I simply wanted to see if I could help him at all."

"Jak Bellowes?" Uncle Yoniff's tone shifted swiftly. Jak's older brother, Rorke, had been one of the moneylender's favored suitors for his niece. "Very well. I'm certain he'll appreciate your concern."

If her uncle had struck on the absurd notion that she had some affection for yet another of Garn Bellowes's sons, Mardi saw no reason at the moment to contradict him. She had as little intention of marrying Jak as she had his brother. Once Mardi freed herself from Yoniff's control, who she chose would be her decision alone.

She wasted no more precious time, hurrying out the front door while her uncle yet stood there, watching her like some dread guardian of the afterlife. The delay had not been a long one, but already Mardi saw that she was too late. The crowd had all but dispersed and the knight and his steed were nowhere to be seen.

The stables. Perhaps he's in the hostel stables. The young woman started in that direction, only to nearly collide a moment later with a tall, shadowed figure who gripped her by the arm and waist with too much familiarity.

"Mardi! You've been keeping yourself cloistered away too much of late, love!"

She thanked the heavens that it was too dark for him to make out the blush she felt spread over her cheeks. "Daniel . . . I've had a lot to think about." Mardi tried to peer past him at the inn, wondering if the noble knight might be sitting in the common room. "I heard a commotion and came out to see what it was. I thought I saw Jak clutching his hand."

Daniel's handsome face twisted into a smirk. "I just sent him off to his father not a moment ago. The fool will try to put his hand where it doesn't belong . . . something most of the girls will vouch for."

He had still not loosened his hold on her and Mardi found herself reluctant to struggle. Her feelings for Daniel Taran had become mixed at best; sometimes he seemed the only one who understood her, yet other times the young merchant appeared to embody everything she thought was wrong with Rundin. There was no denying that she was drawn to him, but whether that was a path she dared take the gentlewoman could not say just yet.

"What happened to him?" she finally managed to ask.

A chuckle. "Some old warhound rode into town on this monster of a mount. Nasty sort that's probably taken one too many blows to the head. The rider, I mean. You should see the rusty relics he had his animal carrying. Have to admit, though, he had a fairly interesting jeweled sword . . . probably stolen off a corpse . . . and when I pointed it out to Jak, the poor fool got it into his head that he wanted to see it, to hold it."

Mardi heard only part of his story. His description of the knight hardly matched her own vision, but Daniel had been standing right there. Could she have been that mistaken? Had her own imagination caused her to start fashioning her own dream visions? She had been so certain that the figure she had seen was so much more than a grizzled old war veteran. There had been something . . . magical . . . about him.

Or is it just your own desperation? she chided herself.

"Where've you gone this time, Mardi, my love? I know that distant look well enough."

Mardi stirred, at last finding the strength to gently free herself from Daniel's strong grip. "I was just thinking of poor Jak."

"Then he'll consider that one good outcome of his encounter with that devilish beast!" At her puzzled expression, he smiled. "You didn't hear me after all, did you? When 'poor Jak' tried to pull the blade free, the infernal creature bit him! Near cleaved his hand in two with just a snap!"

The knight's mount had defended his property. It made perfect sense if the animal was a trained warhorse. Mardi had heard tales of warriors and their loyal steeds, the latter fighting to their very last breath to preserve their masters' lives. Few humans would be so loyal, especially these days.

"He should've known such an animal would be trained to watch over its master's belongings."

Daniel laughed. "So much for your sympathies, but come, you shouldn't be out now. Old Yoniff must be out of his wits."

"My uncle need only worry about himself." Mardi's back stiffened. "I will do what I will do. I'm no small child."

"Now the last is certainly true, I'm happy to say." With gentle pressure, the merchant turned her from the inn. "Still, as there's nothing more to see, why don't I walk you back home?"

"What happened to the knight?" Mardi blurted, again glancing back.

"Knight? More likely a battlefield scavenger from the looks of him. Don't worry about that one. I think Benjamin sent him down to the big stables. Wouldn't have that monster with his other guests' animals. Don't even know if Arno, as good a soul as he is, will let that beast stay the night." Daniel shrugged. "Doesn't really matter, does it? Tomorrow man and beast'll be gone from here and the only memory'll be poor Jak's scars."

His words rang true to her, so much so that Mardi silently

scolded herself for her runaway imagination. Of course knights such as the one she had pictured no longer rode the lands. Scavengers and scoundrels abounded, though, and it had probably been for the best that Daniel had been there to stop her from making a fool of herself.

Before Mardi realized it, they had neared her uncle's home. Daniel peered around, evidently seeking Yoniff, then suddenly whirled her around so that only a few inches separated their faces.

"I heard that you did it. You bought the schoolhouse."

"Yes." It was all the gentlewoman could manage. Again she felt her face flush.

"You could've waited like I asked. I would've bought it for you . . . afterward."

The sensation spread. What she felt for Daniel she could not exactly put into words. Not love . . . not yet . . . but his presence left her disoriented. He was the only one who understood her fears, who listened with interest to her words. Oh, the children she taught did, too, but only where it concerned their lessons. Daniel listened and shared thoughts as well. Mardi knew he wanted to marry her, but still she held back.

He leaned forward to kiss her and, despite her conflicting emotions, Mardi made no attempt to stop him.

The distant howl of a wolf shattered the quiet.

Mardi jerked back as if bitten. The cry sent a chill through her even though she had heard wolves a few times during her life.

"Just an animal," Daniel whispered, clearly trying to bring back the moment. "Probably calling his mate. Bound to be a few wolves still wandering about, even if we haven't seen any for a while."

The howl did not repeat, but its memory lingered over her. Something about it so shook her that the continued advances of the young merchant seemed quite shallow and hardly appropriate.

"I've got to go inside." She slipped free of his hands and darted through the doorway while Daniel Taran stood where she had left him, still trying to recover from her abrupt change of mood. Mardi closed the door behind her and ran up to her apartment, paying no attention to her uncle's sudden presence at his own doorway.

"Mardina—" was all she heard before securing herself in her quarters. Yoniff apparently thought better of disturbing her, for she did not hear him climb the stairs. She gave thanks, needing to be alone with her thoughts.

The echoes of the howl reverberated within her head, adding yet more noise to the din of conflicting emotions concerning Daniel and her growing defiance of her uncle. Curiously, Mardi Sinclair felt calm only when she thought of the noble figure she believed she had seen twice now, the same figure that Daniel had called warhound and battlefield scavenger. Unable to resume her packing, Mardi lay atop her soft, down-filled bed and stared at the ceiling until sleep at last overtook her.

And in her sleep, she dreamt of battling knights—one clad in silver, one in crimson, and both armed with mighty, jeweled blades—and of a great charcoal-black leviathan, a dragon, who laughed, not at the efforts of the two combatants, but at Mardi herself. With the knights still at war, the dragon reached for her dream self—still clad in the very clothes she had gone to bed in—and, as the bloodstained talons closed around her body, asked, *Do you taste it yet? Are you ready, are you straining, to taste the blood of battle?*

She might have answered, but in her dream a hand suddenly thrust itself between the talons and her body. The dragon, hissing, faded to smoke. The two paladins vanished just as each swung a killing blow at the other. A soothing voice, not her own, whispered, *Sleep.*

By morning, Mardi would not even remember the dream.

III

THE GATHERING CLOUDS

Four corners to the room, four candles. One candle stood only a third the height of the others, but it needed only to last until morning, when Evan could find a replacement. He had not needed them for months, not since the castle in Lorinaar, and so had not thought to check them until now . . . when it was too late to do anything. Evan supposed he could have asked the innkeeper for a single candle but felt foolish even considering it. So far, he had sensed no more than the briefest taint of Novaris's legacy, and that from the source he expected.

Yet . . .

Evan was no sorcerer or wizard, not in the common definitions of the words. The gifts granted him—or curses as he thought them—gave the knight some advantage, but they were in their own ways as unpredictable and unreliable as the mocking steed he rode. They had kept him alive, yet because of them Evan had also found himself in the most dire of situations.

Novaris. Centuros. Two sides of the same coin as far as Evan Wytherling was concerned. He had become what he had become because of the pair, and no power in the world could ever free him of their touch. The best he could hope for was to someday complete his quest, whatever its final outcome.

He sat at the window, his chair tilted so he could also eye the corner where the smallest of the candles burned away. The jeweled sword lay across his lap, his hand never straying from the encrusted hilt. Evan did not expect to need the dire blade, but time had shown him that even the most innocent of locations could turn treacherous.

For five hours the knight watched the darkened town, five hours marking each man or animal passing by the church. The priest himself appeared twice early in the watch, retiring to rooms located in the building connected to the house of worship. One man, an old soul, had been the priest's only visitor. As for those homes and businesses nearest the church, they had been, as expected, dark and quiet.

It was, to the eye, a tranquil, picturesque town. Broad-beamed houses with wooden-slat roofs and polished faces, cobblestone streets lit by well-tended oil lamps atop wrought-iron poles, and, in the distance, gently rising hills covered with green forest. In every way, a fairy tale town.

From what Evan Wytherling had noted so far, most of the inhabitants did not even know the full origin of the name Pretor's Hill. Some knew that a battle had been waged here once and that Pretor had been one of those in command of the winning side, but that was all. Many suspected the tale nothing more than myth. The dire legacies of the war against Novaris had been lost to the ages. Only Evan and Valentin understood the truth.

Do you know I am here yet, Valentin? Have you sensed me? Evan wished he could make Valentin come to him, but that would be impossible, of course, given the other's condition. However, it would not be long before their confrontation; Evan needed to learn only a little more before the meeting so he could determine which of Valentin's words were lies and which were only half truths.

The candles flickered. Evan studied each, but none seemed different. He stifled a yawn, then returned his gaze to the window. The three nights before his arrival here had been unsettling ones, the prospect of renewing his acquaintance with Valentin weighing heavily on his soul. That Evan could not trust his own mind, his own thoughts, when it came to Valentin made his task that much more daunting.

Soon. Very soon. What will you have to tell me, Valentin? Why do I feel as if the underworld is about to swallow this land whole?

Another hour passed. Evan had the lay of the town center memorized now, but something about the arrangement of the town's roads and buildings nagged at him. Nevertheless he at least knew where he might best walk unnoticed and which positions might likely prove defendable if the growing anxiety he felt revealed itself to be a true harbinger.

Another yawn. To abandon his task now made absolute sense, yet Evan Wytherling lingered at the window. Tired as he might be, Evan distrusted the calm night. Earlier, as he had departed the company of the over-amiable smith, the veteran knight had heard the howl of a single wolf. While an unremarkable and quite natural sound in so wooded a region, and one that had not even so much as tweaked his senses then, the cry lingered in his mind. Something would happen this night or the next and Evan wanted to be prepared.

Weariness tugged at him again and moments later the fatigued knight began to fade despite his efforts. No one save a single figure that Evan had already marked as a local had passed within sight for at least two hours. Now and then a bird called out, but none with the horribly familiar caw of a carrion crow. All was peaceful.

So much different than the first time he had come to this land. The armies had only begun maneuvering about one another, Pretor and Haggad moving bodies into position in preparation for their terrible game. The sorcerers and wizards remained in the rear. Novaris knew even he would be vulnerable if he strayed too close to the front; on the other side, Centuros ruminated and philosophized about the long-term consequences of war in general, as had ever been his constant and quite annoying habit.

The ghosts warred, the echoes enshrouding Evan. Haggad led his elite warriors forward, his sinister Knights of the Veil. Their garish horned helms—painted with blood—and thick silk masks hid the faces of women dedicated to the craft of killing. Pretor's brave silver-and-blue Rundin Guard would meet them in a clash that left few survivors on either side.

Wallmyrian archers, long practiced at shooting across wild waters at pirate vessels, reaped death on the front lines of the sorcerer-king's forces. The black lancers of Eskreet, mercenaries long in the pay of Novaris, responded by tearing through hapless infantrymen. Sorcery lit the skies above, a hauntingly colorful display meant to add further carnage. Dragons darted about, some with riders, as they sought to avoid the spells while attacking whatever prey made itself visible.

Sword in hand, Evan turned on the nearest rider. The man had only a moment to be startled before the blade buried itself in his throat. Tears swelled in Evan's eyes as he sought the next victim. He would kill more that day than in all his life prior and each death would weigh heavily on his soul.

The battle mounted. Time and time again, Evan swung, sometimes attacking, sometimes defending. The expressions of those he fought seemed ever identical; betrayed, furious, desperate. They all fought to the death, and each thrust of the sword sent a numbing wave of regret and loathing through the knight as he finished his terrible deed.

A shadow draped over him. Talons sought to rake his flesh near the right shoulder. The knight reacted instinctively, turning his sword at the last moment and striking not the man before him but the beast behind.

A snarl. A yelp of pain cutting through the nightmare.

The battle flickered away, the last ghosts receding to the darkness of Evan Wytherling's memories.

He stood in the midst of the room, his chair lying on its back.

The inn! his jumbled mind fought to remind him. *This is the inn, not the battle! The battle is long past, long fought!*

Yet . . . moisture soaked his right arm. Evan touched the area, found his fingers stained crimson. There were fresh gashes on his shoulder where his clothing had been torn away. Belated pain jarred him, but Evan fought it down. He focused his gaze on the edge of his sword, unstained by even the slightest drop of blood.

A whiff of smoke infiltrated his senses. He looked to the side and saw that the smallest of the candles had gone out.

Sword at the ready, Evan approached the shadowy corner. With the tip of the blade, he traced the edge of the gray wall down to the planks of the floor. As solid and unassuming as any of the other corners.

It could have been that while trapped within his own haunted memories he had injured himself, but Evan believed otherwise. The wounds on his shoulder could have been inflicted by neither his sword nor his own hand. They bore the unmistakable marks of a clawed beast, something lupine, perhaps.

A wolf's cry in the night . . .

Evan retrieved the faulty candle with his free hand, keeping his blade pointed at the corner. He scraped excess wax clear of the wick, then, retreating to an adjacent corner, relit the candle with one of the others. Evan did not relax until all four flames jutted high from their appointed positions and even then kept his sword out.

The room secured, Evan Wytherling unbolted his door and peered outside. The narrow hall remained dark and still. Neither the other guests nor the proprietors appeared to have noticed the noise issuing from his quarters. Curious and most convenient. Did one of them know more? Likely not, but Evan vowed he would study his fellow guests closer come the morning.

Clearly his fears concerning Pretor's Hill were more than simply imagination. First the crows, now the claws. Add to them the girl, the cry of the wolf. Forces were gathering . . . had gathered . . . in this site of the epic battle. The stench of Novaris's sorcery might not be evident, but still it saturated the town.

"I have been a fool," the weary knight whispered. Only now did he see that he had been led around by the nose all these years. While he had searched in vain in the West, following dead-end trails, Novaris's legacy had awaited him here, gathering strength. "And are you here as well, sorcerer-king?" Evan dourly said to the shadows.

He had no choice but to speak with Valentin as soon as

possible. Of anyone, Valentin would know best what Novaris had set in motion. Only Valentin could enlighten him . . . or further muddy the truth.

A faint shift in the darkness without hinted at the slow coming of day. Evan's brow furrowed. Had he been so lost among the ghosts of his past that he had missed the last hours of night? A very, very troublesome notion. He needed his faculties at their sharpest when dealing with Valentin.

Sheathing his sword, the knight retired to the bed. No more attacks would come, not this close to dawn. The candles would protect him during the remaining minutes of darkness. All Evan needed were a few hours of sleep . . . but only after he bound the wound. It was not a deep one, but who could say what foulness might infect him if he did not treat it? The weapons of Novaris came in many forms, including those that could easily kill a man from within.

It took but a few minutes to deal with the wound. Evan fell back and closed his eyes, mind churning. He would have to confront Valentin to find out what Novaris had done. It might even be that Valentin could tell him where the sorcerer-king lurked now, provided Novaris still lived after all this time. Whatever had been set in motion could have taken years to reach this point, possibly longer, living well beyond its creator.

Was it then too late to change it?

Tomorrow night, then. Tomorrow night I shall endeavor to renew our acquaintance, Valentin . . . and you shall tell me what I need to know.

It was done. She had freed herself from his control.

Mardi Sinclair surveyed the cramped living quarters in the back of the schoolhouse. Smaller even than her apartment in her uncle's abode, they still seemed so wonderful. They were hers, not his. Even if Yoniff did follow through with his threats, they would surely somehow remain hers. She had planned very carefully for this moment.

A bedroom painted ivory, a narrow kitchen, and a tiny drawing room; that was the extent of her holdings. She could pump water out back. The bedroom had a basin and bed, the kitchen a cedar butcher-block table, four shield-backed chairs, and a cramped cast-iron stove against the main wall and right next to the door leading outside. Mardi would have to make do with many changes; for one thing, the two serving women her uncle kept were no longer at her beck and call.

The bed she had culled from her apartment, the piece having once belonged to her parents. The school building was slightly drafty, but the rich blue-and-white down comforter atop the bed would keep her snuggled warm at night.

On the long shelf that ran the length of one side of the bedroom she had placed her precious books. Paulo Centuros's slim volumes held a place of honor that would enable Mardi to reach for them when she relaxed in bed. Near them stood other volumes the teacher particularly prized, all of them on similar themes.

The great change in her life both exhilarated and intimidated Mardi. In Pretor's Hill it was unheard of for a young, unmarried woman of her station to go out on her own, even if that only meant living in the very building where she taught children. Her new residence required more responsibility, too, for in purchasing this place Mardi had also agreed to take on the rest of the teaching chores, including mathematics, writing, and more. Daunting, but not beyond her. She had excelled at the university and at last some of that education would serve a purpose. The elder generation of Pretor's Hill might be beyond her saving, but the children would grow up with a different outlook, one that did not focus only on material matters. In some small way, she would make a difference here.

At least, Mardi hoped so.

There would be no lessons this day. Mardi had arranged everything to make the transition as smooth as possible. Yoniff, ever against her desire, had refused any aid when she had started moving. In the end, Mardi had brought all her smaller belongings herself, her satisfaction growing with each item transferred to her new home. The bed and a few other pieces she had paid some local youths to cart over.

Although morning had come, Mardi had to light a small lamp. The weather had turned, gray clouds covering the sky, stronger winds tossing leaves about. She had even been forced to wear a long woolen cloak over her green cotton dress while outside, the temperature a good margin below what it should have been for this time of year. Still, despite the inhospitable weather, the gentlewoman felt warm inside.

She also felt hunger. She had not yet been able to gather food. The market would be open now and it behooved her to shop early, while the best items were still in stock.

As Mardi departed the building, she scared off a pair of baleful crows from her step. The malevolent-looking creatures took to the nearest tree, then cawed angrily at her from the safety of their new posts. Mardi ignored the birds, more intent on her task. Her stomach growled.

A throng already filled the wide, five-sided marketplace by the time Mardi, empty wicker basket in hand, arrived. Perhaps it had something to do with the weather, but she immediately noticed that the mood among her fellows had become rather sour. To be sure there were the usual sounds of gaiety and haggling, but mixed in were too many disgruntled faces and petty arguments. People pulled cloaks tight and on occasion glared at one another in what seemed suspicion. A fishmonger's wife in a stained yellow apron snapped at another woman in a manner that certainly had to cost her a good sale, but she seemed not to care. Two men nearly came to blows over a chicken even though Mardi could not see the difference between it and the others hanging nearby.

Despite such incidents, she still found it a joy to shop for herself. Each item the teacher added to the covered basket was for her use alone. However, she did not buy without giving her purchases much thought. Mardi knew she had to stock her tiny kitchen with care; she had to rely on her own earnings from here on, not those of her uncle.

As the morning aged, Mardi Sinclair began raiding her own basket while she hunted for other necessities. It was while she searched for a second apple within that the young gentlewoman nearly collided with someone. Mardi had only a glimpse of a cloaked shoulder, then heard a worn yet somehow gentle voice beg pardon. Collecting herself, she looked up in time to see a tall, familiar figure disappearing among the milling townsfolk.

The apple fell forgotten into the basket.

Mardi tried to follow after him, the better to get a look at his face, but now everyone slowed her. One after another, townsfolk found reason to pause in her way . . . or so it at least felt. Only by sheer effort did Mardi keep her objective in sight and even then she could not be certain it was the same person. Yet . . . it had to be.

The knight. The very selfsame knight she had caught sight of from the window of her old apartment. Despite Daniel's easy dismissal of the stranger as simply an old battlefield scavenger, Mardi Sinclair felt certain he was so much more.

You're being ridiculous, she chided. *Daniel wouldn't lie to you about something so insignificant.* Nevertheless, the gentlewoman continued to hunt after the knight. She had to satisfy her own curiosity, no matter how foolish it felt.

A bulky figure clad in a leather work apron stepped in front of Mardi. "A fine deerskin pouch, young lady?"

His form entirely blocked her view. With some irritation, Mardi involuntarily snapped, "No! I don't want any of your goods!"

Instead of stepping back, the man took great umbrage at her words. The round, almost ursine face grimaced and the beady brown eyes below the thick brow suddenly glared savage. "You saying my leatherwork's no good, woman? You saying that I do shoddy craftsmanship?"

"No! I—"

He nearly thrust the pouch in her face. "Where do you get off looking down on my hard work? If you think that I'll just let you talk so about my goods in public like that, so high and mighty gentlewoman, I'll—"

"Let me by!" Mardi tried to slip by him, but he blocked her path again. Although she did not personally know him, Mardi had seen the leather worker many, many times in the market and he had always struck her as a moderately peaceful man. Why take to such anger simply because she did not want to purchase his works?

"I'll not!" With his free hand, he took hold of her arm.

What overcame her next, Mardi Sinclair could not say. Suddenly the basket fell to the ground. Her left hand caught the man by the throat, her right his arm. Although in Mardi's eyes she only grazed his throat, the man coughed violently. He released his hold and began choking.

Mardi stepped back, stunned at what she had done. Her victim fell to his knees still trying to breathe. His face turned purple with the effort. A stout, plain-faced woman came from behind the stall and rushed to his side.

Although she had only been defending herself, Mardi felt moved to help. "Please, let me—"

"Get away from my husband, witch!"

The woman looked prepared to tear her eyes out. Mardi did not want to abandon the man for fear she would later find out she had killed him. She did not even understand what she had done to him, so instinctive had been her reaction.

At last the vendor slowly regained his breath. The moment Mardi saw that he would recover, she backed away into the surrounding crowd. Best to stay clear and hope things quieted over. No one even paid her much attention, for which the stunned teacher was grateful. Mardi felt distraught enough without having to face other accusers as well.

Away from the scene of her terrifying fury, Mardi tried to focus on the knight again. Unfortunately, he appeared to be gone. How could anyone vanish with such swiftness? Pretor's Hill had grown to be a good-sized town, but it was no Coramas.

"So, here you are!"

She tried to turn, but arms had already encircled her from behind. She pried her attacker's hands away and spun around— only to discover Daniel, dressed resplendently in high leather boots, black pants, and tailed jacket with a white silk shirt showing underneath the last. Mardi reddened.

Eyebrows knotted in confusion, Daniel asked, "What've I done?"

"It's not you . . . it's not."

He gingerly touched both her shoulders and looked into her eyes. "Are you all right? What's happened?"

She could not speak of the incident with the vendor now, in part for fear he would not understand. "I'm sorry . . . give me a moment." She turned away and began to walk slowly.

"I'd gladly give you my entire lifetime, you know that, Mardi," Daniel said, staying close.

She managed a smile.

Daniel smiled back, looking as if he genuinely meant it.

Mardi took a good look at him as they strolled through the square. He wore formal clothes such as his father wore whenever he presented himself in the name of official guild business, only with slight touches that spoke of his own personality. While the black coat bore the yellow sash of the merchant guild, the sash itself had been embroidered with a small green crescent, the symbol of the university in Coramas. Daniel had studied there just before Mardi. He also wore his matching cloak at a jaunty angle, not straight over each shoulder as was the norm among his elders. Like most of his clothing, Daniel's present outfit had been tailored in Coramas. However, in a sign of his family's wealth and connections, the young merchant's knee-high leather boots had been imported from far-off Tepis. Mardi thought the boots made him look something like a dashing cavalry officer in the Rundin Guard.

"I was hunting for you so that I could apologize for not

helping this morning, Mardi. I realized that you'd probably need assistance moving and I did more than once promise you I'd do my part." Seeing her again glance at his finery, the merchant stepped back to display himself better for her. "As you can see, guild business came up. I found out last night after I returned home. Needless to say, I feel very guilty and I'd understand if you'd never forgive me for my sin."

The last he said with that smile she rarely could resist. Beyond that, she could not be angry at someone so concerned for her. It had not been his fault that he had been unable to come to her aid. "You don't have to apologize to me, Daniel."

"Wonderful." He took her arm in his. "Shall we continue your shopping, then? Afterward, we can return to your new home and you can show me around."

"There's very little to see. A kitchen, a tiny bedroom, and not much else. Besides, it would be unseemly if I let you in without someone else present."

"Unseemly? My dear, lovely Mardi, we were trained in Coramas, not this provincial little place. If we choose to see one another in your home, what of it? In the capital, it would mean nothing."

"But we're in Pretor's Hill now," the gentlewoman reminded him, politely disengaging his arm from hers, "and my students have parents who wouldn't care for a teacher who acts so freely with unmarried men."

"Then marry me."

She paled, struck dumb by the seriousness of his tone, the intense stare of his piercing silver-blue eyes. He had bandied words with her in the past, hinting of his intentions, but this was the first time Daniel had ever asked her outright.

"Daniel—"

Clad as he was, with his thick pale-blond hair dangling just over each shoulder, he could have been one of the champions from the days of Paulo Centuros, not a landowner and the son of the wealthiest of merchants. A finer catch no woman could ask for, so

43

her uncle would have said . . . and perhaps that was one reason she could not say yes.

"You'd have the best, love, and could do whatever you want. Teach the little ragamuffins to read or do your own tapestry work. The choice is yours. My father would welcome the match, I know; you being Yoniff's niece would do it even if you were as ugly as old Jak—"

"How charming."

A chuckle. "But he'd prefer to have a wellborn beauty for his favorite son."

Trust not in the face of prosperity, the glib tongue of princes with promises of gold. The words flowed through Mardi Sinclair's mind without invitation; Paulo Centuros's words from the book she had been reading in the woods only yesterday. Why they came unbidden she did not know. Nonetheless, their very presence dampened the mood, ensuring that she could give her suitor but one answer.

"I'm sorry, Daniel. I . . . I really am, but I can't marry you just yet."

An expression crossed his face, an expression so dark that for a moment Mardi feared he would strike her. It vanished almost as quickly as it had appeared, but long enough to become burned into her memory.

"I completely understand, love." Daniel Taran smiled, no trace whatsoever remaining of his brief fury. "You've got so much going on now. I won't give up, though."

Without warning, he bent down and kissed her. Mardi froze, emotions in yet further conflict. The young merchant smiled again, adding, "I definitely won't give up."

Adjusting his cloak, Daniel strode off into the throng, more than one feminine gaze following his departure. Mardi turned away, trying to reorient herself. What had she seen in his face? Never had she known Daniel to show such a temper. He had always been suave, a man of learning and fine breeding. This new part of him frightened Mardi, especially since it seemed that he had barely kept it in check. What would have happened if he had not held back?

What was the matter with everyone? Tempers flared so readily these days. Pretor's Hill had always had its share of volatile souls, but even more so now, if she were any judge. Even Mardi had proven vulnerable.

Perhaps it's just my nerves. With so much change in her life and her uncle's constant threats hanging over her head, Mardi Sinclair suspected that she might just be a little more sensitive to what went on around her. Perhaps people also missed the wonderful warmth of the recently passed summer. Thus far, the fall weather had been cold and more than a little damp. Likely people would settle down once they grew used to the change.

That had to be it. Mardi forced herself to settle down and renew her shopping, but her mind now shifted back to her earlier quest. Once more she had missed her opportunity to see for herself this visitor to her town. Why his presence so interested her, Mardi Sinclair could not say, but the urge bordered almost on obsession. Without realizing it, the gentlewoman found herself already walking in the same direction she had last seen him go.

By now he had to be far away, but if not, then maybe Mardi could satisfy her curiosity and move on with other matters. She expected disappointment; Daniel's description made more sense than her own fanciful visions. Still, it would eat at her until she either found him or learned that he had departed . . .

At that moment, something foul fluttered at her face, cawing harshly in her ear.

Mardi gasped, then stumbled back. The huge black form of a bird filled her vision. She dropped the basket as she tried to fight off the monstrous avian. The blackbird refused to retreat, snapping at her and clawing at her face.

"Please!" she screamed in terror. "Someone help me!"

A few hours of sleep had ever sufficed for Evan. He had risen shortly after the proprietors had, coming downstairs just as they had finished organizing the morning meal. Evan paid for the simplest fare, then immediately departed to reconnoiter the town, especially the areas most immediate to the church. Many eyes watched him as he toured Pretor's Hill, but none that Evan Wytherling judged to be a danger to him.

Yet . . . sometimes he sensed something amiss. The day had already grown more overcast than the previous. The wind, too, had picked up some. But most of the townsfolk seemed not to notice anything out of the ordinary, so Evan reluctantly chose to judge the shift in weather as normal until he could learn otherwise.

Every now and then, the carrion crows materialized. One here on a fence, two there on a rooftop, another picking at some refuse in the street. Evan wondered if they watched him, but all had kept their distance and so he had done nothing to pursue the matter.

In any town, the two best places to hunt for information had most often turned out to be the inns and the marketplace. Generally, the market proved more active this early in the day, the best place for even a warhound such as him to mix inconspicuously with the general population. At least some of the townsfolk had to be easier to deal with than Evan's hosts.

He had learned quickly the essentials of life in Pretor's Hill. A town council ruled here, five men chosen from among the best families. They passed laws, gave speeches, and introduced proclamations. Evan had soon forgotten their names, so interchangeable did the men sound when spoken of by those he had questioned. Besides, the true power appeared to be in the hands of the magistrate, a conservative elder by the name of Drulane. Drulane had the ear of the king's man, someone known as Lord Steppenwald. Evan had learned little about Steppenwald; most folk could not even recall ever having caught more than a glimpse of him. The knight gathered that the king's man stood tall and might arrive without notice, but other than that no one could say more. He made a mental note to learn more about Coramas's representative in these remote parts. Steppenwald, should he visit during the knight's hopefully brief stay, might prove a better source of information than even the inhabitants. Certainly Coramas could not have forgotten the significance of the battle against Novaris.

But the memories and gratitude of kings can be short-lived, Paulo Centuros had told Evan Wytherling shortly before sending the knight on this endless quest. *And the memories of their successors even more so.*

While there was much Evan would have argued over with Centuros, this was one notion he could not. In the course of pursuing Novaris, he had run across more than his fair share of kings and others with memories shorter than the blink of an eye. More than once he had barely escaped those mercurial moods. The protections granted him by Centuros did not make him invulnerable, they only forced him to efforts he would have otherwise chosen to forego.

His mind was engaged in such thoughts when he once again came across the young woman from the forest.

She did not notice him, her mind apparently on her morning shopping. He observed her for a moment, noting that she moved more like a hunter than some wealthy landowner's pampered daughter. Her hair, again braided, seemed almost to glitter. The eyes, he saw at last, were a rich, alert cocoa brown, almost exotic. She walked with a fascinating but contradictory mix of surety and indecision.

For some reason he could not explain, Evan continued to watch her. Only belatedly did he suddenly realize his focus had been so great that she was about to walk into him. At the last moment, she noticed him in turn. Evan managed an apology, then made a hasty retreat. As he did, long-suppressed memories of another woman abruptly stirred memories that he quickly buried again.

Evan had gone but a short distance when he heard the flap of wings, the caw of the blackbird, and a startled exclamation from the selfsame woman from whom he had fled. He whirled, dagger at the ready, wondering what he would do and why he had to be the one to do it. The answer to the second part came first, for when the knight returned to the scene, the first thing he noticed was that although most of those around could see the woman's predicament, they had so far done nothing. Fear, curiosity, even disinterest marked the faces of the throng; but among them not one moved to aid the woman.

He did not hesitate with the dagger, aiming and tossing with a precision borne of too many years of training and far too many moments of necessity. The blade buried itself deep into the monstrous avian, the largest of the carrion crows that the knight had so far marked. Momentum sent both blade and bird hurtling past the gentlewoman.

Mardi stared wide-eyed at the jeweled hilt of a dagger that had embedded itself so deep in the avian's breast that it had pinned the corpse to the post.

While her struggle had not attracted the attention of those around her, the actions of her sudden champion had. Small wonder, too, for coming toward Mardi was one who, despite a lack of armor, had to be the selfsame knight for whom she had been searching.

Vision and reality mixed. No gleaming paladin this one, but also no scavenger of the battlefield dead. A veteran campaigner, true, possibly nearly as old as her uncle, yet there lurked within him both a sense of youth and a great weariness.

Under a much-used cloak, the knight wore a simple tunic colored blue-gray. His pants were a darker gray, formfitting, and disappeared just above the shin into a pair of heavy, weather-beaten black boots. The similarity in colors made her immediately compare him to Daniel, and, despite the difference in age and life, the battle-weary figure before her came out the better against the wealthy merchant's son.

To her wonderment, he walked past her without a word. Ignoring also the startled townsfolk, who only now seemed to realize that one of their own had been assaulted, the knight reached out and pulled the dagger free. He shook the grotesque corpse from the blade, allowing the dead avian to drop unceremoniously to the cobblestones, then wiped off the dagger with a small piece of cloth.

As he sheathed his weapon, his eyes at last narrowed on her.

"A most offensive fowl, my lady. I hope he did not mar your features."

"No, I . . . thank you." Mardi could not help staring at him. Life had etched itself deep into the knight, marking every inch of him, every movement he made. She could never have mistaken him for anything less than what he was. He might have stepped out of the works of Paulo Centuros.

The knight approached her, so imposing that she could scarce believe he was real. "There is blood from the bird on your cheek, my lady."

His hand proved surprisingly gentle as he wiped a small spot from the left side of her face. His gaze flicked away momentarily, as if he were embarrassed by his own presumptuousness. Mardi remained still, uncertain as to how she should speak to him.

"Not the most humanitarian town," the knight at last commented, eyes turning briefly to the marketplace, where most of Mardi's fellow citizens had already returned to their own interests. "A telling sign, that."

Mardi realized he had been talking to himself as much as to her. She opened her mouth, but still nothing of significance emerged. "Thank you . . . again."

"I did nothing much." Without warning, he turned and started away.

She stood watching, unable at first to keep up with the shifting events around her. Then, with a curious determination,

Mardi Sinclair steadied herself and hurried after him, her basket and the blackbird all but forgotten.

The hand that but a minute later retrieved the bloody remains of the antagonistic avian wore a glove of the finest leather, a glove that had been custom fashioned not only because of its wearer's august station but also the massive size of the hand. Near the wrist of the glove, two small gems, one crimson, one ebony, had been sewn in, one next to the other. The gems twinkled despite an overcast sky.

The other gloved hand held tight to the jeweled head of an elegantly curled wooden cane, upon which two stones—the same crimson and ebony—represented the eyes of a beast, a dragon.

Inspection of the bird took but a breath, perhaps two, then the wearer of the glove allowed the remnants to fall again to the cobblestones. A heavy brown boot, also finely crafted, came down and ground the feathered carcass until nothing recognizable remained.

With one tap of the dragon-head cane, the massive figure turned and calmly walked away in the direction opposite where Mardi Sinclair and Evan Wytherling had gone.

The gentlewoman followed Evan now, something he did not need. He had been fool enough when he had chosen to aid her, drawing yet more attention to himself too early in the game. At one time, Valentin would have laughed at his chivalry . . . or perhaps more at his lack of desire to try to reap some benefit from the grateful young woman. Valentin had always stuck to the task, no matter how onerous, and had not allowed himself to be drawn into another's troubles.

The entire situation struck Evan as ludicrous. He had come

seeking information from the locals and yet now ran from one who might be able to provide him with many of the details still missing. Yet, Evan could not remain near her; he still was unsure if she presented any danger to him, and her resemblance to that other stirred thoughts and emotions he no longer cared to relive.

Not for the first time, Evan Wytherling wished he had never heard of sorcerers, much less lived among them.

"Stand where you are."

A wall of armored flesh blocked his path, four men taller than the knight and clad in the gray and silver garb he had come to recognize as that of the town watch. The two tallest had identical features reminiscent of wild boars, if such a description did not give offense to the animals in question. Neither face contained even an iota of compassion. The other pair, while not as severe in looks as the monstrous twins, matched their dour moods.

A shorter, bearded man, evidently the officer in charge, stepped up to the knight. "The magistrate desires to see you."

So they had indeed come for him. Although this surely could not be a common occurrence in Pretor's Hill, Evan marveled at the disinterest most of the inhabitants around him displayed even now. No one seemed to care about or even find extraordinary any of the unsettling events going on around them. Did huge carrion crows regularly attempt to savage unsuspecting travelers? Did the town watch take every outsider into custody without regard to whether they had actually committed any wrongdoing? If so, then perhaps it was too late to save Pretor's Hill from itself.

Evan's hand did not move so much as a hair's breadth toward the dagger. He did not regret having left the sword in his room; after the incident outside the inn, the knight had judged it better to keep the weapon out of sight. The men before him seemed uncommonly eager for some excuse to use their own blades, worn but still worthy enough weapons in the hands of giants such as them.

"I have done nothing." Interesting that the magistrate, the one who truly ruled Pretor's Hill, should desire his company so suddenly. Had he been watched by another while he had been surreptitiously questioning those in the market?

The officer remained straight-faced. "The magistrate desires to see you. Now."

Running afoul of the town watch had not been part of his plan, but he could not refuse, not without destroying any chance he had to make sense of matters. Perhaps Magistrate Drulane might even prove to be the one with the answers he needed. Evan doubted that the man intended him any permanent trouble at this point. Curiosity, that had to be it. The magistrate needed to know who this rare outsider was and what disruption he might cause in the official's little kingdom.

Perhaps he might even enlighten me about this king's man, Steppenwald. Drulane seemed the only one who knew anything about the representative from Coramas.

"I will not fight you," he finally said, noting that patience did not appear a virtue among any of the watchmen.

A hint of disappointment crossed the faces of the brutes, but the officer simply nodded. "Arms wide."

Evan obeyed. Searching his prisoner, the bearded man removed Evan's dagger and thrust it into his own belt. He then thoroughly frisked Evan for any other weapons. Briefly the man touched the pale deerskin pouch on the knight's left side, but, clearly believing it empty, left it where it hung. The knight hid his relief. Without the wizard's pouch, he would have been bereft of funds.

"This way." With Evan surrounded, they marched from the marketplace, then through a maze of narrow streets that disoriented even the experienced tracker. Once again, Evan Wytherling wondered about the design of the town. The region near the church had struck him as peculiar; so now did this. Some pattern of angles existed, but why and what purpose it served remained as yet unclear.

Their myriad path eventually ended at the steps of a rectangular, stone-front building as dour as the knight's companions. The offices and likely residence of the town magistrate stood three floors tall with jutting bay windows in front and false parapets at the roof. Time and soot had darkened the structure to an ashy brown, giving it a depressive air that surely had to dampen the already low spirits of those brought here under less than favorable circumstances.

The plain bronze door to the magistrate's abode opened as the group started up the steps, and a skeletal, well-clad man with a fringe of white hair confronted the small group. Evan's doubts that this man could be Drulane were verified a moment later by the watch officer, who immediately greeted the thin figure as Master Casperin.

Casperin studied the knight with only mild interest. "What have we here?"

"The magistrate desires to see him."

"With good reason, no doubt." Master Casperin dismissed both the matter and the band without another word, stalking past the knight and his companions as if on his way to some important appointment.

The path clear, the watch marched Evan into the building and down a red-carpeted marble corridor with bone-white walls that gave way to double oak doors guarded by two men. The bearded officer approached and knocked on one of the doors. A muffled voice called from within. The officer entered, then reappeared less than a minute later.

"Bring him in."

Evan's guards pushed him forward and the officer ushered him in, closing the door behind them. Evan straightened, keeping his head high as he entered the magistrate's chambers. He briefly surveyed the room from end to end, instinctively estimating distances to windows and what items he might use to defend himself before finally focusing on the extravagant, dark oak desk and the gnarled man behind it.

"Bring him forward," Magistrate Drulane commanded in a rasping voice. The white-haired, elderly man coughed twice, then quickly drank from a small silver glass filled with what Evan guessed to be wine. Drulane coughed twice more, than peered at the knight through watery brown eyes. To the man who had brought Evan to him, he ordered, "You are dismissed."

The officer looked uncomfortable. "Magistrate—"

"Concern noted," Drulane interjected, never once shifting his gaze from the prisoner. "Now go, Bulrik."

Bulrik saluted, then turned. Evan found himself alone with the gnarled man. For the first time he saw that near the magistrate's left hand lay the dagger the officer had taken from him. That Drulane knew how to use such a weapon with effectiveness would not have surprised him.

"What is your name, paladin?"

No one had used such a term for Evan in many years, and he felt no right to be called by such even now. "I am no paladin. I was a knight, Evan Wytherling by name, if you must know."

"Evan Wytherling . . ." Drulane picked up the dagger and toyed with it, pressing the tip gently into his right index finger. To Evan's surprise, a drop of blood splattered on a sheet of paper below the hand. The generously nosed, gnomish man continued on as if not noticing the wound. "Evan Wytherling . . ." He coughed once, but settled down again. "Paladin. This dagger. The questions that my sources say you asked of my people. The coins which Master Casperin, a very knowledgeable man where money is concerned, says were minted before Pretor's Hill even existed."

Trying to follow Drulane's words, Evan felt some concern. The man knew much about him, no doubt more than simply what was said.

Drulane coughed again and this time set down the dagger in order to take another sip from the glass. When his malady had at last settled again, he once more stared at the knight with eyes that, although watery, showed no loss of the intelligence that enabled the magistrate to rule his town. "Evan Wytherling . . . have you come to save us?"

IV

SORCERY STIRRING

A stunned Mardi watched as Bulrik, Drulane's favored officer, took the knight away. Why would the magistrate want to take him into custody? Was it because he was a stranger? Surely the man had done nothing wrong since his arrival; to the contrary, only he had made any move to rescue her from the mad bird. She thought of approaching the watch officer and insisting he let the traveler be, but Bulrik and his men would only have laughed in her face.

The magistrate did not simply pull strangers off the street. While there had always been much about Drulane that Mardi had not cared for, particularly his interest in her and her money, she had generally respected the manner in which he performed his duties. The town council membership changed with the wind, but Drulane ever remained Drulane. Such actions as this did not befit him.

What can I do? Nothing came to mind. Had she ever shown interest in the magistrate's attention, Mardi might have influence on the man, but her rejection of any approach on his part meant he would do nothing for her.

She followed the knight and his captors until they reached their destination, Drulane's residence. Mardi paused near the corner of a squat, redbrick building across from the magistrate's— a fortuitous decision, for in the next moment Drulane's door opened and out stepped her uncle. Mardi moved to the side to avoid being seen and watched as Yoniff glanced at the knight, then spoke briefly with Bulrik before departing.

Whether her uncle had anything to do with the knight's arrest or had been instead speaking with the magistrate about her earlier rebellion, Mardi could not say. As Bulrik led the others in, Mardi briefly debated waiting where she was or following after Yoniff. She quickly decided that she would learn little enough from her uncle.

Why am I doing this? Mardi did not know anything about the warrior save that he had rescued her from the demented bird. Yet at the same time she felt that she knew him, as if they shared some link. Absurd, but Mardi could not shake the feeling. She had to speak with him, find out more and make sense of what she felt.

Peel away the layers and you will find the truth, Paulo Centuros had written in the book she had been reading. *Peel away the truth and you will find the lies upon which it was built.*

Mardi shook her head, trying to clear away the disturbing words. She leaned against the building and watched the doorway. If the knight did not emerge after a short time, then she would go inside and do her best to set him free. Drulane had no reason to hold the man for very long . . . no reason, she suspected, to hold him at all.

So what did Drulane want of the outsider?

Evan met the magistrate's steady gaze. "I do not understand."

"No?" Drulane swept his hand over the injured appendage. When Evan could see the finger again, he noted that the wound no longer existed. The magistrate then reached for the dagger, picking it up by thumb and forefinger at the hilt. He touched the point against the polished desktop and proceeded to spin the weapon. The dagger whirled faster and faster, remaining ever in place without any sign of slowing.

The knight's brow furrowed. More sorcery, albeit of a minor sort. Still, Evan had neither smelled nor sensed its presence, which disturbed him far more than he dared let on to the magistrate. This close, the wizard's gift should have alerted him to Drulane's abilities, no matter how minute. That it had not meant trouble indeed; if he could not rely on what he knew, then the quest shifted even more to Novaris's advantage.

"It will continue to spin until I will it not to," the magistrate rasped, "and yet . . . and yet I am no spellcaster, my honorable friend."

The blade had its enchantments, but none enabling it to perform such a useless task. Evan remained silent, knowing that Drulane would go on.

"There are many who say that sorcery is a dying thing, at least in Rundin. Greylion IV, whose avid interests had always been of the more mundane sciences, refused to allow those with sorcerous potential to be taught at the great schools in Coramas. Backward, chaotic, a discipline designed to keep those without ability in the darkness . . . those were his general"—Drulane paused to cough twice—"general words. Ironic that so progressive a kingdom as ours would reject the magic arts, don't you think?"

"I have no opinion on the subject."

Watery eyes narrowed. "None?" The dagger stopped spinning but remained upright. "None. Fascinating. Perhaps I am wrong, my honorable friend. Perhaps you are simply here by coincidence." The dagger dropped with a clatter onto the desk as Drulane stared unblinking into Evan's eyes. "I do not believe in coincidence."

For nearly a minute the knight and his host simply studied one another. Evan wondered at the magistrate's motives and intentions. Too many had seen Evan Wytherling as a tool to be used as they pleased without thought of consequence. Some Evan had fought, others he had used in turn so long as it suited the quest. Which of these Drulane might be he could not guess. However, he began to suspect that the man before him, while more knowledgeable than most about matters in Pretor's Hill, still knew too little about the terrible truth.

"I am no spellcaster, Evan Wytherling. I lack any such ability and yet I can do this thing. My mother, she had no ability, either, but she knew how to read the signs of troubling times and this she taught me as a child." A fit of coughing struck the gnarled man, forcing him to drink again. He seemed not to care a whit what Evan did in the meantime, although Evan knew better than to try to escape or even assault his host. Clearing his throat, Drulane at last continued, "I have seen birds of black flock as they do only on the battlefield, shadows move when they should not, and heard whispers where no one stands. Last night I heard a beast roar like thunder, but no one else seems to have."

If he expected a response from Evan, then the knight disappointed him, despite growing interest. Evan believed everything that the magistrate had heard or observed. Drulane did not strike him as a man given to fantasizing such dark happenings. That Drulane did not understand what he experienced, Evan Wytherling sympathized. Much had he experienced over the years of his quest that still mystified and perturbed him. Novaris and Centuros had not been the only powers loose upon the lands, and some of those other powers had not been of human origin. Possibly the magistrate's occurrences, too, had such origins, although Evan still suspected the handiwork of the ancient sorcerer-king in this. Even if Novaris truly had died some time in the past, his legacy lived on, of that Evan was certain.

"Pretor's Hill has a past," Evan finally remarked.

The twisted man blinked, clearly surprised that his guest had deigned to comment at last. He nodded, leaning back into the simple dark oak chair so very austere in comparison to the elegant desk with its scrollwork edges and lion-paw feet. "I know Pretor's past. I know about the war. The sorcerers. The bloodshed." He touched the hilt of Evan's dagger. "I have collected artifacts, my honorable friend. I know the banners and marks of every general, every master, who fought in that epic struggle."

Drulane knew much but could not know them all. To know more might be dangerous for the magistrate, so Evan would not enlighten the man on those gaps.

"I do not believe the age of wizards, sorcerers, dragons, and demons has passed Rundin, Evan Wytherling." With a sudden move that surprised even the trained fighter for a moment, Drulane swept up the dagger in his hand and threw it at the figure before him. Evan caught the glittering weapon inches before it would have struck his chest . . . hilt-first. Maintaining his gaze on the magistrate, he returned the dagger to its rightful place.

"I would leave candles in the corners of shadowed rooms," he said, giving Drulane the best advice he could offer.

"I do. My mother taught me that, also. She taught me much, my honorable friend, but I sometimes wonder if it is enough for what seems to be happening here." The magistrate coughed, then casually turned away from his guest. "May your visit to our fair town be fruitful . . . and blessedly short."

Evan heard the dismissal in the man's voice. They had reached some sort of silent agreement for the time being. Drulane would do nothing about Evan for now except no doubt have him watched. If the watchers did not hinder him or place his mission at risk, Evan would ignore them. If otherwise, then it was likely he and the magistrate would be having a second—and not so cordial—meeting.

"Pretor's Hill was the site of much powerful and devious sorcery, Evan Wytherling," the knight's host abruptly added, looking back at him. "I understand that and somehow I think you understand it even better than me." Drulane did not ask for verification of his suspicions. He clearly wanted to know more about the man before him but would not press for now. "Sorcery does not die easily. Sometimes it lingers on and on and on . . ."

"It does."

"Bulrik will not delay your departure."

Evan started to turn, then paused to ask, "What does Lord Steppenwald think of this?"

A transformation came over the magistrate, one so complete that the veteran knight could barely hold his surprise in check. The watery yet ever-attentive eyes lost some of their focus. The gnarled man straightened even though it clearly pained him to do so. With one hand he tapped slowly on the desk, the sounds forming a pattern that repeated itself after every fourth beat.

"Master Steppenwald has not visited Pretor's Hill in some weeks." The tapping continued. "I have told him nothing."

The magistrate's eyes shifted to their former state. The thrumming ended in midbeat. Drulane's gaze turned to papers on his desk and he began to work as if Evan did not stand before him.

The knight departed the magistrate's chamber in silence, knowing he had learned more than he had bargained for and understanding less by the moment. The elder man's reaction had not been what he had expected. Drulane's transformation had smelled of mesmerism or something even more sinister. What part did this Steppenwald play in Pretor's Hill? If it involved sorcery, why had Evan not sensed it, just as he had not sensed the powers his host had displayed?

Drulane claimed no natural skills and Evan believed him, but the spinning dagger and the healing of the wound required more than passing ability. What would enable an unTalented, as spellcasters were wont to call those without sorcerous ability, to perform such acts?

Bulrik and the giants stood at attention in the outer hall, not so much as flickering an eyelid as the knight passed. Evan had little time to admire their professional manner, his thoughts still aswirl. He had come to Pretor's Hill seeking information, but more and more he feared that what he had found would reveal itself to be a danger as great as that of facing the sorcerer-king himself.

"Damn you, Centuros . . ." the weary knight muttered as he left the building. "I have done far more than you deserve. I have fulfilled my mission a thousand times save that I cannot prove Novaris dead. I have nearly died that many times in the process and still your curse insists I go on and on . . ."

A shadow of movement caught his attention as he walked into the street. Evan's hand slowly slipped toward his dagger. In the daytime, even with so overcast a heaven, he did not expect anything more deadly than armed sentinels, albeit clumsy ones in this case. That they lacked much in the way of stealth made the knight wonder if he had misjudged the magistrate's resources. Certainly if Drulane had wanted him watched he would have chosen more subtle methods and better-trained observers.

Keeping careful track of his would-be shadow, Evan crossed the main avenue, heading toward an alley. So far he had marked only one possible pursuer, but there yet might be more. Either way, he had no intention of letting this game continue; there was little doubt in the knight's mind that this was a threat readily handled. He increased his pace in a casual manner, as if simply on his way to some appointment. Behind him he heard the light tapping of shoes as whoever followed fought to match his speed. Now his curiosity overtook his natural caution. What sort of assassin or spy followed in shoes that echoed as loud as thunder on the cobblestones?

He turned into the alley, immediately measuring the narrow, moss-accented passage for the best defensive positions. Three likely spots caught his eye. But then something about the sound of the nearing footsteps gave Evan pause.

The tap-tap of his pursuer's shoes grew louder. Evan drew the dagger on the chance that he might be wrong, then flattened himself against the wall that would longest protect him from view.

The figure that turned into the alley without even pausing stood at least a foot shorter than him. Evan raised the dagger to throat level, seizing the hunter's arm at the same time.

She gasped and tried to wriggle free. The knight tightened his grip and waited until his prisoner's efforts at last subsided.

"You did not scream."

"What point would there have been?" she asked, fear giving way to defiance. "Besides, I don't think you'll use that."

He would not have, but it surprised him that she would be so trusting. As Evan had suspected, his tracker had been the selfsame gentlewoman he had rescued in the market. She had to be more naive than he had originally thought her. "Why did you follow me?"

"He let you go. Drulane, I mean. Why did he drag you inside

in the first place? Was it something to do with my uncle?"

Evan released his grip. "I asked you a question."

She took a deep breath, then exhaled. Her demeanor again reminded him of that other, lost to him so long ago. He wanted to retreat from her, but suspected that she would continue to hound him. That struck him as strange, for even the magistrate wanted little to do with an outsider. Only the smith and this woman exhibited any openness.

"I . . . I don't really know why I followed you. I guess . . . I guess I wanted to see if you were real."

"I am. Your curiosity is now satisfied." Evan put away the dagger and turned from her. "Good day, my lady."

"Wait!" The young woman took hold of his arm, a riskier act than she realized. "Wait. I'm sorry. Please . . . may I just talk with you?"

Evan would not be rid of her until she had her way. He resigned himself to the encounter, trying to think of a manner by which he could shorten their conversation as politely as possible. The knight had little time for useless prattle. Drulane had stirred a hornet's nest within him. "If you can keep up with me, you may speak."

Before she could thank him he had already started off. Although turned about by the mad route Drulane's men had used, Evan recalled the general direction of the market. From there he could readily find his way to the inn and the stable where his horse awaited him.

"Are you really a knight?"

It would have been tempting to give her the answer he felt most true, but she would not have understood his sense of disgrace any more than Centuros had. "I am."

"You're not from Rundin, are you? I mean, you have a slight accent and your face isn't right."

Her simple description of his face nearly made him smile for the first time in months. "No. My face is not right."

She evidently realized her error. "No. I mean that you don't

62

look like—"

"I am not from Rundin. I was born much farther southwest." He did not elaborate. Why speak of a kingdom long eradicated from history? Even if she recognized the name, what would it mean to her?

The wind picked up as they walked, forcing the gentlewoman to pull her cloak tighter around her throat. Evan kept his eyes from her as much as possible; she reminded him of that other and yet there was more to it. Something about the woman herself struck him as familiar. He did not like that; too many complications made for too many mistakes of judgment.

"My name is . . . Mardi Sinclair." A pause followed, one in which she expected him to tell her his name. When that did not happen, she finally asked him for it.

"My name would mean nothing to you, my lady, but if you must have it, it is Evan Wytherling." Pretor's name she would have recognized, of course, and possibly Paulo Centuros, Novaris, and even maybe Haggad and a few others. His, she would not have, for which Evan found himself both grateful and yet a little disappointed.

She asked him simple questions about some of the other lands he had visited, which he answered as simply as possible. The woman clearly had other, more penetrating questions she desired to ask, but had not yet garnered enough courage to do so.

It took longer than Evan had hoped, but at last they reached the marketplace. Unfortunately, his companion seemed not yet ready to part from him. Determined to be rid of her, Evan picked up his pace. Beside him, Mardi Sinclair began to breathe more rapidly, but she matched him step for step, her shoes repeating the same tap-tap sound over and over.

"Why are you in Pretor's Hill, Evan Wytherling?"

So she had finally found the strength. "It is where my path took me."

"No one comes to Pretor's Hill unless they have to," she retorted. "Even the king's man comes but once a season or so, sometimes less."

Mention of the enigmatic Steppenwald caught his attention. "Has he been here of late, this king's man?"

Unlike the magistrate, Mardi Sinclair did not grow distant when asked about the representative from Coramas. "Steppenwald? No . . . not that I can recall. I think two or three months past he might've been here for a short time."

Which meant that Steppenwald might not visit Pretor's Hill again until much too late. Evan's interest in the conversation dwindled.

"What made you decide to become a knight? Honor? Duty?"

Her sudden question, so naive it might have been asked by a child, still caused a darkness within him to stir to waking. With effort, he forced most of it down again. "A tradition outmoded," Evan finally replied. "A family notion."

She seemed not to hear the bleakness in his tone, the regrets in each word. Had he had the choice to relive his life, Evan would have fled far away from the family traditions that had led him to take up the mantle of the knighthood. If not for tradition, he would possibly have lived a shorter, albeit certainly happier existence. No Paulo Centuros. No Novaris.

No cursed quest.

"My uncle's idea of tradition is to make certain that as much money as possible remains in the family under his guidance. You met him on the steps of the magistrate's building."

The skeletal man. A distinct contrast existed between the two relatives, but such trivial matters were of no concern to him. Evan grew tempted to tell her to cease her nattering and go, but the words would not leave his mouth. It slowly dawned on the knight that some minute part of him enjoyed her company just a bit. The realization made him more uneasy.

" 'Bound by tradition, we are trapped in lives without meaning of their own. Guided by tradition, we learn that which will help us grow strong.' "

Mardi Sinclair's comment, clearly a quote, caused an

inexplicable dread to wash over Evan Wytherling. He slowed his pace slightly as he reorganized his thoughts and regained control of his emotions. His companion walked beside him blithely unaware of what he had just suffered through. Evan studied her, but saw no guile.

"Words of wisdom, my lady," he commented cautiously. "Your thoughts or another's?"

"A man who once claimed to be a wizard." Her expression became more animated as she warmed to the subject. "He lived well over a century ago, when people still believed in causes and lived to better their souls, not their purses."

The inn at last came into sight, but Evan chose not to go there. He had to stop at Arno's stables. Evan's horse would be growing impatient. If he did not take the creature out and let him run, there might not be a stable left by nightfall.

"Ideals were still alive then," the golden-haired woman continued. "Men fought for beliefs and took up challenges that most in Rundin these days would flee from or ignore."

"Men fought to survive," he snapped back without thinking. "Men fought for gain. Just as they always have done and always will."

His vehemence silenced her for a time. Evan knew he had angered her, but still she did not abandon him. A very strong-willed woman. He admired the trait as much as it also irritated him. What was he to do with this woman? Did she really simply plan to talk of ideals and honor? He wondered exactly what foolish ideals her head had been filled with and, more important, who had filled it with them.

"It wasn't always like that," Mardi pushed, sounding just a little disappointed in him. "It still isn't. Some of us who were educated at the university are trying to revive that spirit, revive the soul that once made Rundin so great. There's more in the world than profit and anger. You of all people should know that, Sir Wytherling."

"School ideals fade rapidly in the true world, Mardi Sinclair."

Despite his training, he found his bitterness rising. "Pampered scholars would do better to first experience the harsh realities before pontificating on the way things should be."

"Paulo Centuros was no pampered scholar. He was a wizard who fought for Rundin at the risk of his life and then they rewarded him by exiling him from the kingdom!"

Paulo Centuros . . . Evan might have known. The glib phrases, the nonsensical philosophizing, it matched the rotund wizard's way. Centuros could talk about how the world should be; he had always had the power to make it so, at least when the knight had known him. Evan felt a twinge of satisfaction upon hearing that some king of Rundin had finally tired of his prattling and found some method by which to oust Centuros from his domain.

The new information did not free Evan of his quest, though, and he could not allow this educated but clearly inexperienced woman to trouble him any longer with her incessant desire to talk about fairy tale worlds. The stable lay just before them. He needed to take the beast out and at last survey a part of the region he had so far avoided. Evan wanted no one near when he scouted the eastern ridges.

He turned to face her just as it seemed she might begin yet another defense of the cursed wizard. "I have ridden across more lands than you could name, Mardi Sinclair. I have my beliefs, my experiences, my tragedies. If they conflict with the wondrous philosophies of the august Paulo Centuros, I cannot help that fact. I am not a character penned into an epic; I am flesh and blood, and flesh and blood is much weaker than the imagination. Live your dreams if you desire, my lady, for they will soon enough evaporate in the light of reality."

Before she could reply, Evan vanished into the stable. Inside, he paused and listened carefully, relieved yet also a little disappointed when Mardi Sinclair did not follow him in. Her devotion to the ideals of the wizard had pushed him too far, forcing him to recall the truth of the times she dreamt about. Causes and honor, two ghosts far less substantial than those that haunted him so often. The only thing that had mattered to him in the end had been survival . . . and even that gift had proved a tainted one, forcing him toward yet darker choices and foul actions.

Bone pale, the monstrous steed stood out even in the shadows of the far end of the stable. As Arno had promised, the other horses had been kept away from the beast. His mount did not seem at all put out by the shunning, but the moment he sighted Evan, the baleful gaze the knight knew so well returned. The damnable beast snorted, then kicked at the stable gate; a gentle reproof, all things considered, for the horse could have just as easily kicked the gate off its hinges had he so desired.

"I was delayed," Evan offered, aware that no excuse would assuage the beast's feelings. Evan went about the task of saddling his animal. He had nearly finished when he heard heavy steps coming toward him.

"Sir Wytherling, sir," Arno called, a great grin across his features. "Would've helped you if I'd heard you come! Don't know where those stable boys have got to, but if you need—"

"No help was required, smith." Evan started to lead his mount to the stable's entrance, Arno's incessant good mood further vexing him. How could anyone be so pleasant all the time?

"He's been no trouble at all, Sir Wytherling, no trouble at all! Will you be bringing him back this evening?"

"I do not know." By rights, it should take him only a couple of hours to scout the ridge, but one never knew what one might find . . . or what might find him in turn.

"Well, if you come late, bash on the door out back! I'll be there to help open the stable for you!"

With a curt nod of gratitude, Evan nearly dragged the beast outside. The monster kept to a leisurely pace, as if enjoying his rider's discomfort around the smith. Evan glared at the steed as he finally mounted. Had he had any other choice, he would have chosen a thousand other horses over the one forced upon him—

"There's nothing wrong with dreams," a familiar voice insisted.

Evan cursed under his breath. He had not seen Mardi Sinclair when he had come out of the stable and so had assumed he would not be bothered by her again. Now not only had she slipped silently up to him, but his mount, supposedly skilled at keeping strangers from approaching too near, had decided to forget he had such wondrous abilities. Worse, the horse now eyed her with what the veteran campaigner would have termed friendliness.

"There is nothing wrong with dreams," he finally agreed. "So long as you differentiate them from reality, my lady."

She stood no more than arm's length from the head of the horse, a distance that would not have protected her in the least had the beast decided to treat her as he had the inquisitive Jak. However, the towering animal had the nerve to simply sniff in her direction in apparent curiosity, causing her to reach out to pet him on the muzzle. As with Arno, he reacted with satisfaction, not savagery.

"A beautiful animal," the gentlewoman remarked. Looking up at Evan, she added, "I don't understand you. I would've thought that you were different. You must've had a dream, an ideal, to be willing to push so hard, to train so long to become a knight. I don't mean a knight like those prettily painted peacocks attending the ceremonies for the king in Coramas; I doubt they've ever fought for anything more significant than a good place at the royal table! You, though, I know that you must have once believed, had to have once dreamt, to have come so far! You must have seen that there were more important ideals than profit and—"

"Come to me with your sword bloodied by your first kill, Mardi Sinclair, with your best friends dead in the field, and then speak to me about ideals, beliefs, and other fantasies. I think you will see different, then."

That said, he urged the horse forward. To his relief, the creature obeyed without hesitation. Evan did not look back, knowing that the gentlewoman would still be there. Her eyes burned into his back. He suspected that he had not heard the last of her preaching. Had Evan been like her once? Probably so, but that naive young soul had died so long ago that the weary knight barely recalled him.

The wind picked up as he rode, an even chillier wind than the one before his detainment by the magistrate. Evan pulled up the hood of his travel cloak, wishing he had his helmet instead. The visit to the ridge would stir more ghosts, especially after the infernal conversation he had just suffered through. Mardi Sinclair's talk of heroes and ideals had cut him to the quick, more than he would have ever admitted to her.

The horse slowed before the inn, but it took Evan a moment to understand why. He had left the sword in his room. Would it be better to retrieve it . . . just in case? The knight planned to be back before dark and surely the only danger to him now would be the ghosts of his own memory—

He suddenly dismounted and, without a glance back to the stable, hurried inside. As Evan Wytherling recalled all too well from the past . . . memories could kill more swiftly than solid foes.

Daniel had been correct. Fool that she had been, Mardi had actually thought the stranger something more than the scavenger Daniel had described. To her, though, Evan Wytherling had revealed himself as even worse than that. The knight was a shell of what he had once been; a soulless, fatalistic wanderer with no guidance, no hope. He would fit in well in this modern world in which she had been forced to live.

"Damn you, Evan Wytherling!" Mardi whispered as she watched. "Damn you!" She watched him dismount and hurry inside Benjamin Jakes's inn, then forced her gaze away. Better to get on with her own life. She might not agree with everything her uncle believed in, but Mardi did know that there were times when some causes had to be abandoned. Sir Wytherling had forever lost his dreams; she could do nothing to change that. There were those, however, who still followed theirs and it was up to her to nurture them.

And so, Mardi abandoned the stables in favor of returning to the school. The children were her shining hope and she had spent too much time neglecting them. Tomorrow lessons would begin again and Mardi only now realized how many things still had to be prepared before then.

Fortune smiled upon her for once, for neither her uncle nor anyone else she was loath to meet stopped her on the way to her precious new home. Mardi slipped inside and headed to her bedroom, taking great relief from the simple surroundings. Now she stood in her world. Here she did not have to think of disillusioned knights and money-minded uncles. Here she could strengthen her resolve, look to the words of Paulo Centuros and the others to—

Where were her books?

She was aghast. Emptiness greeted her from the wall-length oak shelf. Every book, from those by Centuros to even the rare dictionary she had brought back from Coramas, had vanished. Not one leaf remained. Mardi turned about, finding nothing else in the room changed. Only her books, her precious books, had been removed.

Her hand went to her pouch. No, not all her books. The one slim volume she had been carrying around remained hers, but only because she had forgotten to put it away. The realization brought her some slight comfort, but it could not entirely erase the loss of the rest of her collection. Who would be so arrogant, so criminal, as to steal her most precious belongings?

"Uncle Yoniff . . . how could you?" It had to be him. No one else would dare come into the school, into her home.

Growing fury spurred her back into the streets. She had not actually believed that Yoniff would have the audacity. Mardi had even hoped he might leave her be despite his earlier threats. So much for his words of care and family. Now she knew that he only cared about keeping her and her money under his complete control.

When she arrived, it was to find Yoniff Casperin sitting at his desk, quill in hand, ledger at the ready. Two harried-looking younger men, his apprentices, worked feverishly at smaller tables. From his intense concentration, Mardi gathered he had been working to make up for the time he had lost visiting first the magistrate and then her home.

The elder man finally noticed her. "Mardina—"

"How could you, Uncle?" she snapped. "Did you think that you could win me over by thievery and threat?"

Yoniff stood up, expression first puzzled, then insulted. He dropped his quill and quickly pulled her aside, whispering, "Mardina! Are you insane, girl? This is hardly the time or place to spout such nonsense! I've too much business to attend to. I still have to ride out to Master Taran's holding this evening to complete the arrangements of an important deal we've worked on—"

"But this is the time and the place, Uncle Yoniff! You made it so!" She had not only his full attention but now also that of the two apprentices and a servant. "How dare you steal my books from me—"

"What?" Yoniff drew himself up to his full height and stared down at his niece like the angel of death come to claim her. His look of indignation appeared so genuine that Mardi faltered, finally ceasing to speak altogether. Yoniff quickly filled the silence, continuing, "Come with me into my apartment."

He led her back, sparing just enough of his time to glare the two apprentices and the servant back to work. Mardi tried to regain her earlier fury, but her uncle's expression kept her confused. She knew Yoniff well enough to read his emotions, and he had seemed very honest and open in his outrage.

"Let me understand this, Mardina," the balding man hissed the moment they were in his spartan quarters. Yoniff's home perfectly reflected his appearance. Functional furnishings and few personal items. A simple bookcase lined one wall, each shelf filled with records of his business. A small, circular table of dark oak flanked by two matching frame chairs held one of only two brass oil lamps in the room. The wooden floor had been covered in great part by a braided, oval rug of brown with golden specks. On the far end of the chamber, a door led to the moneylender's bedroom. Other than the rug, the only color in the sitting room came from several small decorative items his niece had given to him over the years. "You are accusing me . . . me . . . of stealing from you? Stealing your blasted little books?"

"You did," she insisted, but the forces the young woman had mustered before no longer served her. Her accusations grew weaker. "You did . . ."

The indignation he had earlier displayed could not be matched by the look of sadness that suddenly spread from his eyes to the rest of his face, softening the harsh scarecrow appearance. "Mardina . . ." As pale as he was, Yoniff turned even more so. "Mardina . . . whatever our differences . . . you would think that I would stoop so low as to invade your quarters and take those things I know you hold most precious?"

"You were going to burn one book!" Her fury rekindled.

"Never! It was a hollow threat, Mardina! I wouldn't have burned it even if you hadn't threatened me in turn! I only wanted to shake you up! I was furious, but I still knew better—"

"But you had to have taken the books . . . this morning after I went out—"

"This morning?" She could see him calculating. "Mardina, you know how precisely I keep to my schedule. I've that pair out in front and several other visitors who'll attest to my time here. The only moment I was away was due to the summons of the magistrate. Some drifter's been passing very old coins around . . . but good coins and of interest to collectors, I might add." Yoniff's eyes glazed a little as he warmed to a favored subject. "There were coins from Rundin, of course, but also Tepis, Wallmyre, and a handful of kingdoms elsewhere . . . some I'd never even heard of. The youngest coin had to be fifty years. The ones from here were minted at least two hundred years ago, if not longer." He exhaled. "Drulane wanted to know if they were as real as they looked. When I offered to buy the lot, he took that as evidence they were."

Mardi's uncle looked down at his niece, giving her a rare and fleeting smile. "You know how far it is from here to Drulane's. I can find enough witnesses to prove I'd no time to do as you accuse, Mardina, if that's what you want."

"No." She believed him now. Her face went red with humiliation. Mardi's uncharacteristic fury had only led her to worsen the situation between her uncle and herself. She turned away from Yoniff, not wanting him to see her shame. "No . . . I'm sorry . . ."

"Mardina . . ." Yoniff put a comforting hand on her shoulder, which made her feel all the worse for the accusations she had flung at him.

"I'm sorry . . ." she blurted again, pulling away. Keeping her gaze down, she abandoned his apartment and raced through the building. The apprentices looked up, but Mardi paid them little mind. How could she have been so presumptuous?

The caustic words she and Evan Wytherling had tossed at one another had to be partly the cause for her quick loss of temper. Had Mardi not been bitter about the knight's disillusionment with the world and the path he had taken, surely she would have thought through the matter of the theft.

Who then had stolen her books? Not her uncle and certainly not the knight, however much the latter clearly held Paulo Centuros in disdain. Mardi could think of no one who would have performed such a heinous act and yet someone had.

She headed back to the school, this time determined to carefully investigate the scene. Some clue had to remain. Someone might have even noticed a figure lurking by one of the doors. True, such hopes might only be so much air, but Mardi Sinclair held tight to them. She had no other choice.

The blackbirds had returned to the school, four massive, brash forms perched in various locations near the door. Mardi paused, recalling the savage attack in the market. This time, however, she felt ready for the creatures; surprise had left her vulnerable to the one bird. The young woman drew her cloak around her, pulling the hood up. She carried no knife, but from her pouch she retrieved a pair of sharp scissors she often kept on her for school projects. While not as keen as a blade, they would serve to ward off the avians should they decide to torment her again.

In a nearby tree, two of the birds were methodically tearing apart some scrap between them. One of the others pecked at the ground. The last eyed her as if Mardi had transformed into some tasty worm. She kept her gaze for the most part on that one, although each of the others received fair attention.

"Away with you!" Waving her hands did nothing to disturb the huge blackbirds. The pair in the tree Mardi ignored, concentrating at the moment on the one that pecked at the ground, since it blocked her path to the door. Perhaps if she ignored it in turn, walked on as if it were not even there, the bird would move out of the way before she trampled it. Certainly it had to have that much sense.

Scissors in hand, she closed in on the pecking bird. The other avian continued to watch her but made no move. Mardi waited for the one on her path to finally step out of the way, but it continued to peck at some small, wrinkled tidbit. A few more steps and she would be upon it.

Perhaps if she kicked the scrap away the bird would follow. Edging her foot forward, she prepared herself for the avian's possible reactions. If it flew at her, Mardi had the scissors ready, but she hoped it would not come to that.

Still the bird attacked the scrap, finding something so alluring about it that even the human's close presence did not disturb the arrogant creature. Mardi steadied herself for the kick, focusing on the bit of trash to avoid striking the bird unless absolutely necessary.

There were words on the scrap. An entire page of words.

"Away!" Without thinking, Mardi kicked in the direction of the blackbird, who darted into the sky with a raucous caw. She retrieved the ragged sheet, quickly studying what remained of the printing.

The piece had come from one of her books.

One of the other birds cawed, a sound almost like laughter. Mardi turned, staring at the two avians above. As shredded as their prize had become, she thought she noticed printing on it.

A child giggled from somewhere.

Mardi turned in a complete circle, not at first finding the source. Then another child giggled, this time enabling her to track them around the corner of a nearby building.

Two grinning youths confronted her there.

"Talis? Bret?" Confused, she started toward the pair, wondering why they were watching her. The two boys had been among her most avid students, prize pupils and strong readers themselves.

Both boys had their hands behind their backs, as if hiding something. Talis, the taller of the two, adjusted position. As he did, part of what he kept hidden briefly revealed itself.

A book. Dismayed, Mardi at last saw what lay at their feet. Scraps of paper, most of them torn and crumpled. Behind the pair, other pieces and even a cover lay visible.

"Bret! Talis! What's the meaning of this?" She could scarcely believe the sight. Not only had the two boys apparently stolen her prize books, but they had decided it would be amusing to destroy them right by her home. "What've you done?"

Giggling again, Bret threw the savaged remnants of the book he had been holding at his teacher. Talis followed suit, then, as Mardi ducked the flying tomes, both boys ran off, still laughing.

Mardi started to give pursuit, then faltered. Her dreams lay before her, scattered to the elements. She counted shreds from at least half a dozen of her books and knew that most of the rest lay among the chaos. Falling to her knees, the distraught woman gathered up pages, trying to salvage whatever she could. The boys had been thorough, however. Little remained intact and what did had no use without the rest.

But why had they done this? Talis and Bret had always been quiet, attentive souls. Mardi had other students more suited to the roles of vicious pranksters.

She had no answer for their vandalism. If they returned tomorrow to be taught, perhaps she might force an answer from them then, but, in truth, Mardi doubted she would see either lad for quite some time unless she went to their homes. They would surely have the sense to realize that she would not soon forget this.

Evan Wytherling's bitter attitude came to mind. How he would have loved this spectacle, pure proof of the folly of her beliefs. Mardi felt some relief that he had departed the town for a time. At least the knight would not find the young woman kneeling on the ground, retrieving her tattered treasures. She could not have survived that humiliation.

From their perches, the four blackbirds watched for a time as Mardi tried to salvage the remnants of her books. Then, as one, three of the birds flew off, heading to the north. The last, the one that had watched her with the most interest since her return to the school, departed a minute later, heading east. It flew swiftly, avoiding any of its brethren it came across. In a few breaths, the crow had flown beyond the town and deep into the woods. At last the avian located its destination, a tightly packed grove of trees perhaps a half hour by foot from Pretor's Hill. The crow circled once, then descended.

In the woods awaited a rider, a massive figure atop a huge gray stallion with black spots. He looked up, saw the crow, and raised his left arm high.

"There you are, there you are. I was just on my way back from a short excursion when I thought I heard you calling me."

The blackbird alighted onto the outstretched arm, where the man rewarded it with a meaty treat. A gloved hand reached up and stroked the feathers, the ebony and crimson gems in the wrist of the glove seemingly glittering with life of their own.

"Now then," the avian's master rumbled. "Tell me, tell me

what you've seen of late, my little one."

V

STEPPENWALD

The chill that shook Evan as he neared his destination had nothing to do with the weather. Rather, the memories and ghosts from what had taken place here assailed him worse than they had just prior to his discovery of the town. He heard the clash of arms as clearly as if the armies battled now, and even the smell of blood seemed once more fresh.

Ahead and far to his right, near a small rise where a bent ash grew, lay the area where Haggad and his surviving officers had made their last stand. Three men would die at the snowy-eyed general's hand before overwhelming forces dragged him down and someone with a sharpened ax removed the cursing Haggad's head from his body. The still-glaring head would decorate a pike and travel the lands for weeks, by order of the monarchs of the three united kingdoms, not Paulo Centuros. Evan gave the wizard credit for trying to heal the wounds of the defeated as quickly as those of the victors. The kings, on the other hand, had been more than eager to flaunt the victory that magic and treachery had in great part afforded them.

Beyond the site of Haggad's death lay the area where the sorcerer-king's most loyal knights had perished, betrayed by one of their own. Their bodies no doubt still lay in what now had become a shallow, foliage-covered gap between two weathered mountains. They had been slaughtered to a man, many in the end not even realizing that there had been a traitor in their midst.

Good and evil are the same face, Centuros had told him after the end of the struggle. *Especially in battle, when all that matters is victory regardless of cost.*

It had been one of the few times that Evan could recall hearing outright disgust in the wizard's voice. However, that had not prevented Paulo Centuros from perpetrating certain deeds that even Novaris would have found disquieting.

Several carrion crows attended the knight as he rode. They made no move to disturb him, perhaps having discovered the fates of two of their brethren. Certainly they did not desire to come within biting distance, for Evan's mount from time to time eyed the avians as if contemplating which would make the best morsel.

Then the birds were forgotten as the arched ridge he had sought reared up before him, roaring.

The knight blinked, shaking off the ghosts for the moment. The ridge did indeed stand before him, as did the huge rounded mound, his actual destination, just a few yards beyond. The movement and the cry had been products of his own mind, though; memories related to what had taken place at this spot.

Here had been buried the most savage, the most gargantuan of the dragons, fearsome Grimyr . . . killed by Evan's own hand.

Unable to burn so resilient a form, they had at last buried it whole, leaving the remains to time, the elements, and the servants of decay. The mossy mound rivaled the ridge in size and scope and those unfamiliar with its origins might have marked it as either a natural formation or, if they were more keen of eye, the burial mound of some lost kingdom. Both suggestions would have been equally far from the facts, though. Only one who had actually witnessed the astounding event unfold could have believed the truth.

"Grimyr . . ." He almost expected the horrific leviathan to rise up from the primitive crypt and take revenge. The great dragon had seemed unstoppable, a force with no equal. Yet Centuros, of course, had divined his area of weakness and given Evan the method by which to kill the beast; a slim, silver lance tipped with dragonscale, the one substance readily able to pierce the tough hide. The scale used had come from Grimyr's own molting, which made the weapon his true nemesis.

The weary knight still recalled the searing heat, the angry roar, the huge paws that had tried to crush him to a bloody pulp. The battle, surprisingly enough, had been a brief one, lasting, Evan Wytherling later realized, but two or three minutes.

In the end, Grimyr's own belief in his invulnerability had led to the behemoth's death. He could not comprehend that a weapon existed that could kill him, especially protected as he had been by the many intricate spells cast by Novaris. Swooping down upon Evan, he had unleashed a torrent of flame that should have not only melted metal and flesh but burned the knight's bones to cinders. Of course, Evan, too, had been swathed in spells, and though the heat had been more than any creature should have been forced to bear, he had struggled through it, lance at the ready. Beneath him, the accursed steed, yet another gift from the wizard, had also suffered, but it, too, had pushed on.

Startled by his failure, Grimyr had grown enraged. If dragon flame could not stop the tiny figures, then brute strength and jaws large enough to swallow both horse and rider whole would do.

"Thisss one will peel the shell from you, Man Wytherling, then feassst upon your flesh!" the leviathan roared. "Grimyr will gnaw upon your bonesss and clean the remnants from hisss teeth with your little pick!"

Evan said nothing, trusting to the lance because Paulo Centuros had given him no choice. If it did not mortally wound the fire-black dragon on the first strike, then Grimyr would make good on his promise.

The sky had filled with dragon. Grimyr had become Evan Wytherling's world. The huge claws reached out, the terrible maw opened, the red, inhuman orbs fixed on the human and his mount—

And at last the tip of the lance pierced the thick hide of the leviathan, the dragonscale edge enabling the weapon to sink in as easily as if the monster had been created from whipped honey. Evan released the lance immediately, turning his mount away at the same time. Grimyr's progress continued unimpeded, but not as the dragon had intended. The sky-blanketing wings faltered, the roar cut off . . . to be replaced by a harsh, thundering cough.

The knight's mount needed no urging to run, for although the lance lay deep in the leviathan's chest, so great a beast was Grimyr that he still threatened to destroy the pair by crushing them under his immense weight. Mortally wounded, Grimyr sought to pull the enchanted weapon free, but his efforts only pushed it deeper. He roared, sending flame in every direction and creating an inferno that would burn clean the area for miles around before it died down.

At last the dragon's weakening movements turned him from the escaping knight. Grimyr struck the ground but yards from Evan, the collision spewing torrents of rock and dirt over the human. The great dragon roared one last time, a sound that still reverberated in Evan Wytherling's mind to this day . . . and then collapsed in a terrible heap, still writhing. Although dead already, Grimyr would continue to writhe for hours to come, wreaking yet more havoc on the already-devastated landscape and keeping the victors from his massive corpse.

Now wild, flowering plants and small oak and ash trees covered the mound that marked the dragon's last resting place. Evan suspected that during high summer pairs of lovers might come here and eat a meal while gazing into one another's eyes. Nothing here gave notice that the most terrible of beasts, second in evil only to his masters, had breathed his last on this spot.

Dismounting, the knight took sword in hand and walked around the front edge of the unnatural hill. What he expected to find he did not know, but his senses tingled just a little. Grimyr, like all dragons, had been a creature at least in part magic, so some traces after all this time did not surprise Evan.

The wind howled, mimicking in its own way the dragon's last mournful roar. Since approaching this area, Evan had noted that the clouds had darkened, possibly hinting at storm weather. He hoped it would hold long enough for him to scout the entire area.

Novaris, like Centuros, had been a scholar in his field. The death site of such a beast as Grimyr might possibly have interested him, especially if he had found some use for the rotting scales or the blackened bones that no doubt were all that remained. Dragons were of value in some aspects of sorcery and wizardry, although many mages shunned use of their parts because of the unpredictability of the results. Centuros had declined any trophy from Grimyr on the basis that the creature had been too long tainted by the many spells the sorcerer-king had placed over him through the years. That, however, would not have prevented Novaris, who had been legendary in his pursuit of the elements of magic so often shunned by the more cautious, from possibly seeking some use of the decaying corpse.

Behind him, the pallid steed snorted and pawed at the ground. The animal eyed the area with as much distaste as his rider.

"Not long. I will not be long." That he felt the need to give some sort of comfort to the creature spoke volumes about his own unease.

Evan trudged through the foliage, gaze darting around as he sought some sign, visible or not, that his elusive quarry had returned here ahead of him. He also watched for evidence he could trace to the peculiar happenings in Pretor's Hill, perhaps a spot where Novaris had taken old dragon bones and cast a spell. There had to be some clue somewhere around the battlefield and this seemed to be the best place. He did not want to face Valentin with nothing to show but his own suspicions.

The cold weather had caused the trees to drop much of their leaves early, forcing the knight to sometimes stumble over hidden gullies and rocks. Evan counted each step as he walked the perimeter of the mound, both anxious to reach the end and yet afraid he would find nothing of use to him by the time he did. One matter the knight did note, although it did not necessarily signify any evidence of the sorcerer-king's work, was that the carrion crows had flown off at some point since he had arrived. The trees remained barren of any life, much less avian ones. In the distance came the occasional call of some bird, but none seemed at all interested in flocking to those trees nearest Grimyr's resting place.

Midway around, the knight paused to survey the area beyond. Trees, bushes, and hills met his gaze. Everywhere he looked, Evan saw more of the same, an untouched wilderness. If Novaris had returned here and made use of the dragon's remains, then he had performed his spellwork somewhere far from this spot. Of course, it was highly possible that the sorcerer-king had never even come back. For all Evan knew, Novaris lay dead in some other land or, if he had not actually escaped the final day of the battle, under the tons of earth that Centuros and his associates had dropped upon the bulk of the enemy forces crossing from the south.

Perhaps I should ride there. *Perhaps I might find your bones where the grand wizard failed.* What irony it would be if Evan discovered that his quarry had lain dead here all these years and no one had known it. What a jest it would have made of both Paulo Centuros and the knight's quest.

But no, he could not believe that the sorcerer-king had died so easily. Novaris had survived that day.

With a sigh of resignation, Evan Wytherling continued his trek. The wind stung his weathered cheeks as he walked, encouraging him to finish swiftly. The weary knight kicked aside some of the brown, curled leaves, trying to vent his frustration.

His horse greeted him with a snort as he came into sight again. Evan did not acknowledge the beast, determined to maintain his vigil until he had covered the entire distance. At this point Evan did not expect much, but perhaps under the dead foliage he might at least find a minute clue, some bit of refuse the sorcerer-king might have left in haste.

The sky continued to darken, so much so that it almost seemed that night had chosen to fall hours early. Evan Wytherling frowned, not at all certain the weather would hold. He still wanted to ride farther up toward the old pass, inspect the location where Novaris had last been sighted during the climax of the battle. Evan doubted he would find much there, but it remained the only location left to him after the mound.

A flicker of movement in the trees beyond caught his attention.

The knight at first gave no hint of noticing. He continued on toward his mount, who, with his keener senses, also seemed to note the presence in the forest. Evan listened carefully, but whatever moved out there moved in absolute silence. He tightened his grip on the jeweled sword and readied himself.

With a sudden turn, the knight bounded toward the trees. Again he saw a shadow of movement, then nothing. Sword before him, Evan darted past the first thick trees, trying to spot his quarry. Once more, he caught a glimpse of a form, possibly human, possibly not, before it vanished behind some more distant trunks.

Whatever he hunted moved with incredible speed. The knight pushed harder, knowing he would need every ounce of determination just to keep pace. Behind him he heard the horse whinny, but Evan had no time to return. By the time he mounted and rode back, the shadowy figure would be long gone.

Naked branches scarred his face, obscured his view, but still he pursued. Several times the knight had to strike with his blade in order to clear his path. Nothing, however, appeared to impede the path of his prey, for it moved and dodged with ease, yet still managed to keep its identity a secret. Evan began to wonder if he hunted anything at all save his own ghosts. In this place that was all too real a possibility.

He nearly tripped over a hidden tree root, saving himself at the last moment by dropping the sword. Had he failed to do so, Evan would have likely struck his head on a massive rock half-buried in the ground before him. The knight quickly retrieved his weapon, but now he had no idea as to which direction his quarry had run.

The figure briefly moved into sight again as it ran. Still Evan could not identify it, but at least it had not gotten much farther away. He took up the chase again, determined once and for all to discover the truth.

When next the shadow came into view, Evan Wytherling realized that the gap had shrunk. The pair of them had begun an uphill climb and perhaps his quarry did not have the stamina of one who had lived on the battlefields for most of his life. If so, the chase would not continue for much longer.

Now he heard breathing . . . or at least what he took to be breathing. It sounded more like an animal huffing than a human gasping, but from what little Evan had discerned the one he pursued ran on two legs at least most of the time. That the other might not be human he had already accepted; his long and harrowing experience had introduced him to a world of which mankind had only been a minor part at times.

The growing darkness and the strong, chilling wind made it harder to keep track, but fortunately each glimpse Evan got revealed that less and less distance remained between them. A minute or two more and the knight would be upon his elusive adversary.

His foot came down not on solid earth, but rather air.

Evan clutched at the nearest branches, the sword flying from his grip as he sought to grab hold of something secure. One hand found a hold, but the other garnered only loose, fragmented foliage. The knight hung suspended briefly, then his hold started to give way.

Neither foot found any support. Straining, Evan focused on a small outcropping, seizing it with his free hand. Much of it crumbled under his desperate grip. The other hand lost hold and the knight began to fall.

Evan bounced against the trunk of a tree, crashing through several smaller branches before colliding with a much thicker one that finally held. Half-senseless, he yet managed to wrap one arm around the quivering limb. His legs came around, striking the trunk again, but the knight held on.

Fighting the tremendous agony that accompanied each movement, Evan Wytherling wrapped his other arm around the branch, then slowly tried to pull himself up. The branch shook but held his shifting weight.

Lying on top, facedown, Evan took a minute to recover from his fall and assess his predicament. Far below, he could see the rocky woodland landscape, certain to break many a bone at the very least should he jump. The knight had been played for a fool and rightly so. His quarry had known of the sudden, long drop and led him to it like the proverbial lamb to the slaughter. Only pure luck and desperation had saved the knight from plummeting to the hard earth. Possibly the fall would not have killed him, but it would certainly have left him vulnerable to the elements, not to mention his unseen adversary.

A tiny shower of rock and dirt made him look up. A long, pale head peered down at him, then gave a snort of derision. Evan started to call to the horse, but the frustrating beast vanished again.

His breath returned, the knight cautiously began his descent. Evan could see no foe above or below but did not trust that his quarry had fled after the nefarious trap had been sprung. True, his mount's brief presence indicated that the area should be safe now, but one should never assume too much.

It took several minutes of aching effort before he at last reached the bottom. Evan leaned against the trunk, again seeking to recover his breath. No foe attacked, for which he was grateful. His only weapon remained the dagger in his belt, which the knight doubted would have sufficed against whoever or whatever had tricked him.

The sword lay several yards away, the tip half-buried in the soil. It had not been damaged at all, of course. Still, Evan felt some relief as he looked it over. He had feared that it had been taken by his unknown quarry.

He turned, sensing movement behind him. A moon-colored form materialized out of the woods, his horse come to him. The beast snorted, giving him a look that said much about his opinion of Evan's antics. The battered fighter kept his expression set, refusing to be reprimanded by the animal. He sheathed his sword, then mounted, body still aching.

As he rode back to the region of the mound, he thought over what had happened. There was no place his quarry could have run save off the same edge he had gone and yet Evan had seen nothing. Clearly the horse had come across nothing either or else the knight surely would have heard the encounter.

What did I follow? Did I follow anything? Had he imagined the movement? Surely not.

"Chasing after shadows . . . Valentin would love that, would he not?"

The horse snorted, giving no further opinion on the matter. They reached the mound and after Evan Wytherling had surveyed the area briefly from horseback—finding no trail save his own, of course—the knight decided to proceed on to Pretor's Hill before the storm that clearly threatened poured down upon him. He had accomplished nothing here besides nearly breaking his neck following a will-o'-the-wisp. Whether Novaris had returned to the scene of the leviathan's death at some point in the past meant nothing if Evan could find no clue to the sorcerer-king's present whereabouts. After Valentin he would return here, next time better prepared.

Rumbling laughter made his body stiffen in the saddle.

The knight swore. Not laughter, but thunder. For a moment, in the knight's mind it had sounded like something more. The laughter of a giant. The laughter of Grimyr, the dragon.

Evan twisted in the saddle, studying the mound intently but seeing and sensing nothing out of the ordinary. Then, with a grip so tight his knuckles strained, he turned and urged the horse on, not looking back.

The storm builds swiftly, Magistrate Drulane thought as he attempted to look over his papers. He had been unable to concentrate since his meeting with the outsider. The conversation should have gone differently, but neither of them had been fully trustful of the other. This man, this Evan Wytherling, knew far more than Drulane had initially suspected, of that the magistrate had grown certain. He should have questioned him longer, offered him more. Something was terribly amiss in Pretor's Hill, his town, and Drulane would not rest until he knew what that might be.

The creak of the door made him look up. He had no appointments set for now, no matters to settle. Who would disturb him now, so close to dinner?

The papers dropped from his hands. "My lord! I hardly expected you!"

"Magistrate." His unexpected guest moved smoothly for a man of such monumental proportions. The doors closed behind the massive figure as he strode forward, the floorboards creaking under the strain of each step. Drulane's gaze flicked momentarily to the elegant dragon-head cane, an object that always drew his attention for some unfathomable reason.

Belatedly he recalled that proprieties demanded he stand in the presence of such an august personage. His guest, however, waved him down with one gloved hand. The gloves alone would have cost Drulane a fortune, and they were but a small part of a trousseau half-seen under the stylish gray travel cloak that itself spoke of the riches of far-off Coramas and beyond. The lined deep-blue jacket and matching pants had been made to the specific proportions of its wearer. In fact, all of the clothes had been crafted specifically with the wearer in mind. The white shirt hidden beneath the gray vest could only be rare silk, as had to be the cravat. The boots, of so fine a leather as the magistrate had not seen since in the audience of the king, fairly shone, so clean and new did they appear despite the long journey through which they had no doubt just suffered.

The prodigious figure seated himself in the one chair that Drulane ever kept available for just such a rare visit. The man smoothed his vest, then his well-trimmed, silvering beard. With a sweep of his hand, he removed from his head the broad-rimmed hat that had left the eyes shadowed; narrow, silver-gray eyes that seemed to see the magistrate's very thoughts.

"I've only just arrived, Drulane, only just arrived."

The elderly man could barely tear his gaze from those eyes. "Yes, my lord."

Gloved hands rested on the head of the dragon, the gems at the wrist glittering in the light of the magistrate's lamps. The mismatched eyes of the dragon stared at Drulane. "Things seem to be a bit livelier of late. Stakes seem to be getting higher."

"Yes, my lord Steppenwald."

The immense figure leaned forward, expression more that of a predatory feline than a man. "There's a stranger in town, a stranger. You met with him."

Drulane desired greatly to take a drink in order to clear his throat, but his hand did not seem to work. "Yes . . . yes, I did. He only just arrived the other night."

"You have a name for him, a name?"

"Evan Wytherling. A knight. My sources indicate he's spent much time out West, although, my lord, I think he's familiar with this region as well." The magistrate could keep nothing from the king's man, nothing at all. All Steppenwald had to do was look at him and the answers came flowing forth.

"Evan Wytherling . . ." Lord Steppenwald leaned back, a peculiar expression briefly crossing his features. Drulane, had he had the opportunity to study it closer, might have described the expression as a mix of consternation, disbelief, suspicion, and, although it conflicted, growing satisfaction. "Evan Wytherling, you say . . ."

"Yes, my lord."

"A knight. You're sure, a knight?" Steppenwald waved a gloved hand, cutting off the magistrate's response. "Yes, of course, he's a knight, yes, of course. I should know that, I should." The king's man stroked his beard. "Tell me of your discussion. Word for word."

The magistrate did, recalling the encounter with an eye for detail that only Steppenwald could make him bring forth. Drulane's description of the spinning blade brought a chuckle from the immense figure, but Steppenwald's humor faded soon after. By the time Drulane had finished, the imposing figure looked contemplative.

"I would never have thought to see the day, never," he whispered half to himself.

"Beg pardon, my lord?"

Steppenwald rose, his girth not at all causing him to strain in the effort. "Thank you, magistrate. I've much to think upon, much to think upon."

For the first time since the other's arrival, Drulane began to relax just a little. "Will you be staying the night, Lord Steppenwald?"

The king's man gazed down upon him, silver-gray eyes wide and innocent. "Stay the night, Drulane? I've not even arrived . . ."

The magistrate stiffened, unable to look away. "Yes, my lord."

"In fact, as I've not even arrived, I was never here, which means this visit has never taken place."

"Never taken place. Yes, Lord Steppenwald."

Turning, the elegantly clad giant stepped toward the doors, which opened as he neared. Steppenwald calmly walked past the sentries beyond, cane tapping lightly on the wood floor with every other step. Two of the men closed the doors behind him, their own gazes never leaving the walls across from them.

Magistrate Drulane blinked, then quickly poured himself a drink for his dry throat. He had enough to do without daydreaming at his desk. With this Evan Wytherling in town, he suspected that matters would soon take a decisive and not at all pleasant course.

He had to come to a decision of his own before that happened, before events wrested control of Pretor's Hill from him.

Before Lord Steppenwald visited.

Despite all that had happened to her, despite even the terrible weather that threatened, Mardi Sinclair still made certain to attend services. She did not consider herself zealous in her beliefs, but at the same time the young woman never missed the midweek evening service. This evening especially Mardi desired to attend. Perhaps it had to do with the stability of the services or the compassion of the priest, Father Gerard. While not a brimstone preacher like some, he still conveyed a strong belief to his flock. Some of the priests Mardi had come across in Coramas could have learned from his earnest manner.

Still, even Father Gerard's sermons could not explain her feelings tonight. Mardi simply had to be there.

Yoniff had never understood. His business had always been his religion. Once in a while he attended, but one could never predict. While not certain she wished to see him so soon after her accusations, Mardi still wished he would include in this evening one of his occasional visits to the church.

Clad in a prim brown dress and cloak and seated in a polished oak pew toward the back, the teacher observed her fellow townsfolk as they entered. Many surly moods tonight, even in a house of worship. She had not spotted the families of either of the two boys who had stolen and vandalized her collection, for which she found herself both relieved and disappointed. Mardi had to address the incident soon. She had gathered all the fragments and shreds and stored them in the school to show the parents what the two had done. She intended to ask them to stop by on the morrow.

While not nearly as extravagant as the great cathedrals of Coramas, the church in Pretor's Hill remained an edifice of which the townsfolk had always been proud. Simple, yes, with solid stone walls built by the first hardy settlers at least a century past. Long, narrow windows, "archer slits," some of the older menfolk who had served in the king's armies jokingly called them, allowed enough light in during the day, even with the stained-glass panes to mute it. For evening services, a rotating group of church volunteers lit large brass oil lamps with spherical bases hanging next to the windows.

Twin columns of plain oak pews lined each side with one wide aisle in between. The stone floor, perhaps crafted by someone with a gift for mosaics, did not have a long carpet down the center but rather a well-worn crimson and silver pattern much akin to a banner that ran from the entrance to the pulpit. In keeping with their apparent taste for lasting things, the original church designers had even crafted the pulpit of stone, creating a high, arched platform that even the rare clerical visitor from the capital admired with open envy.

A balding, somewhat cherubic figure, Father Gerard stepped forth. "Welcome to this house . . ."

The moment the priest began speaking, a strange sensation welled up within Mardi. The sermon, the entire church, blurred. She tried to rise but at first could not. Father Gerard and the townsfolk transformed into vague reflections of themselves, completely oblivious to what was happening to her.

From the stone floor erupted a deep darkness, a darkness with a vaguely reptilian cast to its shape.

Burning, monstrous eyes bore into her very soul. The fiend roared—revealing row upon row of long, sharp teeth—and reached out toward Mardi Sinclair with great talons of sinister shadow. At the same time, the rattle of weapons and the screams of men dying in combat assailed the gentlewoman's ears.

Suddenly Mardi could move again. She gazed down and saw that in her hand she held a sword and shield, both of pure silver light. Her clothing became silver armor that gleamed, armor almost living, so free did it allow her movements. Around Mardi, other indistinct but gleaming forms moved to combat the darkness. She charged forward, knowing that the darkness must be kept back.

A piece of that darkness broke away, then another. Wolves of shadow, they pounced upon her from both sides. Mardi brought the blade, now a familiar jeweled sword, down, sweeping across the necks of both shadows. The wolves howled as the blade struck, then faded as so much smoke.

I will not be denied . . . an inhuman voice hissed. The reptilian form shifted, becoming a shadow man, a handsome, bearded figure with features hazy yet somehow so beguiling that Mardi Sinclair's resolve momentarily faltered. He reached out a hand, and the voice she had heard before came again but this time softer. *I will not be denied . . .*

She almost reached for the hand, but then another gently took hold of hers from behind. A voice both familiar and strange whispered, *Trust not the open hand when the other cannot be seen . . .*

Only then did Mardi look down to the right and realize that the shadow man held a sword in his right hand. She barely parried the treacherous attack.

The shadow man faded, his words echoing as he became but a nebulous mist. *I will not be denied . . .*

"Go in peace."

She stirred, suddenly jerked back to the church service. The last words had been spoken by Father Gerard and now everyone around her had stood up to leave. Mardi realized that she had missed the entire service, caught up in some dream where she had become a warrior maiden, a paladin. Yet the dream had left her perspiring and her hands clenched tight, as if they still held sword and shield.

What happened to me? She slowly rose, looking about her to see if anyone had noticed her peculiar behavior. No one acted as if they had, although at first Mardi thought that perhaps Father Gerard might have. A troubled expression covered the priest's generally kindly face, but after a moment the young woman decided she had not been the reason. Father Gerard eyed his flock in general as if not at all satisfied with the outcome of the sermon. Another time Mardi might have gone up to speak with him, but tonight she simply wanted to get away.

Once in the streets, Mardi slowly began to feel normal again. How could she have remained in that dream for the entire service? Why had she even dreamt like that at all?

It took her little time to reach the school, but once there she felt uneasy about going inside. Mardi bundled herself up against the cold, damp air and went to saddle her horse. Although reluctant, the mare gave in and soon the pair rode through the town, heading in the direction of Mardi's favorite reading spot.

Why am I doing this? It made no sense to ride to there, not in this weather, but she had nowhere else to go. Mardi knew only that she had to ride; she had to move.

They had nearly reached the western end of town when a wolf howled.

Mardi twisted in the saddle, realizing immediately that the cry had come from behind her. An inexplicable dread filled her, and she knew she had to quickly turn the horse around. Her mount struggled briefly, a bit confused at first by the change. Mardi's anxiety heightened with the delay. She did not know why, but she had to hurry.

Not at all concerned about riding wildly through town, Mardi Sinclair urged the horse to a full gallop. A fine mist now accompanied the harsh, chill wind, dampening her face. She pulled the hood of her cloak close but could not entirely avoid getting wet.

The foul weather created one advantage for her: Mardi came across few townsfolk as she raced along. While on the one hand it would have likely been good for her to gather others to follow her, Mardi did not want to spend precious time trying to persuade them to go somewhere for no good reason.

Pretor's Hill finally gave way to the forest edge. The mare slowed, clearly desiring to journey no further, but Mardi forced the animal on.

A second howl, now much nearer, shook her to the bone. She screamed in the horse's ear, trying to get the creature to run faster.

Thunder rumbled and a lightning bolt briefly illuminated the sky. Although the sun had not completely set, it might as well have already vanished for all the light it cast. Mardi wished she had had the opportunity to grab a lantern; she feared she might race right past her destination without even knowing it.

Some of the greater landowners had holdings out this direction, including Daniel's father. Had something terrible happened to Daniel? Mardi had not seen him since early in the day; perhaps he had been riding back home and some wolf had spooked his horse . . .

Deep within, the gentlewoman knew she was insane to ride out here simply because of the howl of a wolf. The animal might be doing something so mundane as calling to its mate. Mardi risked her own life by her impetuous and inexplicable act and did not even know if anyone else might actually be in danger. She had only her feelings to go by . . . that and the dream in the church, which disturbed her even now.

The mist grew into a powerful rain, made more terrible by the biting wind and the growing dark. Mardi turned her face away to wipe the water from her eyes and saw that Pretor's Hill had already all but vanished from sight. Surely it would be best for her to turn around.

She turned her gaze forward again just in time to discover the dark, bulky form that lay directly across her path.

Her mount stumbled to a halt, nearly throwing Mardi from the saddle. Mardi fought the mare for control, then anxiously studied the corpse. Lightning played, but the young woman did not need it to recognize that the dead beast had clearly been another horse. She could not tell how it had perished, save that its death had not been gentle.

But what had happened to the rider?

Holding the reins in one hand, Mardi dismounted for a closer look. The dead horse lay at an awkward angle and only when she took a step toward the huge corpse did Mardi Sinclair see that its throat had been torn out.

She had been a fool to come out here alone. If a wolf had done this, it had to be monstrous in size. Holding her cloak tight, Mardi looked anxiously around.

A booted foot just beyond the nearest tree snared her unwilling gaze.

"My God . . ." The words came out a hoarse whisper. Mardi wished she could summon up some of the strength and determination of her dream, but the sight of the boot froze her where she stood.

The mare, more and more nervous, pulled at the reins. Mardi wrapped them tight around her hand. She had to come to grips with matters. Whoever lay there might be dead, but they also might just be injured. If so, they would need her aid.

"Come!" Her horse reluctantly following, the gentlewoman walked carefully around the dead animal. Mardi's gaze continued to return to the still form of the rider, but she could not yet make out his identity. A tall man, that was all she could tell. The head and shoulders remained obscured by foliage.

Still holding the reins, Mardi leaned down to investigate. She knew she would likely recognize the person and that further unnerved her. The body lay so still, Mardi feared that he had to be dead. Not since her family's demise had she been this close to death . . .

With one tentative hand she reached out to touch the nearest damp boot. Had she seen them before?

Mardi's mare began tugging frantically on the reins again. She understood the animal's anxiety; she no more wanted to be here than the horse did, but now she had no choice. Rising, Mardi tried to calm the animal. "Easy! Easy!"

A shadowy form leapt from the trees nearest them, a form lupine . . . yet nearly human.

The mare whirled in fright, pulling an unprepared Mardi forward. She tumbled to the ground and would have been dragged across the path had she not lost her grip. The horse raced off, unmindful of the danger to her mistress.

Panicked, Mardi tried to rise, but the ground had grown so muddy that she continually slipped to her knees. She heard a low growl and faint movement, then looked up in time to see the murky figure coming upon her. It growled deeper and lunged toward her. Mardi tried to pull herself away, but her fingers only sank into the muddy earth. The vaguely seen image of a face both human and wolf—and more the horrific for the combination—filled her wide-eyed gaze.

Mardi reached with a trembling hand for her pouch, seeking the scissors, but she knew she would not find the tool in time—

A cloaked figure who moved like a ghost among the trees appeared beside her, brandishing a sword. The lupine creature, still more shadow than substance, backed away a step but then paused, as if unable or unwilling to retreat any farther.

Then, with a cry both lupine and human, it pounced on Mardi Sinclair's defender.

The hooded swordsman appeared briefly taken back by the creature's advance but met the assault with his blade. As shadowy as the monster seemed, it presented a target impossible for the cloaked figure to miss. He thrust, striking his adversary full in the chest.

To Mardi's astonishment, the blade slipped through unimpeded. A peculiar sound, almost a sigh of great relief, escaped the shadow beast as the sword drove through. The creature writhed, flailing on the weapon like a fish on a hook.

Then, unbelievably, the monstrous beast, still quivering madly, faded away.

The swordsman stood still, clearly transfixed for the moment by this outcome. Then he turned and for the first time the

97

gentlewoman saw that her rescuer had been none other than the knight, Evan Wytherling.

A look of remorse crossed his weathered features the moment he caught sight of her. His eyes shifted from Mardi to the unmoving rider, then back to her. Slowly he reached out a hand, which she took.

"Are you well? Did it strike you?"

"No . . . I'm . . . I'm all right . . . just muddy . . . it . . . what was it?"

He did not seem to hear her question, his thoughts clearly elsewhere. He helped her to her feet. At the same time, a familiar pale shape emerged from the same direction he had. The knight's tall horse, moving along as if he knew exactly what his master wanted.

"We must get you back to town . . . to your home . . ."

Town. Home. For one of the few times in her recent life, Mardi looked forward to returning to Pretor's Hill. However, as Evan Wytherling attempted to lead her to his steed, she halted, realizing that they had one matter yet to address.

"The rider. That . . . monster . . . must've attacked him, too. We can't go until we see what we can do with—"

"He is dead, my lady."

"Dead . . ." She had thought so, thus the notion did not disturb her as much as it might have. "Still, we can't leave him lying there. We have to bring him back or, at the very least, find out who he is so we can tell his family. They might be worried sick about him already!"

She felt his body stiffen, then heard him exhale, as if in resignation. Likely he had seen so much death during his life that taking any more time with this one corpse seemed a waste to him, but Mardi had a responsibility to others. At least they had to know who to alert.

He turned her so that their faces were suddenly less than a foot apart. This close, the gentlewoman could see the lines, the scars, and, most of all, the eyes that had experienced so much. She felt saddened by what she saw and yet also drawn to it in some way.

"My lady Sinclair, forgive me," he began, abruptly looking down to the earth. "I only met him once and briefly, but I fear . . . I fear that the dead man can be none other . . . than your uncle."

VI

DREAMS

"A terrible business, this," the magistrate whispered as he stared down at what remained of Yoniff Casperin. That Drulane, accompanied by Bulrik and the twins, would leave his home to personally inspect the body that Mardi and Evan had brought to the church spoke much about both the dead man's position in the town and his friendship with the magistrate. The knight watched with some interest as the gnarled figure reached out to remove the cloth that covered Casperin's remains.

The woman at Evan's side gasped and turned away. Strong as she could be, Mardi Sinclair could not again face the horror of her uncle's terrible fate. Evan had tried his best to prevent her from gazing upon the ruined form in the woods, but she had demanded to see proof that it had indeed been her uncle. With no other choice left to him, Evan had brought her over to the corpse, then turned it over.

It amazed him that she had been strong enough to help him secure the body after what she had seen. The beast . . . he still did not know what to call it . . . had torn out the elder man's throat much the way it had the horse's. A good portion of Yoniff Casperin's face had gone the way of the throat, leaving behind a blood-soaked horror that would, Evan did not doubt, haunt the man's niece forever.

Now, in the priest's residence, she turned not to the holy man but to the knight for comfort. Evan stared down helplessly at her as she buried her face in his chest. Despite his own garments, he felt the warmth of her body, a sensation rare to him. With much trepidation he put one arm around her, hoping the effort would be enough. Mardi responded by pressing more firmly against him.

"Please be gentle with him, your honor," the priest urged.

"I'll not bother him at all, Father," Drulane responded, a brief glare at the priest reminding the man that the magistrate knew how to handle his own work. Nonetheless, Drulane's visage paled some as he studied the victim. "Nasty work, this."

Behind the magistrate, one of the twin behemoths swallowed nervously. Evan wondered if they had ever faced something so terrible as this before.

"We must gather a hunt together," the magistrate muttered. He leaned forward to study the throat. "We can't allow this to happen again."

"But I understand this gentleman dispatched the wolf already." The priest did not know what to make of Evan. He treated the knight in a cordial manner but clearly found his presence disturbing.

Drulane favored Evan with a suspicious glance. "Yes, so he said before."

Mardi Sinclair had made no objection when Evan had earlier told the priest that a simple wolf had caused the deaths of both horse and rider. Father Gerard did not question the story.

The magistrate, on the other hand, clearly did not believe it but chose to pretend otherwise before both the priest and his own men. Evan did not doubt that Drulane would interrogate him soon enough. As for Bulrik and the twins, the knight suspected that they, too, found the tale of a wolf at least a bit suspect.

"There may be more than one, an entire pack, perhaps, or just one mate. A hunt is necessary, if only to assuage the fears of the good townsfolk." Drulane straightened as best he could and gently dropped the cloth back over Yoniff Casperin's ruined face. He turned to Mardi Sinclair, who had not moved. "Mardina, my dear, you've my deepest sympathy for this tragedy. You know in what regard I held your uncle. I'd like you to consider me available at any time should you need someone to turn to for guidance."

To Evan's relief, the gentlewoman removed herself from

him. She faced the magistrate, wiping away tears. "Thank you, Master Drulane, but I'll be all right—"

A clatter beyond the door caused all within to turn and look. The door swung open and a barrel-chested man with long silver hair tied in a braid barged inside. Behind him followed the young man whose friend Evan's mount had nearly dismembered. Both had clearly just come from a lengthy ride, for they dripped puddles onto the floor of the priest's abode.

"Magistrate Drulane! I've only, just only, mind you, heard terrible news that I cannot, cannot, believe! Is the good moneylender indeed dead? Murdered, as I've heard?"

The young man behind put a hand on his companion's shoulder. "Father, have a care. Mardi's here—"

"Mardina!" The imposing man marched over to Evan and the woman, unmindful of the trail he left behind. He seized her hands in his own and leaned so near that the knight almost thought he intended to kiss her. Evan found himself tempted to push the man back to arm's length. "Mardina! So terrible. You must let us care for you in this time of your distress—"

To the veteran warrior's relief, Mardi Sinclair found her voice and nerve again. "Master Taran . . . I thank you for your concern, but I . . . I'll be fine."

"Nonsense! You're almost family! I'll—"

"Master Taran." Although barely reaching the other man's shoulder, the magistrate had a presence about him that allowed the soft-spoken words to readily cut off the bellow of the merchant. "May I ask how you come to know of this tragedy so swiftly? Mistress Sinclair and her companion only brought her uncle to my attention less than an hour ago."

"Why, I came into town looking, looking, mind you, for Casperin when he failed to appear at my home this evening. We had business, important business. Must've barely missed Mardina and this"—Master Taran eyed Evan for the first time, swiftly finding him wanting—"this other returning. My son and I rode to Casperin's home, found him long absent, but then when we rode to

Benjamin Jakes's inn for something to warm us, we heard the horrible news!"

Evan silently swore. Despite the weather and the darkness, others had witnessed their return with their terrible cargo. He supposed it had been inevitable but had hoped to slow the course of the news at least for a time. By morning at least a dozen different tales would be spread around Pretor's Hill, each more fanciful than the last and none of them even approaching the awful truth.

From his reaction, Magistrate Drulane clearly thought something similar. "I'll have to nip this in the bud. For your information, Master Taran, a wolf, possibly two, attacked and overcame both Yoniff and his mount. I daresay they caught the animal by surprise and Yoniff fell, injuring himself. That made him easy prey for the wolves once they had the horse down. Mardina and this man, Sir Wytherling, claim that one's dead, so I imagine only one remains. A hunt will be formed and we'll either catch the animal or drive it out of our region forever."

"A wolf?" The younger Taran joined his father, his gaze assessing Evan. "We heard he had been murdered . . . by some outsider."

"Then you'd best forget that story now, Daniel Taran, for nothing human killed Yoniff Casperin. This was done by a beast."

"Men can become beasts, especially if they've been trained to be one." Daniel studied Evan. "How is it you came to be so nearby, anyway, sir knight? A fortuitous circumstance, that. Pity you didn't happen upon Master Casperin before this alleged wolf took down both him and his horse—"

"Sir Wytherling's already explained his role, Daniel," the magistrate interjected. "But for your sake and to get this matter over with, I'll repeat what he said. He'd been out for some time and found the body on his way back. Seeing poor Yoniff dead, he thought to find the wolf or wolves nearby and dispatch them, which he did to one . . . as Mistress Sinclair will attest."

"That's . . . that's so, Daniel."

"Hmmph . . ." Despite his obvious reluctance to accept the explanation, the knight's accuser quieted for the moment.

Evan pondered the younger man's intentions; Daniel Taran would have dearly loved to place the blame for the death on him. The reason why became clear a moment later when Taran's eyes shifted to Mardi Sinclair. The merchant's son coveted the woman.

Not completely understanding why he chose to act as he now did, Evan Wytherling put a comforting arm around his companion. To his surprise, the action did not startle her, but Daniel Taran's eyes smoldered. Evan studied the blond man as the latter forced his ire down. Beneath the elegant and educated exterior lurked a burgeoning storm that would at some point soon burst forth.

"It was a wolf, plain and simple." The magistrate shook his head. "Mardina, if you've no objections, I'll make the arrangements for your uncle's funeral. I'll see to it that he'll be sent off in a proper manner, I promise you."

"Thank you . . . I'd appreciate that, I think."

"I'll also attend to the matter of his estate. In case you didn't know, he planned for me to do that."

"I was fairly certain, Magistrate. You were good friends."

"Yes . . ." Drulane coughed. "The latter should be a simple matter, you being his only heir."

Both Tarans stirred, a pair of predatory peacocks. Evan had a sudden desire to send father and son back through the door, the flat of his sword urging them to great speed.

Talk of inheritance caused Mardi Sinclair to shiver again. Father Gerard noticed. "Mistress Sinclair, I think it would be best if you perhaps tried to get some rest now. You may leave the duties involving your uncle in the hands of the magistrate and myself."

"A good recommendation," Master Taran declared, sweeping toward the knight's companion. "Come, Mardina! I insist that you stay with us. You shouldn't be alone, you know, after a terrible time such as this."

Daniel Taran stepped in front of his father, facing Mardi. As the younger merchant took her hands in his own, Evan sought to control himself from pulling her free.

She rescued herself again. "I thank you both, but I really just want to go back to my own home."

"The school?" The blond young man gave her an incredulous look. "That's no place for you, Mardi, especially alone."

The last word he stressed with a glance toward Evan, as if insinuating something more. If he thought to goad the veteran knight, however, he failed miserably. Evan had stood fast against more suitable adversaries than this arrogant pup.

"I'll . . . I'll be fine. Really, I want to go there." To everyone's surprise, including his own, the gentlewoman looked up at the weary knight and asked, "Will you take me back there now, Sir Wytherling?"

"Mardi! You scarcely know this scavenger—"

"He saved my life, Daniel." She spoke quietly but with a firmness in her voice that would not allow argument. "He's rescued me twice now. I think I know him enough."

Magistrate Drulane broke in before anyone could say something that would further fray tempers. "Yes, by all means have Sir Wytherling take you to your home, Mardina, but before that allow me to arrange to have my housekeeper, Mistress Arden, meet you at the school. I insist that she keep you company for at least this night, if not more."

"Please, no, I need no one—"

"Thank you, Magistrate," Evan interjected, ignoring the gentlewoman's sudden stare. "Your kindness is greatly appreciated."

Mardi Sinclair looked nearly ready to demand how he could dare speak for her, but at the last moment held her peace. Instead, she turned back to Drulane and nodded her agreement. Her acquiescence further incensed Daniel Taran and only the elder merchant's quick action no doubt prevented the son from making a greater spectacle of himself.

"A fine notion, Magistrate Drulane," Master Taran announced, one warning hand already on his son's forearm. The young merchant stiffened and the vein in his neck grew visible as he fought to restrain himself. Evan wondered if anyone else noted the fury barely held in check. "Fine, indeed. Mardina will be able to sleep in peace, then." He patted his frustrated progeny on the shoulder, adding in an even more exuberant voice, "Well, Daniel, nothing for us to do here, then, is there? Time we were on our way back home!"

"Yes, father." The vein receded.

Master Taran took one of Mardi Sinclair's hands and kissed it lightly. The younger Taran followed suit, all traces of madness vanished in an instant. His gaze briefly crossed that of Evan, then fixed on the gentlewoman. "I'll look in on you tomorrow, Mardi. I've got a new book you'll want to see, too. Came in with some new dress materials my father ordered from Coramas. If you come back with me tomorrow, you can look them over as well. Only the latest cloths!"

"I'll . . . maybe, Daniel. We'll see."

"All I can hope for." With a flourish of his cloak, Daniel Taran exited after his father.

Drulane signaled to one of the twins, giving him orders to locate the housekeeper and inform her of her new duties. The magistrate then turned his attention to his friend's niece and her rescuer. "I, too, will look in on you tomorrow, Mardina. Purely formal matters."

"I understand."

"Sir Wytherling." The hunched man's tone grew colder. "We will be seeing one another again soon."

"At your service, Magistrate."

"Sleep well, Mardina."

Although Mardi Sinclair left the church wearing a stolid expression, Evan sensed that his companion verged on a breakdown. After retrieving his mount, he walked in silence beside her, trying to fathom her various emotions. Shock, certainly, and anguish, too. Fear also had to be present, but fear wore many faces, turned in many directions.

Not until they had reached the school did she speak. "I want to thank you for your help in bringing my uncle back here."

"Your gratitude is unnecessary, my lady."

" 'My lady.' " A rueful smile momentarily graced her lips. A tear plummeted down her cheek. "The paladin slays the beast, thereby saving the lady from death. Just like in the tales, only no one remembers those the beast slaughtered before its own death. No one ever talks about the loved ones lost . . ."

"Lady Sinclair—"

"My name is Mardi. Not Lady Sinclair, not Mardina." She turned from him. "I need to get inside."

The magistrate's housekeeper had yet to appear. Evan stepped back but did not depart. He could not, not after what the two of them had faced. Visions of the wolf shadow haunted him and no doubt haunted her much more. There were methods by which he could help protect her in her own home, give her a sense of security, but only if she allowed him to implement them.

Mardi opened the door, then paused as if recalling something distasteful. She stepped back, staring at the darkness within. "What was it, Sir Wytherling? What killed my uncle?"

"I truly do not know, Lady—Mardi. I truly do not know." That he had some suspicions, recalled vague tales, Evan would not tell her. "I have fought nothing like it before."

"I'm afraid to go inside," the young gentlewoman at last admitted. "I'm afraid to go inside a place I know so well because I fear that it might be in there, waiting."

An opening that he himself could not have better devised. Evan released his horse's reins, knowing full well the accursed creature would not go far. "I can help you sleep well, Mardi."

Her intent eyes shook his resolve a bit. "How?"

"I will light your way." He reached into one of the pouches on his belt, suddenly fearful that what he sought had been lost during his near mishap by the mound. His fear proved insubstantial, for Evan immediately felt one of the smooth cylindrical objects he sought. With hidden relief, the knight pulled forth his prize. "First with this."

A slight giggle escaped her as she stared at the candle. Not the talisman to ward off evil that she had no doubt expected. Evan located his tinderbox and, keeping the candle out of the wind and moisture, lit the wick. Tiny as the candle looked, the flame illuminated the doorway for several yards inside.

Although he did not draw his sword for fear that his companion would realize his precautions all too real, Evan Wytherling kept his free hand near his dagger, knowing he could draw it quickly. Fortunately, Mardi's home consisted of barely more space than many monasteries allowed their monks and with not much more in the way of major furnishings. It did not take more than a minute or two for the sharp-eyed swordsman to decide that nothing lurked nearby.

Emboldened, the young woman moved to a door that had to lead to her sleeping quarters. Evan did not stop her, but he kept close behind, ready to pull her back.

The room she slept in proved as harmless as the two prior. The knight paused at the entrance out of respect for the proprieties. Mardi eventually realized his hesitation and rewarded him with a tired smile.

"For one so disillusioned, Sir Wytherling, you've proven many times this day to still be a knight most honorable and chivalrous, a credit to your ancient calling."

"Disillusionment does not preclude the preservation of lives nor does it always mean complete abandonment of all of one's tenets."

She looked around. "I hope that Mistress Arden comes soon. I thought . . . I thought I'd be more likely to sleep in these quarters rather than stay in my uncle's home, even in my old rooms. Now, though, I don't know if I could sleep anywhere ever again."

"Sleep will come." Evan handed her the candle, which she used to light her lamps. "It may take some time, but it will come."

"I hope so." She put the candle down, then stared at her room. "I keep seeing that . . . that horrific beast. I keep thinking it'll rise out of the shadows."

Her comment reminded him that he had not finished securing her room. Evan reached once more into his pouch, hoping he could convince Mardi of what he planned before the possibly meddlesome housekeeper arrived. "This is an old method, but, as I promised, it should help you with the shadows and your desire to sleep."

"What is it?"

Opening his hand to her, the knight revealed another candle. In response to the young woman's puzzled expression, he explained, "It is said that placing a lit candle in the corners of one's chamber can ward off evil spirits." Evan gave her a smile that hid his true concern for her safety. "Yet another fanciful tale, true, but for one so recently touched by the violent death of a loved one, driving away the shadows can greatly aid in garnering some relief and relaxation."

She weighed his words carefully, glancing at the corners from time to time. Evan kept his gaze on her but focused his attention on the various sounds from without the school. Did he hear footsteps? How much longer before the magistrate's servant interrupted?

"Strange . . ." Mardi pursed her lips. "I must've heard of that story before. It sounds so familiar." The smile returned. "Mistress Arden might think me a child, but I'd like to do just as you suggested. I don't think I have enough candles—"

"I have more." During his sojourn in the market, Evan had restocked his supply. He had just enough for her needs and his own. Tomorrow he would purchase more; candles might prove very valuable in the days to come. "Please forgive my intrusion."

With her permission, he entered the room. Utilizing the candle already lit, Evan Wytherling moved from corner to corner, positioning each new candle securely. Mardi supplied him with small plates upon which to place them, the better to prevent a fire from starting if one candle tipped over. It took a short time to completely secure the room to his tastes.

"I feel . . . I feel better somehow just seeing them." Mardi inspected each corner. "There are no deep shadows."

No deep shadows. Evan exhaled quietly, more secure about her safety. Whether she was in danger of a night visitation such as he had suffered in his room was debatable, but now at least the knight could feel that he had done what he could beyond guarding her quarters himself. As trusting as Mardi Sinclair had become, he doubted her trust would have extended itself that far. Evan was still an outsider, not to mention a man. Pretor's Hill still respected proprieties.

A harsh knock from without made both turn. Evan felt a tingle and stiffened. With one hand on the hilt of his dagger, he moved cautiously to the outer door, opening it after a slight hesitation.

One of the brutish twin guards filled the frame, piggish eyes narrowing upon sighting the knight. Mardi stepped into view behind Evan, drawing the huge man's attention.

"I've brought the judge's woman," the behemoth grumbled.

A tall, narrow woman with pinched features and a vague look of suspicion wended her way around the immense guard. She wore simple, dark clothing of good make with no adornments whatsoever. Her graying hair had been tied up in a tight bun.

"Mistress Sinclair. My most abject sorrow over the death of your uncle. He was an industrious man." Even her words came out plain, unemotional. Evan wondered if perhaps with a guardian such as this the magistrate hoped that any shadowy stalkers would themselves be frightened away.

Her feet hidden beneath her skirt, Mistress Arden glided into the room, continuing her inspection. She came to the bedroom door and noted the candles. Evan expected some word of protest, but the magistrate's housekeeper merely turned and asked, "The chair in the first room. Do you have any objections to my bringing it into the bedroom? It looks to be the most comfortable in which to sit while you sleep."

"Really, Mistress Arden, I don't want to put you out. I

appreciate everything the magistrate's done, but—"

"If Master Drulane considers it important for me to stay with you this night or even longer, I'm certain he has good reason." To the housekeeper, this statement ended any further discussion. She returned to the outer room, where the guard still waited, and pointed at the chair. The giant picked up the piece of furniture, replacing it where it best suited Mistress Arden.

"Thank you, Grel. You may leave us now." She turned to Evan. "You as well. I will attend to matters here."

Again the knight felt a tingle. Mistress Arden might be the magistrate's housekeeper—a notion he found debatable now—but she also wielded the powers of a minor sorceress. Drulane could not have been ignorant of this fact. Evan's estimation of the man rose. Drulane understood the stakes better than the veteran warrior had assumed.

Mardi briefly took hold of his wrist. "Thank you, Sir Wytherling."

"I did little enough."

Before she could protest his remark, Evan departed. Behind him, eyes ever watchful, came the guard, Grel.

"You bring trouble. You should leave Pretor's Hill."

Evan ignored the man, instead taking the reins of his horse in hand and heading for the stables. He sensed the giant continuing to watch him, one hand no doubt on the great weapon at his side. Grel would not attack, not this time. Bulrik and his men feared the magistrate and would never dare to take such initiative on their own. Whatever their own dislikes, they would wait until ordered to act. So far, though, Drulane and Evan were on the same side . . . but that could easily change.

"She should be safe for tonight," he whispered once certain that the guard could not hear him. "The magistrate's woman bears power of her own. Candles were also lit."

The horse snorted. Evan Wytherling continued on in silence, pondering the day's events. A death, a futile hunt, and now his chance to speak with Valentin lost again. If Novaris or his shade haunted this land, he no doubt laughed at the knight's ineptitude. Even the death, if it could be called that, of the shadow creature did not make up for the victories the darkness could so far claim.

As he neared the inn, Evan glanced at the church, so innocent, so steadfast. Light still shone from within where the body of Mardi's uncle lay. Tomorrow they would surely move the body elsewhere.

Tomorrow, then, the knight decided, knowing this time he could not allow himself to be thwarted. *Tomorrow I must do it . . . or Pretor's Hill and all within will surely suffer.*

Mistress Arden unnerved Mardi but, at the same time, also gave the younger woman a sense of increased security. Mardi had doubted that she would sleep even for a minute, but as soon as her head touched the pillow, it was all she could do to stay awake long enough to watch the somber housekeeper settle herself into the chair.

The housekeeper reached up with her left hand and, to the weary young woman's momentary curiosity, drew some symbol with her finger. Mardi tried to decipher the symbol, but exhaustion caught up with her before she could. Her last glimpse of Mistress Arden was of the elder woman turning her direction, then the room and consciousness vanished in a comfortable fog.

How long she slept or whether she dreamt, Mardi Sinclair could not say. She only knew that she suddenly jolted to consciousness again, yet did not so much as move a finger or break the rhythm of her breathing. A sense of foreboding touched her.

Through slitted eyes, Mardi studied the bedroom as best she could. Mistress Arden remained seated, but her head hung forward. At first Mardi feared that the other woman had died, but then she saw that the housekeeper only slept. An exhalation of relief escaped Mardi, one that she immediately swallowed as a flicker of movement caught her attention.

112

A shadow.

She sat up in the bed, fists tight at her sides, fully expecting to find the shadow creature from the woods about to murder the two of them. Mardi could see its claws, feel them ready to tear through her throat as they had done to her uncle. The magistrate and Evan Wytherling would find the corpses in the morning, the two women's blood splattered over every wall.

But the beast is dead! her mind shouted at her. *He slew it! The knight slew it!*

Only then did Mardi acknowledge what her eyes saw. A shadow moved, but only the shadow caused by the flicker of a candle as melted wax dripped down. She quickly turned about, studying the other candles in turn and finding them still lit as well. No monster lurked save her own fear.

She collapsed back onto the bed, feeling very, very foolish and grateful that Mistress Arden had not woken. Mardi relaxed again, awaiting sleep.

However, her mind, now active, would not so readily relinquish itself back to sleep. Mardi found herself thinking of the knight and his deeds. What did she know of him? The question struck her as odd at this hour, tired as she was, but she nonetheless pursued the answer. She realized that he had fought in many wars, had witnessed far more than she ever would, and knew more, truth be told, than what could be learned in a lifetime at the university in Coramas.

Not enough. Surely Mardi knew more about him than that. What about the man within the armor? He wore a mask of disillusionment, but clearly his dedication to protecting others had not diminished over the years. Given a cause, Mardi felt certain that Evan would pursue it to its end, no matter what the effort or how long it took him to accomplish it. She had watched him during the brief, horrific struggle with the lupine monster in the woods; Evan Wytherling had stood fast, never once giving ground regardless of the threat. It had been the beast that had given way.

Weariness returned. Still not satisfied with her answer but too tired to continue, Mardi closed her eyes and started to drift off. Her last thoughts before sleeping concerned Evan and his reasons for coming to Pretor's Hill in the first place. Had he some specific intention in mind? How could she find out?

In her dreams, plans began to form.

Sweat beaded on his forehead. He took a silken handkerchief from his breast pocket and wiped the moisture away. The girl should not have been such trouble, even protected as she had been by both the blasted candles and the witch woman. She should have been easy to invade, especially as deep as she had slept, so worn down by her earlier grief.

Still, she had not only answered his question to a point, but now his own notions had been implanted in her mind. She would do some of the groundwork for him.

Of course, he left nothing to chance. Even with the girl prepared, it would do to investigate the knight next. With that hellish mount at last ensconced in the stables, Sir Evan Wytherling had to be asleep or at least very near it. He would prove trickier by far than the girl. The knight had to have safeguards far beyond those he had supplied to this Mardi Sinclair.

A wry grin filled Steppenwald's face. As his mother had always liked to remind him, he dearly loved a challenge . . . and now he faced one of the greatest of all.

Candles in place, Evan chose this night to make use of the simple bed. He did not, however, strip off his clothes, not even his boots. That could be done in short time in the morning, when he knew it was safe to do so. After the hellish encounter in the woods, Evan intended to be prepared for the possibility of some new stalker.

He did not relish sleep, had not in many years. Sleep could

bring him temporary relief, but as often it brought the ghosts back in greater force. Sometimes he relived the entire battle, sometimes he lived only those portions that sickened him most. Whichever the case, Evan tended to wake in a full sweat, hands generally attempting to wend off phantom blades or the jaws of a dragon.

Sleep he must, though, and so with reluctance Evan closed his eyes. He prayed this would be one of the nights in which he slept without dreaming but did not expect it to be so. Too much had happened. Too much would happen in the days ahead.

The first moments of sleep touched him as a gentle haze, which Evan gratefully entered. The nothingness soothed him, caressed him, and for a time enabled the knight to forget his endless quest.

His relief did not last long.

Once more he rode among the others, leading them through the pass he himself had scouted. Time was of the essence; if they did not cut off the enemy before their forces were pushed back, the tide of battle would turn from them. Evan and his force were among the elite their side had to offer, the most loyal men sworn to fulfill their mission even at the cost of their own lives. Evan had been chosen their leader because he had always been most dedicated to the cause, had proved himself time and time again.

"How much farther?" one warrior in dark blue, Marcus by name, called out to him. "How much farther, damn it? We should've been out of this blasted pass by now!"

They all knew that to be fact. Evan tried to mask his emotions. He, too, knew that they should have been through long before. Had things gone exactly as planned, the knights should have been coming up on the unsuspecting enemy at this point, yet all that lay before them was more of the same treacherous passage.

"We've gone wrong somewhere!" Marcus cried out. "We must've taken the wrong fork back there!"

"No!" Evan returned, hands clenched. "This is the correct route!"

"It can't be—"

Marcus vanished. The other knights faded. As the very pass itself dwindled to fog, Evan Wytherling drew his sword and stood in the saddle. Something was wrong. Even in dreaming he knew the end of this vision and this was not it.

A pressure built up around him, an intrusive force that desired to reach within his very being and twist him around. A terrible fear, a terrible memory, shook Evan, and he swung at the air, seeking to cut down the invisible invader.

His vehemence, if not his blade, seemed to startle it for a moment, but then it pushed harder, trying to, as he felt it, peel away his skull so it could find his mind.

"Not again! I will not have it done again! In God's name, leave me be!"

Now on foot, with nothing but fog surrounding him, Evan thrust his sword over and over, seeking in vain his attacker. The pressure on his mind continued to build, so much so that he expected his head to burst at any moment.

Phantoms from his past materialized and vanished in the fog. A knight he had slain in the course of the battle. Savage General Haggad holding up his bloody weapon, a grin on his face. A carrion crow as large as a man.

Some of the phantoms had no link to the war, to the terrible battle. A waiflike figure with pointed ears, seeming in need of holding, caring . . . yet Evan knew that to come too close to the creature had meant death for a score and more men. A cloaked figure with a mask resembling the face of a beautiful woman, but who, beneath it, had no face of her own and even less soul.

There came a short, laughing man who tossed knives around in the air as if they were a living part of him. He had never missed, so he had often said to Evan . . . until that one fateful encounter in the swamplands when it had mattered most. Evan had never found his body, but the memory remained one of those terrible ones ever burned into his mind.

"You were always so sentimental . . ."

Evan's blood froze. He did not have to turn to see who spoke.

Only one voice ever cut through him so much.

"Novaris."

With a strength borne of desperation and hope, Evan Wytherling swung the jeweled blade in the direction from which the voice had come—

And woke up.

He gripped the sword tight and leapt from the bed. Evan stared first at the doorway, then turned to the window. He threw it open, then thrust his head out.

The streets of Pretor's Hill were empty. A few dim lights attempted to illuminate the murky dark, but the rain had left in its wake a mist too reminiscent of his terrible dream.

The dream . . . it had not simply been the product of his regrets, of his guilt. Someone, something, had invaded his mind, sought to know his innermost secrets. This attack had been different than the one the previous evening. Then only death had been sought. Why this sudden change . . . or were the two attacks connected at all?

As he pulled back inside, Evan experienced a brief tingle, one so faint that he nearly ignored it at first. By the time he realized just what he had felt, the sensation had passed into memory. The knight sought in vain for another trace, but none existed.

All sorcerers, all wizards, all spellcasters of any ability bore unique signatures in their power. Sometimes in the wake of their spellcasting, they left traces of power that those with the Sight could detect, hence the tingles that Evan Wytherling felt now and then. Some traces lingered on forever; others, if cast with stealth in mind, vanished swiftly.

Mistress Arden, although having some ability, had made no attempt to shield her power from him, possibly because she had not known he would be sensitive to it. This night visitor had taken great pains to protect himself from Evan's notice but had not entirely succeeded. Of course, while it somewhat comforted Evan to know that the wizard's gift had not entirely abandoned him, the knowledge it brought him now did little to ease the veteran knight's mind. If anything, it only added to a situation already fraught with too many questions and too many contradictions, for although the trace had been short-lived, it had borne a signature that in many aspects reminded him of one spellcaster in particular.

Paulo Centuros.

VII

A HUNT FOR ANSWERS

Yoniff Casperin's body had been placed in state in the church prior to what would be a swift but elegant funeral. At the same time, a hunting party, led by the erstwhile Officer Bulrik, searched the countryside for the mythical wolf or wolves that might still remain behind. Evan admired the speed and efficiency with which Drulane orchestrated the events, deciding that in another age, another time, the hunched man would have made a worthy commander on the field of battle. He only hoped that Drulane understood that his town and people were already at war, but against a foe that the locals could not possibly fathom.

On account of the hunt, Evan had seen nothing of Mardi Sinclair since the night before and hoped to keep it that way for as long as possible. He could do no more for her than he already had and believed that his presence would only serve to remind her of what had befallen her uncle. Enough reminders abounded without him adding to the toll.

Of course, Evan knew that he also avoided her for the memories and emotions she stirred within him. The quest the wizard had forced upon him had not left him bereft of the appreciation of women, but his sense of honor—outmoded, Valentin had always said—still held sway . . . or so the knight kept telling himself. In truth, he could not bear being reminded that beneath the facade, Evan Wytherling still retained human emotions, still recalled too well memories of another place and another woman. Such weaknesses left him open to attack, left the wizard's almighty quest in danger if Evan did not keep himself under control.

Now more than ever he needed control. If Novaris did not lurk here, some legacy of his did. This was the closest the weary knight had come to his prey in many a year. Evan could not let matters slip from him any more than they already had.

To be free of the quest at last . . . that was all Evan Wytherling *truly* wanted.

The knight had been given an active part in the hunt. The magistrate had insisted on this and Evan had readily acquiesced. Like the knight, Drulane understood that they hunted will-o'-the-wisps, but he had to pretend otherwise lest the townsfolk wonder. As Evan had been Mardi Sinclair's rescuer, it seemed only natural that he would be the one to lead them to the site of her uncle's death. Of course, no beast's body remained for the hunters to discover, but the magistrate had suggested in advance that some scavenger might have already dragged off the supposed wolf's carcass. Drulane wanted no question to remain.

Still, not all had taken his last suggestion to heart. Daniel Taran, his sire, and Garn Bellowes, father of the unfortunate Jak, joined the group early, bringing with them a good number of retainers. The Tarans and their neighbor seemed of a different mind from the start. More often than not Evan found one of the three much too near for his tastes. Bellowes especially followed the knight about as if hunting him, not the wolf. The short, whiskered merchant eyed Evan with open hostility, possibly blaming him for his son's mishap. Fortunately, since both were on horseback through much of the search, the man never came too close. Likely he rightly suspected that the knight's devilish steed would treat him much as it had his errant offspring.

As expected, they found nothing, although Evan did grow nervous as the hunters entered the vicinity of the mound. Daniel Taran rode over the very top of the unnatural hill without even realizing what lay buried beneath. His father and Garn Bellowes circled around the mound with as little interest in the landscape as they had in actually finding wolves. The other hunters milled about, more than half of them probably not at all certain how to find a track, much less read it.

Near sundown, Bulrik removed his helm and, peering around at the scattered members of his hunt, called out, "That's it, then! The sun's nearly gone! Best to call an end to it now!"

"Waste of time, anyway," muttered the younger Taran, eyes alighting momentarily on Evan, who had pulled up next to the officer. "There's no wolf within miles. I'm beginning to doubt there ever was."

"Not a wolf hunt at all," Garn Bellowes snapped, his voice surprisingly high-pitched for such a stocky man. "More like a wild goose chase."

"I'm obeying the magistrate's orders, that's all." Bulrik stared at them from behind a mask of indifference.

"So you are." Bellowes nodded to the Tarans. "Feodor, Daniel, I'll see the pair of you at Master Casperin's funeral. You"—he pointed at the officer—"tell Drulane that I'll be seeing him soon after it about a matter of justice." This time he glanced Evan's way, rewarding the knight with a fleeting glare.

Bulrik only nodded. The merchant rode off, followed by his retainers. Others left immediately after. The Tarans remained, a dozen strong men with them. Bulrik's own six guards gathered behind the officer, facing the Tarans' force. Evan made no move toward his weapon, watching the unspoken confrontation and knowing it centered on him.

"Mind you, I'll be speaking with your master, too," the elder Taran commented, also glancing at the knight. "Matters important to the late, lamented Yoniff's family, too."

"The magistrate makes himself available to his people as much as he humanly can," Bulrik commented blandly. "If he has time, he'll be glad to hear your concerns."

"He'll have time. He'll have time." Signaling the others, Feodor Taran led his party off, his son remaining behind long enough to smirk at the knight.

When no one remained with Evan Wytherling but the magistrate's men, the officer turned to him. "Magistrate Drulane is not done with you, knight. Expect to speak with him before long." Bulrik's tone indicated that a refusal would be out of the question. "He's requested that until then you remain in your room at the inn as much as possible."

Evan said nothing, urging the baleful steed toward town. After a moment, he heard the guards follow. He had expected nothing less. When questioned, Evan would give the magistrate some of what he desired to know and hope it would be enough to assuage the man. He wanted to meet with the magistrate for his own reasons, chief among them being his curiosity as to whether he could detect some trace similar to what he had sensed last night. The knight did not suspect that Drulane was in actuality Paulo Centuros in elaborate magical guise, but perhaps there existed a link between the two that Evan had so far missed. A slim possibility, but one worth investigating.

The watch officer and his men gradually surrounded Evan as they rode. The knight did not fear his escort, but he did keep a careful watch on the surrounding trees. The Tarans and Garn Bellowes had acted with more animosity than should have been warranted. Daniel and his father clearly saw him as some obstacle to their goal, presumably Mardi Sinclair's marriage to the son, but they had to be fools if they thought Evan would take her away from them. As for Master Bellowes, had he branded the knight an enemy simply because his son had been bitten by Evan's horse? Absurd, yes, but what other reason did the man have for his actions?

Not for the first time, Evan pondered the behavior of most of the town's citizenry. Since his arrival he had noted the majority to be arrogant, unthinking, and hostile, especially toward strangers. Even those whose business should have required an appearance of friendliness, such as Benjamin Jakes, could not bring themselves to so much as pretend. The greatest exceptions to this parade of animosity had so far been Arno, whose simplicity might be his saving grace, the magistrate, whose motives were yet questionable, and, of course, Mardi Sinclair.

The matter still weighed heavily upon Evan as he and his escort reached town. The watch abandoned him shortly thereafter, returning, no doubt, to their quarters. Evan rode on to the smithy, keeping his gaze for the most part on the path ahead. The knight could not help but notice that his appearance now drew even more attention than it had when first he had arrived in Pretor's Hill. It seemed that everyone he passed marked him for one reason or another. Evan forced his hand away from the hilt of his sword despite feeling as if he had entered enemy territory.

Dismounting, the warrior led his beast toward the stables. The clang of hammer against anvil gave notice of Arno hard at work, so the knight chose not to disturb the man. One of the young boys who worked at the stables hurried toward him, but Evan waved him off. He needed no assistance in caring for the damnable steed. The horse could almost take care of itself.

A single lantern at the entrance provided minimal illumination. The other mounts shifted in discomfort as the pair passed through, save one; an animal in one of the farthest stalls showed no fear of the knight's creature.

Gray for the most part save for a generous sprinkling of black spots along the flanks, the muscular stallion stood nearly as tall as the baleful steed. The thick ebony mane and tail had been most neatly groomed. As they neared, the animal gave an arrogant snort, as if challenging the newcomers. Fortunately for Evan, his own mount did not take up the gauntlet.

The king's man, Steppenwald, he's got himself a magnificent animal, a Neulander Spotted as nearly as many hands as yours . . . So Arno had told him the first time they had met. Evan Wytherling paused, studying the animal. How very unlikely that another traveler owning such an expensive, well-kept steed would arrive in Pretor's Hill at this time. To be sure, the animal might belong to another, but the knight found himself doubting that the Neulander's master could be anyone other than the king's man, the mysterious Steppenwald.

Once certain that his own mount's needs had been cared for,

Evan turned his attention to the Neulander. The haughty stallion snorted again as he approached, kicking the stall once in threat. Evan studied the beast from a nearby stall.

A strong, broad animal. Evan had seen its kind before, but never so large. Although slightly shorter than his own mount, the Neulander clearly came out the more muscular, the more sturdy. That spoke of a rider who himself had to be of greater proportions than the norm. If this stallion belonged to Steppenwald, then surely it would not be difficult to pick the king's man out of a crowd.

The continued clanging reminded him that he had one source of information available to him this very moment. Abandoning the stalls, Evan sought out the smith. Arno had to have been here when the newcomer had arrived, which meant he might even know where the Neulander's owner was now.

Arno looked up as he entered but did not pause in his work. Evan patiently waited while the smith finished working on a shoe, aware that his quarry would be going nowhere so long as the spotted stallion remained in the stall.

As ever, the smith proved in a good mood. He did apologize, however, for being unable to give his visitor much of his time at the moment. "So much work and my apprentice ill, but if you've got yourself a simple question, sir knight—"

"The Neulander Spotted in the stables. Is it the one belonging to Lord Steppenwald?"

Arno reached for one of his tools, brow furrowed. "You must be mistaking something, Sir Wytherling. There's no Spotted in my stables. Lord Steppenwald's Ghost is the only Spotted I ever see in Pretor's Hill and I'd certainly recall him coming."

"Perhaps one of the stable boys took care of him."

"I'd still be seeing the horse and his lordship when they came in." The beefy man put the tool down. "But maybe I'd better look for myself. Make sure the boys've done a proper job if Lord Steppenwald has come like you said."

The smith wiped his hands and trundled past Evan, who followed close behind. "Rolf! Come here!"

The same lad Evan had seen earlier rushed over. He had a sullen look, as if he wished he were elsewhere.

"Rolf! Did you see his Lordship Steppenwald today? Maybe on his big spotted steed?"

"No, Master Arno. No."

"And you've not been running off to play games with those two friends of yours?"

The boy shook his head with great vigor. "I've been here all, day, Master Arno, I swear!"

"All right. Back to your duties, then." The smith shrugged as the boy ran off. "He's been a pretty reliable lad, I'll tell you, Sir Wytherling, though I'd be the first to admit he's been careless a few times these past few days." He rubbed his thick jaw in thought. "Maybe we'll go take a look ourselves."

The knight squinted, the stable seeming murkier than previous despite the fact that the first lantern still hung lit at the entrance. Arno seized a second lantern so the pair could better see the stalls farther back.

"Easy . . . easy . . ." Arno murmured to the other horses in passing. He held the lantern high, peering into each stall. Occasionally the smith would gently pat an animal or inspect the cleanliness of its surroundings. Evan Wytherling's patience grew thinner with each pause. The murky darkness remained strong, still obscuring the stall where he had discovered the Neulander Spotted. An uneasiness touched the knight.

"Where was this Spotted?" Arno swung the light around, at last illuminating the stall in question.

It was empty.

Evan took a step nearer and felt a slight tingle. He backed up, sweeping his gaze across the other horses boarded nearby. All seemed in order, much to his hidden frustration. It would do no good searching the other stalls. "I must have been mistaken."

The other man frowned. "Hard to mistake a Neulander Spotted, at least, hard for me. Hard to mistake seeing a horse at all."

"The shadows must have confused me. I apologize for taking you from your work."

"My work . . ." The smith's eyes widened. "I must be getting back . . . unless you'll still be needing me, Sir Wytherling . . ."

"No. I have wasted enough of your time, it appears."

"Think nothing of it, Sir Wytherling, sir. Nothing of it." Swinging the lantern around, the massive man rushed from the stables. Evan paid his departure scant attention, already interested in the mysterious disappearance.

The tingle returned when once again he stepped toward the stall. It never grew very strong, more the hint of something than the thing itself. Any good-sized mount would have tramped down the straw.

He returned to his own horse, who had stood watching his antics in what had probably been amusement. Evan touched the animal lightly on the muzzle. "The horse was there."

The baleful steed snorted.

"Now it no longer is. Did someone retrieve it?"

This time, the knight's mount remained still, silent.

"Did it simply vanish?"

Again, the foul steed remained silent.

"You know as little as I." Evan sighed, turning once more to stare at the empty stall. He had not imagined the Spotted, not at all. The knight approached, but the tingle did not recur. Fool that he had been, Evan had not earlier paid enough mind to the signature of the trace. Now he had lost a possible clue.

I saw the stallion. A Neulander Spotted. The very type of horse ridden by this Lord Steppenwald, the king's so elusive man.

"Who are you, Steppenwald?" he whispered, running his hand along the gate of the stall. Not the slightest trace remained of the sorcery that had made a full-grown stallion disappear. Yet the fact that sorcery and the king's man were somehow linked intrigued him. Officially, Rundin had forbidden sorcery. Interesting that one of its own would be so immersed in it.

He wondered what Drulane might or might not know about

this possible visit. More important, as Evan departed the stables for the inn, he wondered what Steppenwald himself knew . . . and what danger that knowledge might pose for both the knight and his quest.

The most unnerving part of her uncle's funeral did not turn out to be the service itself, but rather the relentless wave of sympathy afterward that threatened to engulf Mardi whole. The death of a prominent citizen such as Yoniff Casperin meant that everyone with even the slightest reason to be there had to also speak with his only relative. Hand after hand touched her. Voice after voice assaulted her, murmuring words she found ever hollow.

To be certain, many of those who attended had to have felt genuine sympathy, but Mardi quickly lost the ability to judge. Too often those who came to her came because they owed the moneylender and now sought the opportunity to wipe away their debt. She had never known such pettiness in all her life in Pretor's Hill, and it shocked her to think that people she had known for so long could be so callous.

"Mardi, Mardi . . ." Arms engulfed her, almost cutting off her breath. Belatedly she realized that the arms belonged to Daniel, but where once she might have welcomed their comfort, now the bereaved gentlewoman found them only stifling.

"I'm all right, Daniel," She struggled out of his grip, pretending at the same time to be reaching for a handkerchief from her belt pouch.

"Far from it, from what I see." He started to reach for her, then evidently thought better of it. Instead, he offered her a handkerchief of his own, which she forced herself to take in order to avoid further confrontation. "You've kept to yourself all through the services . . . and before that for that matter. It's not good. Father insists . . . I insist . . . that you come spend some time with us at the holding. Being away from town'll do you good and

Mother'll be pleased to have you for company—"

"I—" Mardi tried to form a response that would not leave Daniel angry and bitter. Behind him she could also see his parents, Mistress Taran a properly thin, vacant-looking woman who seemed ever an appendage of her husband. On a rare occasion, Mardi had seen the woman who was buried within, a woman who had once had a spirit of her own. Now she mirrored her husband's moods.

Magistrate Drulane unexpectedly came to her rescue. "My dear Mardina, I hate to disturb you at this time, but there are one or two matters I still need to discuss with you. If you could?"

The gnarled man steered her away with gentle strength, ignoring the frustrated glance of the young merchant. Mardi allowed herself to be drawn outside even though discussing her uncle's affairs was not a subject she looked forward to.

"Many a young woman would consider Daniel Taran a fine match," the magistrate commented quietly. "Perhaps you do, Mardina?"

"I . . . I really haven't given it much thought."

The watery eyes narrowed just a bit. "No, I don't think you have . . . not lately."

She bristled, suddenly wondering if he thought to renew his own attempts to court her now that he had some control over her uncle's affairs. Mardi appreciated the aid he had given her thus far, but if Drulane thought this presented him the right to make her his, he would find himself sorely mistaken.

"I've made arrangements for your uncle's business that, with your approval, can be completed in a day or two. It'll leave you with quite a tidy sum, I think . . . unless you've some reason for retaining his business yourself?"

"No. No, that would be appreciated." Mardi calmed herself.

"Fine, fine. Have you considered moving back to Coramas, my dear? You certainly have the money now. I know how much you enjoyed your time there. It might be better for you. I can give you letters of introduction so that you might have a proper place to stay. You could also meet the right people."

Mardi's gaze drifted beyond, seeing nothing but memories. Sometimes she had thought of returning to Coramas, recalling the friends, the excitement, and the opportunities to learn. However, Mardi had not been able to bring herself to depart, Pretor's Hill always pulling her back. Even during her years of study, she had often found herself yearning to see her home again. It had puzzled her at times, for she had found the town lacking in so much.

"No. I don't want to leave."

"A pity."

The peculiar tone in his voice, a tone hinting that he would have much preferred she take up his suggestion, shook her from her reverie. Her gaze had already begun to shift back to the magistrate when she caught sight of a distant figure. All thought of the magistrate, his suggestion, and even, momentarily, the funeral of her uncle, were swept away as she recognized the pale knight.

He had been watching the church, of that she was certain. The moment he realized that her eyes had found him, Evan Wytherling abandoned his post at the street corner and started for the inn, where he had a room. His movements were smooth, seemingly uncaring, but she suspected different. He had not meant to be noticed by her.

A great urge to speak with him filled Mardi. She wanted to know more about the man who had rescued her not once but twice now. The urge pressed on her, almost making Mardi Sinclair tear herself free of the magistrate's grip and run after the knight.

Inwardly straining, Mardi instead politely separated herself from Drulane. "I must beg your forgiveness, Magistrate, but I've a matter to attend to."

The elderly man showed no offense, but as he bowed farewell to her, Drulane added in a quiet voice, "Be careful around him, Mardina. He's accompanied by many ghosts."

She paused a moment, thinking to ask him what he meant by that, but the magistrate immediately turned away. After that, the urge to pursue Evan Wytherling proved too much to resist. Mardi hurried after the tall figure, hoping she would catch him before he reached the inn.

That proved no race at all, for as the veteran knight neared his destination, several men emerged and immediately swarmed him. Evan paused, visibly assessing each newcomer. Mardi bit her lip and instinctively sought a place to secrete herself, recognizing that more than one member of the group worked for Garn Bellowes. She slipped around the corner of a nearby building, then peered out. A moment later, Jak Bellowes, hand neatly bandaged, joined the pack surrounding the outsider. Unlike his parents, he had not attended Uncle Yoniff's funeral.

"The scavenger . . ." Jak sneered. Whereas his whiskered father sometimes reminded Mardi of a cat, the younger Bellowes had a more pronounced canine appearance. "You're bad luck for this town, you know that?"

To the surprise of both his accuser and Mardi, the knight nodded slightly. "Perhaps I am."

His reply momentarily took the group by surprise. Finally recovering from his astonishment, Jak pressed his advantage. "Funny, my father said they couldn't find any trace of a wolf carcass. No blood, nothing. You'd think a beast that big would leave some remains behind even if another one'd dragged it away . . ."

"Maybe it weren't a wolf what killed the money man, Jak," one member of the pack spouted, sounding very much as if he had been tutored in advance on what to say.

"Aye, a man could kill a man like that, especially if killing were his life trade."

Mardi looked around, hoping that Drulane had not yet departed, but hardly anyone who had been at the funeral remained in sight, Jak's family included. She debated shouting or running for help, but before she had the opportunity to decide which course might be best, one of Jak's other companions, clearly impetuous, swung a fist at the knight. Although Evan could not have possibly seen the attack coming, he still dodged in time, then twisted in the man's direction. He caught the fist and wrist with both hands, turning them sharply. His attacker cried out in pain. The knight did not pause, kicking the other's legs out from under him.

Even as the first man fell, two others launched themselves on the outsider. The first tumbled back a second later, choking, the leathered edge of Evan's flat hand having caught him in the throat. The second managed to snare the veteran warrior's other arm, but without his partner to help him, he proved unprepared for the knight's fist.

"Pile on him!" Jak called, not at all attempting to leave the safety of his position. "All of you, you fools!"

They fell on the knight from all sides, at least seven that Mardi could count. Two received blows that slowed their advances, but Evan could not stem the tide after that. He disappeared under an avalanche of fists.

All thought of finding help vanished from the gentlewoman's mind. Possessed by something she did not understand, Mardi abandoned her place of safety and charged the combatants. Jak looked up and, upon recognizing her, started toward her.

She reached the first of the men and pulled him away from the group. Mardi drove a fist into the face of the stunned attacker, who collapsed into two of his companions.

"What in blazes do you think you're doing, woman?" Jak cried, seizing her wrist.

She glared at him, recognizing and yet not recognizing Daniel's friend. As he fought to push her hand aside, Mardi brought down the heel of her shoe on his foot. Jak cursed but did not let go. He tried to grab her other wrist, but Mardi moved fast, punching him hard in the stomach. Gasping, Jak Bellowes released his hold and folded over, fighting for breath.

Her brief interference had bought Evan some relief. One more man lay unconscious near the knight, but the remaining ruffians had regrouped. Mardi caught a brief glimpse of a knife. Unmindful of her awkward clothing, she threw herself at the nearest of Jak's associates, sending one man into another.

Evan Wytherling seized the hand that held the knife and turned it sharply. His foe yelped. His booted foot buried itself in the chest of another foe to his side.

"What's the meaning of this? Stop! I command you!"

Rough hands pulled Mardi Sinclair back. She nearly punched the man who had seized her, only at the last moment recognizing Bulrik. As the watch officer drew her from the group, his giant underlings strode into the fray and began dragging out the combatants.

"Easy, Mistress Sinclair! Please!"

"Let go of me!" Shaking free of the officer, Mardi went to the knight. Blood dripped from a gash on his forehead and a small cut on his lip, but otherwise he had come through unharmed. Compared to his adversaries, who fought for breath, he seemed not at all winded.

Evan took hold of her hand before she could touch one of the bruises and in a whisper warned, "You would do best to separate yourself from me, my lady. You will gain no friends from any association with one such as myself."

"I don't care about that. Let me see what they did to you."

"It will heal. It always does." Gently pushing her aside, Evan confronted Bulrik. "You will want to take me to see the magistrate, I presume?"

The other man looked sorely tempted, but to Mardi's astonishment, he shook his head. "Go about your business. It's clear who's at fault here. The magistrate'll know all that happened, you can count on that." The officer grunted. "Besides, you'll likely be seeing him soon enough, anyway."

The knight made no reply to the last statement, possibly out of respect to Mardi. Drulane had not yet questioned the man further about her uncle's horrible death. She knew the magistrate wanted better details than the ones they had earlier provided; surely, he knew that no ordinary wolf could have taken a man on horseback so easily.

"Let's go, you lot." Bulrik's men herded Jak and his

companions together and, despite the young landowner's protests about his station, dragged them off in the direction of Drulane's offices.

Evan watched them vanish. "They will be free before the night comes, will they not?"

"Probably. Jak's father will see to that. Drulane will do what he can, though. They won't escape some punishment."

"That was not my concern." He started to walk off, then paused to look at her. "Thank you, Mardi Sinclair. I admit to some surprise concerning both your skills and your willingness to use them."

She had surprised herself as well. Yet again Mardi had reacted as if some warrior maiden instead of the educated young woman she was. Where the skills had come from, she still could not say. No one in Coramas had ever taught her any such abilities. Certainly the university would not have considered it part of a gentlewoman's curriculum.

"I don't know what came over me," Mardi finally managed.

"Of that I am certain." Evan stared at her with such intensity that Mardi could feel her face reddening with embarrassment. Perhaps the knight, too, noticed, for he suddenly turned his gaze in the direction of the church. "My condolences again over the death of your uncle. The funeral was not too painful, I hope."

"Everyone tried to be kind."

"Which would only make it more painful. He will be buried today?"

"No. Rundin tradition requires the body to remain in a place of viewing for one day after funerals. I don't know why, but that's the way it's always been. He'll be buried tomorrow." It surprised her that she could speak so plainly about Yoniff's final disposal. She truly missed her uncle.

"Yes, I had forgotten that. Surely, though, no one will disturb his rest tonight. Only the priest, Father Gerard will be about after sunset."

She shivered even though this had been one of the warmer

133

days in the past week. "No, there shouldn't be anyone else, but it's tradition."

"Tradition can be cumbersome." Evan Wytherling absently touched his lip where one of the men had struck him. Mardi thought it looked better than she had first believed; the skin had barely broken.

The fatigued knight started up the steps to the inn. Mardi's heart quickened. She wanted to find out more about him, but if she did nothing to stop him she would lose her best opportunity.

"Sir Wytherling. It's . . . it's getting dark. Would you be so kind as to escort me home again?"

"My lady?" The tall figure gazed down on her, clearly surprised by her request. Mardi herself could barely mask her own astonishment at her boldness. The night they had brought back her uncle's body she had definitely needed an escort. The shock of discovery had almost left her numb. Now, though, despite the funeral having just ended, Mardi could have readily made her way home alone. To ask the knight to escort her such a short distance might give him the wrong impression as to her interests.

What *were* her interests? She wanted to know more about the man, but so much so that she had to risk her reputation?

"Of course I will escort you, my lady. Forgive me for being remiss." He joined her while she still struggled with her inner demons, presenting his arm. "Your grief would still be strong and the funeral must have weighed heavily upon you. You should not be out alone just now."

Mardi took the arm, thankful that Evan had offered his own reasons for her sudden request. They walked slowly along, the knight allowing the gentlewoman to set the pace.

After a few steps Mardi began to question him. "How long have you been a knight, Sir Wytherling?"

"Too much of my life, my lady."

"I thought I asked you to call me Mardi."

"Then I am Evan . . . Mardi." The shadow of a smile flickered across his face, vanishing so swiftly that his companion barely had time to marvel over its existence.

After several seconds she realized that he had not answered her question, but by then another that interested her more had already formed. "You once visited Pretor's Hill before, didn't you?"

She felt the slightest bit of tensing in the muscles of his arm. "I have visited this region."

Another question readily formed, one that made no sense to her yet seemed also strangely appropriate. "Did you ever meet Paulo Centuros?"

This time she sensed no reaction, but Evan's answer came slowly. "Paulo Centuros lived well over a century and more ago."

"But wizards are said to live much longer than the rest of us. You might've met him."

"I have been far in the West for many years, my—Mardi. It is unlikely I would have come across him there."

"What about Novaris . . . the sorcerer-king?"

She might have struck him a blow as hard as any she had struck against Jak. For the first time, the veteran warrior looked confused, unable to shield his emotions. Mardi, too, felt somewhat disoriented. Where had the name "Novaris" come from? One of her books, surely, although she could not recall ever reading of the man.

"Novaris did battle with your wizard during the great wars," Evan said at last, the confusion gone from his face. "Like Centuros, he would have been of a time long before now. Your grandfather's grandfather might have fought against him. We are here."

"What?" His last words caught her by surprise. She looked ahead, saw that the school stood before them much too soon. Deeper, more striking questions fluttered through her mind, but if she asked them now, Mardi feared she might push Evan permanently away. Still, perhaps just one more . . .

A woman's voice cut through her concerns, dousing any hope of continuing her inquiry. "Mistress Sinclair. I trust the proceedings did not take too much out of you. I knew I should've accompanied you, young lady."

Mistress Arden stood by the door, hands clasped in a manner that Mardi found somewhat imperious. For just the slimmest of moments anger at the elder woman swelled within Mardi, an anger so intense that she barely had the wherewithal to hold it in check. Her reaction frightened her; the magistrate's woman had treated her with only dignity and concern. Mardi owed her no animosity. That she had not accompanied the young gentlewoman to the funeral had been at Mardi's own request. Mardi had wanted to show some strength before her fellow townsfolk.

"I will leave you here now." Her escort bowed, then briefly surveyed the school. "No crows. How curious."

Mardi heard the words, but they did not register with her in her frustrated state. Would she never have the opportunity to learn about the man? Would they forever be meeting for just a few moments, then going their separate ways?

"Come inside, Mistress Sinclair. The day is waning and this eternal dampness creeps into everyone."

Already the knight had started off, leaving her to the ministrations of Drulane's housekeeper. Mardi watched him walk away, stiff, proud, yet also with what she imagined to be a tremendous burden on his shoulders. Evan Wytherling carried many secrets and some of the scars from them ran deep, very deep.

Whatever it took, she would discover each of those secrets. Mardi had to . . . even if she did not understand why.

One who did understand why watched nearby, the shadows around him so deep that despite his girth neither the women nor the errant knight could ever have noticed him. Even the slight gleam from the mismatched eyes of his dragon-head cane barely penetrated the impossible gloom.

A disappointing foray, yes, disappointing, Steppenwald

decided. He had hoped that using the already-bitter Jak Bellowes to soften up the knight would leave Evan Wytherling open to suggestion. Steppenwald greatly approved of suggestion, especially when it was his own. He had encountered unexpected resistance during his initial attempt to probe the inner recesses of the knight's mind. The man's will had been strong, but something else within had also protected Sir Wytherling, something with an annoyingly familiar trace to it.

Does he even know, this paladin of less than a virtuous past? He must, he must. Not even Paulo could've erased that much. Does he chafe under the bit? Would he change what was, what will be?

His burning gaze fixed on the school, where the woman lived. She, too, bore some curious traits, especially her sudden burst to action when the fools had fallen on the knight. No one could have taught this Mardi Sinclair what she knew about combat and yet she moved with veteran grace. Steppenwald could think of at least one other reason why that might be, but the reason did not satisfy him.

Conundrums, puzzles, and mysteries. Mother, dear, you should see this, you should. What a mad mess. But I'll tidy it up, and perhaps, just perhaps, I'll have the key to a quandary of my own.

He strode out of the darkness, pausing briefly to stare at the inn, then at the church. Perhaps it might be time to let the knight take a hand, see where that led. If he was any judge of character, and Steppenwald believed himself so, then Evan Wytherling had but one recourse. He would seek out the best source of information available to him. Surprising that he had not yet done so, but perhaps the fates had conspired against him, as exampled by the death of the moneylender Yoniff Casperin.

Steppenwald tapped the cane lightly on the cobblestone road, still eyeing the church. *Yes, he must do it. He'll go and visit old Valentin. No other choice.*

The gigantic man tapped the cane once more, then pointed the eyes of the dragon to a location just to his left. The mismatched pair gleamed bright.

A cloud of dust swirled up from the ground, a cloud that swiftly formed an equine shape. In but the blink of an eye, the arrogant Neulander Spotted formed before his master.

"Aah, good Ghost, good Ghost," the king's man murmured. Evan Wytherling had seen through the glamour Steppenwald had cast in the stables, quite a surprise. Steppenwald liked the surprises to come *from* him, not *to* him. Still, before long, he would not have to keep his presence all that much a secret. After all this time, matters were moving quickly. Something would break very soon. When it did, Evan Wytherling would certainly be in the midst of it.

Mounting, Steppenwald surveyed the street. A few folk were about, but unless he chose to draw attention to himself, he knew they would not even see him.

Evan Wytherling would surely visit Valentin, but in the meantime, Steppenwald had a journey of his own to make, the one he had postponed when his avian messenger had come to report to him. With a last glance in the direction of the inn, he turned the stallion Ghost around and rode swiftly and unnoticed out of Pretor's Hill . . . in the very direction that would lead him straight to the final resting place of the dragon Grimyr.

VIII

VALENTIN

It must be now. It cannot wait any longer.

The priest had to be asleep by now. Evan had watched and waited, marking the lights of various buildings as they had flickered out. The lamp of Father Gerard had remained on longer than most, a somewhat vexing sight. The good father had a burial to perform on the morrow and in the knight's mind that meant the man should have gone to bed early. Instead, Father Gerard had remained up well into the evening, finally dousing his light just when Evan had come to fear that the priest intended to remain awake forever.

The inn had long since quieted. A good thing, for Evan doubted that Master Jakes, who had, absurdly, blamed the knight for the actions of Garn Bellowes's son, would have readily accepted the spectacle his tenant now presented.

With his fondness for history, Magistrate Drulane might have appreciated the touches Evan Wytherling had added. The clothes in which Evan had clad himself were of a fashion far past, when once a younger man had still fully believed in the canons of the knighthood. The faded silver and black jerkin he wore bore the embroidered fighting gryphon crest, the emblem of a house lost to time. The shirt beneath remained smooth and silken despite the long period during which it had remained packed away. As with the jerkin, the pants, too, were silver and black, creating a proud house uniform fit for the most formal occasions.

Evan adjusted his boots, trying not to recall that the last such occasion had been the funerals of his own family. Those ghosts, too, haunted him, but for different reasons. Had he not followed his ancestors into the knighthood, the House of Wytherling might still stand, albeit under most difficult circumstances.

Anyone who had watched him ride into town would have been hard-pressed to see exactly where he could have stored these garments. Another "gift" from Paulo Centuros, a tiny pouch, lay with the mouth open and its strings dangling off the bed. At a glance, the pouch looked large enough to contain a deck of playing cards and no more . . . but wizards could create fascinating and troubling toys. The garments were not all that Evan stored within, only the most mundane.

In his scabbard the jeweled sword glittered even in the faint candlelight. Hands now gloved, Evan departed his room, moving silently through the darkened inn. The outer doors squeaked as he walked out into the night, but not enough to disturb the deep slumber of Master and Mistress Jakes.

The watch had but minutes ago passed this area, ensuring Evan of complete privacy. He paused only long enough to survey the vicinity, then marched directly toward the church.

A part of him, a great part of him, wanted nothing more than to turn to the stables, retrieve his horse, and ride off, never looking back. How the thought of confronting Valentin still shook him. Valentin would laugh at that.

I will be strong. He can do nothing to me. He can do nothing to anyone. Evan only wished he could believe that.

The chill wind that had taken root in Pretor's Hill seemed eager to push him on to his intended destination. A crow cawed, its laughter mocking his hesitancy. The knight looked around but could not locate the bird. Still, Evan found something comforting in the fact that the crows had reappeared. When he had noticed them missing from the area surrounding the school, he had wondered over their sudden absence.

You are stalling. In truth, Evan Wytherling had been stalling since his arrival. He admitted to himself now that he possibly could have visited Valentin before this had he not found a viable excuse each time he had considered it.

He drew the sword free, pointing the tip at the doors. For a single breath, the jewels flared bright. From within came the faint sound of metal shifting, then, with a slight creak, the doors slowly swung back.

Evan lowered the blade and advanced inside, the doors closing behind him. He blinked, allowing his eyes to adjust to the greater gloom within. Far up ahead, on a dais, stood the open coffin in which lay Mardi's uncle. To its left he made out the stone pulpit from which Father Gerard had no doubt performed the funeral. On the far wall stood the doorway leading to the priest's personal quarters.

The sword out before him, Evan walked down the aisle, counting each step as he went. Silently he also asked forgiveness for bearing the drawn weapon in this place, but he had had no choice. He could not reach his destination without it.

Ten steps. Fifteen. Twenty. After two more, the knight paused. He recalculated the distance he had gone since entering, finding his first estimate correct. Evan visually measured the distance to each wall, then the ceiling as well.

Interesting. Did you have a hand in this, too, Valentin? The tip of the sword hovered over a spot on the floor that, to his keen eye, had to be the exact center of the chamber. Coincidence? Evan had trouble believing that.

He shifted his grip on the hilt, holding the sword blade-down as if intending to thrust it with both hands into the heart of some invisible foe lying at his feet. Evan shut his eyes and whispered words Centuros had given to him on that fateful day, words that the knight had hoped never to use again.

The full force of his strength behind him, Evan Wytherling plunged the sword into the stone floor.

It should have bounced off or even shattered, in the process raising a clamor that would have roused the priest, but instead the blade sank deep, as if thrust into soft mud. The jewels blazed, momentarily illuminating the interior of the church.

The stone floor cracked, a fissure forming where blade had

bit into rock.

Evan quickly retrieved his weapon, knowing that the events he had set in motion would not stop until they had run their course. Already the fissure had grown in length, nearly reaching the pulpit. He stepped back, watching with unblinking eyes as the fissure in the aisle widened, spreading until it threatened the pews on each side. From within the gap a dim azure light burst forth, both beckoning and warning him.

Throughout it all, the silence of the night remained unbroken. Ever efficient, Paulo Centuros had taken the possible need for quiet into account, even if he could not have predicted an entire town being built around this place.

The knight moved toward the fissure and gazed down. A stairway formed from earth and stone led into its heart. Mist swirled from deep within, rising up and spreading throughout the chamber.

With his sword once more at the ready, Evan Wytherling descended into the fissure.

The steps were crude, sometimes treacherous, but with care he managed his way into the depths without incident. Evan happened to glance at his hand. In the bluish light, his skin took on a deathly sheen, an image that began to stir up the ghosts of memory again. Evan heard the roar of Haggad's voice as the general whipped his soldiers forward, the snarl of dragons as they fought in the air, the cries of the dying. Ever the cries of the dying. They were the strongest of all the ghosts, for many of those deaths the weary knight blamed on himself.

The ravaged floor of the church already lay several yards above him by the time he caught sight of the bottom of the stairway. He paused, took a deep breath, and finished the descent. Ahead lay a narrow corridor leading to his destination.

A half-shadowed form rose before him, filling his view from floor to ceiling.

It had a face yet not a face, the only truly visible features dark, soulless eyes that sought to peel away at his sanity. It moved like a man, but one twisted and deformed by forces most could only envision in their nightmares. A hand more reptilian than human beckoned to him, offering him release from life.

But Centuros had planned for unwanted intruders.

"You will not have me . . ." Evan did not raise the sword, but rather drew a symbol in the air with his free hand. "You will know your place."

He drew a line through the symbol and as he did it took visible form. A glittering yellow star surrounded by two emerald circles, one within the other. The dark eyes turned from the human, staring intently at the floating image. Evan pointed to his left and the symbol moved accordingly. The half-shadowed figure followed suit, seemingly enraptured by the mystic vision before it.

The ward the rotund spellcaster had taught Evan would keep the guardian fascinated for as long as the knight needed. He felt some pity for the creature even though he knew it had been formed from nothingness and did not know true life. Yet the guardian and he were both prisoners of sorts, trapped into missions they could not escape.

With one last glance to assure himself that the ward would hold, Evan passed the creature.

And then a voice still so familiar after these many years boomed from beyond, "Come, come, my old and dear friend! Don't think that you might be disturbing me! I've long awaited your return!"

With those words, the floodgates to Evan's memories opened wide . . . Haggad, Pretor, Centuros, Grimyr, and even the ever-distant form of the sorcerer-king Novaris bombarded the stricken knight. He watched the fire-black dragon incinerate a band of foot soldiers, the stench of burning flesh engulfing him. Grimyr became Haggad, who dragged an enemy close, then thrust his blade through the fearful man's throat. Haggad in turn became Novaris, casting spells and watching from his remote position, ever a tall, hooded figure seemingly made more out of the cloth of his robe than of flesh and blood.

The hooded head turned toward him and, though no mouth could be seen, Evan knew with certainty that Novaris smiled. *You will always bear my mark . . .*

"No . . ." Barely a whisper, but the knight immediately seized hold of that tiny grain of defiance. He remembered what Paulo Centuros had told him before the battle, that Novaris could not bend him, that Evan would remain true to the cause the wizard had set for him. "I must be strong . . ."

Raising his sword, the knight cut through the ghosts surrounding him. Novaris and the others vanished, returning to the recesses of his mind.

Hands shaking, Evan lowered the sword. He took a deep breath, calming himself. The memories could not hurt him. They could not.

He waits, Evan reminded himself. *The longer I delay, the more he will suspect my weakness.*

That did it. The knight took another deep breath, made certain that his hands were steady . . . and entered.

"Aah . . . and there you are, Evan! I thought I'd have to wait here forever before you deigned to visit your old companion again!"

The light that had enabled Evan to reach his destination also lit the chamber, a magic illumination with no physical source. Evan marched in, eyes and expression set.

"You took so long getting here that I thought you might've changed your mind and turned tail. My, my. The years haven't been so very kind to you, have they? Certainly I can see the mark they've left upon you even from here . . ."

Evan's macabre host stood in the center of the old cavern, arms outstretched. He still wore the crimson armor that had been his signature, not that the choice to wear it in this place had been his. A visored helm lay to one side, as if tossed there carelessly, enabling Evan Wytherling to closely study the face he already knew too well. Where Evan's hair had begun to silver, his counterpart's long, thick mane remained as black as the soulless eyes of the guardian, save for twin streaks of gray in the short beard. In contrast to the darkness of the hair, the crimson knight's pale skin made Evan's seem tanned. No pigment remained. The only color left could be found in the eyes, a disquieting amber that many in the past had sworn gleamed in battle.

Although Evan stood tall, the ebony-tressed figure still looked down at his visitor. The crimson knight smiled, a sight that could charm a maiden or chill a foe. "So very good to see you, Evan, old companion. I would greet you with open arms, but, as you know, I could not then close them."

In truth, he could not. The arms remained outstretched because they were bound by thin gold links that reached to the opposing walls. So, too, had been bound the ankles. Yet even though the links appeared barely strong enough to hold a child, much less a knight in full battle armor, the bearded prisoner could not break them. Evan recalled how hard the other had tried when first Paulo Centuros had bound him, struggling so hard that in the end they had left him screaming in frustration.

"But I suppose even if I were free, it might be hard to reach you with this pigsticker in the way . . . and therein lies the heart of the matter, doesn't it?" The prisoner leaned his head back and laughed, a harsh bark that echoed throughout the chamber. It was the laughter of the dead . . . or one who by all rights should have been dead long ago, for protruding from the captive knight's chest was the broken end of a lance.

The lance had belonged to a footman, from whose stiff, bloody hand it had been drawn. While not the enchanted weapon that had brought down Grimyr, when wielded by one who knew how best to utilize it, the lance could pierce the strongest of armors. So it had done in the hands of Evan Wytherling, piercing breastplate, flesh, and bone and not ceasing until it had passed through the dark heart and struck the armor behind. At that point it had snapped in two, leaving a shaft more than a foot long sticking out of the screaming knight's chest.

And yet . . . and yet the man before him had refused to die.

Pretor and Centuros had left him screaming for a day while they had determined their next course. The corpse of Novaris could not be found among the dead sorcerers in his enclave, although with so much destruction in that region, he might have been buried under tons of rubble. In the end, because they suspected what they could not prove and because of all of Novaris's servants he had been the most reviled, they had bound him and left him here, at the site where he had last served his dark master. For his heinous crimes alone, for all those he had helped slaughter, they had even left the crimson knight impaled, knowing that with his legs and arms outstretched, he could never remove the object of his torment.

They had also left him as bait, just in case his master did one day return.

He had been a madman when Evan had first met him and the years of isolation and pain had only served to hone that madness.

Evan made no attempt whatsoever to sheath the sword, despite knowing he should not need it here. "Hello, Valentin."

Once more Mardi found herself girded for war. Men cried out and dragons roared. A veiled figure in armor slashed at her, and as she parried the attack she realized that her adversary was also female. Mardi thrust in turn, and where her opponent had failed, she succeeded. Screaming, the veiled Amazon faded into mist.

As she paused in the midst of battle to regain her breath, a familiar voice echoed in her ears. *The warrior should ever look in the mirror if he desires to know the face that will most often betray him.*

The dream ended with that. The next Mardi knew, she sat in bed, staring at the sleeping form of Mistress Arden. A tingle coursed through her and she rose. As had happened the previous night, Drulane's housekeeper did not stir, but this time Mardi did not question her fortune. She felt an immense urge to step outside, and Mistress Arden's mysteriously deep slumber meant that the only obstacle to doing as she desired had already been removed.

She donned the simplest of her clothes, never during that time questioning her actions. Clad in a thick brown cloak, the gentlewoman slipped out the door, pausing just beyond. None of the malevolent crows were about, yet Mardi knew they could not be far. She walked around the area of the doorway, trying to organize her thoughts. The night remained moist and chill, but Mardi barely noticed it at first. Something had driven her outside, but she could not say what.

Gazing out at the darkened streets, Mardi felt the urge gradually lessen. As the seconds passed, the dampness and cold began to affect her. More awake now than when she had first stepped out, Mardi started debating whether she should return to the comfort of her bed.

A sudden movement in the street put an end to all such thoughts.

Instinct made her press against the wall, although as she did the gentlewoman felt foolish. Her embarrassment faded away, though, when Mardi saw who it was she had sensed. Evan Wytherling.

Sword in hand, the knight marched with purpose toward the church, seeming ready to do battle with some great threat. That struck her as odd, for what could threaten him from within the church? Certainly Father Gerard posed no danger, nor, especially, her uncle. What interest then could the building hold for the determined figure?

Pulling the cloak close, Mardi Sinclair followed. She kept far back, having learned at least one lesson from her first attempt to track the knight.

Curiosity turned to amazement as, a moment later, Evan Wytherling pointed his blade at the church doors. The jewels on the hilt blazed briefly in glory, then, as they dimmed, the doors opened of their own accord. Sorcery. Mardi had heard the tales, watched false magicians ply their trade at fairs, but never before had she come across anything even remotely real. Progressive as

Rundin could be, where sorcery had been concerned all of the kings since the days of Paulo Centuros had condemned it.

She stood there, marveling so much at the deed that it took some time for it to dawn on her that her quarry had long since entered the building.

Seeing that only they two were about, Mardi rushed to the church. The doors had closed behind him, but one stood slightly ajar. With great caution, the gentlewoman put a hand to the door and slowly, ever so slowly, attempted to push it open a crack. A crow cawed from nearby, startling her and making Mardi push harder than she had meant. Mardi felt a brief obstruction, as if she had just thrust herself through some invisible wall, then the door gave way.

The dim blue glow that bathed her as she entered nearly caused Mardi to retreat. No light she had ever known glowed so. She blinked, then saw an even more unnerving sight, the source of that unearthly illumination.

The glow could not have been real and yet she did not doubt its existence. A chasm had somehow opened up in the center of the church. Had she felt a tremor earlier? The light emanated from deep within. Mardi stared at the terrible fissure for some time, knowing without a doubt that the man she followed could only have descended into it.

I should wake Father Gerard! He should know about this. But she knew the priest's skills would avail her little at this juncture and any interference might somehow place Evan in jeopardy.

Forcing herself to the edge of the fissure, the gentlewoman looked down. A crude stairway led into the crevice, disappearing into the blue mist but a short distance below her. Mardi tried peering through the mist, hoping to see the bottom, but failed. She hesitated at the first step, wanting very much to turn back, but curiosity propelled her forward. She slowly descended.

The jagged walls loomed uncomfortably close. She imagined them suddenly pushing together, crushing her. The graphic vision nearly made her retreat, but then Mardi heard the voice. Evan's voice. Slowly she made her way, straining to see some end to her descent.

Mardi did not see the horrific creature until it was too late. A scream caught in her throat as she raised an arm to defend herself.

But the monster remained perfectly still, staring past her at a tiny glowing symbol that floated in the air. The unnerving eyes of the creature were fixed upon it, seemingly fascinated.

Sorcery.

Realizing that Evan Wytherling must have been the one who had put this terrible creature at bay, Mardi lost a bit of her fear. The man she followed had been a veteran knight, after all. He had been trained to face great odds, fight off danger using both wits and a sword arm. Even a monster such as this had been no match for the paladin.

However, just as she began to calm down, for the second time someone spoke . . . but not Evan. The muffled voice had a cultured sense to it yet also bore more than a touch of madness. Mardi froze, listening. Only when Evan's voice, calm and steady, reentered the conversation, did she dare breathe again.

"Hello, Valentin," she heard clearly. The knight talked as if to an old, lost friend, not some mysterious denizen of this underworld. She crept forward, at last peeking around the final corner.

Evan stood but a few scant yards ahead, his back to her. Yet Mardi Sinclair's gaze lingered on him only a second, for the one with whom he spoke demanded her attention simply by his presence. Another knight, this one clad in crimson, stood chained in the center of the chamber. With his ebony hair and fine features, she could not deny that he was handsome . . . and yet looking close at his face, at his eyes, Mardi felt a deep uneasiness. The disconcerting amber eyes enhanced the crimson knight's pallid tone. The one called Valentin reminded Mardi Sinclair of nothing less than a corpse that did not yet acknowledge the fact it had died.

Mardi tore her gaze from his face . . . and at last caught a glimpse of the lance protruding from his breastplate.

She barely stifled a gasp. When she had silently proclaimed this man a thing worse than the half-shadowed monster, she had come closer to the truth than she could have ever imagined.

" 'Hello, Valentin.' " The imprisoned knight chuckled. "Evan, my dear friend, you never change. Proper and polite. The epitome of the knighthood. I admired those qualities in you even if at times they proved cumbersome for you." His expression sobered. "And have you come at last to kill me?"

"No, Valentin, I have not."

"Of course not." Bitterness tinged the prisoner's words. "You would never do something so unchivalrous as kill a defenseless man, would you?" When the other knight did not immediately respond, he continued, "It can never be over between us until I am dead, old friend. As long as I . . . live isn't the right word, is it? As long as I exist, you will be forced to repeat your mistakes while you futilely try to redeem yourself."

Although the men were clearly enemies, they spoke as if they had once been close friends, brothers in arms. Had that been the case . . . and how long ago? This cavern existed below the church and Mardi knew the building had to be well over a century old. That would mean that Evan and the crimson knight themselves had to be . . . to be . . .

Evan spoke again, sparing her, at least for the moment, from thinking more about the implications. He ignored completely the other's suggestions, instead asking, "What have you done, Valentin? The stench over this town, this town that should not even be here, is clearly evident."

Valentin smiled. It did nothing to shake the image Mardi had formed of him. "Now, Evan. What could I've possibly done, old comrade?" He rattled the golden chains. "I'm clearly not in a state to do much of anything except wait."

"Wait? Wait for what? I have seen the carrion crows, Valentin, the scavengers of the battlefield. Why would they come where no battle plays out? Do they remember so very long ago?

Did their elders whisper to them about the feast they once had? I find that a little extraordinary."

"Birds will gather where they will, my friend. Even the butcher birds."

"And the people, Valentin? They are, for any town, a mercurial lot, prone to sudden anger, in some cases even violence. At other times, they will not even lift a finger to aid one of their own who is in distress."

The pale prisoner chuckled again. "I'm also to be blamed for the poor attitudes of townsfolk? Evan, dear Evan, what a monster you must think me."

Mardi, too, had difficulty accepting Evan Wytherling's accusations at first. Not only did she find it hard to believe that this imprisoned warrior could have done anything to threaten Pretor's Hill, but how could Evan think that one man, however despicable, could affect the very minds of her friends and neighbors?

And yet . . . the man in the market had attacked her simply because she had not wanted to buy his goods. She, in turn, had almost beaten him to death. Later still, not one person other than the knight had raised so much as a finger in her defense when the blackbird had clawed at her face.

No! It's ridiculous to even think . . . To think a mere man, even one as unnerving as this Valentin, had the power to affect others' very thoughts and actions was ludicrous.

The darkness knows no bounds and those who believe they understand the limits of its power will forever be cursed to fall prey in the end. The words of Paulo Centuros rang so loudly through her head that Mardi briefly feared the two knights would hear them. She looked again at Valentin, stared long at the broken lance buried impossibly deep. Her breathing faltered. The truth of what she saw fairly screamed at her to acknowledge it. This was no man; no mortal man could have survived such a horrific strike. This had to be a creature of the darkness, a creature, Mardi decided, probably even more foul than the thing that had killed her uncle.

"I know exactly what you are, Valentin." Evan took a step toward the bearded figure. "You are as damned a soul as I."

"Then kill me!" the crimson knight spat. "Kill me and save both of us any more of this futile posturing!"

To Mardi's horrified fascination, Evan appeared ready to grant Valentin's request. He raised his blade high. The chained knight's amber gaze shifted to the weapon and anticipation lit the snow-colored features. Mardi, too, found herself urging Evan to strike down the monster, end the thing that Evan himself claimed cursed Pretor's Hill.

The sword came down . . . to rest at Evan's side. "I cannot. I cannot kill you."

Valentin's expression shifted from hope to anger to mockery. "No . . . you couldn't. That would mean disappointing your master, wouldn't it? But which master do I mean? Aah, yes, it would have to be that fat sausage roll Paulo Centuros, wouldn't it? The wizard who can kill with words and kindness." Valentin again rattled his chains. "Novaris, now he would never have accepted so weak-willed a servant. The sorcerer-king, praise him, desired and respected only those with backbone, a good weapon, and, by all means, a sense of loyalty, especially after they had given him an oath of fealty sworn on their swords." He cocked his head. "Tell me. What sort of oath did you swear on the robe of the fat one?"

Mardi could not see Evan's visage clearly, but even from where she stood she could sense the change in him. He moved as if Valentin had struck him a mortal blow, unable to speak at first. When he at last did reply, it came out in a hoarse whisper that Mardi had to strain to hear. "Damn you."

"As you've pointed out, I already am." The crimson knight shut his eyes. "Your visit quickly grows tiresome and I've so much to do. If that is all you want, you've my permission to leave."

Evan would not leave, though. He straightened, the grip on his sword tightening at the same time. "Where is he, Valentin? Where is Novaris? I sense his evil here and if he has been back to this place then he would have come to you."

Amber eyes opened to slits. "If he had come back, do you think I would be here for you to visit? Do you think my master would've left his most loyal servant stretched apart like this?"

"If it would serve his purpose, yes."

"Then if it would serve his purpose, I would be pleased to remain so imprisoned for as long as necessary."

"You owe him nothing now, Valentin."

"And what do I owe you?" The crimson knight glanced down at the lance. "Oh, yes. This. These marvelous chains, too. I thank you."

"Where is he?"

"He is dead to you, Evan, just as you are dead to me."

"That is no answer, Valentin."

The other only stared.

The weary knight reached out with his free hand, almost but not quite touching the lance. Mardi thought he might pull it out, but at the last Evan's fingers curled inward, empty. "I do what I must."

Surprisingly, Valentin's expression actually softened slightly. "Yes. The good wizard saw to that, didn't he? It should have been different, friend. It should have been glorious."

"I implore you one last time, Valentin. What is happening here? If what I think, you must stop it. I know you must have a free hand in it, even if still bound physically. I have seen patterns upon patterns in the very design of this town and even killed a wolfish beast formed from the shadows of your master's darkness, but this must be only the beginning. What do the patterns mean? What lurks in the woods? How many more must die or be twisted in the name of Novaris? How long must this land suffer his legacy?"

"If this land should be cursed, it should suffer for eternity, Evan." The amber eyes flashed. "As should you."

The other knight turned away so that Valentin could not see his expression, thereby giving Mardi a fleeting view. The torment twisting his features stunned her, so much so that she barely pulled herself out of sight in time. She leaned against the rocky wall, the vision of Evan Wytherling's face still burned in her mind. What had Valentin meant by his last comment that would so pain his adversary?

"I see I have wasted both our times in coming here," Evan said at last. Mardi carefully peered around the corner. He had turned backed to Valentin, whose amber eyes watched unblinking. "I thought your seclusion here might open you up to redeeming yourself, to making amends in part by telling me the truth, but I see that once again my notions proved naive."

"You should've known me better. You once did."

"Yes. I did. Now I do not know you at all."

Valentin chuckled, all vestiges of sympathy gone. "You're on a quest with but one end, my friend. You will lose all again; you know that."

Evan shook his head. "I will unweave what has been wrought here, Valentin, and you will have suffered for your master for naught."

This amused the crimson-clad prisoner yet more. "I wish you the best of luck, knowing that you'll fail miserably in this, Evan. Just as you failed your oath so long ago."

Evan raised the jeweled sword in mock salute. "Forgive me for disturbing you, Valentin. I will leave you to your thoughts. I hope that they will keep you occupied until Judgment Day. For the goodness of your soul, though, I wish you had answered my questions. You will need every good deed however slight if you hope to at least lessen your damnation."

He turned to depart, clearly disappointed in the results of this unsettling visitation. Mardi began to retreat, not wanting the knight to realize he had been followed. Confusion racked her; she no longer knew what to think about Evan. He knew this Valentin too well, this creature jailed beneath the grounds of the church. If the crimson knight was no mortal, what did that say of Evan? There had been no war here in her lifetime, but some of the elders talked of battles fought in this region during the time of their own grandparents' lives or even earlier. It explained all too well the archaic armor and the somewhat formal speech.

Valentin called out, stopping Mardi just before she would have taken her first step up the stairway. "I'm truly sorry that I couldn't be more help in answering your precious questions, Evan! Perhaps next time, you might ask old Grimyr!"

She heard a scuffling sound behind her and the clatter of a heavy metallic object striking the rocky floor of Valentin's chamber. Mardi found herself turning back, knowing that the latter noise could only have been Evan Wytherling's sword falling from his grip. The unreasonable fear that he had somehow been attacked by the chained Valentin locked her in place.

Evan stood at the mouth of the cavern chamber facing his adversary. The glittering sword, seemingly unnoticed, lay at his feet.

"Grimyr is dead, Valentin. Of that I can swear . . . as you should be able to, also." He retrieved his weapon, his tone growing colder. "You had your chance. I will put up with no more of your games. Enjoy eternity, Valentin."

Now Mardi quickly retreated, knowing that this time Evan would not pause. As she hurried up the treacherous steps, she heard behind her Valentin's mocking laughter. It chilled her, sent a sensation of growing anxiety racing up and down her spine. Mardi ran through the church, flinging open the doors without care and darting out into the cool, moist night. She wished that she had never woken, never followed Evan into the church. Her world had been chaotic enough before this; now the gentlewoman did not know if she could go on. Surely before long she would go mad . . . if that had not already happened. Mardi no longer even trusted her own mind.

She rushed toward the school and the safety of her bed, but before she could reach it, a crow cawed from just ahead of her. The sound startled her and she backed away, stumbling against another building. An avian form swooped down, grazing her hand with its wing as it passed. Without thinking, the young woman ran blindly back into the street.

A human wall blocked her path. A gloved hand caught one of her own. Mardi blinked away moisture, looked up.

"Why are you out here this late?"

She looked up into a face that briefly revealed itself as Evan Wytherling's but in her shock as quickly shifted into something more sinister . . . Valentin's. Mardi Sinclair knew that the crimson knight had not escaped his tomb and yet could not keep herself from fearing that he had.

Without thinking, she screamed, and when from surprise the figure before her released his grip, Mardi dashed by him, wanting only to escape.

"Mardi!" He took up pursuit, which only served to heighten her anxiety. She raced past the stable and Arno's smithy, then farther on. Valentin's laughter echoed in her ears.

Deep within, Mardi struggled to reassert control over herself, but her efforts thus far proved futile. An overriding and abnormal panic pushed her forward even when she had passed the outer edge of town and only the dark woods remained before her. If she kept running, the irrational part of her insisted, she could leave everything behind her.

Yet despite constant defeat, her true self continued to try to rally her, to make her see fact, not fantasy. *Calm yourself! Think! The woods are where Yoniff died! Evan is not the monster! The monster lies below the church and its name is Valentin!*

Mardi faltered but still could not bring herself to stop. Yet now she did realize the potential predicament she had just thrust herself into. She had run out in the woods alone during the dead of night, an act that would have been foolish even during the most peaceful of evenings and especially so considering the gruesome fate of her uncle. Even if no beast or bandit awaited her, moving through the treacherous dark brought with it the risk of breaking her neck by tripping over a tree root or stepping in a depression.

She heard the fluttering of wings just before the black form nearly collided with her face. Mardi swung out with her hands, warding off the huge avian form but receiving several stinging scratches in her right forearm in return. A second bird dove down upon her from behind, pulling on her hair. The gentlewoman tried to grab the attacker, but it rose just above her reach, returning the moment she let down her guard.

In desperation, Mardi ducked under a low branch. The bird cawed in anger, the higher branches of the tree preventing it from readily returning to its assault. Mardi took the opportunity to draw her cloak tighter. In the trees she could hear what she swore had to be a full flock.

Racing frantically among the trees, Mardi tried to summon the anger that had aided her in the past, but it would not rise. She could only hope that somehow she could lose her aerial pursuers. The gentlewoman also assumed Evan Wytherling hunted her, possibly to keep her from revealing his secrets to anyone.

Let not fear blind one from the fact that the impossible is not always the enemy. The reality in which one believes may often be the true foe . . . An enigmatic quote, yet it soothed her somewhat, just as the ancient wizard's writings often tended to do. Mardi seized the thin thread of hope and tried her best to focus on his words, thinking that they might further aid in calming her.

It seemed to work. Her thoughts organized. The fear lessened. She no longer felt so disoriented.

Coming to rest against a nearby tree, Mardi decided to face the birds. For the first time she recalled that in one of the pockets of this cloak she had placed a tiny knife. Breath coming in gasps, the vicious caws of the birds resounding louder and louder in her ears, Mardi fumbled for the knife. There would be no more running from the birds. If she had to cut her way through, she would.

Belief in oneself is the key. Anger is but a lock. Odd, Mardi could not recall where she had read that particular quote, but it could not have been more appropriate. She would face the crows on her own terms.

Only . . . where were they?

Silence filled the woods. Not only had the cawing and

fluttering of wings ceased, but so had every other woodland sound with the exception of the rush of the chill wind. Mardi looked up, trying to locate the birds in the treetops, but as far as she could see—and admittedly she could not see much—the branches were bare of even the tiniest sparrow.

She lowered the blade, exhaling in some relief. The birds had fled, perhaps seeing that she had decided to fight rather than run this time. A sense of triumph filled her. Here at last Mardi had taken a stand and succeeded.

She was ready for a confrontation. She had faced the birds and now she would face Evan. Her fear of him had faded and now she wanted answers more than anything else. Her thoughts clearer, Mardi recalled some of the knight's conversation with the monster Valentin. Evan had sounded concerned for Pretor's Hill. He wanted to help her fellow townsfolk, although in Mardi's opinion he could have done that best by dispatching the crimson prisoner there and then. If something threatened her community, in her mind Valentin had to be an integral part of it.

I have to wring the truth from Evan. I have to find out what's happening to us. The knight had not been far behind her when she had fled into the woods. Mardi suspected that if she backtracked, she would come across him before very long. She was surprised he had not found her first. She could not have gotten that far ahead—

Something caused the foliage before her to rustle, something much larger than a bird. Mardi raised the tiny knife, then lowered it as a tall, night-enshrouded form moved toward her through the woods. It had to be Evan.

"I'm not afraid of you! Not anymore. I just want to know what's hap—"

Another dark form joined the first, then a third added itself to the ranks.

Mardi pressed back against the tree, her arm fully extended as she sought to ward off the newcomers with the now-inadequate weapon. In her excitement, the gentlewoman had forgotten that she and the knight might not be so alone in the woods after all.

One of the lupine shadows howled, then all three lunged at her.

IX

EVAN'S TALE

The horrific image of what had been left of her uncle flashing through her mind, the gentlewoman shakily wielded her small knife at the lunging abomination. She squeezed her eyes shut, certain of her gruesome end. She had no one to blame for this but herself, her curiosity worse than that of the proverbial cat.

Her eyes shot open as the meager blade met the shadowy horror.

With a blood-freezing howl, the lupine creature tore away from the knife, rolling away in agony as if Mardi had gutted it with a strong, wicked sword. It writhed on the ground, turning over and over. The claws sought for the wound as if trying to pull something free. Beyond it, the remaining pair paused, vague countenances unreadable.

The night is the most fair of allies and enemies, for it cloaks friend and foe alike. Another of Paulo Centuros's cryptic sayings, but for some reason it made Mardi unclasp her cloak. Knife still extended, she used one hand to remove the garment. The other creatures had recovered, no longer bothering with their dying comrade. They sought her and only her.

What did she intend with the cloak? Now that she had it off, Mardi held it like a shield, but that did not seem correct. She should have been doing something else with it, something that would help her against these fearsome foes.

As she struggled with her thoughts, from the tangled woods burst a majestic figure wielding a jeweled sword. It was Evan Wytherling, after all, once more come to defend her foolhardy life.

Mardi's heart leapt as Evan confronted the lupine creatures, drawing their attention from her. The knight held the pair at bay, their claws unable to reach past the length of the sword. "Slip behind me as soon as you can," he commanded her.

Mardi moved to obey . . . then halted as she spotted another figure just beyond where Evan stood.

"Sir Wytherling! Evan! There's another behind—"

Too late. The creature leapt from its hiding place, seeking the pale warrior's throat.

Evan turned and the other pair pounced on him. Mardi Sinclair reacted instinctively, tossing her voluminous cloak over them in an effort to at least slow them. The cloak flew unerringly over the two beasts' heads, billowing, widening. In fact, it seemed far, far wider than the anxious gentlewoman recalled it, spreading so much that she thought it might completely engulf the abominations.

The knight's blade severed one clawed appendage of the nearest wolf creature but did not slow the beast's attack. Evan's monstrous adversary rode him to the ground, snarling. Undeterred, Evan reached with one hand for the throat of the murky beast, forcing the head back.

Mardi noticed this only in part, her attention taken by the wondrous work of the cloak, which had grown so great that it had indeed enshrouded the other pair from head to foot. They clearly struggled, but even their murderous claws appeared unable to open the way to freedom. With only one clawed hand, Evan's foe could no longer match him. Avoiding the creature's snapping teeth, the knight at last managed to lift his blade and drive it into the beast's side. The lupine horror howled sharply, then slumped atop Evan. He pushed it aside and rolled to his feet.

His eyes widened as he noticed what had overcome the other attackers. Evan glanced at Mardi, but she could not explain. She watched as the knight again fixed on the shapes within the vast garment, blade poised ready. A breath later, he drove the sword into her cloak. From within came an almost-human cry that quickly died away. One of the forms dropped.

Again Evan Wytherling struck and again came a howl. Mardi watched with some guilt, knowing that the creatures had not had any chance against the knight's actions. Still, they had acted with far less remorse—interested only in slaughter—and would have continued their bloody efforts if freed.

As he removed his blade, the second figure sank to the ground, the cloak falling with it. Mardi waited for the garment to come to rest on the two slain abominations, but instead it continued on, falling flat against the earth as if covering nothing. Stunned, she slowly stepped forward, looking for some trace of the two beasts in the folds.

Evan prodded the cloak with the tip of his weapon, then raised one side of it. Underneath there remained not a trace of the pair.

"What happened?" she murmured. "Where—where are they?"

"Returned to the darkness which cursed them," he replied, his words as enigmatic as those of the fabled wizard.

Looking around, Mardi discovered that the other two had likewise disappeared. Nowhere could she find any trace that would suggest she had even been attacked. Only her cloak now marked the place of battle.

Evan picked up the garment and returned it to her. Mardi took it, noticing that the cloak had shrunk to its original size.

"My apologies for ruining it . . . Mardi."

The dying creatures might have left no trace, but his sword had. Two well-placed slits revealed a good night's sewing ahead. Nonetheless, she accepted the cloth gratefully, knowing that it would still cover her. The night felt exceptionally cold, more so now that Mardi's anxiety had dissipated some. She wrapped the cloak around her, then looked to Evan for guidance.

"This is twice now," he finally said. "You have been very, very fortunate to survive." Evan pulled away his gaze, which had lingered far too long on her face. "We must get you home . . . and you must not ask questions. You must forget this night, Mardi

162

Sinclair."

"How can I forget it? What happened in the church? Who's Valentin? Who are you, Evan?"

His expression stiffened. He was silent for a moment, clearly digesting the revelation that she had somehow followed him down below the church. Finally, he slowly answered, "You must forget because it is best. What happened in the church did not happen. There is no Valentin and I am but a battle-scarred warrior who will be gone soon from your life." Silver and brown hair tossed about slightly from the wind, the knight reached for her, pausing when he noticed that Mardi still held the small knife. "You defended yourself well," Evan remarked.

"I was fortunate . . . it . . . it leapt onto the blade."

"And simply died of its wound . . ." Evan glanced at the small blade a moment more, then seemed to push the matter aside. "Come, we need to return. Others no doubt heard the howls at least."

She refused to move. "I can't forget what happened . . . and I won't go unless you promise to tell me the truth."

He looked exasperated with her, so much so that Mardi nearly gave in. Fortunately, Evan then sighed and began to speak. "Very well. I have no real choice, do I? You have heard and, I suspect, even seen Valentin"—he watched for her reaction and she nodded grimly—"and while I might be able to dissuade you on other matters, where he is concerned I truly cannot hope that you will forget. Valentin leaves his mark simply by his existence."

A voice from the direction of Pretor's Hill prevented him from saying more. Evan gently took Mardi by the arm and began to lead her back. She wanted to ask him questions but could tell by the set of his jaw that he would say nothing now.

As they neared the town, she saw that several men had gathered near the edge, torches and weapons ready. Most were of the watch, Bulrik commanding them. A few other men of the town had joined the half dozen or so regular officers and they seemed to be listening to some last-minute instructions. Mardi heard

Drulane's man mention "wolves" and "fools rushing about with swords and pitchforks."

"This way," Evan whispered, pulling her away from the watch. They skirted the town until the knight seemed satisfied that no one would see them, then flitted past darkened buildings until they at last arrived at the back of the schoolhouse.

Mardi nearly opened the door, then recalled Mistress Arden. "The magistrate's woman is asleep in my bedroom. I . . . I think that she's under some sort of sleep spell."

"Do you fear for her? Shall I try to wake her?"

She thought about it and, for reasons she could not comprehend, decided not. If someone had wanted to do Mistress Arden any harm, they could have used some spell more dire than one to make her slumber. "I suppose not. I think . . . I think that she'll just sleep until morning."

"And yet it disturbs me that something clearly reached her within your home even with the protection I set . . ." He fingered the hilt of his sword, which he had sheathed on their way into town.

They heard men muttering and the sound of footsteps. Mardi immediately opened the door, but instead of leading Evan into her quarters, she turned him toward the schoolroom. Once there, they waited in the dark while the men passed, then Mardi lit an oil lamp. The gentlewoman placed it on one of the crude tables used for a desk.

The knight looked uneasy. "I should leave you now. Rest as best you can; matters will seem less frightful come the dawn—"

Amazed and also a little vexed, she exclaimed, "You promised me the truth! You promised to tell me what sort of horror surrounds Pretor's Hill! You owe me that!"

Wincing at her rising voice, Evan signaled for peace. Pale eyes studied the flame in the lamp. At last he exhaled, replying, "What I could tell you would not suffice to ease your fears and would, in all likelihood, fuel their flames."

"I'll be the judge of that!" Mardi snapped, her voice rising again.

From outside there came the not so very distant voices of men on the hunt. Evan clamped a hand over her mouth. Mardi reached up to pull it away, then paused as the voices neared her door.

"What about the knight?" someone asked. "What about the outsider?"

She could not make out the reply, only its threatening tone. The voices dwindled as the men strode off. Evan kept his hand on her mouth for a minute more, then gently removed it, apologizing. "This is not a night when thoughts run calm. Those you know as friends may not be so this eve and I fear it will only get worse."

"Why? What do you know?"

"Too little. Only that I have been duped for so very long. He has led me around like a fool."

Her expression hardened. "Who has? Valentin?"

"Valentin, yes. His master possibly more so, but Valentin most definitely yes. This has his mark on it."

"Who is he, Evan? What is he to you, to my home?"

He could not look at her. "Valentin is me. Valentin is vengeance. He is the legacy of a time long past, a horror long thought dead." The pale man grimaced. "He is my failure."

Mardi paused, trying to formulate her next question, trying to prepare herself for the consequences of his answer. What she had heard and seen made her suspect much, but only Evan Wytherling could verify her mad notions. "Were you . . . was he . . . were you both a part of the battle fought here . . . two centuries ago?"

His gaze drifted back to her, weary hazel eyes seeing something beyond her, something across the passage of time. "He should have died then, but the spell that bound him to Grimyr proved so terribly strong. Even the wizard, the great and powerful wizard, could not separate man from beast. Had Centuros only done that, perhaps none of this would have come to pass . . ."

Centuros . . . Mardi had her answer, to a point. She opened her mouth to ask more, but the knight went on, caught up in a past he could clearly never escape. "Valentin always persevered, always dug in, refused to accept defeat. He was Novaris's favorite for that, even above Haggad, who would slaughter legions in the name of his master. The sorcerer-king chose well when he chose Valentin and Valentin chose well when he chose Grimyr."

An image burst through Mardi's thoughts, the crimson knight astride a fire-black dragon so fearsome that its very presence could send hardened men to their knees in panic. Man and dragon reacted as one, almost as if they shared a soul . . . if two such as these could ever have souls.

Evan's voice shattered the image. Caught up in his own reverie, he did not notice Mardi fighting to calm herself. "It came to the point when Paulo Centuros knew that he could not defeat Novaris if he did not first defeat Valentin and Grimyr. That task . . . that task he set upon me."

"Why you?"

Something in his eyes troubled her. "I knew Valentin's ways best. I knew how he would think. To some, Valentin was evil incarnate, but to those who served him loyally, he was a true master, a true and resolute commander. In that trait lay the weakness that the wizard chose to exploit."

Again she sensed bitterness in his tone, as if he still did not approve of what Paulo Centuros had decided so many years before. Of course, as a knight, Evan's notions of honor and fairness had likely conflicted with those of a wizard; Centuros would have been willing to stretch the limits of honor if it meant defeating the enemy. That made sense to Mardi, but she could see how Evan Wytherling might feel otherwise.

"The wizard . . ." Evan muttered, no doubt seeing the rotund form of the man in his mind. "Paulo Centuros always knew what had to be done, even if others did not want it done that way. He came to the king of Rundin just as the first rumblings of war grew in the southern climes of the land. He showed the monarch what had become of the harsh, hilly realm of Torea beyond the mountain passes that had been closed for some thirty years. Centuros revealed to the mortal how a sorcerer, a tall, thin, cowled figure, had taken the king of Torea by the throat and caused him to explode before the eyes of the man's own court—"

So old Brathius finally got what he deserved, eh? came a voice in Mardi's head. The room seemed to swim around her and Evan Wytherling faded a little. The image of a throne room and two misty figures in confrontation grew stronger. She tried to focus her attention on her companion, but the image would not be ignored.

You miss the point, Your Majesty, and the point is always the deadliest part of the weapon, the second figure responded. *The sorcerer Novaris is now lord of that southern realm and his power is already absolute.*

The first form remained defiant. *He wouldn't dare come north, magician. Our armies are the finest in all the realms and we have treaties with both Tepis and Wallmyre. To attack one is to attack all. The sorcerer barely has reign over his own kingdom; he could hardly concern himself with anything else at the moment!*

The second replied, *He concerns himself with nothing else but a drive northward. King Ulrich, and all of Torea will march for his cause!*

The taller figure, who appeared to be a man upon an elaborate chair, waved off such fears. *Go back to your books, magician, and leave the rule of kingdoms to those God has chosen by right of birth . . .*

A sleeping lion will wake much hungered, Your Majesty—

Mardi shivered as the images abruptly dissolved and she found herself again listening to Evan's version of the tale. What had happened to her? Why did she have visions such as this? In every way they frightened her as much as the dragon in the church had.

"It is said that Centuros came every other day to warn the king of Rundin of the impending danger, but after two years, his words fell more and more on uncaring ears. The king himself died peacefully some twelve years later, and his son, equally obstinate, at last forbade the wizard to come unless he had some proof of his words." Evan's grimace grew. "Paulo Centuros preached preparation for thirty-odd years but no one would listen, forgetting that wizards see beyond the day-to-day, perceiving instead the far future.

"In the end, the wizard proved correct . . . as he always did. The young king now grown old discovered that when the armies of darkness began pouring into the southernmost tip of Rundin, laying waste to all in their path. At the head of that force rode Valentin atop Grimyr and, below, Valentin's elite and fanatical corps of knights."

Attempting to remain focused on Evan and the true world, Mardi realized that his digression concerning Paulo Centuros had been anything but that. The weary knight appeared to be trying to explain both to her and yet again to himself why he would follow the suggestions of one who did not necessarily understand honor the way one of Evan's calling did. Evan had obeyed the wizard in all things because the wizard had proved from the beginning to be the only one who could see the truth about the coming war and what it would entail.

"Novaris's armies presented a foe such as the northern kingdoms had never encountered. Most were human, yes, but there were other things: goblins, trolls, morags, and creatures nameless. There were dragons, too, although none so terrible as Grimyr. Yet, ever it became apparent that Valentin led the way; Valentin gave force to the commands of his master. Of course, the vicious General Haggad had his own important role, but it had been Valentin who guided Grimyr and commanded the knights most feared on the battlefield.

"Even the sorcery of never-seen Novaris did not put so much fear into the king of Rundin and his two allies, for, despite their misgivings concerning the rotund spellcaster, they soon saw that Centuros was every bit the equal of his rival. When Novaris brought forth his acolytes and temporarily shifted the tide, the wizard summoned his own, pushing back the dark magic. True, men died in droves on the field of battle as the powers of the two fell upon them, but to kings such deaths meant little if, in the long run, their side triumphed.

"By themselves, the kings would have lost their war, the ax-men of chill Tepis, the archers of seaborne Wallmyre, and the swordmasters of Rundin itself wasted by leaders who did not understand this new and horrible sort of battle. Only one Rundin general met with Centuros's approval, the soft-spoken giant Argus Pretor. Pretor had quickly made a reputation for himself so when it came time to deal with Valentin and his knights, Centuros turned to the general for assistance. Pretor, in turn, brought the wizard the one who could help them deal with the crimson warrior . . . and that person is me.

"I knew of Valentin, you see," Evan explained. "I had known of some of his early exploits and studied them." He hesitated for no good reason that Mardi could think, then quickly added, "Pretor and the wizard charged me with the task of leading Valentin and his followers, even the dragon, into a trap. I performed that task, Valentin's knights perishing to a man. For Grimyr, Centuros gave me a magical weapon, which pierced the leviathan's heart but was torn from my hands in the process. Valentin survived that attack, but as he came at me, I seized a dead foot soldier's lance and thrust it through his chest. But Novaris had ensured that he would not die."

Curiously, the further Evan delved into the final conflict with Valentin, the sparser his tale grew. Mardi sought to ask questions, such as how he had trapped the knights or why Valentin let him come so close with so terrible a weapon, but the knight went on, cutting his story to the very bones. Evan gave the final moments of the battle and, indeed, the war an almost cursory pass.

"Novaris's force collapsed without Valentin and Grimyr. Pretor cut off Haggad's retreat. Making use of the confusion, Centuros and his acolytes struck hard at the sorcerer's own position, a place not that far to the south of here where the mountains just begin. Power unimaginable by mortal men struck the peaks from which the sorcerer-king and his followers had launched their own barbarous assaults. You may have noticed the ragged sides of those mountains. Novaris's own sorcerers died en masse, but he . . . his body was never found." The silver knight inhaled, pressing yet swifter with his story. "As for Valentin, since the lance had failed they then tried to cut off his head just as they had that of Haggad, but the ax would always turn away and soon the victors tired of the effort. Centuros then hit upon a notion of his own, one with which the kings acquiesced. You saw the fate to which the kindly wizard condemned the knight. Shortly after that, I swore to the task of finding Valentin's master, for we could not be certain that, if he lived, he might not rise up again. Centuros taught me, showed me methods of tracking beyond mortal ken. He even set some spells upon me to aid my efforts. Since that time, I have hunted, going ever west until west I could no longer go, for that was where the trail originally led . . . so I thought. Only then did I return here, to question Valentin, the notion that Novaris might have returned to rescue his most loyal servant often nagging at me over the years."

"Did he not return to Torea?"

"He dared not. He could not have stood against the alliance, much less the wizard, at that point. What would he want of the shattered land, anyway? Does it even exist as a sovereign kingdom now?"

Mardi pondered the regions to the south. Rundin as she knew it continued that direction long past the mountains of which Evan had spoken, ending only, if she recalled her geography lessons, when it reached the sandy domain of Saduun. The blond woman said as much to the knight.

"A token prize for Rundin, then. I suspected it would fall such. Tepis and Wallmyre would have wanted nothing to do with such an unsightly and useless land." He suddenly pulled away. "The night has grown silent. I must go now."

"Wait—" Mardi had so many questions still, Evan's story not at all satisfactory. "What about—?"

In her bedroom, Mistress Arden stirred. Mardi turned, wondering how to explain Evan's presence. As she looked away, she belatedly realized that the veteran warrior had already slipped toward the door. By the time Mardi turned back, he had stepped out.

"Sleep well, my lady," Evan whispered, shutting the door before she could stop him.

Mardi reached for the handle, but as she did, the room shifted. She felt herself floating, losing all connection to her surroundings. The door, the room, her entire home faded.

She stood on the top edge of a hillside, staring down at a scene of incredible carnage. Two fearsome armies clashed, men from both sides screaming as they were cut down. Although deeply overcast, the sky grew bright on occasion as what clearly had to be magic spells ripped open the earth or attempted to bring down one of the massive leather-winged forms in combat above.

Among the warriors moved those not borne of mankind. Tall, narrow elves fought on one side, grotesque, muscular scaled creatures that could only be trolls on the other. Beyond the trolls were helmed monsters much akin to them but taller, more animalistic, and with ears like bat wings. Morags, Mardi vaguely recalled from the fairy tales of her youth.

She tried to turn from the scene, but her body would not obey. A hand came up to rub her chin, a thick male hand half-covered by a long forest-green sleeve.

"We've got the one you want, wizard."

"Aah, splendid, splendid," Mardi's mouth abruptly uttered. Suddenly her view swung around, turning away from the battle to face a small band of grimy, disheveled figures, veterans of the war beyond. Most were clad in chain mail and breastplates with what looked like a variation of the Rundin emblem, two lions guarding a golden crown. Two other figures, a young man and a stone-faced older woman, wore pale-green robes with cowls that hid much of their features. Their heads were tilted slightly forward in what Mardi Sinclair at last realized had to be obeisance to her . . . or to the owner of the body from which she watched.

Then her eyes drifted to the one in the center of the group, the one who stood above the others, silver armor tarnished but no less impressive. Only a touch of gray marred his long brown hair and, while worn, his features had a much more youthful cast to them than she recalled.

Evan.

He wore a sullen but respectful look on his face, clearly ignoring all but Mardi. She tried to speak to him, but the mouth she wore would not obey her.

Yet, it did speak other words. "So, Sir Wytherling, are you now amenable to the task at hand? War waits for no man, yet we have waited for you."

The stone-faced woman snapped a finger. The soldiers retreated, visibly relieved to place some distance between Mardi and themselves. Evan stepped forward, never glancing away. The two robed figures moved aside but kept a wary eye on the knight.

"Your lackeys have prepared me well, Centuros," he finally replied, a curiously dead tone to his voice. "You should be proud of them."

Centuros? Mardi wanted to gasp, but could not. She realized that she must be seeing the time of the great war against the sorcerer-king . . . but from the very body of Paulo Centuros? How? Why?

The questions faded to the background as the wizard spoke. "The teacher is always proud of a good pupil, but even more so of a delinquent one who redeems himself."

Mardi did not understand the sentiment, but Evan apparently did. His eyes narrowed, the only sign of what she imagined had to be anger.

When the knight did not answer, Paulo Centuros went on. "The spells of protection are all cast? Do you feel any different?"

"You would know."

Again the barely concealed anger. Mardi tried to understand the curious relationship between the wizard and warrior. They were both allies in a war against evil, yet clearly Evan despised the wizard.

Her right arm rose up, her fingers splayed. "Step forward, Sir Wytherling."

He did, albeit with much reluctance. Evan did not stop until he stood within an inch or two of the outstretched appendage. The silver knight stared at the hand as if seeing a poisonous adder. This near, Mardi could see his eyes, read his emotions deeper, and what she saw disturbed her greatly . . . for Evan Wytherling looked at the wizard's open hand in unrestrained fear.

"The tool is prepared, now the tool must be honed." With that utterance, the heavyset spellcaster reached out, not for Evan's chest, but for his forehead.

Evan grunted and the muscles in his face twitched, yet he remained otherwise still, staring into the eyes of the wizard. A swell of sympathy made Mardi want to embrace him, comfort him, but still she could only observe as Paulo Centuros worked his wizardry on the warrior. Outwardly, Evan appeared untouched, but Mardi sensed that something within the paladin had forever changed . . . and not in a way that the knight approved.

The rotund mage at last lowered his hand. Evan sighed and his body relaxed some as Centuros broke contact.

"You are ready. You must not fail, you know."

The knight stared. "I cannot fail."

"Your steed has been prepared for you."

For some reason, this simple statement sent renewed consternation through Sir Wytherling. The eyes narrowed ever so slightly in what Mardi thought might have been dismay or disgust.

"The lance is also prepared. Use it only when the time is right. Until then, the sword provided you earlier will do in all other matters."

"I understand everything." Again, a trace of inexplicable

bitterness.

"Destiny is in your hands, Evan Wytherling," Paulo Centuros concluded. "You will shape tomorrow, as a sculptor shapes a piece of marble. Consider the masterpiece you create . . ."

Those words said, the wizard waved his round hand, dismissing the warrior. Evan turned from him . . . and Mardi . . . without so much as the slightest bow. The soldiers who had accompanied him let the silver knight pass before following. The two subordinate wizards attempted to join them, but Centuros cleared his throat slightly, catching their attention.

Mardi did not like the two other spellcasters. They had an almost unsavory look about them, as if they obeyed out of lack of choice, nothing more.

"See to it that destiny favors us," the senior wizard muttered. "Whatever the cost may be to him . . ."

The woman frowned. "How can we—?"

"Mistress Sinclair! Were you thinking of stepping out in the middle of the night? You should know better than that!"

Mardi blinked, seeing once more her own fingers touching the handle of the door. The vision of Evan Wytherling and Paulo Centuros on the eve of the great battle had vanished, although the sounds of war still echoed slightly in her head.

Mistress Arden, shawl wrapped around her shoulders, stood behind Mardi, eyeing the younger woman as if she had taken leave of her senses. Mardi wondered if perhaps the magistrate's servant had the right of it. Certainly nothing would better explain what had just happened to her.

"Actually," she finally began, having recovered her voice, "I've already been out." Mardi knew that she had to admit as much. If Mistress Arden looked any closer, the older woman would certainly see the traces of moisture and dirt on her clothing. "I just needed a little fresh air. You caught me just checking to make certain that I had shut the door properly."

"You dressed and departed without me hearing you?"

That she had done so without waking Mistress Arden had clearly ruffled Mardi's companion. Drulane's servant probably slept very lightly in general, one of his reasons for sending her in the first place. Mardi suddenly felt guilty for having left her own home without permission.

"I'm so very sorry! I needed air and thought to be back in bed without your noticing. I did not mean to worry you—"

"Worry me?" The elder woman sniffed. "I have nothing to fear, young lady. It's you who should be thinking about your own well-being."

"I said I'm sorry." Her vehemence startled her, but Mardi could no longer tolerate the other's attitude. She strode past the disapproving Mistress Arden, heading directly to her bedroom.

Behind her she could hear the magistrate's servant following, but Mardi no longer thought of the woman's matriarchal attitude. Although Mistress Arden could not see it, Mardi could hardly even stand. The night's events had taken their toll, this most disturbing and recent vision the final straw. Why had Mardi been condemned to suffer these visions amid so much other horror?

And how had she become linked to what threatened her town?

Evan wended his way back to the inn, wary at all times of the torch-bearing figures stalking through the town. The horrific death of Mardi Sinclair's uncle aside, Evan thought the townsfolk far more uneasy than their present situation warranted, more so since their distrust appeared to focus much in his direction. More than once he heard himself mentioned, as if somehow these proceedings had all been his fault. True, they could not and, he hoped, would *never* know of Valentin, but it seemed unreasonable that they should all choose Evan as the devil in their midst.

Valentin, you have a hand in this . . . Somehow the crimson knight's baleful will had touched almost everyone in the vicinity. Such a feat required tremendous magical power and, without his master here, Valentin had no such power. By himself, the other warrior had wielded little more magic than Evan. His greatest link to such forces had perished with its source, the dragon Grimyr, now little more than bones and old scale . . .

Scale. Wizards often sought dragonscale for their spells. If Novaris had not ransacked the beast's grave, then perhaps some residual link between the knight and his monstrous companion remained, enough of a link to enable Valentin to spread his corrupting influence over Pretor's Hill. Perhaps . . . perhaps the sorcerer-king had even strengthened this link himself before departing the region.

Too many suppositions. Evan blamed magic for the many questions plaguing him. A good strong arm and a sharp sword, those were things a knight understood. Even after all this time, magic served only to fog the situations he faced.

Evan paused just before the inn, watching as another party with torches stalked by. They looked to be tiring out at last, their burning ire cooling. Some already mumbled about returning to their beds. The silver knight relaxed slightly. He had feared that his visit to Valentin might have served to hasten matters. The people of Pretor's Hill were not yet completely lost.

As the party vanished into the night, Evan started toward the inn. No lamps shone within, meaning that either Master Jakes slept or he had not yet returned home. In either case, it gave Evan the opportunity to return to his room unnoticed.

Soft but steady hoofbeats sent him falling back into the darkness.

Even in the dark he recognized the muscular gray stallion with the black spots on the flank. The arrogant steed shook his head as he turned and for a moment Evan Wytherling feared that the horse sensed him. However, with a shake of his ebony mane, the animal moved on past, heading for the stable.

Atop the animal rode a man of incredible girth. Beneath the fancy garments lay a body well muscled and stout. Evan could make out only some of the face, but what he saw told him that here rode a man most dangerous, a man used to events acceding to his will.

So . . . Steppenwald. Curious that the king's representative should choose this time for a ride; Evan could clearly see that he had not been a part of the search. Steppenwald—and this could be no other than the elusive figure—clearly cared little for whatever stirred the folk of Pretor's Hill, perhaps because he knew more than they did about the truth.

Did he? Evan frowned. While some clues pointed to suspicious activities on the part of the man, that did not necessarily mean that Steppenwald knew anything about Valentin or the danger to the town.

Somehow, the silver knight could not convince himself of the royal agent's complete innocence. Despite the nearness of sanctuary, Evan Wytherling turned and began to follow Steppenwald. Evan had faced Valentin and learned little; if he now confronted this figure, perhaps he might yet discover enough to turn the course of events and save Mardi Sinclair's home.

And will that redeem me? Evan suddenly wondered as he crept toward the stables. *Will that satisfy your will, wizard? Likely not.* Nothing would free the weary knight of his quest save the final, absolute certainty that Novaris himself was dead.

But certainly removing Novaris's curse from this region would at least help.

Steppenwald dismounted as he reached the stable doors. From the side of the saddle, he seized a cane topped with a grip that resembled some beast the knight could not make out. Steppenwald clearly did not need the cane to walk, though; Evan marveled at the ease with which the massive rider moved. He contemplated confronting the man now, but did not want to be disturbed by the magistrate's officers. Best to let Steppenwald enter first. Besides, Evan sensed something unnatural surrounding the king's representative. Magic enveloped Steppenwald, and although the watcher sensed only the barest traces, he suspected the gigantic man wielded more power than those traces indicated.

There was also something familiar about the signature of those traces . . .

Although the doors should have been bolted, they swung open readily enough when Steppenwald touched them. Reins in one hand, the giant led his huge stallion inside. Steppenwald left the doors open. It was possibly a trap, but Evan did not care. Drawing his sword, he took one last look around, then darted in after his quarry.

He caught sight of the black tail and spotted flank of the Neulander as man and animal vanished into the darkened stable. Evan wondered what Steppenwald made of his own baleful steed. Had he inspected the knight's horse? Would he see the truth when he stared into the damnable steed's eyes? Would Steppenwald realize what the beast was?

The darkness obscured his view of the king's man, but Evan could think of few places within where the massive figure could secrete himself.

Evan had taken only a few steps when blinding light washed through the tall wooden building. The veteran warrior wielded his sword before him, fighting for time as his sight slowly returned. Intense but mercifully brief heat singed him and for a moment he wondered whether the stables had caught fire.

However, the coolness of the night suddenly returned. Evan blinked, silently cursing. If not a fire, then the light could have been caused by only one thing.

Once more in darkness, he quickly sought out the nearest oil lamp. The lamp lit, Evan Wytherling swung it around to survey the remainder of the room.

Both Lord Steppenwald and the spotted Neulander were nowhere to be seen.

X

A TEST OF WILLS

In the sealed chamber that had been so long his prison that it had become his home, Valentin smiled.

Drulane did not look up as Evan Wytherling entered.

"Tell me about your Lord Steppenwald, Magistrate."

If anything, the new day matched well the knight's sour disposition. The dark clouds and high winds only added to Evan's certainty that the time of reckoning had drawn very, very near.

"The king's man?" Drulane finally asked, the gnarled figure still perusing papers on his desk. "He is the word of our monarch in these parts."

Exasperated, Evan pressed. "But what do you know of him? Who is he truly?"

The aging magistrate looked up, his expression almost matching his undesired guest's. "Lord Steppenwald has been the king's representative for as long as I can recall. He is efficient, determined, and commanding."

The words came out as if by rote. The knight stepped closer, leaning on the desk. "Does he wield magic?"

Drulane looked stunned. "A royal representative of Rundin? Wield magic? The king would not permit it!"

"Are you certain of that?"

"Most emphatically." The crooked man leaned forward, staring deep. "Why such questions?"

Instead of answering the magistrate's not-unreasonable

query, Evan continued on with his own interrogation. "Lord Steppenwald. Is he a big man? A man of great proportion, stout of build?"

"Be careful not to say that last in his presence! He would have the right to bring you in on charges!"

"For simply that?"

Drulane leaned back. "He is the king's man."

They were back to that again, but Evan would not be deterred. "He is a giant to many, is he not?" When he at last saw acknowledgment in the other's eyes, the impatient knight went on. "A noble beard, also, plus clothes the likes of which only tremendous wealth can afford. He also uses a walking stick, one surely crafted by an artisan—"

"It sounds much like his lordship," the seated man admitted. "But it can't be him because Lord Steppenwald has not been to these parts in some time."

"I saw him last night."

Drulane pursed his lips. "Exactly what are you driving at, paladin? We've weightier concerns than Lord Steppenwald, although I, for one, might find his arrival fortuitous . . . and speaking of this last night, what do you know of it? There are reports of howls much like the ones heard prior to Master Casperin's death and claims of figures hurrying through the dark, two-legged figures. I suspect one of them to be you."

"There were many out last night. The people of Pretor's Hill seem very light sleepers."

"Yes, nerves have grown even more frayed in the past few days. You would especially need to take care, paladin."

"I've tried to stay out of the way."

"You need to try harder. There are limitations to even my control of matters these days." He indicated the papers before him. "Landowners encroaching on one another's properties. Theft. Altercations. Rare things in Pretor's Hill until very recently. Now it seems as if half the folk think their neighbors are attempting treachery behind their backs . . ."

"And your town was never like this before?"

The elderly magistrate looked offended. "We don't claim to be saints, Sir Wytherling, but the people of Pretor's Hill have always been there for one another." His eyes narrowed. "Now then, you were outside last night, weren't you?"

Evan saw no point in lying. Limited as he was, Drulane still represented his only real ally other than Mardi . . . and what could she do? "I was."

"And what did you see?"

He chose still to evade mention of Valentin, but of the other danger, Evan gladly spoke. "The howls were real. The creatures that murdered Master Casperin still stalk the land. I slew three and saw another die, but I fear that there must be more."

"They are not wolves, then, as you first said."

"You knew they were not even then."

"Too true." The magistrate tapped his fingers on his desktop. "I imagine shadows more, paladin"—he ignored the slight widening of the knight's eyes at this description—"shadows with fangs and claws and as much men as they are beasts. Would that be a fair image?"

"You have seen them?"

"Only in my mind's eye," Evan's companion returned enigmatically. "I dream of them, dream also of blackbirds that turn into scaly behemoths borne from the primal flames. I even dream sometimes of a warrior clad in blood with eyes that seem to seek my soul." Drulane began to tap his fingers again. "And for many reasons I believe that all of these will come to my home even if their forms may differ from what I dream . . ."

Evan could not respond at first, digesting the man's jarring words, the descriptions that included even Valentin and long-dead Grimyr. Even if Magistrate Drulane consciously knew a part of the truth, his subconscious clearly delved deeper.

"I would send everyone away," the hunched figure added when his visitor did not speak, "and face alone whatever was to come, paladin, but you know the impossibility of doing that. I

181

couldn't convince everyone on my own . . . and they would certainly not listen to you."

"Would they listen to Lord Steppenwald?"

"If he were here, perhaps, and if I had persuaded him of the facts as I see it. It would be a difficult attempt where he's concerned, too, paladin, considering I likely know little more than the tip of the mountain."

The knight took a breath and eyed the magistrate. He found it tempting to confide in someone other than Mardi Sinclair, but what he could tell Drulane would do the man little good. At this point, he hoped only to stir Steppenwald to new action. He wanted to see what the king's representative would do upon hearing that the knight had been asking about him.

"If you'll not pursue a better course, Sir Wytherling, then I must ask you to depart. I had hoped we might be trusted allies, but now I see that not to be the case. I wonder what you hide from me and what harm that'll do to my people—"

"I share what I can, Magistrate, just as I hope you do." Evan bowed to the man and departed. He hoped that Drulane would stay out of his way and keep the rest of the town from interfering as Evan dealt with Valentin's curse.

He also needed to unravel the mystery behind Steppenwald . . . and Mardi, too. He knew not yet what role she played in all of this, but somehow she looked to be more than simply a hapless bystander. Events had too often centered around her in one way or another.

As Evan walked to the inn he tried to reconcile himself with the hope that by instigating the debacle of a conversation with the magistrate, he might draw Steppenwald out. The man might yet prove an ally, but if he did not, then Evan would have to deal with him before striking against Valentin.

Through the apple-sized sphere of light resting on his gloved palm,

Steppenwald surveyed the dwindling figure of the knight as the man departed Drulane's office. He waited to see if this Evan Wytherling would turn and speak once more with Steppenwald's dupe, but, no, the knight pressed on, vanishing.

Steppenwald crushed the sphere into nonexistence, both disappointed and vexed. Evan Wytherling had not said nearly enough of consequence and then actually had the audacity to try to bait him into revealing himself. Steppenwald would reveal himself when he chose, in the method he chose. He had not yet made a judgment, not yet decided which hand he should play, although he leaned close to a possible decision.

A notion occurred to him, a notion that made him smile. Steppenwald pursed his lips, beginning to smile. "Perhaps I should, perhaps I should . . ."

Steppenwald liked to think himself daring and certainly this notion could be considered that. Set certain events into motion, let the players play against one another at a pace that he, not they, set. Then he could choose the one he needed, the one who could guarantee that when all was said and done, it would be Steppenwald who gained everything.

The immense man tapped the dragon-head cane on the ground. "Very well, sir knight. You'll get what you want, get what you want . . . but you may not like it."

It had grown more overcast and, if possible, darker, even though midday had barely come. Mardi Sinclair bundled the collar of her cloak and scurried through the town, avoiding eye contact as much as possible.

Under normal circumstances, Mardi would have gone to see Father Gerard for guidance, but the fact that the devilish Valentin mocked the world from below the very foundation of the church had left her untrusting of the sanctity of even that building. Father Gerard had a demon beneath his feet and did not even know it.

She had also thought of the magistrate, but despite his infatuation with her she suspected that Drulane would only think her mad. More to the point, if she mentioned any of Evan's part in the matter, the gentlewoman worried that the magistrate might deal unkindly with him.

That left only Evan, whose entire role she did not yet understand, and possibly—

"Daniel?" Mardi glimpsed the tall, well-clad figure as he strode past. He wore an expression of determination, one that kept her from repeating his name louder. Clearly oblivious to her presence, the young merchant and landowner hurried on, as if late for some important business. His rich, gold-lined cloak fluttered in the growing wind and at another time Mardi might have imagined him akin to a heroic prince. Now she pictured him more as an executioner.

Driven by some force she did not understand, the blond woman put aside her own concerns and began pacing Daniel. No longer did she think of confiding in him, whatever his feelings toward her. Too much his present expression reminded her of the momentary beast he had become, of the beast she herself had become on recent occasion.

Daniel suddenly halted, standing as if prepared to go to war. Mardi peered past him, saw Evan heading toward the inn where he stayed. The young merchant's hands clenched, almost as if Daniel had the knight's throat. This had to be more than jealousy; he had never shown himself to be so violent in the past.

With an abruptness that caught Mardi completely unaware, Daniel turned to his right and headed toward the marketplace. Mardi hesitated, caught between wanting to speak with Evan and wondering what the younger Taran was about. Her hesitation cost her as both men vanished, Daniel around a corner and Evan into the inn. She could not very well visit the knight in his room, so Mardi tried to locate the landowner. However, despite his height and imposing appearance, she could see no sign of him.

As Mardi pondered what to do next, a sense of unease

washed over her. She glanced to each side, almost expecting the dragon of her dreams to come charging down the street. At first she noticed nothing amiss, but then an image her eyes had skirted past registered.

A man. An immense man. A figure she vaguely knew.

Mardi spun her gaze back and again caught sight of the elegant clothes that could have been fashioned only in a great city such as Coramas, caught sight of the immense figure. He stood silent, but watchful, visibly pleased by the unpleasant day as if he himself had planned it to be so.

"Lord Steppenwald?" she mouthed.

To her astonishment, his eyes immediately focused on her. They flashed briefly in what might have been equal surprise, then shifted to amusement. The king's man reached up with a gloved hand to tip his hat to her just as a small group of passersby came between the two, obscuring her view of the royal visitor.

The blond woman blinked, confused. Why had she stood here daydreaming when she should have been pursuing Daniel? Now Mardi had completely lost him . . . and for what? Vaguely she recalled something catching her attention, but what it had been Mardi could not recall. Nothing overly important, otherwise it would not have so soon slipped her mind.

She felt an urge to go to Evan despite the improprieties of speaking with him in his room. He needed to be warned . . . yet what exactly Mardi had to warn him about, she could not say. The urge grew so tremendous, though, that Mardi ceased questioning it.

The crowds thickened as she sought to make her way to the inn, more and more people finding their paths coinciding with hers. What started as a brisk pace slowed to less than a crawl, then a stop. Voices rose, unintelligible voices but clearly angered ones.

A crowd had gathered in front of the inn . . . and Mardi did not have to ask for what reason her fellow townsfolk had come together.

Forcing her way through, she managed to get close enough to see the entrance. Master Jakes stood near the doorway, but he had not positioned himself there as staunch defender. Instead, the innkeeper stood to the side, obviously stating that he would not act against the throng.

A moment later, her worst fear was realized as four of the town's burliest men dragged out Evan Wytherling.

He did not fight them, but at the same time he made no effort to ease their burden. The four men who held him had their hands full and all watched him with unease.

"It's his doing!" someone shouted. "He's brought death and evil to our town!"

The crowd found this to their agreement, although Mardi thought the statement absurd. Only she knew to what extent dark forces threatened Pretor's Hill; most of her fellow townsfolk had only her Uncle Yoniff's grisly death and the foul weather upon which to blame a wave of evil. She had not blamed Evan in any way for her uncle. Why, then, such a violent, abrupt reaction this day? The sudden birth of this mob made absolutely no sense.

Mardi had the nagging sensation that she should know more, but, try as she might, her memory failed her. Something she had just seen . . .

"I have harmed no one," the knight calmly announced.

His words might as well have been carried away by the strengthening winds, for the crowd reacted as if he had said nothing, continuing their own shouts of condemnation. The charges grew more dubious with each passing breath—milk curdling for no reason, voices speaking where no one stood, slaughtered animals rising up and running about for several minutes, and on and on. Mardi doubted that most, if any, of these events had actually occurred, being not at all in tune with what she had faced. It almost seemed as if her fellow townsfolk mouthed words they did not even understand they were speaking.

The wind continued to whip around the area, a slight mist adding to the already-horrendous day. Despite this, none of those around her seemed at all inclined to depart.

"It's black magic!" a masculine voice cried. "He's a warlock as dark as hell and should be burned!"

Mardi gasped, recognizing the speaker. Peering over the shoulder of one of her neighbors, she saw Daniel, one hand raised in a fist, the other carrying a flickering torch. The look of intense hatred he had worn before had resurfaced tenfold stronger.

"He killed Yoniff Casperin!" Daniel cried, pointing an accusatory finger at Evan. "There were no wolves! Has anyone seen a wolf?" When the others shook their heads, he continued, "The howls are always in the distance! Wolves don't attack people, much less a grown man on a horse! *There*'s the animal in our midst! *There*'s the monster we've got to fear!"

His words rallied the mob. Evan's captors dragged him down the steps while the good Master Jakes watched. Mardi could not believe the actions of her friends and neighbors. She knew they could be distrustful at times, especially of outsiders, but this all verged on some sort of sudden madness!

She forced her way toward the young merchant, hoping to somehow make him see sanity. "Daniel! Daniel!"

He glanced her way, the hatred turning to determination. "This has to be done, Mardi! He's cast a glamour over you, but once we've sent his evil spirit to Hell, you'll be free again to marry me!"

"Are you insane? That makes no sense!"

"It makes every sense!" He swept away from her, moving to confront the captured paladin. "Warlock! Thing of evil!"

To her horror, Evan Wytherling did nothing to deny the fantastic charges. The weathered knight stared at Daniel with somber hazel eyes. Despite Mardi's nearness, his gaze never once turned her way, although she knew without a doubt that he was aware of her presence.

"We should burn him here and now," someone called.

Mardi gasped. Where were Bulrik and his men? Why were they not here to stop this? At any given time, one of them should have been patrolling this area.

"We won't be bothered by the watch," Daniel Taran said,

looking directly at Mardi. Chills ran up and down her spine. Had she asked it aloud? "And the magistrate'll see the right of it once we're done."

With that, the mob pulled Evan forward. Shouts filled the area, causing curious folk not already involved to watch the gathering. A few looked aghast, but most of those simply hurried off, as if their absence assuaged their part of the guilt.

Mardi seized Daniel's arm. "Think what you're doing!"

He stared into her eyes, never blinking. "I'm doing this for us."

She saw that he actually believed what he said, which only added to her horror. The young landowner pulled away, returning once more to commanding the crowd. Mardi fell back, unsure of what to do. Already some had gathered materials for a makeshift bonfire. Did she have time to run to Drulane's office? Would he even do anything?

"What is this terrible thing you do?"

A voice of reason at last. Mardi Sinclair's hopes rose as Father Gerard, eyes wide with astonishment and dismay, strode toward the throng. He looked at what had been built, then at the prisoner.

"Purging Pretor's Hill of a demon, Father," Daniel returned. "I would've thought that obvious!"

"This is a human being!" The priest tried to pull Evan free, but the men holding the knight would not release their grips. "Such savageness is of times long past, times better forgotten!"

"This is a warlock, Father, and we're not supposed to suffer them to live!"

"Do not misquote such words to me, Brother Taran! Now release him!"

Daniel looked around, pointed at two men, one of them Jak Bellowes. "Keep the priest out of harm's way while we do his work for him."

"See here—" Before Father Gerard could protest further, the pair had seized him by the arms and pulled him back. When he continued to protest, Jak put his wounded hand over the priest's mouth.

"It's almost ready!" one of Daniel's cohorts yelled.

They had positioned a pole at the site where, during festival times, banners were often raised. Already a good pile of tinder and such lay waiting. At a command from Daniel, the knight's captors dragged Evan to the pole, where they bound him in place.

This could not be happening. Mardi stood aghast, trying to drum up the physical strength she had summoned spontaneously in the past few days, desperate to put an end to this travesty before something irreversible happened. After a moment, she felt a tingling in her chest, a tingling that spread rapidly over her torso. She felt a locked door—for lack of a better description—suddenly open. Mardi raised a hand as Daniel bent near the tinder, knowing that she had to prevent him from starting the blaze no matter what the cost to her—

People at the rear of the crowd shrieked. Mardi turned just as a great horse seemed to materialize among the throng. At first she thought the stallion Evan's bone-white phantom, but then she noted the difference in shading and the telltale spots on his flank. The mighty steed had reared up, but as he came down, she and the rest saw upon his back a gigantic, well-clad figure with penetrating eyes and an expression anything but pleasant.

"What's this, what's this? Is this any sort of tableau for a visitor to confront, to confront, mind you, as he first enters your fair town?"

"Lord Steppenwald!" Who first called out the name of the king of Rundin's royal representative, Mardi could not say, not even if it had been her. The titanic rider urged his mount forward a few paces, cutting a path through the suddenly subdued crowd. Even Daniel appeared momentarily stripped of his madness, although he still held the torch near the bound knight.

"I was under the assumption," Steppenwald went on, "that royal justice still prevailed in these far parts. What crimes has this man committed that demand such horrendous, horrendous reactions from the community?"

No one could find their voice until Daniel at last muttered, "He killed a man."

Steppenwald's head snapped toward Daniel. "Which man?"

"The moneylender Yoniff Casperin." Emboldened a bit, Daniel swung around and pointed at Mardi. "Her uncle!"

Lord Steppenwald turned the spotted stallion toward her. His eyes met those of the gentlewoman, ensnaring them. Mardi experienced a brief sense of vertigo. "And you are, my lady . . . ?"

No one save Evan had ever called her by such a title, but coming from the immense rider the term made Mardi feel uneasy, undeserving. She felt the need to curtsy. "Mardi—Mardina Sinclair, my lord."

"Mardina Sinclair . . . do you know that this man slew your uncle? Can you state it as fact?"

"He did no such thing!" She uttered the denial with such vehemence that even Lord Steppenwald bent back in mild surprise. Ignoring the looks of those around her, Mardi added, "If anything, Sir Wytherling, a veteran warrior, would have tried to save my uncle! He saved me from the very beast that had killed Uncle Yoniff. Had he not been there, I would have been ripped to shreds, just like—just like—"

She faltered, her guilt for the arguments she and her uncle had suffered just prior to his death swelling up again. To her relief, though, the king's representative filled in the silence.

"And Magistrate Drulane? He judged this man not to be responsible?" When no one replied, Steppenwald nodded sagely. "So I thought! Are there then any, any crimes that can be squarely placed, squarely placed, mind you, at the feet of this outsider?"

A few people muttered, but when the gaze of the king's representative fell upon them, they ceased, their eyes cast earthward. Even Daniel had lost much of his steam. He looked around as if trying to find a place to dispose of the torch.

"The magistrate's men will be here shortly," Steppenwald declared with such firmness that no one doubted his word. "It would be prudent if all trace of this near travesty vanished before then." For the first time he looked at Evan. "And someone should start with unbinding the would-be victim . . ."

Mardi darted toward the knight, immediately working on his bonds. Evan did not acknowledge her efforts, instead maintaining his attention on the newcomer. "A timely rescue, my Lord Steppenwald."

The massive rider tipped his hat. "Fortuitous, fortuitous."

Most of the crowd had already wisely melted away. As Mardi freed Evan's hands, she also noted that Daniel had at last found some water with which to douse the torch. His expression puzzled her some, the madness and anger giving way to an apathetic, somewhat sleepy look.

Looking around, the gentlewoman noticed similar expressions on others, even those involved in dismantling the makeshift execution spot. Two men brought down the pole without so much as a glimmer of regret or remorse; they simply carried it off.

Evan rubbed his wrists, finally looking at Mardi. "My gratitude."

He seemed almost as nonchalant as the rest, which served to infuriate her a little. Did he not realize how close he had come to being horribly murdered? "How can you take this so calm? They almost burned you alive!"

"But Lord Steppenwald made certain that they would not . . . is that not so, my lord?"

The bearded giant chuckled slightly. "Of course, of course. We can't have such occurrences in fair Rundin! This is a land of peace now, isn't it?"

"And for some time now, so they say."

Mardi eyed the two men, feeling as if she missed half of their conversation. They talked as if they knew each other far better than two men who had just met under dire circumstances. Again, the absurdity of the events surrounding her threatened to overwhelm the young woman. Her head began to pound and she almost wished that she had never involved herself, never had to confront the darkness that had become so much a part of her town, her people.

Steppenwald looked around, nodding his approval at the almost-pristine area. Only the presence of the three left any trace that something terrible had nearly taken place. Even Mardi found it harder and harder to believe that Evan had nearly been killed.

At that moment, Bulrik and three officers, the two giants included, marched into sight. They did not seem in any hurry and, in fact, might have marched on if not for Bulrik immediately recognizing the king's man.

"Lord Steppenwald! My lord! How long've you been in Pretor's Hill? The magistrate, he didn't tell me you'd be coming!"

"I've only just arrived, Bulrik, only just arrived! Good to see you, man! No need to tell old Drulane I'm here; he'll know soon enough, soon enough!"

Bulrik saluted. "Yes, my lord!"

Steppenwald indicated the other officers. "Keeping Pretor's Hill good and safe, I see, lad! Go on with your duties, then! Wouldn't want to be the cause of any mischief going unnoticed, eh?"

The lead officer saluted again. Steppenwald and Evan watched Bulrik and the others march off while Mardi continued her mental struggle. Bulrik had clearly heard nothing about the attempt on the knight and neither the king's man nor the veteran warrior had so much as hinted about it to Drulane's aide. She truly began to wonder if she had imagined the entire incident.

"And so," Steppenwald intoned when only the three of them remained. "I think I've done in this matter all I need do! Sir Wytherling, I hope you find your remaining time in Pretor's Hill to your fascination! A good day to you, paladin, a good day to you!" He tipped his hat to Mardi, smiling with teeth that reminded her of the dragon from her dreams. "And to you, fair lady! Best, I think, you forget this horrid little event, just as the rest of the town should . . . don't you agree, Sir Wytherling?"

Evan did not smile. "For her safety, yes, Lord Steppenwald."

192

"Capital! So glad, so very glad, you agree . . ." With that, the Promethean rider tugged hard on the spotted steed's reins, turning the great beast. As the Neulander horse shifted, Mardi for the first time noticed the elaborate cane hanging from the back of the saddle. The cane vanished from sight as Steppenwald's animal continued to turn, but, as fleeting as the glance had been, Mardi doubted that she could ever forget the crafted piece on the handle, the dragon with the mismatched eyes. She almost believed that those eyes had stared back at her.

The stallion trotted off in the direction of the magistrate's domain. Mardi continued to watch the dwindling figures, more and more experiencing a peculiar sense of detachment.

She felt a hand gently touch her shoulder. "Mardi . . ."

Starting, she turned to see Evan looking down at her with concern and compassion. He flinched when he realized he had frightened her.

"I'm sorry," Mardi immediately said. "My mind was elsewhere. Don't be angry with yourself!"

His features looked so worn, so tired, that she almost reached up to touch his cheek in the hope that it would give him some comfort. Only the fear that he might reject her action kept her from doing so. "I am angry with myself for other reasons, Mardi. You should not have been drawn into this. I have acted like a fool. He was correct about one thing; best you forget what happened here just now. Besides, I suspected even in the beginning that it would not end in my burning. He merely wanted to learn, possibly to drop the gauntlet, but—"

Her brow furrowed; her thoughts felt murky. Something had slipped away from her, but what? "What are you talking about, Evan?"

Now it became his turn to look confused, if only for a moment. "The mob? The stake?"

"Oh, the ones last night? Did they pursue you after you left me?"

His expression turned neutral. "You should get out of this

193

wind and wet mist, Mardi Sinclair. Nothing dire will happen today. After I leave you, I plan to return to my room, there to recoup my own strength for the days ahead."

"But I wanted to ask you—" The blond woman paused, not at all certain what she had wanted to ask. The entire day so far seemed mostly a blur.

Evan took her by the shoulders, touching her so lightly she wondered if he believed her made of glass. "You have not yet recovered from the night. Go home. Rest. Let sleep blanket your confusion."

Her head pounded as she turned from him. Rest sounded very good at the moment. Mardi wondered if she had caught ill from being out the night before. A small worry compared to Valentin and . . . and . . .

"Steppenwald . . ." A raging storm could have struck then and Mardi would not have noticed it. Within the space of less than a minute, she had all but forgotten what had just happened to Evan, all but forgotten the mob, the stake, and Daniel trying to set the bound knight ablaze. Equally curious, she remembered Steppenwald saying, "Best, I think, you forget..." And forget she had—at that exact moment.

Mardi felt cold.

She whirled about, catching Evan watching her. He frowned as she came toward him, tired eyes narrowing.

"Mardi. You should go home and rest—"

"Stop it!" The furious woman raised a hand, cutting him off from any protest. "Not this time. Not again. Not because either you or he said I should!"

"My lady—"

She walked up to him, only inches between them. This close, the gentlewoman almost faltered, but the resurrecting memories of how her town had suddenly turned mad gave her enough determination to press the knight. "He did something to me, Evan! He did something . . . I think . . . to everyone! Made them all go away, made them forget!"

"You are imagining—"

"I'm imagining nothing. Lord Steppenwald looked at everyone and they simply walked away. You can't deny that." She stared deep, looking beyond the weary eyes, demanding the attention of the man within. "He had power over all of us, Evan, even you."

The wind tore at their cloaks, threw their hair to the side. The knight finally blinked, then nodded slowly. "His power was not absolute . . . but strong."

"Is he a wizard, then? I didn't think that they existed any more!"

"He is a wizard . . . and something more, though I cannot put my finger on it." Evan pulled her nearer, his voice dropping to a whisper. "I would beg you to go running to Coramas if not for the fact that he comes from there. Mardi, you must stay far from him; he has already noted you with far too much interest. Almost as much interest as he has in me."

"But Lord Steppenwald is the king's man! You saw how he stopped the madness! He might—he might make an ally if you'd just explain the truth! If anyone would understand, it should be surely be him!"

"Him?" A humorless chuckle escaped the knight. He shook his head, briefly looking skyward. "Mardi Sinclair, you see the surface but not beneath it! You see the mask, but not the face!" The somber eyes focused squarely on her. "Mardi, your Lord Steppenwald not only had the power to end this scene of madness . . . he also had the power to create it."

"That can't be!"

His expression told her otherwise. "His timely rescue confirmed the suspicions I had. Lord Steppenwald has been here for at least two days, my lady; I have seen his horse and his trail. I sought to draw him out, see what he desired, but he turned my attempt into a thrust of his own, showing me that he, not I, held the advantage. He caused this sudden rage among your people, though I suspect he only stirred up what has been bubbling since Valentin made his move. In fact, I would not doubt that Steppenwald knows as much, if not more, than I about what is rapidly eating away at the soul of Pretor's Hill . . . and I fear he may be disinclined to do anything to stop it."

XI

RETURN TO VALENTIN

No one remembered. No one recalled.

The residents of Pretor's Hill went on with their lives, more evidence to Evan of Steppenwald's hold on these people. Only Mardi, who had already proved herself different than the rest, regained the memories. Evan did not even bother to see if the magistrate knew anything; if Steppenwald had complete control over anyone, it had to be Drulane.

Once again, Evan realized he had made several miscalculations. He had hoped Drulane of some use, but that would not be. And he failed to keep Mardi from becoming a part of this unholy war against the legacy of Novaris. Now Evan had underestimated this Steppenwald, did not even know what piece of the puzzle the man represented.

Initially, Evan had wondered if perhaps the gargantuan man might have been the sorcerer-king in disguise, but while something about Steppenwald vaguely reminded him of Novaris, other elements contradicted such a notion. At the same time Steppenwald certainly could be no pawn of Valentin. They had to be two distinct players with overlapping concerns . . . but what were those concerns and why here and now? Why had everything come together so timely, almost as if waiting for Evan himself to arrive?

A fearful notion occurred to him, one he had to verify quickly with the only source available to him.

It had taken some effort to persuade Mardi to return to her normal routine. At the moment, it appeared that Steppenwald meant her no harm—on the surface yet another contradiction—and the foul weather had grown so fierce that only the most determined were about. Even now the rain poured steadily down, limiting visibility to very short distances. The young woman had finally relented only because of the weather, and Evan prayed that it would continue to remain poor, for Mardi Sinclair would certainly come seeking him the moment it let up.

In the meantime, Evan had to deal with one certain matter . . . Valentin. He would have preferred to wait for the darkness, but Steppenwald's audacity had accelerated matters.

As he reached the steps of the church, Evan hesitated. He would have to make certain that Father Gerard did not interfere, and that would require actions for which the knight might never forgive himself. True, he already had centuries of sin upon his shoulders, but Evan hated especially the thought of causing harm to the priest. Father Gerard had been the only person other than Mardi to come to his aid and one of a handful of people besides the gentlewoman who had treated him without suspicion.

At the doors, he pulled free his sword, which he had retrieved after seeing Mardi to her home. Evan cast his gaze about the area, seeing no one near the church who might wonder at an armed figure entering. One tap of the sword's hilt against the doors caused them to open. The knight slipped inside, then not only bolted the door, but used a spell to seal the entrance as well.

He contemplated going straight to Valentin, but his experience with Mardi had taught Evan that nothing could be taken for granted. Moving silently through the church, Evan reached the door leading to the priest's personal chambers. Once more, he tapped on the door with the hilt of the glistening blade.

From within, Father Gerard started to utter a greeting, but his voice faltered as the door swung open without his aid. Evan gazed down at the kindly man, who sat perched at a simple desk, writing.

"I thought I'd bolted that door," the priest said, his brow furrowed. Then, remembering he had a visitor, Father Gerard rose, right hand outstretched. "Welcome, sir knight. Forgive my lapse of manner . . ."

Clearly the priest did not recall any better than the rest of the townsfolk what had earlier happened. Evan took that as a good sign; it meant Gerard was as susceptible as any. Lowering the sword, he reached out as if intending to grasp the priest's proffered hand.

The moment Father Gerard came within reach, the knight stretched forward, touching the priest on the chest. The balding man hesitated in confusion, giving Evan the moment he needed to draw the necessary symbol.

Gerard froze in midgesture.

Evan exhaled. "Forgive me, Father."

The spell would keep the priest in place for as long as Evan needed, and leave him with no memory of the visit.

He departed the chamber, heading to the entrance to Valentin's prison. Evan buried the sword in the stone, then impatiently waited. For all the magic surrounding its hidden existence, the opening crevice did not impress him at the moment. His only interest lay in the crimson knight and the mysterious representative from Coramas.

The guardian approached Evan, ready to rend him to pieces, but the graying warrior left the unfortunate creature in a state not unlike that of Father Gerard. Evan went on, noting this time that Valentin remained unsettlingly silent as his counterpart approached the chamber. As a precaution, Evan readied the sword for combat. One never knew what to expect with Valentin.

"A second visit so soon?" the crimson figure cooed. "Are we again dedicated comrades, stalwart friends?"

Valentin kept his head down, staring up at Evan from beneath his dark brow. The knowing smile that ever set the silver knight on edge remained fixed. The imprisoned figure leaned forward in his bonds, as if testing their strength.

"I would not have returned, Valentin, if I did not think present matters of interest to both of us. After all, you are dedicated to the legacy of your master, are you not?"

"As you were . . . once."

Evan refused to let the other goad him. "I have been thinking, Valentin, thinking about the timing. It has been so very long since Novaris, since Centuros, since the battle royal. All this time and yet the evil that you somehow spread only now comes to fruition and with a sudden swiftness."

"All good things come to those who wait," the ebony-bearded ghoul returned with a shake of the lance in his chest. "Your fat wizard probably said that at one point or another. Seems he spouted just about every cliché . . ."

Evan took a chance. "You have been waiting for me, have you not? Oh, the evil had already seeped in, but you stepped up matters only when I drew near. You have been waiting for me to return. Perhaps Novaris did not plan it that way, but you, Valentin, you did."

The dark knight chuckled. "Oh, yes, I've had nothing better to do with myself lo these many, many years but to wait for you, my dear friend. The anticipation kept me going all this time! How highly you still think of yourself!"

"Perhaps I am wrong, but I think not. In any case, all your plans, all your master's plans, may be for naught, Valentin, if Steppenwald has his way."

Evan waited, wanting to see the other's reaction to the casual use of the name. Valentin's expression did not shift, but the prisoner remained silent for a breath longer than necessary. "And what of Steppenwald?"

"You know him not, do you?"

"I know Steppenwald well enough. He visits now and then." The crimson warrior's tone remained neutral, neither revealing the lie of Valentin's words nor the truth of them. "You've become acquainted with him, I see."

"He acquainted himself with me. His interest in this region is great; I think he has plans of his own for it and its people."

"Steppenwald will do what Steppenwald will do . . . just as I do, Evan."

"You must find it like old times to deal with him. He reminds me much of Haggad. Thinner than a ghost with the mind of a devil."

Valentin shrugged as best he could. "There may be some blood link between them."

The imprisoned knight had neither corrected nor even mocked Evan's outrageous description of the king's man. Obviously Valentin did not know Steppenwald, probably had never even sensed the huge stranger's presence. Evan stored the knowledge away, trying now to see if he could pry any other information out of his counterpart.

"He seems an ally not to be trusted, though. I would venture to say that some of the things I have seen him do would hardly be in keeping with Novaris's legacy . . . nor your dreams as well."

"He'll not overstep his bounds." Had there been a slight hint of anxiety in Valentin's tone? The dark-haired figure straightened, the better to meet Evan Wytherling's gaze. "And he can certainly be trusted better than some I knew, eh? There've been some who would stab their closest comrade in the back."

"Are you drawing your powers from the bones of Grimyr, Valentin?"

He had hoped that the sudden question would cause his counterpart to momentarily drop the mask. Valentin, however, merely cocked his head and smiled anew. "Why not ask Grimyr? He could answer that as well as I."

Again the nonsensical answer. Valentin would have him chase out again to the mound to see if any residual magic remained in the buried, decaying carcass of the huge, fire-black beast. Evan silently cursed; he would gain no more here. The most important fact he had at least verified. Valentin did not know Steppenwald and that alone gave the silver knight some satisfaction. For all that the crimson warrior had given Evan to ponder, now Valentin would have to worry about a possible wild card in the deck.

"Perhaps I will," Evan returned with just a hint of flippancy. "When I do, I shall give him your regards, Valentin, just as I will to Steppenwald."

Evan turned and left, picturing the pale, bearded prisoner's reserve at last slip a little as Valentin contemplated the repercussions of Steppenwald's arrival. Valentin would not be able to rest now . . . and that, in the end, would serve Evan.

No words of mockery followed him as he left the chamber, but before he could reach the jagged steps, Valentin called out after him. "Evan! I would speak a moment more with you . . . After all, what more do either of us have but the other?"

Against his better judgment, he did as the crimson knight requested. Valentin watched him with eyes filled not with vengeance and madness, but something more unsettling that Evan could not name.

"We can end this now," the chained warrior whispered. "We can end the battle, end the feud."

"Give me Novaris, then."

"I can't do that!" Valentin spat out. "For all I know, he may be dead by now. It's been far too long since I last saw him. Oh, his spells live on, but then, you know how far in advance the cowled one often planned."

Evan did. Novaris clearly laid out the false path to the West even before the great battle just in case he lost and needed to send his enemies off on the wrong track. "I must find him, Valentin. You know that."

"You can have something just as good here, Evan. All you need to do is kill me. Paulo Centuros could not do it, but you, deep down, know the key . . . remember?" He twisted so that the broken lance thrust through his chest formed a line of contact directly between them. This close, the silver knight could see how labored Valentin's breathing was; the weapon had pierced not only the heart but the side of one lung as well. It amazed Evan that his counterpart could exist in this state even with magic to keep him from death. Evan started to reach out, whether to try to remove the lance or drive it deeper, he could not say. Valentin held his breath.

Let not the war be lost in order to achieve an easy victory in one battle . . .

He silently cursed Centuros as the wizard's words ripped through his brain. Evan pulled back his hand, immediately turning from Valentin for fear the other knight could see the agony evinced on his face.

"A plague on you, then!" the crimson figure roared. "Twice now asked and twice now rejected, there'll never be an offer of peace again between us!"

"I know." Evan stalked away, trying to maintain an appearance of determination. Inside his mind, though, he replayed again and again what would happen if he finally put an end to Valentin's suffering. He could have saved Pretor's Hill with one swift, decisive act . . . but no. The ghost of Paulo Centuros had whipped him back as usual. The thrice-cursed wizard had decreed the path his hunter would follow and Evan could not veer from it, whatever the consequences.

"On your head all their lives, then!"

Evan Wytherling reached the steps, hurrying up them in order to escape the condemnations. The last thing he heard was Valentin's laughter again, but this time tinged with bitterness and regret. Even after Evan had reached the top and sealed once more the path to the crimson knight, he could hear Valentin's words and laugh echoing in his thoughts.

I might have ended it here, at least, with minimal danger to the innocents . . . What Valentin had said had been partially true; Evan did think he knew—or rather, remembered—the secret to ending the other knight's agony . . . but to commit the act would leave him without the only link he had to Novaris.

Evan released the spell on the priest and the church entrance. Father Gerard would go to his bed and sleep, waking in the morning with no knowledge of the visit. Everything had to look normal even now, despite the encroaching evil.

With great caution he slowly opened one of the tall entrance doors. The endless rain poured down, which meant he faced little danger of some passing inhabitant noticing his stealthy exit. The wind howled yet stronger—if such a thing could be believed—

causing Evan to pull the collar of his cloak tighter even as he stepped out into the foul elements.

The baleful gaze of the knight's bone-pale steed met his eyes.

The harsh rain seemed to little touch the animal, but the wind madly tossed the creature's mane about, making the locks resemble a nest of writhing serpents. The creature snorted as Evan neared, possibly impatient. The human swore under his breath; he hoped no one had looked out of their homes. No one could possibly miss so huge an animal even in this weather.

"You should not be here," he muttered. "I know you dislike the stables, but that cannot be helped. We are among others now."

A pair of colorless orbs stared him down. Evan shook his head, knowing that the creature would do as he liked whatever his rider's hope. Still, the beast rarely displayed himself so without some reason.

"Is there something amiss?" His thoughts went to Steppenwald, who even Valentin did not know. He had assumed that the mysterious representative from Coramas would not act for now, having satisfied himself with showing Evan what power he wielded.

The steed turned to the side, indicating that Evan should mount. That could mean only a journey of some distance. The knight leapt onto the saddle, knowing that the pallid steed would not act frivolously. Both were bound to this quest.

They started off at a slow but steady pace, the beast clearly trying not to draw any more attention. A little late for that, Evan thought. Whatever had agitated his equine companion, it had to be of significance.

And then, as they turned in the direction leading to Grimyr's burial mound, he saw the reason.

Lightning crackled in the distance, but lightning flying skyward, not to the earth. Those who did not know to watch might not have realized the reverse direction of the bolts, but Evan's senses had been sharpened by too many decades of running afoul of magic.

"Steppenwald, do you think?" he whispered.

The horse shook his mane as if tossing off the building moisture, but Evan understood that his question had been answered.

An awful thought struck him. "Novaris?"

This time, the animal simply stared ahead, neither denying nor agreeing with the choice. Novaris. As good or bad a guess as any. Whatever the source, the location Evan knew too well. It had to be somewhere near the vicinity of the mound. Perhaps that had been why Valentin had more than once insisted that his rival go speak to the dead dragon. Either the sorcerer-king or some other wielder of power had to be making use of the inherent magic that still lingered in the scales and bones of the reptilian leviathan.

Valentin might have had a puppet of some sort to do the physical work his chains forbade him. Steppenwald, too, might have a pawn among the townsfolk. Such manipulation was certainly not unheard of; too often sorcerers and the like used certain of the unTalented as conduits. In the end, those mortal folk generally paid the highest of prices, burned from within by powers they could not normally wield.

Whatever the source of the magical display, Evan had to seek it out. Only then would he perhaps be able to untangle some part of the web draped over Pretor's Hill, a web already grown too vast and intricate.

Mardi Sinclair stared at the rain, wondering how she could have let the knight persuade her to stay here. Instead of finding relief, the gentlewoman felt only claustrophobia as the walls, the town, and the rain closed in on her.

The tableau in the square remained fixed in her memory, especially Lord Steppenwald's part in it. Try as she might, she could not push his face away. He had been a part of the town's life for as long as she could recall, the hand of the king reaching out to govern his farthest subjects. Yet, Rundin's monarchs did not look favorably on magic and the latest certainly would have chosen no man who wielded it the way Steppenwald did.

Of course, the king might not have realized that his representative had such arcane skills, but Mardi had at last come to the conclusion that perhaps Steppenwald might not even be what he appeared. Perhaps the people here only believed he served the kingdom. More likely, the elegantly clad giant served only himself.

Did the magistrate know? Surely not. For all his faults, Drulane would never have been a part of this, Mardi felt certain. In fact, the more she thought about it, the more she pondered how he would react if he heard that the man he had served for so long might be a fraud, a threat to Rundin.

She rose, determined that he would know. Evan might not be willing to trust anyone, but Drulane cared about his town; he would take action once he heard the truth.

A few moments later, Mardi scurried through the downpour, hooded cloak wrapped around her. The storm forced her to move slowly and more than once she nearly slipped on wet stone. Only one other person crossed her path during the trek, a drenched figure who hurried into one of the homes near the magistrate's sanctum. The rest of the townsfolk knew enough to stay out of the rain.

Mardi reached her destination just as the intense rain began to penetrate her cloak. Shivering, she started up the steps.

A pair of hooded, short-tempered guards, one heavyset and the other barely out of his youth, halted her at the entrance.

"Who's that there?" the heavyset one growled.

"Please!" Mardi pulled back her hood a little. "Mistress Mardina Sinclair to see the magistrate!"

Despite her attempt at formality, the guards did not take her seriously. "The magistrate's at his meal," the younger one muttered. "You can see him during normal hours tomorrow."

"It is a matter of import!"

Both guards were armed with swords and while Mardi did

not believe they would harm her, the younger officer did raise his slightly, no doubt hoping to discourage the newcomer from disturbing their master. However, his companion suddenly blinked, peering closer at Mardi.

"Sinclair . . . You're the money man's niece . . ."

"I am Master Casperin's niece, yes."

He looked at his younger counterpart, a crooked smile momentarily playing. "You know, Alfrid . . . her . . ."

Recognition dawned in the face of the other officer. "Oh, the one himself fancies—"

His partner cut him off with a glare. Mardi thanked the heavens that the dark day and her hood helped mask some of her embarrassment. Arriving at a time like this, she suspected she had just started a rumor she would have to suffer for some weeks to come.

"Go right in, then," the bulky officer told her, eyes innocent.

"Thank you." With as much dignity as she could muster, the gentlewoman entered. As the doors closed behind her, Mardi could hear the pair talking. Embarrassment overtaken by repulsion, she rushed on, ignoring the other guards in the corridor.

Despite what the sentries had told her, Mardi did not find the gnarled figure eating, but rather staring out a window at the rain. He turned as she entered, acting as if he had expected her all along.

"My dear Mardina, a bright spot on an otherwise oppressive day. What, though, could bring you to me in such horrific weather?" A cynical smile briefly crossed his elderly features. "I know it could not be what I would choose it to be . . ."

For both their sakes she did not respond to his last statement. "Magistrate, I think you are the only one I can turn to."

"I? What about Sir Wytherling? Surely he better fits the roll of savior of damsels in distress than a twisted old man. Failing that, you could turn to the irrepressible, younger Taran, although I'd hoped your tastes better than that."

"Magistrate! This is serious!" She rushed up to him, almost taking his arm. "I shouldn't have come here, but you're the only one other than Evan who might be able to do something!"

"I'm honored. What might this task be?"

"Magistrate . . . Master Drulane . . . do you know what happened earlier this day? Do you know how Evan Wytherling was nearly burned alive . . . and Lord Steppenwald's part in it?"

Drulane's eyes widened, then narrowed, as Mardi spoke. He did not answer her questions, instead leading her to a chair. The magistrate chose not to seat himself, looming over his guest like an inquisitor. He coughed long, then, recapturing his breath, said, "I do not and if it were anyone other than you I would give it no thought! Please . . . tell me this fantastic tale."

She did, leaving out no detail. Curiously, Drulane seemed not at all surprised save when she mentioned Steppenwald and the belief that he had played a hand in orchestrating, not ending, the foul incident. He asked no questions and Mardi began to wonder if the crooked man simply humored her.

His first words after she had finished her story set aside that concern. "Worse than I could've feared," he muttered, half speaking to himself. "Worse than I could've ever feared. Madness, indeed. Yet . . . Lord Steppenwald? The king's representative? I've worked with the man for twenty . . . is it thirty years . . . no . . . he would be older than he is . . . or would that explain it . . ."

"Master Drulane . . . have you seen Lord Steppenwald today? He rode off in the direction of your office."

"His lordship has not visited me . . . I think. You've left me curious now." The magistrate seemed particularly unsettled, as if putting together past matters and finding that they all had a common thread.

Mardi recalled how she had nearly forgotten her own encounter with Steppenwald. Could the same have happened to Drulane?

"Where is Evan Wytherling now, Mardina?"

She fought to hide her sudden anxiety. The magistrate evidently knew nothing about Valentin, either. Should she tell him? Evan clearly had decided that Drulane did not need to know, but should his decision be hers?

"He's away." Even as she replied, she knew he would suspect her vague answer.

"Away . . ." Drulane slowly paced the area between the window and his desk. "An inopportune time. I would've liked to have questioned him on this matter, my dear Mardina."

The magistrate fixed his watery eyes on her own. Uncomfortable under his gaze, Mardi glanced toward the far corner of Drulane's office, where the lamps lit the chamber least.

She blinked. Did she see a figure in the shadows? "Who is that?"

Drulane coughed, then eyed the dark corner. "What are you talking about, Mardina? There's no one there."

For a moment, what he said rang true. No one stood in the shadows. However, when Mardi blinked, the shape reformed, a monumental figure clad in elegant attire and holding a cane. Even obscured much by the darkness, the figure could be only one person.

"All right, then, Drulane," rumbled the watcher. "Cease the protests."

To her horror, the elder magistrate froze, arms at his side. He looked as if he needed to cough, yet somehow held back.

The tap of the cane against the floor made her turn back to the shadowed man. He doffed his broad-rimmed hat, which had all but covered the upper half of his face. The silver of his hair matched that in his trim beard. "Sharp eyes, my dear lady Sinclair, sharp eyes."

Lord Steppenwald moved toward her. He was clad much like she had last seen him, even down to the jeweled gloves. Once more the mismatched eyes of the dragon-head cane briefly snared her attention, almost alive.

The king's man raised the cane up, bringing Mardi's gaze back to his face. Narrow, silver-gray eyes narrowed yet further. "Beautiful, strong of mind. An enchanting combination . . . at any other time."

"Lord S-steppenwald . . ." Mardi Sinclair tried to recover. "It is good to see you, my—"

"No, young woman, I daresay it's not at all good to see me, not at all good."

She started for the doors. Steppenwald raised the cane high. The eyes flashed and suddenly the entryway glowed crimson. Mardi hesitated, certain that to touch the ensorcelled doors would invite strong repercussions.

"Beautiful, strong-willed, and intelligent," the human leviathan murmured. "Wise not to touch, my lady . . . oh, and don't even hope for the guards; they know even less what's happening than my dear friend the magistrate."

Mention of Drulane made Mardi glance at the older man again. Despite clear discomfort, Drulane stood as straight and still as possible.

"Dear me, dear me!" Steppenwald almost sounded truly sympathetic. "What was I thinking, what was I thinking . . ."

At a gesture from the bearded aristocrat, Drulane abruptly turned and walked to his desk. The magistrate seated himself, then leaned forward slightly. Although his expression remained empty, Mardi thought his body relaxed a little.

"Now, then, to you." Steppenwald raised the cane. "Don't make me fetch you, my lady Sinclair . . ."

The mismatched eyes flashed. The young woman immediately stepped forward, stopping when she stood just out of arm's reach of the towering figure. Evan's revelations concerning Steppenwald's part in the attack continuously spun through her head. What horror did he now plan for her?

"I expected the paladin to be able to override a simple spell of forgetting, but certainly not you, little one. Oh, once, perhaps, but then after our brief glance at one another, you refused, refused, mind you, to forget my little test for our friend in silver. I would've left you alone even then, but here you are once more, attempting to play havoc with my carefully arranged masterpiece!"

"I don't have any idea what you mean!"

210

"Probably half-true, but unfortunately, half-false as well." He leaned forward until but a few inches were left between their faces, the silver-gray eyes filled with a coldness that Steppenwald's hardy form and cultured manner attempted futilely to belie. Here stood a man who could have let Evan burn alive if it suited his purposes. Here stood a man who had complete mastery over Mardi's life. "I find you very intriguing, very intriguing."

From within, she suddenly felt an intense buildup, a surge of fury. Mardi fought it down, fearful of what Lord Steppenwald might do in return. Her stomach churned with the effort.

The gargantuan wizard must have noticed something in her expression, for his eyes shifted. "Something ails you, my dear? Can't have that, can't have that."

He snapped his fingers and an immense, padded chair, which the suffering gentlewoman realized must have been designed with him in mind, slid over behind her, nearly bowling her into it. Mardi tried to regain her balance, but the eyes of the dragon suddenly bloomed before her as Steppenwald thrust the head of the cane toward her. She fell back, landing in the soft, almost suffocating chair.

"Better now, better now . . ." The bearded aristocrat leaned on the cane with one giant hand, a jovial smile that would have been pleasant on any other person spread across his wide features. "I think it's time we got to know one another, Lady Sinclair! I knew your family, I did. Your uncle, to be sure, a man of many monetary talents. Your mother, too, if I recall." He tugged on his mustache. "I begin to suspect I should have gotten to know her better. Somehow I feel she was a part of this . . . perhaps still is."

She steeled herself. "I've nothing to tell you!"

"Oh, but no, no, my dear! You've much to tell me, much to tell me . . ." With a snap of his fingers, a narrower chair scurried over to his left. Steppenwald planted a boot in the seat cushion, causing the unfortunate bit of furniture to squeak loudly under the crushing weight. "We shall talk of battles past and battles still in play! We shall talk of knights errant and erring knights! Most of all, we shall talk of Sir Evan Wytherling, a paladin most in shadow, most in shadow, and the tales, true and false, he may have told his lady fair . . ."

XII

GHOSTS OF THE MOUND

The bone-pale steed raced through the rising woods seemingly oblivious to the storming weather. Evan Wytherling, not so fortunate, held on to the reins with one hand while he sought to shield his face with the other. He wished that he had been allowed the time to completely clad himself for battle, but the damnable steed had insisted on the need for urgency and with that Evan could not argue.

The thunder brought back ghosts of the battle, great war spells cast by the vying wizards and sorcerers. Half-glimpsed shadows in the dark woods reminded him of the death that had lurked around every corner during the fight and, it seemed, lurked even to this day. The drenched knight saw no sign of the lupine creatures, but he did not doubt that they were somewhere near.

He had his sword, though, his sword, his wits, and the cursed animal beneath him. Evan had survived equipped with much less during other heinous encounters, and yet, as they approached the region of Grimyr's final resting place, he could not help but wish that Centuros and Pretor rode behind him. Magic and steel; Evan would need both at his back.

Occasionally lightning flashed, but mostly of the mundane variety. Now and then, though, one of the wicked earth-borne bolts touched the heavens, resurrecting his anxieties.

Is that you, Novaris? Have I found you at last? He imagined the gaunt, cowled figure, arms raised dramatically, drawing forth the residue of magic still remaining in the rotted corpse of the dragon. In truth, though, it seemed more likely that the sorcerer-king would be nowhere to be found, that this could be yet another wild-goose chase . . . or a trap.

Evan glanced back in the direction of the town. He hated having left Mardi alone back there, but if she followed his advice and stayed home, she would be safe. So long as Steppenwald did not know that the gentlewoman had broken free from his mesmerism, Evan would not have to worry about her.

Still, she had a habit of being too independent . . .

Lightning crackled nearby, splitting a tree, which nearly fell across his path. Evan's steed did not hesitate, racing as swiftly as the wind toward his destination despite the fact that the bolt that had almost hit the pair had come not from above but from before them.

Evan drew the jeweled blade, certain that someone or something already expected him.

Perhaps a hundred yards or so from the dragon's mound, the baleful animal at last halted to a slow trot. The knight noted his mount's wariness as they approached the vicinity, almost as if the horse sensed something he could not.

"What is it?" Evan whispered.

The damnable steed's only reply came in a dismissive flick of the ears. Evan frowned, at last peering out into the wet, foggy gloom for answers.

Someone whispered.

He turned in the saddle, seeking the speaker, only to be snared by another voice coming from the opposite direction. Both spoke unintelligibly, but with tones of urgency.

A pale figure moved through the trees, seemingly unconcerned by either the downpour or the lightning. The knight leaned forward, squinting. It took Evan a moment to recognize the fur-clad form of an ax-man from Tepis—a warrior from the battle some two centuries before. The fur had been stained by something dark and the figure's head wobbled as if not entirely attached. No living being this, but rather some specter wandering the earth.

Despite his mount's disagreement, he forced the animal toward the murky figure. What part this apparition played Evan did not know. He grew tired of unanswered mystery after unanswered mystery—

The ashen steed drew up short as a veiled, feminine figure in armor burst forward from the brush, waving her sword. She made not a sound and when the horse rose up and kicked at the horned helm of the attacker, his hooves went through her. She continued on, one of Haggad's lithe and deadly Knights of the Veil, swinging at foes Evan could not see.

He shivered, the ghosts of memory a faint thing compared to this. The worn knight shifted his gaze and through rain-drenched eyes watched as his most ancient nightmares more and more took on form and fury. From the mists emerged a Wallmyrian archer, his gut spilled open by a sword, readying his bow for another volley. The empty stare of death greeted Evan when he sought the man's eyes.

Beyond the archer, a knight in old Rundin wear straggled along, one leg twisted, armor soaked in blood, and half his head and helm missing.

And in the background, the whispers and the thunder of the storm gave way to the mournful wail of battle horns.

A bolt of lightning from the vicinity of the mound struck the earth nearby, startling man and mount and briefly illuminating the area for a mile around. In that instant of light, Evan Wytherling beheld a sight so blood-freezing that he nearly turned and fled, whatever the consequences to his tarnished honor and his cursed quest.

The dead had come in force to replay their roles in the great battle.

They formed from mist, from rain, from thin air. Elfin warriors with skin paler than even in life marched toward the mountains, some without limbs, some without heads, some crawling along with only one hand to push them forward. Trolls pincushioned with longbow shafts tottered toward them, grotesque faces made more so by death. A scorched and mangled skeleton swung at an almost perfectly preserved Rundin warrior.

From above came the roar of a dragon. Evan immediately looked up, but saw nothing but the overcast heaven. He returned his gaze to the ground just in time to notice one ghost in particular, a ghost who stared *back* . . . no mean feat as the wraith's massive head lay cradled in his arm.

"Come to play, boy?" sneered the bony, snow-eyed visage. In his other hand he waved a wicked, toothed sword stained with dried blood. "We've waited long for you . . ."

Evan fought to control his mounting distress as he greeted the foul apparition in turn. "Hello, General."

"Meek as a kitten! You've been away from good bloodshed far too long, boy! No more fire in your gut . . . just water!" The rail-thin specter tapped his steel-gray breastplate where a dozen or more heavy swords had been driven into his torso. "Look at me, boy! I don't even have a gut anymore and yet I'm still more alive than you!" The gaunt face cracked into a skeletal smile again. "Why don't you come down and play a little? I'll get the fire going in you again . . . before I split your gullet . . ."

Control yourself, Evan urged. The macabre figure before him could not hurt the knight; none of these apparitions could. They were phantasms called up by latent magic seeping from the cairn of Grimyr. At worst, they might steer him toward madness if Evan gave them substance with his fear. Even the monstrous figure before him, one of those best guaranteed to strike at his innermost being, did not really exist as a threat. The veteran knight had faced far more dangerous ghosts and knew the difference. "You are long dead, General Haggad. Go back to your rest."

"But I'm not done with this world yet, boy . . . and not with you, either. You owe for a lot of deaths." The wraith held his nearly hairless head up high, the better for Evan to see the soulless eyes, the outline of the bone beneath the very thin layer of dead flesh. "You owe Novaris, especially."

The silver knight's skin tingled. Evan pulled quickly on the reins, trying to urge his mount elsewhere. The horse obeyed without argument, perhaps sensing the same danger that his rider had.

A bolt struck the drenched earth a scant distance from them.

The force threw the stunned crusader from his horse. Evan heard the animal shriek, then he himself cried out as he bounced against rock and wood. His outfit did little to cushion the blow; he doubted that even his full armor would have aided. The stunned knight rolled forward, unable to stop and yet somehow still managing to hold on to his weapon.

Another bolt struck, ripping open the earth and unleashing a new element to the storm already raging, a torrential rain of dirt and stone. Clumps of dirt pelted Evan as he tried to stop himself. A crevice opened before him and the knight nearly tumbled into it, but at the last moment Evan managed to drive the tip of his sword into the remaining ground. He held on and wiped his eyes clear, finding himself staring into a black chasm that seemed to go on forever.

The rain continued to torment him, but no new bolt struck. Gasping, Evan pushed himself up to his knees, looking for Haggad. The ghost had vanished. All the ghosts had vanished, as had his horse. Laying his blade on his knees, the bedraggled warrior pulled off one muddied glove, put two fingers in his mouth, and let loose a high whistle. A moment later, he heard whinnying, but from impossibly far away.

Forcing himself to his feet, Evan again surveyed the region. The phantom warriors had indeed vanished, but somehow he knew that he had not seen the last of them.

A lupine howl cut through the storm, a howl answered immediately by one just like it, then another, then another, and another still. From all sides.

Evan immediately whistled again, but once more the reply came from too far away. The shadowy steed should have been able to reach his rider by now, and that they still remained separated by so much distance indicated that something interfered. Estimating the direction from which the horse's call had come, the mud-soaked knight trudged on, sword at the ready for whatever he would next face.

The howls grew nearer. Evan picked up his pace. He suspected the creatures would not be so easy to deal with this time, not with the numbers that he estimated hunted him and certainly not with so much power radiating from the vicinity of the mound. As with the wraiths, the wolves were clearly tied to Grimyr's tomb.

Thinking of that, Evan paused. Through the abilities Centuros had bequeathed upon him, he found he did sense some evidence of Novaris's magic, but it still seemed too faint, too old. The sorcerer-king must have set this trap long, long ago, which meant Evan had a good chance of outwitting it; the spell had to stay true to how it had been cast, unlike a thinking creature.

A more opportune decision Evan could not have made, for just then, a dark form with claws and teeth leapt upon him, humanlike eyes glaring into his own. Knight and beast rolled once, then Evan kicked at the lower torso of his attacker, freeing himself. He brought the blade up, cutting into the stomach region. As before, no blood, no organs, spilled forth, yet the creature howled as if dealt a deadly blow, then, with a sigh, evaporated.

By now they had to know that to face his sword directly meant their doom and yet still they most often tried to charge him. Did they not fear the weapon?

From both his left and right came a new pair seemingly forming out of thin air. Swinging the sword wide with both hands, Evan Wytherling severed the head of one monster, then cut across the chest of the second. The first fell, fading even as it hit the drenched and ruined ground, but the second staggered toward its intended prey as if driven by a force it could not fight. Evan felt little pride as he finished the wounded shadow beast, his adversary moving so clumsily that the knight simply thrust his jeweled blade through it to the hilt.

The hair on his neck rose as shadows in every direction separated from the surrounding trees and moved in on him. Evan glanced around, saw that he stood surrounded by more than a dozen of the murky demons. Vulnerable they might be, but sheer numbers would tell a sorrowful end to his tale after all, unless . . .

He had never cast the spell with so little preparation, but all his years of working the wizard's magic had to help him now. Muttering the words of power under his breath, Evan spun in a circle, dragging the tip of his sword over the earth. In the wake of the blade's path, a faint blue line of light grew into being.

Perhaps realizing what he intended, one of the beasts leapt toward the remaining open area. Evan muttered faster, completing the spell, then tugged the tip of the sword until it touched the beginning of the blue loop.

Airborne, the lupine monstrosity could not halt its attack. It fell across the glowing boundary that raggedly encircled the desperate knight. No cry. No gore. No ash. Its entire body simply evaporated inch by inch as the spell's victim crossed.

A second creature pulled back just before it would have committed itself. One of the half-seen monsters snarled, others following. They jostled as if trying to urge some of their members forward, but no one desired to achieve the fate of the first. As willing as they were to directly chance his sword, they clearly saw no value in throwing themselves uselessly at such a barrier.

Protected for the moment, Evan fell to one knee, gasping again for breath. Still the rain poured down, giving him little respite. Nonetheless, the knight took what rest he could get, ever, of course, keeping his eye on the beasts.

This had turned out to be a very personal trap, he realized, but one that should have been beyond Valentin's abilities. That Valentin could affect the town, Evan understood. The crimson warrior lay imprisoned directly underneath its center . . . and Evan now recalled at least in part the pattern Pretor's Hill itself created. The town's layout formed a sign of power, one that amplified a spell cast in its center. No coincidence, that. Novaris's hand surely had prompted the early settlers to assist in building the method of their own destruction.

Still, could the spell have been so well set that Valentin could reach out even here and cause such disaster for his adversary? The only other explanation seemed less likely. For all his attention to detail, even the sorcerer-king would have been hard-pressed to put together such an elaborate spell designed to last centuries and strike only when Evan appeared. Surely Novaris, if he lived, had not been so fearful of one determined yet weary warrior?

Questions and more questions, none of which he should have been presently wasting his time on. The creatures would not simply stand and watch; they were more than animal. Evan had a disturbing feeling that he knew more about them than he thought he did. He sensed a familiarity that went deep, went back to a time before he had been sent upon this endless quest.

At that moment, the faint voices began again . . . but this time there were words that Evan could make out.

whywhywhywhywhywhy . . .

lostlostlostlostlost . . .

betrayedbetrayedbetrayedbetrayed . . .

lostlostlostlostlost . . .

whywhywhywhywhywhy . . .

The sword slipped from Evan Wytherling's frozen hand. He knew not the names, but he knew the voices. They were voices from the war belonging to men he had once fought beside in that previous life. Evan clutched his ears, not wanting to hear those voices, be reminded that their owners had all perished in that battle, their lives, so many lives, wasted because of the ambitions of one sorcerer.

Nothing shielded his ears from the voices, though. They seeped through his clenched hands, ripped into the cloth of the hood of his cloak, repeating endlessly words of condemnation.

The lupine hunters crouched close, possibly waiting to see if through madness Evan himself might cross the barrier.

"This is not real," he muttered at last, almost throwing the words at the watching pack. "This is a spell of yours, Novaris, a spell to make your enemies do themselves in! I am stronger than it!"

Yet no sooner had he uttered his defiance when the next and even more foul step of his torture commenced, for the indistinct faces of the furred horrors surrounding him shifted, grew somewhat identifiable. They were not, however, the faces of beasts, but rather those of men, lost men, dead men. Slaughtered, left for the carrion crows. Each and every one of them.

Evan knew them all by face, if not by name.

And each mouthed the same words over and over . . .

why . . . lost . . .

betrayal . . .

He shut his eyes, trying to will the faces and words away. Memories welled up within, adding to his desperate situation. Faces Evan had not recalled in decades passed through his mind. Bloody skirmishes long fought replayed themselves. The whispered words continued on in the background, now accompanied by the low, consistent beat of war drums and the mournful wail of horns signaling the doomed into battle.

Despite his strong struggles, Evan Wytherling found himself slipping deeper into despair. He had never imagined reaching such a point and certainly not here. Emotions he had cast aside for so very long poured forth, the guilt of two hundred years at last seeking its due in full. The stricken knight grabbed for the hilt of the sword, uncertain at that moment whether he needed it to fend off foes or put an end to his own miserable condition.

From beyond the circle came a familiar cry, one that ripped through his despair, tore him from his descent into relentless guilt. Evan looked up in time to see a massive, pale phantom burst through the startled creatures, turning them once more into shadow beasts, not condemning ghosts. Great hooves struck out at the nearest, sparks of magic flying as the lupine horror fell back, stunned.

Reaching forward with the sword, Evan muttered a few words, eradicating the protective circle. The massive stallion charged up to him, turning so that the human could immediately leap onto the saddle. Evan did, then clutched at the reins. One of the beasts sought to pull him back down, but the knight's mount turned again, enabling Evan to strike. His attacker fell back, one arm severed.

The pack reformed, pressing them from two sides. Forced to higher ground, the pallid steed had to fight for footing. Evan noticed burns on the animal's sides, evidence that the steed's attempts to reach him had been fraught with danger. Disturbing enough how quickly this trap had worn the veteran warrior to the core; now Evan saw he could not even rely on the full strength of his companion.

The horse stumbled, something he rarely did. Evan nearly slipped off. He peered around them, trying to judge the landscape. They were within but a few yards of Grimyr's mound.

Another grim notion occurred to him, one that risked much but might save them. Limited though his own skills at magic might be, the tricks Centuros had taught him could still help Evan reverse his dire situation. Given a few moments' respite, he believed he could seize control of the magic spell and turn it. During that attempt he risked leaving himself open to attack, but that might be unavoidable.

Tugging hard on the reins, he steered his mount toward the dragon mound just as the shadows closed. Kicking at the nearest fiends, the animal reluctantly obeyed. Evan himself did not entirely like his choice of action but felt it best. They were already being herded farther and farther from safety.

In the rain the mound almost took on the shadowy shape of the great leviathan buried within. How Grimyr would have roared with anger if he had known that someday Evan would try to use what remained of the dragon's magic against the very power Grimyr had once served. As for Valentin, Evan realized that this might be his chance to put an end to the crimson knight's foul curse. Surely his suspicions had to be correct; Valentin had to be drawing power from this same source through his ancient link to Grimyr.

He sensed the presence of magic, a presence much stronger

than during his previous visit. The moment they reached the edge of the mound, Evan leapt off, landing several feet up its side. The baleful steed snorted, then turned to a defensive position. The horse understood that he had to buy his rider precious time.

The soaked knight climbed farther up, trying to locate the highest point of the mound. He heard the nearby growls of the shadowy beasts and the defiant snort of his horse. Evan knew he did not have long; the stallion could not take them all on.

At last finding a satisfactory position atop the dragon's tomb, Evan prepared to drive his blade into the wet earth. He did not intend opening a passage to the rotting remains of the reptilian beast; instead the sword would act as a focus, as a way of drawing what magic there was to Evan's hand.

"Grasping at straws, boy?"

The suddenness of the voice nearly made the knight stumble backward off the mound. Regaining his footing, he glared at the apparition of General Haggad, who stood but a few feet to his left. The general's cadaverous head smiled from the crook of his arm. As usual, the bloodied, jagged blade remained a fixture in the ghost's other hand.

"You are becoming tiresome, General."

"And you are becoming desperate and pathetic, boy. Give in to your guilt. Give in to the past. This isn't the course you want to take."

Evan kept his expression masked, although inside his anxiety swelled. Haggad could be no less devious in death as in life. "You are nothing but the product of a madman's spell, General. You've failed to drive me mad, so you might as well go."

"I'd like to cut you wide open," the snow-eyed ghoul commented cheerfully, "to see how yellow your blood's become . . ."

The silver knight turned from him. "I have no more time for you, General."

"Then you'll have no more head, boy!"

Evan twisted around, but too late. Haggad's fiendish blade

cut through the air in line with the paladin's throat. Sheer reflex caused Evan to reach up with one hand in a futile attempt to stop the jagged blade, but the general shifted, bringing his wicked weapon over.

The blade sliced completely through Evan's neck.

He gasped, waiting for the blood, waiting for oblivion. Yet, no blood seeped onto his hand, no darkness swallowed him. Slowly the truth dawned on Evan; the sword had not beheaded him. General Haggad's weapon had been as insubstantial as the specter himself.

The wraith laughed, a mocking, chilling sound. The body of the general shook so hard the head nearly toppled from the crook of the arm. "He said I'd be able to have some sport with you even though I couldn't touch you, boy! What a gullible little fool still after all these years!"

Though breathless, heart pounding, Evan composed himself again, realizing that Haggad's tactics had been designed to stall him, nothing more. Restoring the grimness to his features, the knight once more prepared himself for the spell. He lifted his sword. He could do this. He knew enough from Centuros to turn the evil on itself.

"I wouldn't do that if I were you, boy! He wouldn't like that!"

"Who?" Evan mocked, despite his efforts to remain indifferent. "Who? Valentin? Novaris?"

"Novaris? The Master's long gone from here, Wytherling, and Valentin, loyal that he is, is a mad dog, to be sure! No, I mean himself, boy! You know best not to disturb the dead . . ."

Evan reminded himself that he spoke only to a projection, that General Haggad stood there as only the simplest of ghosts. Some could do physical harm, but Haggad could only taunt, pretend. He had no real power over the knight save what Evan gave him . . . and Evan would give no more.

"Your games are over, General," Evan said as he focused on his sword. "Go back to being dead."

"You first, boy."

Just before Evan would have plunged his sword into the ground, the earth beneath his feet suddenly gave way, collapsing inward. Evan stumbled back, arms outstretched as he tried to regain his balance. His blade, which made contact with only air, was unnaturally propelled upward and over, landing far.

He rolled off the mound, collapsing facedown at its base. Groaning, Evan moved slowly, the air knocked from him.

Some distance away, his mount gave out a warning cry.

Darkness enveloped Evan, a darkness deeper than the night and even the storm warranted. With effort, Evan rolled onto his back, seeking his blade.

Laughter not that of the wraith assailed his ears, sent his head pounding. He knew that laugh, knew it erupted from no human source.

Something large and powerful struck him.

Steppenwald tore his gaze from Mardi's eyes. She tried to blink, tried to wipe away the image of his burning orbs, but could not. Mardi could not do anything at all, her body, her will, subject completely to his command.

And yet . . . something within her still struggled, still sought the power the gentlewoman needed to do battle against her fiendish captor. However, Mardi's own fear fought against it, kept it from bursting forth.

"What's this, what's this?" Cane tapping, heavy footsteps causing the floorboards to creak, Steppenwald marched to the nearest window. Mardi could no longer see him, but she could hear the sharp intake of breath, the barely audible curse. She heard him shove aside the curtains, the better to see. A flash of lightning added momentarily to the illumination, creating a monstrous shadow of her captor on the magistrate's floor.

"Interesting, interesting . . ." Steppenwald retreated from the window, tugging on his well-trimmed beard. "A very distinct possibility . . ."

He passed out of Mardi's range of sight again and a moment later the captive woman heard the clinking of glass, the gentle gurgle of liquid being poured. Again she felt the desire to fight, this time succeeding in at least moving her eyes. She doused the sensation. She dared not go against Lord Steppenwald. What chance did she have against so clearly proficient a sorcerer?

The king's man slowly sipped from a goblet. He made a sour face as he swallowed. Steppenwald's dire gaze fell upon the ensorcelled magistrate. "Drulane, you really should see to getting a better brandy! This stuff is hardly worth serving!"

The magistrate remained motionless, staring straight ahead.

Replacing the goblet, Steppenwald returned to the window. He tapped the cane twice on the ground, as if in thought, then raised both hands high.

The window flew open, strong wind and rain immediately blowing in. Papers on Drulane's desk scattered over the far side of the chamber and one of the lamps went out. Mardi felt flicks of moisture on one side of her face.

Yet the storm did not touch Lord Steppenwald, the wind and rain neither blowing free his hat nor dampening his fine garments. The huge figure called out a single word . . . or name, Mardi could not decide which . . . and waited.

A moment later, a singularly ugly carrion crow fluttered into the chamber. He shook himself free of some of the wetness, cawed once to Steppenwald, then leapt up to the man's proffered forearm. The well-clad sorcerer gestured at the window, which shut tight once more.

"Well, my friend? Have you anything to report?"

The blackbird glared at Mardi, seeming to consider long his master's question. Then the crow looked again at Steppenwald and cawed.

"Is that so? Interesting. What about the cairn?"

One caw. The bird shifted uneasily.

Steppenwald frowned at his pet. "And that's all, all you know? Let a little rain and wind get the better of you and yours, you and yours, eh?" If anything, the crow looked even more miserable. "Not a very good day's work, my friend . . ."

He seized the startled bird by the neck. The avian managed one protesting squawk before the massive man twisted its neck around. Mardi could not gasp, but her eyes widened at such outright cruelty. If she had had any lingering doubts about Steppenwald's evil, the bird's murder had eradicated them.

"Filthy creatures . . ." Lord Steppenwald threw the dead avian to the floor. The mangled crow struck the wood and vanished in a sulfurous puff of smoke. "I should've never bothered with them. I shall have to deal with this matter from a different perspective, yes . . ."

He turned toward her with such abruptness that Mardi nearly forgot that Steppenwald might notice the slight change in her condition. She immediately stared ahead, hoping he would not notice if she had to blink.

"We've only just begun with one another, only just begun, my dear lady. A pity to stop so soon, but more immediate affairs demand some personal attention. Still"—the noble waved the cane before her—"even though I can't ensure that you'll forget, I can take a different step, a different step."

He muttered under his breath, using words familiar yet foreign to the gentlewoman. Mardi felt a tingle from both within and without as the peculiar forces inside her tried to come to her defense. She refused, though, at the moment more afraid of the mysteries stirring within than she was of Steppenwald, who had no clear desire yet to kill her.

"If you were not so strong of will, my dear lady, I'd put you in a spell like the good magistrate, I would. Oblivious to my spells or the time under them, at peace in his mind that he's in control of his own destiny." Lord Steppenwald shrugged. "You, alas, will do as I bid, pretend that nothing is amiss . . . but you'll know at all times that I am your puppeteer." He doffed his hat at her, nearly causing Mardi to blink. "We'll talk again very soon, so very soon . . ."

Her body turned, pulling her away from both men. Mardi walked out of the chamber, neither she nor the guards on duty there acting as if anything had been amiss. Nearly all of the magistrate's men had to be under similar spells, although only she evidently had to suffer with the knowledge that her life, her body, would no longer be hers and that Steppenwald could command her whenever and however he pleased.

Mardi entered the storm, on the outside her every movement casual. Yet, when she tried to turn a different direction, her legs continued toward her home.

"Good day, Mistress Sinclair!" a jovial voice called. "Well, perhaps not so good, but not the worst, either!"

Of all the people living in and around Pretor's Hill, trust that Arno would be the only one in a decent mood. Mardi's body paused and her mouth opened. "Good day to you, blacksmith. Forgive me, I must be going."

The gentlewoman's legs started moving again. Inwardly, Mardi Sinclair cursed; she could not even talk to someone of her own volition. Steppenwald had taken even the simplest parts of her life from her.

A thick hand gently took hold of her arm. "Mistress, forgive me, but I've been wondering about Sir Evan and where he might be."

Again her body shifted of its own will. Mardi knew that the only answer Arno would get from her would be a bland, unhelpful one unless she somehow broke Steppenwald's control . . . But how?

The peculiar sensation that had combated with her fear all through Steppenwald's interrogation surged stronger than ever. This time she accepted it, let it at least in part guide her.

"I don't know . . . Arno, I can't . . . anything . . . I . . . help me . . ."

"Mistress Sinclair?"

The sorcerer's spell warred with the fury from within her. The battle proved too much for her already-fragile mind, though. Mardi reached a hand toward the blacksmith . . . then collapsed, unconscious even before falling into the stunned man's arms.

XIII

WHAT LIES BENEATH

Steppenwald stood at the doors of the church, more anxious than he had felt in many, many years. He had contemplated riding directly to the mound, but that would thrust him into a possibly explosive situation of which he knew little enough about. No, before he committed himself to such a path, the gargantuan man desired to know what he might face . . . and the only source of information lay buried deep beneath the foundation of this building.

The insipid priest would not hear him, Steppenwald's spellwork seeing to that. His concern lay only with Valentin.

"Rubbish, rubbish!" the king's man muttered as he waved his cane in the direction of the doors. They opened for him without any hesitation. "He can do nothing to me . . ."

The elegantly clad figure strode through the church until he came to the center. Steppenwald eyed the pattern in the floor, recalling both his research and what he had been told in the past. How boring Rundin had become, to no longer allow such wondrous works of magic! He longed for the past, longed for when wizards and sorcerers had had the freedom to perform their spells without fear of repercussions from those far inferior to them. How he looked forward to the day when he could depart this realm for home . . .

And that would be very soon, if all went as planned. The final player had arrived and now Steppenwald merely had to set into motion select events. Then he could make his choices based on who survived.

Steppenwald brought down the tip of his cane onto the floor.

A spark shot forth as the cane struck. The mismatched eyes of the dragon flashed bright, almost as if with a life of their own.

A severe crack formed in the floor. Steppenwald moved back as the crack became a fissure and the fissure grew into a menacing crevice.

"Fascinating . . ." the sorcerer murmured.

The earth opened up enough to reveal a stairway. Steppenwald remained where he was until the crevice ceased opening and the walls below quit shivering. Then he slowly made his way down, testing the firmness of each step with his cane. His great girth meant that the stairway offered him little room on each side, but Steppenwald felt no anxiety. Only his final destination haunted his thoughts.

He paused at the bottom to reorient himself. A dim light ahead informed him that his quarry lay not far, yet Steppenwald remained cautious. Not only had he not heard any sort of greeting from Valentin—who surely expected a visitor at this point—but he had been warned that at least some sort of trap lay ahead—

A murky form rose from the shadows, reaching out to seize Steppenwald by the throat. Steppenwald, though, moving with speed astonishing for a normal man much less one of his size, retreated a short distance, then thrust with his cane. The tip of the cane caught his monstrous adversary directly in the chest.

The eyes of the dragon glowed bright again. A sharp flash burst forth from the cane.

Blue flames engulfed the guardian. The creature did not scream, but rather simply shook as it perished. The stench assailed Steppenwald's nostrils, but only for a moment. The intense flames swiftly did their foul work, completely consuming the horrific guardian. In but a few seconds, only a small pile of ash remained to mark the creature's passing.

And at last the voice of Valentin broke the silence, the smell of the guardian's passing perhaps informing him that someone other than the good knight had come to pay their respects. "What happens out there? Who comes to visit?"

Lord Steppenwald did not deign to reply, desiring first to face the imprisoned warrior. Slowly, calmly, he walked the short distance to the glowing chamber . . . and there beheld the chained form of the crimson knight.

The sorcerer had imagined Valentin in a thousand different forms, each more astounding than the last, yet still none matched the ghoulish, pale man snared by chains so pathetic and yet so unbreakable. Steppenwald felt a brief shiver course through him, one that he managed to hide from the other. This day had been planned for so very long, yet now Steppenwald could barely focus and that annoyed him. Valentin could do nothing to the sorcerer, only something *for* him.

"You are not Evan," the ebony-haired prisoner calmly remarked. Amber eyes watched Steppenwald without blinking. "But I know you somehow . . ."

Very good. Valentin's incredible detachment revealed a mind still alert, still battle-ready, even after so many years of torturous confinement. That he also felt he knew Steppenwald somehow showed that his higher senses, that which marked him among the Talented, had remained attuned. Small wonder if all that the aristocratic sorcerer had noted about the vicinity of Pretor's Hill had been in part influenced by Valentin. Such effort over the decades would have left him sharp, which meant that perhaps he would serve Steppenwald's needs perfectly.

"You need not concern yourself with who I am, not concern yourself at all," Steppenwald replied, matching the other's calm, "only with what I can perhaps offer you . . ."

Now Valentin chuckled, an act that stretched the dead skin of his face tight, enhancing his skeletal visage. "Have you come to offer me my freedom? You might be surprised at my answer."

The king's man stepped nearer. He noticed the knight's eyes shift ever so briefly to the cane, most likely to the dragon-head handle. Then the gaze returned to Steppenwald's own, but with what seemed just a bit more knowledge to them. Steppenwald tightened his grip but held his expression. "I can offer you freedom, perhaps, or something more if that is what you desire. I can offer you much, so much, but only if I gain in return."

"Not so altruistic are you . . . my dear Steppenwald."

This time, the massive intruder could not stave off his surprise. Belatedly, he realized how this imprisoned warrior knew his name, but by then the deed had been done. Steppenwald had revealed a bit of weakness. "So you know me . . . and that can only be through the auspices of one Sir Evan Wytherling, one Sir Evan Wytherling."

Valentin smiled. "I've other methods . . ."

"But in this case only one, only one." Lord Steppenwald paced slowly in front of the crimson knight. "Well, then, Sir Valentin, let us speak of this errant warrior, your dire predicament, and the culmination of both our dreams . . ."

"And what dream do you have, fat man? What dream could possibly lead you here? What dream do you think would be of any interest to me?"

Steppenwald ignored the insult, knowing something of Valentin's character before this encounter. He clutched his cane tighter, trying to keep his enthusiasm in check. No alliance yet existed before them; Valentin remained a potential enemy, albeit one with limited choices to his actions. Steppenwald could sense the magic around the knight, magic kept shielded from all save those who knew its source.

"I would dream of destiny, of tearing free the yoke, tearing free the yoke, that has been much too long across my back. I would dream of no longer obeying the dictates of one undeserving of my compliance, just as you should, just as you should. I would dream of being my own master, as any man would . . ." The aristocratic titan shrugged. "Nothing more than you must dream, I would say."

"So . . ." began Valentin, macabre smile forming again, "nothing but a lackey, are you? A lackey with dreams of grandeur? I think I know you better now, fat man, and I smell in you a bargain I should not . . . cannot make." The crimson knight rattled his chains. "I'm quite comfortable here for now and, after all, I do have a duty to perform."

Steppenwald found the prisoner's attitude reprehensible. Did the man not understand what he offered? Perhaps Valentin had been down here too long. Perhaps he needed to be shown.

He moved to the broken lance, studying the fractured end first, then tracing with his eyes the path to Valentin's gored chest. Through the impossible rip in the breastplate, Steppenwald could even make out a bit of the knight's pale flesh. The skin there seemed to fold in where the lance had burrowed deep and a black crust surrounded the point of entry, dried blood centuries old. The sorcerer could see that Valentin's chest rose and fell slightly, a labored breathing made more so by the very weight of the broken weapon.

"It must pain you, must pain you dearly," Steppenwald quietly commented. He gently touched the end of the lance, causing Valentin to momentarily shudder. So then, the weapon that pierced the ungodly warrior remained a point of frustration . . . and a possible bargaining chip.

" 'Tis but a scratch . . ."

The aristocratic giant chuckled. "How droll." His fingers traced the broken edge. Steppenwald seized hold of the lance. "Good to see you have kept your sense of humor, kept your sense of humor."

"What do you—?" was as far as Valentin would get.

The eyes of the dragon flared. Valentin, looking into Steppenwald's own eyes, would see that they now matched in color the jewels. Of course, the color of the sorcerer's eyes would hardly be of the utmost importance to the imprisoned knight, considering that Steppenwald now slowly drew the lance fragment from his chest.

Rather, he drew it only partially free. Valentin's breath faltered, either because of the portion still embedded or his burning anticipation that Steppenwald might, in the next moment, at last put an end to his agonizing torture. The immense spellcaster toyed with the lance, turning it around and around, then, just as it seemed

Valentin might speak . . . Steppenwald shoved it back inside.

The knight shrieked, although whether out of anger or pain, Steppenwald could not judge. Valentin glared at him, amber eyes almost but not quite disconcerting the intruder. Steppenwald met his gaze for a moment, then raised the cane up so that the dragon's head distracted his companion.

"How—?" the imprisoned warrior gasped. "How can you do that? Only a few select can even move it, much less bear the power to pull it free!"

"And I am one of those, one of those . . ."

Valentin looked him over, stared for a moment at the cane. Something shifted in his demeanor, something not entirely to Steppenwald's liking. At this point, he should have had the upper hand in any further discussion with the knight, but Valentin appeared to suddenly be focused on something else entirely.

"I know you now, Steppenwald," Valentin finally uttered. "Or perhaps it'd be best if I said I know what you are. More than a lackey, yes, but not so much as you yearn to be! Until your day comes, you'll forever be at the beck and call, won't you? Unable yourself to advance to the station you desire, you need someone who might clear the field for you . . ."

The cursed knight knew. Perhaps not exactly, but he knew enough to judge Steppenwald. "Your answer, then! You know what I can offer and that it is within my abilities!" He slammed the tip of the cane down hard on the ground, sending off blue sparks. "If you will agree to what I need, agree to what I need, then I will grant you your freedom and so much more!"

Valentin closed his eyes, lifted his face to the ceiling. Steppenwald waited breathlessly behind a mask of confidence. He had come this far, dared so much, waited so long . . .

"I must think it over."

"What?" Consternation swept over Steppenwald. Think it over? Madness had indeed infected this condemned soul.

"You'll come again," Valentin suddenly declared. "When the shadowed moon briefly cuts through the shroud enveloping this once-fair land and when the wraiths claim their own. You'll come then and I'll give you the answer."

It became all that Steppenwald could do to restrain himself in the face of such an absurd reply. Did the man think he had so much to offer his visitor? Did Valentin expect that Steppenwald had nothing better to do with his time than come here whenever the imprisoned knight felt the whim? "I think you forget your situation, my good man . . ."

The look that the crimson warrior gave him caused even the gargantuan sorcerer to flinch. "I forget nothing, Master Steppenwald, leastwise those who are my enemies and those who are my allies. For instance, you've not asked a question I know must be on your mind." Valentin tipped forward, allowing the chains to hold him in place. "Surely you must sense what happens even as we speak."

Trying not to grit his teeth in frustration, Steppenwald nodded. "I sense it, I sense it . . . and know that you mean something for Sir Evan Wytherling this eve . . ."

"As I said, fat man, I forget neither my enemies nor my allies . . . and especially not dear Evan . . ."

As Steppenwald had earlier suspected, the magical storm surrounding the region of the dragon mound had been arranged in part for the silver knight's entertainment. It made the sorcerer's decision to come here even more appropriate. Perhaps Valentin had inadvertently solved one quandary, steered Steppenwald to one choice.

Of course, that depended also on the choices made by Evan Wytherling, who seemed quite resilient . . .

"Very well, then, very well," he responded, pretending that all went as originally planned. "Since you are busy this eve, I'll return when you suggest . . . but that will be the last time I set my offer before you, the last time."

"Oh, I don't doubt that."

The king's man turned slightly toward the path leading out, part of his weight resting on the cane. "I will follow your activities tonight with some interest. I want to see how well you deal with your enemies; my own offer may hinge on the results."

Valentin turned his head away, obscuring his expression. "Then, fat man, you'd be disappointed in this night's work, for I've no intention of slaying Evan . . . rather I hope to save him."

Steppenwald's heavy brow furrowed. "What do you mean by that?"

The knight remained silent at first, his gaze away from the massive intruder. Then, just as Steppenwald had at last started for the passage, Valentin's voice echoed through the chamber. "What did you do with the beastly guardian? Did you slay it?"

"Of course." The aristocratic giant glanced over his shoulder to see if Valentin watched him, but the knight had not altered position.

"A pity. It wasn't much of a companion, but at least it was one. I'll miss it . . . but not for long, I suppose."

Steppenwald waited a moment longer, then, when it became clear that Valentin would not speak again, he returned to the steps and began his ascent. His mind raced, going over each word spoken in search of hidden meanings. Valentin's last few statements especially worried him and the ones concerning Evan Wytherling most of all.

Valentin wanted to save the silver knight . . . but from what?

Evan woke to darkness and the stench of the dead. He blinked, trying to adjust to the dark, then realized that he could not see the night because a ceiling of earth obscured it from his sight.

He had been buried alive.

The knowledge, curiously enough, did not frighten Evan as much as it once might have. He had suffered similar fates in the past and at least this time the air, while a bit stifling, could be breathed. Whatever force had done this to him, it had wanted him to live, at least for the time being.

Evan fumbled for his sword but found nothing save an old bone. By the size and shape of it, he judged it to have been once that of a man or elf, those the two races nearest to one another in appearance. The stench did not originate from the bone, nor two others he found. Rather, it seemed to come from somewhere before him.

He lay in a cave or, more apt, a burrow of sorts. Nothing natural had created this underground chamber. Evan recalled the goblins and trolls used by Novaris in the war; had one or more of them survived and fled underground? Surely even those foul creatures did not live so long.

Feeling for the dagger at his belt, Evan found with some relief that he had not been completely disarmed. Not much against the hard hide of a troll or, worse, one of their cousins, the ferocious morags. Still, it lent him some strength . . .

The ceiling hung low, which forced him to crawl on his knees. He felt along the wall with one hand, noting rock and dirt. Occasionally, his hand would come away with small, foul worms attached to it. Maggots. Evan would take the knife, mutter a few words, and quickly burn them away. First the stench, then the bones, and now these creatures, the carrion eaters of the underworld. Truly he had fallen into the land of the dead.

Then a new wave of stench rolled over him, nearly causing the knight to lose the contents of his stomach. Old flesh, rotting and soiled. Where had he ended up?

"Grimyr . . ." he muttered. Of course. Foolish that Evan had not thought of that before. He had been dragged into the leviathan's mound, where the body of the dragon continued to slowly decay even after two centuries. The inherent magic of the beast had no doubt delayed the process to some extent. Of course, that ruled out goblins and trolls as the creatures who lived here, for even they did not have stomach enough to remain close to this putrid odor. Ghouls? Certainly the hungering undead would find such a battlefield to their liking, but surely someone in Pretor's Hill would have discovered their presence before now. Ghouls were never satisfied with the flesh of old corpses . . .

More worms sprouted from the walls of the tiny cave, but these were most definitely unique. They glowed like tiny ghosts and moved as if trying to seek Evan out. He shifted away from them, only to find more burrowing out of the soil at his knees. Evan moved back a short distance, trying to avoid them, but they emerged from everywhere. Gradually, their combined illumination created a dim light that spread through a small portion of his makeshift tomb. Enough for him to see his hands and immediate surroundings, but not near enough to tell the knight where the passage might end.

With great caution, Evan edged forward again, trying not to crush the creatures. However, once again a great, monstrous stench assailed the warrior, forcing him to cover his nose and mouth and try to breathe as shallowly as possible.

"Man Wytherling . . ." rumbled a deep yet strangely hollow voice.

The knight held the tiny blade before him, too stunned to speak. Had he truly heard that voice or had his memories turned on him again?

"Huuuuman . . ."

The words came out as hisses, spoken by a creature that had no trace of humanity itself. As Evan squinted, he noted what seemed movement ahead of him, then the vague shape of something large, something that more than filled the narrow passage.

"How long hasss thisss one waited for thisss moment . . ."

The shape shifted, growing quickly more distinct. Evan Wytherling saw the outline of a snout that belonged to a beast large enough to swallow him whole. He caught a glimpse of talons that could have raked the side of a warhorse, disemboweling the animal in one quick strike. Most horrifying, the weary knight could see the fiery orbs, the reptilian orbs, of a monster he had long thought dead.

The name came out as a gasp. *"Grimyr . . ."*

"Man Wytherling doesss not forget . . ." the shadowy form rasped, again the voice both deep and hollow. "Nor doesss Grimyr forget . . ."

"You are dead!" Evan demanded of the dark shape. "As dead as Haggad! As dead as—"

"Asss Valentin?" Grimyr countered. "Asss Novarisss? Asss you, Man Wytherling?"

Only two humans had the huge fire-black dragon called simply by their names, all others of the species receiving the designation "man" as a sign of the leviathan's contempt for the tiny, weaker creatures. Only Valentin and Novaris had received such an honor, the latter because Grimyr had rightly feared him and the crimson knight because of a bond forged between them at some point in the distant path. Grimyr had always done as Valentin had commanded; they had been as twins, tied together by birth. The dragon would have been willing to die for his rider and had done so . . . or so Evan had thought.

"Thisss one ssstill feelsss the pain, Man Wytherling. Thisss one ssstill sssuffersss your cursssed ssstrike . . ."

Evan heard him only in part, his mind still trying to accept this most terrible of discoveries. He had assumed that someone else, the sorcerer-king or Valentin, had been making use of the dragon's latent power. Never had he suspected that somehow Grimyr had survived his mortal wound, had lain here in wait just as Valentin had.

Yet how could a creature of the air survive all these years penned up beneath the earth? Evan had inspected the area of the mound on his previous visit and would have noticed the sort of chasm needed for a massive dragon to exit to the sky. True, dragons did sleep for years at a time, but not this long. Others of Grimyr's kind would have dug themselves free before this.

Once more he wondered if he faced a specter such as General Haggad, but something told the knight that Grimyr could and would tear him apart if given the opportunity. However, the dragon did hide some secret, or else why did he remain so distant . . . and what created the awful stench of death about him?

"I am sorry that you are pained," Evan finally returned, stalling with conversation. Grimyr had many secrets, one of which was why he had bothered to let the human live at all. Certainly the great dragon had no love for the knight who had run him through. "I had thought the strike quick and true."

"You have thought many untrue thingsss, Man Wytherling. Your mind isss weak and Grimyr would be done with you, but . . . but Valentin sssaysss to forgive that fault . . ."

Forgive? Valentin? Evan did not quite understand what Grimyr meant, but the murky dragon had told him one interesting fact; Valentin and the beast still remained in contact despite their conditions and separation over these past two centuries. How so very strong remained the bond that the macabre pair had woven between them.

"Valentin is most gracious."

The dragon chuckled, a sound that reverberated in the passage. "Valentin isss Valentin . . . and how fortunate for you."

Evan tried to move back a little, give himself some more space, however futile it might prove in the end. He did not trust the sinister behemoth despite Grimyr's loyalty to the other knight. Something in the dragon's voice hinted at a different sort of madness in Grimyr, one that perhaps even Valentin might not understand.

"Valentin sssaid to thisss one that Man Wytherling mussst be pitied, not hated . . . that Man Wytherling would have thingsss different than they were . . ." Grimyr hissed and a wave of fetid breath washed over Evan's face. "Grimyr doesss not think the sssame, but if Valentin ssso sssaysss, thisss one will abide by hisss word . . ."

Evan ran his hand against one wall as if trying to balance himself. In truth, he sought any weakness in the tunnel that he might use to escape the presence of the shadowy dragon. Despite the fact that Valentin apparently did not want him dead, Evan had no doubt that the other knight had picked out some special fate for him.

"Then we have no quarrel anymore," the human replied, maintaining a calm tone. "We shall part ways and never—"

Grimyr hissed. The barely seen talons scraped at the ground, gouging ravines. The chamber shook and bits of earth showered down on Evan. He realized that he had angered the dragon and that the beast now barely kept in check his tremendous fury.

"There will alwaysss be quarrel between thisss one and you, Man Wytherling! Only the word of Valentin givesss you life and only becausse Valentin wishesss to sssave you from yoursssself . . ."

"Wishes to save me?" Evan barely kept his grip on the dagger, completely confounded by Grimyr's words but knowing they could not bode anything good.

"Yesss . . ." The murky figure of the dragon moved slightly closer, but never so much that the illumination of the wriggling worms would bring him clearly into sight. Why did Grimyr despise even the foul light that his magic had likely brought into the mound? "Yesss, Man Wytherling . . . sssave you from yoursssself and the wizard who bound you . . ."

Now the veteran knight finally thought he understood, and what he understood filled him with dread. He backed away some more, only to find that he had reached the end of his side of the tunnel. The worms flowed toward him, ever bathing his area in deathly light. Evan looked at the wall beside him, seeking some other way . . . and found himself staring at the partially buried skull of an armored figure.

"The memoriesss lay buried all around thisss one," Grimyr commented, moving nearer. The earth gave way to the hulking form as he pushed forward. It astounded Evan that the mound had not collapsed over time. Truly the great dragon had remained amazingly still during his two-hundred-year wait. "The memoriesss are all thisss one hasss had . . . until now . . ."

Brandishing the dagger, Evan returned, "The time comes for you to put aside memories, Grimyr."

"Have *you*?" When the human did not instantly reply, the leviathan snorted. "The little tooth will avail you naught . . ."

Evan muttered a few words. The blade began to take on a soft glow of its own, one that the worms instantly shunned. Grimyr, though, seemed not at all impressed by his magic. He moved yet nearer and Evan could sense the dragon summoning magic of his own.

From the ground beneath the graying knight, a skeletal hand shot up and seized one of his ankles.

As he tried to pull away, Evan sensed movement from his side. The grinning skull broke free of the wall, followed by the rest of a suddenly resurrected foe. Sightless eye sockets stared past the knight as the skeleton sought to seize the dagger. The jaw hung open, barely held on by some residual muscle. Despite the ghoulish attacker's fragile appearance, its bony hand gripped Evan's wrist with monstrous strength. The knight knew that no life truly existed in his foe; Grimyr's magic guided the macabre puppet along.

Even as he struggled with the skeleton, something seized his other ankle. The dragon had summoned the nearby dead, forcing their mortal remains if not their spirits to once more fight in the name of Novaris's evil. They would remove for Grimyr the one obstacle to Evan, the enchanted dagger. The knight increased his exertions as his racing mind filled with the horrific images of what Grimyr might do with him.

Twisting his wrist, the skilled veteran freed his blade hand from his unliving foe. Evan wasted not a moment, turning the dagger toward the selfsame attacker and driving the glowing blade into the skull. The dagger sank in as if cutting through air, leaving only the hilt visible.

The skeletal warrior twitched wildly as if suffering some sudden fit. Its left arm fell away, then its right. Armor and bone clattered to the floor of the tunnel, the jaw even slipping free.

Evan shook the skull from the dagger. However, before he could turn the enchanted weapon on one of the hands that had thrust up from the ground, an armored, fleshless limb wrapped itself about his neck, pinning the knight back against the end of the passage. Mere seconds later, another animated hand burst through from the side and wrapped bony fingers about his wrist. The hand squeezed hard, cutting off all circulation and inevitably forcing Evan to release his hold on his only hope.

A tiny crevice opened up in the earth below the dagger and it fell from sight. Immediately thereafter, the crevice repaired itself, leaving no trace of either its brief existence or the magical blade.

Despite his attempts, Evan Wytherling could not free himself from his ghastly bonds. Nonetheless, he did not cease his efforts even when the worms suddenly began to burrow their way back into the earth, leaving him with less and less visibility with each second.

Eventually only Grimyr's blazing orbs remained to fix his gaze upon.

"Valentin wishesss you sssaved, Man Wytherling, and ssso Grimyr will sssave you whether you wish ssso or not . . ."

A lance struck Evan through the head . . . or rather the knight felt such pain. In truth, no physical weapon pierced his forehead; the magic of the dragon had done the deed, delving into the human's mind without concern for his pain. Grimyr would fulfill Valentin's command, but he would do so in his own way.

"Resssissst and it will pain you more."

Even knowing that, the captive knight fought against the intrusion. He formed within his mind a thousand shields, but each of those Grimyr shattered with little effort. Only near the core, only where Evan's mind most lay open did the leviathan actually need to exert effort . . . for here were shields that another had placed long before.

"You will be sssaved!" came the odd, hollow roar of the dragon.

Evan's world turned inside out . . .

He saw General Haggad again, this time the commander's head attached at the neck, as was proper. The general commanded his Knights of the Veil to close on the enemy, the warrior women shrieking as they charged. That they were female no longer mattered to the defenders; the soldiers of the three kingdoms had witnessed the atrocities perpetrated by these wild Amazons.

The foot soldiers of Novaris continued to advance, followed closely by the goblins and the trolls. From the hills, the bat-wing-eared morags threw massive boulders at the nearest of the enemies, the monsters' great strength feared by all save the dragons and wizards.

Against all of these, Evan fought . . . then found himself fighting beside them. Trolls who had been his foes now stood next to him, shield to shield. He shook his head, knowing this to be wrong. Suddenly, Evan changed sides again, this time joining with Rundin swordmasters to sweep away a band of fearsome goblins. The goblins, though, became Tepis ax-men, Evan Wytherling now atop a charger and leading a rank of knights into their midst. He managed to avoid slaying one man, but another swung at him, forcing the knight to defend himself against what should have been an ally.

Sssee the truth . . . came the voice of Grimyr in his mind. *Do not give in to the liesss . . .*

"Whose lies?" Evan demanded, parrying the ax-man's strike. "Yours? Valentin's? Novaris's?"

You will be sssaved from yoursssself!

The ax-man managed to get his weapon around Evan's guard. The blade bit into the armor protecting his leg. Evan shouted in pain as blood poured from the wound. While he tried to recover, the burly warrior struck a second blow, this one aimed at the knight's steed.

Evan and the animal tumbled into a heap.

Ax-wielding figures surrounded him. Evan would have risen and fought them off as best he could, but his wounded leg lay pinned beneath his dying mount, whose neck had nearly been severed. He looked for the sword he had been using, but the blade could not be found.

The swarthy, bearded face of one of the Tepisian soldiers

appeared above him, filling his gaze. The man wore a satisfied grin and held a blood ax high above him.

The knight prepared himself for death.

Suddenly, a horse and rider broke into the crowd, scattering the Tepisians. Someone let out a wild battle cry. An ax-man fell dead beside Evan, his chest bloody. A second man fled, to be followed a moment later by a horse. Evan heard a cry, then the sound of hoofbeats.

The animal came to a halt. The knight could not see his rescuer at all, but he heard the armored figure approach. An ungauntleted hand reached down and took his own, dragging Evan Wytherling free, then pulling him to his feet.

"They'll not be so eager to fight one of my own in so cowardly a manner next time, will they, Evan?"

Valentin, a healthy, tanned Valentin, smiled at him, one good comrade coming to the rescue of his friend. Evan tried to pull his hand away, but Valentin's strength bordered on the magical.

"Careful there, Evan! You'll fall on that injured leg. Come! Your mount is dead. You'd best ride mine. There's room enough for two."

He indicated with his free hand what should have been his horse but to Evan's horrified eyes began to transform into something huge and terribly familiar.

"We fly into battle?" rumbled Grimyr with barely contained eagerness.

The silver knight tried to back away, not wanting to be anywhere near the monster. However, he could not go far, for Valentin's grip remained unbreakable.

"That would depend upon our dear friend here, wouldn't it?" the other warrior asked, his tone losing some of its warmth. "What say you, Evan? Do you still have the stomach for it?"

Evan turned to confront his counterpart, only to stiffen at the sight of Valentin. Now the crimson knight looked as he had last seen him, the skin white as parchment, the amber eyes burning with revenge yet so soulless, the dry blood caked upon the gaping wound going through armor, flesh, and bone . . .

"Come back to us, dear Evan . . ." Valentin said with a deathly smile. "You know you want to . . ."

Look not so often back upon the path you have already tread, began a voice in his head. *But rather where the one before you leads . . .*

Still smiling, Valentin faded. Grimyr hissed . . . then he, too, faded. The battlefield became a misty nothingness, then a dark, stifling cave—

The burning orbs glared at Evan from the blackness. "The fat wizard playsss too many gamesss!" the true Grimyr snarled. "But thisss one will not be blocked by hisss will!"

The spellwork of Paulo Centuros had repelled the efforts of the dragon to delve into Evan's innermost mind. The spellcaster had planned for this day.

The talons scraped again at the earth. "Puny mortal magic will not shield you long, Man Wytherling! Valentin commandsss that you be sssaved, that you sssee the world asss you were meant to sssee!" Grimyr chuckled. "And sssee you shall . . . even if thisss one mussst hurt you a little in the processs . . ."

A storm suddenly raged full force in Evan's head.

The knight screamed.

XIV

GRIMYR

"Mistress Sinclair?"

The anxious voice at last stirred Mardi from deep and terrible dreams of gigantic, fat crows and serpentine dragons with mismatched eyes. She forced herself to open her eyes, finally focusing on the concerned face of dear Arno. The smith had both meaty hands clutched together in obvious panic, the care of a woman clearly outside his normal field of expertise.

"Arno . . . where . . . ?" Mardi could barely make her mouth work and her thoughts yet remained muddled.

"In your home, Mistress Sinclair!" The ugly man reddened. "Atop your bed . . . if you'll be forgiving me, lady . . ."

Her bed. Her home. A small sense of security returned to the young woman. For a moment, all she wanted to do was bury herself in the blankets and forget everything that had happened, but Mardi knew such an act would provide her with no escape.

"Arno . . ." His face remained scarlet. "It's all right. You did the good, caring thing." Mardi looked around. Everything at first looked normal, but then she noticed one thing missing. "Arno . . . have you seen . . . Mistress Arden?"

The burly smith shrugged, a monumental sight. "No one was here, Mistress Sinclair."

It could have been possible that Drulane's woman had simply not stopped by yet, but Mardi could not help but think that this coming night there would be no sign of her. She recalled too vividly what had happened in the magistrate's office, recalled in full her horrifying encounter with the towering Lord Steppenwald.

He had indicated to her that she would recall everything, but that it would forever be locked within. If she tried to tell anyone, her own body would rebel against her, obeying the man's dictates. Yet Mardi had fainted, surely not something Lord Steppenwald had intended. Mardi tried to recall the incident and her conflicting emotions at the time. Her body had sought to obey Steppenwald's spell, but something else within her had attempted to counteract it, the same something that she had managed to keep subdued in the office for fear that her captor would do worse harm.

"What's happening to me?" she murmured.

"Mistress?" Arno's kindly face wore an expression of pure puzzlement.

"Nothing, Arno. I'm sorry for the bother I've been to you." The gentlewoman rose to a sitting position. "I'm much better now. You've no more need to sit with me."

He suddenly rose, looking ashamed. "My apologies! I . . . I'll be going then—"

"No!" She realized that he had misunderstood her. "I'm truly grateful to you, Arno! I don't know what might've happened if you hadn't been there! And certainly I can trust you!"

"That you can!" the smith replied with a series of rapid nods. The more familiar expression of cheerfulness returned. "You can be trusting me, mistress!"

In truth, the smith probably remained one of the very few Mardi could actually rely on at the moment. Magistrate Drulane had proved a colossal blunder; by going to him Mardi had handed herself over to someone who in some ways frightened her more than Valentin, for Lord Steppenwald roamed free, using the king's name to enable him to do as he pleased. He also knew much about the dark events concerning Evan. Not all, certainly, for the lightning outside had disturbed him so much that he had ceased all else in order to investigate it—

The lightning . . . Mardi tried to rise from her bed, but suddenly her arms and legs felt like weights. To her consternation, her hands reached down of their own accord and pulled her blanket up to her neck.

"Thank you again, Master Arno," came her voice, yet not her words. "I think that I'll rest a little. Forgive me if I don't walk you to the door."

While the smith did not appear to bear her any ill will, he certainly revealed some curiosity for her sudden shift. Again looking rather embarrassed, Arno quickly nodded. "Forgive me, Mistress Sinclair! I've been overstaying my welcome, that's for certain! I'll be leaving now."

He immediately backed out, bowing just before he vanished from view. Distressed over her seeming impoliteness, Mardi sought to rise, but still the gentlewoman's body fought against her. Even after she heard Arno shut the door behind him, Mardi could not so much as lift a finger on her own. Despite her vague hopes, it seemed her body yet belonged to Steppenwald.

As if to prove that foul point, her mouth moved again, this time the sorcerer's voice issuing forth. "You will do as I say, do as I say, in all things, Mardina Sinclair! I am your master, now and always . . ."

The single glowing lamp, lit no doubt by the smith, abruptly doused, sending the helpless woman into darkness.

How long Mardi lay there, she could not say. A few minutes, a half hour, maybe even twice that. Outside, the endless storm raged, never once letting up. She had nearly resigned herself to her forced slumber when she heard a peculiar snuffling sound beyond the walls of the school. Renewed fear sought to overwhelm Mardi, the notion that Lord Steppenwald had decided to send some dark beast to finish her off. He might have come to believe, however inaccurate, that Mardi could break free of his spell.

The animalistic sound drifted away and at first the captive teacher thought that perhaps she had been wrong, that it had been only some animal passing by. Then, Mardi Sinclair heard something bump against one of the other walls, perhaps even the outer door. She held her breath, desperate not to draw the mysterious creature's attention.

The door to the outside crashed open.

Under Lord Steppenwald's spell, Mardi could not immediately rise to either investigate or seek escape. She heard the storm come roaring into the school, felt the wind even in her bedroom. Mardi waited for the monster to enter, but only a few scattered leaves made it as far as her door.

Her fingers began to tingle.

The sensation did not pain her, rather it made Mardi Sinclair's skin itch. Despite knowing that she had no mastery over any part of her person, Mardi tried to scratch the offending digits and, to her astonishment, watched them move.

The tingling spread rapidly, moving from her fingers through her entire hand and up past her wrists in the blink of an eye. At the same time, new tingling began in her toes, then spread with eagerness to her ankles and beyond. Wherever the sensation moved, the gentlewoman recovered the use of her body.

Now once more whole, Mardi rose from the bed. She did so with less trepidation, more curious than fearful of what might lurk outside the door. Somehow her apparent freedom from the spells of Lord Steppenwald had to be linked to it . . .

The wind and rain continued to assault the room beyond, the floor nearest the open door drenched. Mardi retrieved her cloak, the only garment dear Arno had dared remove from her person, and stepped to the entrance. Shielding her eyes from the elements, the young woman peered out into the dark, seeking answers.

What she saw was a familiar horse.

Evan Wytherling's ghostly steed stood in the midst of the empty street, one eye focused on her. Mardi somehow knew that the beast awaited her. Covering herself up, she ran toward him.

"You did something, didn't you?" Mardi asked of the animal. He did not speak or even nod, not that she would have been so surprised if he had, but he did blink once ever so slowly. Mardi knew that she should have been unsettled by such a creature, but for some reason she felt only comfort from the steed's nearness.

The horse turned, presenting his flank and the saddle. Only now did it occur to her to wonder what had happened to Evan. "Is he all right?" she asked. "Is he in danger?"

The animal's only reply turned out to be a snort almost derisive in tone. Of course something terrible had happened to his rider; why else would the horse have come to her?

Without further hesitation, Mardi mounted. As soon as she grasped the reins, the ghostly stallion started off toward the wooded hills. Due to the storm, no one noted their departure, for which the gentlewoman especially felt grateful. What a sight she would have been, riding wildly out of town as if the devil himself followed her.

Of course, the devil might very well be ahead of her.

The rain did nothing to deter her mount, but Mardi Sinclair struggled to keep herself under the protection of her cloak as they raced into the woods. Thunder and lightning played havoc with her emotions, each blast making Mardi wonder if Evan had been slain. She also wondered exactly what she could do even if she found him; surely the knight would be better capable of handling any dire situation. How did his mount think Mardi could aid him?

The quill is said to be as mighty as the blade, but in truth it is the hand that wields either that most counts for their strengths . . . Despite the words having been penned by Paulo Centuros, Mardi found little comfort in them this time. A quill would do her no good and she had no sword to wield. She doubted she could even lift a good strong blade such as Evan or the sinister Valentin might use. She had two hands and the small dagger—her scissors Mardi had foolishly removed that morning in order to use them—but they hardly seemed sufficient.

Yet . . . Mardi had slain one of the lupine fiends . . .

A roll of thunder and a brilliant flash of lightning made her gasp. Illuminated in the branches of some of the trees were what Mardi thought to be scores of birds. She peered up at the limbs ahead, but both the rain and the darkness prevented her from verifying her suspicions.

Then a dark form flitted past her face, nearly scratching her cheek. Mardi heard a harsh caw and saw a similar shape fly from tree to tree. Another, far more brief flash of lightning outlined three, maybe four large crows daring the harsh storm by circling above her.

Pulling her hood close, Mardi pressed herself against the damp mane of the horse. The creature appeared oblivious to the swarming blackbirds, intent on reaching some area to the east. The stallion slowed as the rising landscape and dense trees forced it to be more selective about its footing. She hoped they would reach their destination soon, before the birds acted, yet had little desire to see where Evan's animal intended to carry her.

A bird managed to alight on her shoulder, seeking her neck with its hard beak. Gasping, Mardi swung a hand at the avian, momentarily forcing the creature away. However, as soon as she ceased her efforts, the massive crow returned, again trying to get past her hood.

"Away! Go away!"

The bird seemed only to enjoy her reaction and a moment later Mardi's situation worsened as another crow joined in the endeavors of the first. When she would try to shoo away one creature, the other would return to its perch. Already her hood had loose fibers near the throat as the birds methodically tore at the seams.

The horse abruptly shifted direction. Mardi saw no reason for the change until a thick branch suddenly cut across her path, mere inches above her head. The larger of the avian attackers, so intent on returning to task, failed to navigate the branch and collided with such force that even in the storm the harried woman could hear the bones break.

Freed of one menace, Mardi dared not let the second have space in which to breathe. Instead of waving the blackbird off, this time she seized the startled creature and, much to her own astonishment, threw him to the side with all her might. The crow went sailing off, protesting all the while. Not so permanent a solution as that offered by Evan's astounding steed, but at least it enabled her to gather her wits about her.

They had to be near their destination, for the birds flew thick and furious now. Yet, for all their numbers, few could reach the pair at any one time. The path that Evan's horse chose turned more and more tangled, with branches of all twists and bends making navigation difficult. Mardi had to stay pinned to the pale beast's neck in order not to get her face scratched and even then her cloak occasionally snagged on some tree. She wrapped it close to her as best she could and silently prayed for an end to the madness.

One enterprising crow of mammoth proportions managed to speed ahead, coming down on the duo from above. Clearly the avian sought to claw Mardi's face and likely the bird might have achieved such a goal if not for yet another startling reaction by the stallion. As the blackbird dropped, Evan Wytherling's steed kicked forward, briefly propelling himself into the air. Instead of Mardi's visage, the crow flew directly into the warhorse's mouth.

The sound produced as the horse clamped down on the blackbird forced Mardi to shut her eyes and turn away. She felt the animal shake his head once, twice, thrice, then cough. The gentlewoman opened her eyes just in time to see a dark, mangled shape drop beneath the horse.

Immediately after, lightning flashed and the woods gave way in part to a hill, a place Mardi recognized as a rumored burial mound or some such. A few elders in Pretor's Hill had claimed that a great monster killed in a battle had been laid to rest there, but those stories had always been met with amusement from Mardi and other young folk.

Whatever the truth about the hill, it seemed that the bone-pale steed had at least reached the place he had sought. The creature slowed, then trotted around the mound as if seeking something or someone. Mardi joined in the search, assuming that the animal sought his master.

They found someone, but hardly Evan Wytherling. The stallion came up short and actually backed away a few steps. Mardi could not blame him, for what moved toward them frightened her more than either the birds or even the shadow wolves. Here now came a tall, pale figure in metal who carried in his arm nothing less than his head. The head smiled at Mardi in a manner that made her clutch her cloak tighter, as if this foul ghost violated the gentlewoman simply by acknowledging her presence.

"Here now, horse . . ." the mouth uttered, the voice no less chilling than Valentin's but made worse by coming from the crook of the specter's arm. "We can't have that, now can we?"

Evan's mount snorted defiance and tried to go around the macabre figure.

The beheaded warrior raised his open hand . . . and a toothy blade nearly the length of his arm formed from the rain. "Now you know, horse, that I can't be hurting your master . . . but you're quite another story . . ."

He swung, nearly cutting a valley in the stallion's neck. The animal did a peculiar thing then, turning to his side as if presenting Mardi to the ghoul. She swallowed and hung on tight, refusing to believe that the horse had brought her here just to give her up to this monstrous phantasm.

"Oh, that won't help you!" the head mocked. "She's as much use for you as she would be for me in this form!" One snowy eye winked at her. "But I'd have been pleased to try, girl . . ."

Although Mardi tried to move as much to the other side of the horse as she could, the beast would not have that. The horrific ghost attacked again, this time thrusting. He came within an inch of reaching his target, but only because Evan's steed spun about again, clearly trying to present Mardi as best he could to their attacker.

"You're a pretty piece, girl," the ghost remarked, his headless body positioning itself for another strike. "Who knows? Maybe after this night's work, the scaly one might give me something extra!" The face leered. "Could be he might even make this two-legged mount of mine something a bit solid for a time . . ."

Mardi shuddered at his suggestion as the specter laughed wickedly. She tried to urge the horse to flee, but although the animal clearly sought to avoid the weapon, he had no desire to abandon the area.

Evan. The horse had brought her here to find him, of that she had no doubt. Why, then, would he want to sacrifice her to this monstrosity? No, the animal had something else in mind.

Mardi felt a sudden urge to slip from the saddle, an urge so tremendous that she could not fight it. However, she did not dismount away from the headless ghost, but rather in front of him, an act that a part of her knew to be madly reckless. With one swipe of the sword, he could cut her in two . . .

Yet, the specter did no such thing. Instead, the head frowned, then the armored phantom stepped back. "I'll cut you into pieces, my fine bit of wench! You'd best run, for it's your only hope!"

He seemed disinclined to charge her, which Mardi found quite peculiar. Surely she posed no threat.

The first step forward is the first step toward truth. Yet another saying so very much like Paulo Centuros, but not one that the wary gentlewoman recalled ever reading. Still, something about it made so much sense to her that Mardi Sinclair could not help following the words with action. She took a step toward the ghoulish general.

The ghost brandished his sword, but he again retreated a step or two. The snowy eyes met her gaze. "Now you don't have to come to me just yet, girl! Not until I'm done with the cursed animal. Then we'll have us plenty of time together!"

Mardi reached for the tiny dagger she carried, certain, although she knew not how, that she acted correctly. A word sprang out of her mouth, a word she had never heard and did not understand. The ghost, however, seemed to understand it perfectly and his reaction to it startled her. He dropped his head, which rolled to a stop near his booted feet, and swung the sword at her with both hands.

"Damned witch! Begone!"

Another word spouted from her lips, then Mardi did what seemed at first a most foolish thing. She lunged at her inhuman adversary, tiny dagger against jagged blade. The gentlewoman saw the sword come toward her and readied herself to feel the savage bite, but still she pushed forward, trying to at least make contact with the armored torso.

The sword cut through her without so much as leaving a scratch. Mardi felt a slight gust in its wake, but she did not long concern herself with the miracle of her survival. Instead, Mardi pushed the last foot, reaching the ghost's breastplate and managing to get at least the point of her insignificant weapon to touch.

The head, now at her feet, howled with fury and dismay. The dagger glowed a bright red, a red that enveloped the decapitated form. As the young woman watched, the dagger seemed to suck the ethereal figure into its blade, the phantom knight trying to cut her down until the very end.

"Damnable wench!" the head cried as it, too, felt the pull of Mardi's weapon. "By the Fenri, I'll see your bones bleached and used for—"

She did not find out what use the ghost might have for her bones, for at last the head succumbed, vanishing toward the dagger's blade just as the body had done.

The storm raged about Mardi, but she barely noticed it. Falling to one knee, she stared at the tiny weapon and knew that twice now she had done the impossible. First the lupine shadow, now this monstrous specter. Yet the blade she held in her hand had no special qualities to it; it had been forged one among many by a craftsman of competent but unremarkable skill. How could it be so magical?

A snort from behind her reminded Mardi of the horse. She looked up, gazed into the colorless eyes that in some way reminded her of the ghost, and finally murmured, "You knew that it could not harm me, didn't you? You knew that I could better shield you against the ghost than you could me."

The pale steed shook his mane, whether in response to her question or simply to dispose of some of the rain pouring down on him, the woman could not guess. He then moved past her, walking slowly toward the top of the hill. Mardi followed, certain that the animal wanted her to do so.

At what could be considered one of the gentler slopes of the hill, the horse gazed up. Mardi, hood wrapped tight, could not at first see anything. She took a few steps up to get a better view, only to have the stallion's muzzle in her back, nudging her yet farther.

Mardi studied the slope, saw that it presented no difficulties. She wended her way up, pausing only when she realized that Evan's mount had not followed her.

The horse snorted again, as if to say that here she would be on her own. Thinking of the peril the knight must be facing, the gentlewoman made her way along the hillside until at last she located the top.

A howl broke through the thunder and rain, a howl much too near for her taste.

Mardi searched the area, seeking some sign of the knight. What she could make out of the hilltop revealed nothing of Evan. She took a few steps, only to find her feet sinking into the ground; her heart pounded and she picked up her pace, now more careful where she moved.

Something gleamed up ahead in the next flash of lightning. Evan's armor? The drenched woman hurried on, a bit heedless of her footing.

Her right leg sank into the earth up to her knee.

Mardi thrust her hands into the mud, trying to find leverage, and she managed to pull herself up again. As she shook the heavy mud from her hands and leg, her gaze fell upon that which had first attracted her attention. Not the armored form of Evan Wytherling, but rather his jeweled sword. Much of the blade lay buried in the dirt, but the hilt remained fairly free.

She took hold of the hilt with both hands and dragged the weapon free. It proved surprisingly light, so much so that with only a little effort she found she could raise it up to chest level. Mardi doubted that she could have fended off a foe, but at least she might be able to scare them away. By itself, Evan's sword looked impressive enough to keep some adversaries from considering attack.

The tip of the blade abruptly turned of its own volition to her right.

Uncertain about what that meant, Mardi tried to walk a different direction . . . only to have the tip again turn to her right. By this point, Mardi knew that Evan walked in a world where magic and other forces of an arcane nature often held sway, even despite Rundin's official belief that such things had faded with the past or only existed in legend. Could the sword be so tied to Evan that it would lead her to him?

She had no other hope but to believe it so. There was the chance that some dark sorcery toyed with her by manipulating the weapon, but Mardi chose to think otherwise. She needed to find Evan.

Following the blade's lead, the hooded woman crossed the hilltop, ever watching for some sign of the missing knight.

More howls cut through the storm, these nearer yet. Wiping moisture from her eyes, Mardi peered beyond the hill, noticing shapes moving through the trees. No birds these, for they were the size of men and moved on two limbs more often than four. She clutched the hilt tighter, wondering if she would be able to wield the sword well enough to keep them at bay.

The tip suddenly dipped down in front of her.

Stumbling to a halt, the gentlewoman stared at the weapon, waiting for it to rise again. When it would not, she lifted it high. "Don't stop now! Show me!"

Again the point dropped earthward, nearly ripping the hilt from her struggling grip.

Why had the sword failed her now? It had dragged her nearly the length and breadth of this mound, but now it would only point down, certainly not a proper direction.

She tried to urge the sword to renewed action by simply stepping past the area in which it now pointed, but to her dismay her left foot sank into the ground . . . and continued to sink. Mardi realized that if she did not do something quickly, the earth might swallow her up completely.

Dropping the sword, Mardi used both hands to claw at the ground around her, ground that proved frustratingly soft under her fingers. Nonetheless, she gradually made some progress, finally dragging herself back a couple yards, where she then stared accusingly at the depression left in her wake.

Then something occurred to her. If Evan had come this way, perhaps he had fallen through a similar depression . . . burying him alive.

"Dear God, no . . ." She crawled to the sword, heedless of the mud. The horse had given her no idea as to what to expect and so she had only the blade for a shovel. Hardly a useful digging tool, but if Evan still lived, and a pocket of air still supported him, then she had to start immediately.

Rising, Mardi held the blade first like the very shovel she required, but that did not feel right. She also worried that the sharp edge would cut her hands to ribbons even before she managed a foot deep. Her only option was to hold the hilt with both hands and point the sword down, to try to at least open an air hole for Evan; then, she could slice through and clear more earth away.

More howls echoed around her, so near now that Mardi almost expected the creatures to fall upon her at any moment, adding to her desperation. She raised Evan's jeweled sword as high as she could . . . then used every bit of strength she could muster to bury it deep in the hill.

Lightning—lightning from the ground—flashed bright blue as the blade bit in.

The earth opened wide.

Sweat dripped over Evan's face as he strained against Grimyr's intrusion into his mind. Images of his past swarmed around him, mixing and shaping. He felt the dragon's reptilian presence slither deep, only to be repelled by the last barrier, the one put there by the wizard so many years ago.

"Again you resssissst . . ." rumbled the shadowy leviathan. The two burning embers retreated slightly as the dragon considered. "Valentin desssiresss you sssaved, but you will not allow that! Grimyr will have to teach you, then, the folly of your defiance! Even if thisss one mussst kill you, you will be sssaved!"

The knight gripped the earth beneath his hands, trying to prepare himself for what would surely be Grimyr's most terrible effort yet. Evan wondered how long even Centuros's spells could stand up against the beast. More to the point, he wondered how long he himself would be able to withstand them. Clearly, Grimyr cared little at this point if he injured or killed the knight in the process. Valentin might take him to task for it, but in the end only Evan would truly suffer.

Again the dark magic of the dragon began to eat at his thoughts. The weary knight stiffened.

"Laughable . . ." came the deep yet hollow voice. Again the stench of Grimyr's breath threatened to do what his magic had not. "Only one shield protectsss you true, Man Wytherling, and that shield will fall thisss time whether I mussst rip your mind apart or—"

The mound exploded.

Dirt and rock rained down on both dragon and knight. Grimyr roared. Moisture buffeted Evan's face and he realized that a hole had been torn open above him.

"Evan!" a voice called from above, almost imperceptible over the dragon's roar.

Reflexes took command. The knight turned around, dragging himself toward the opening as quickly as he could. It would be only a matter of moments before—

"Man Wytherling! You will not leave Grimyr!"

A discharge of rocky earth pelted Evan from behind. He heard the rumble of stone being pushed away and knew that the dragon pursued him. Fortunately, Grimyr's greater girth slowed him down a little, giving the knight some desperate hope.

The storm above made his climb trickier as he neared the top, rain and mud turning every hold into a tentative one. Below him, he heard the great beast roar again, then the scratching of Grimyr's talons on stone. Once more, a wave of fetid breath overtook him, nearly causing Evan to slip back down into the darkness of the mound.

Lightning flashed, revealing a cloaked figure bearing a sword. The knight tensed, thinking that his path had been blocked by another monstrous foe. Then, a voice heaven-sent came down to him from above.

"Evan! Is that you?"

"Mardi!" Now he recognized not only her but the weapon in her hands. "Mardi! Drop the sword to me!"

"But you'll never catch it!"

Grimyr's rumbling indicated that the dragon had to be right behind him. The mound shook, nearly sending Evan Wytherling to his long-overdue doom. "Slide it hilt-first toward me! Do it now, please!"

She fell to one knee, then set the sword against the side of the hole. The jewels in the hilt glittered even when no lightning illuminated them.

"Are you ready?" the young woman called.

Evan pulled himself a bit higher . . . just as barely visible claws tore at the wall where he had just hung. "Do it!"

Mardi Sinclair released the sword. The weapon clattered its way down toward the knight, but began to drift to his left. He shifted position, trying to meet it.

Grimyr roared, so close now that the sound shook Evan. The knight slipped, managing to regain his hold only after falling back several feet.

"You will not essscape Grimyr!"

Something snagged his left leg just above the ankle, then squeezed. Letting out a gasp, Evan searched for the sword and saw that it was sliding down the rock wall farther to the left. Knowing he had but one chance, the veteran warrior released his hold.

What held him dragged Evan down, but by releasing his hold, the knight was able to twist more to the side. The hilt slid within his reach. Evan grabbed it and lost hold momentarily as Grimyr pulled him into utter darkness.

"What do you—?" the murky form roared.

Bringing the blade around, the silver knight swung hard at what held him, two of Grimyr's lengthy talons. The dragon must have realized his danger, for the burning orbs widened and the talons released the human's ankles. Nonetheless, Evan managed to strike one, sending out golden sparks.

Grimyr cried out and pulled away, but Evan did not immediately take advantage of his release. The sparks had illuminated some little bit of the leviathan's paw and what the knight had glimpsed had startled him. Evan could have sworn that on the paw barely *any* flesh remained . . .

"Cursssed flea! Valentin be damned! Thisss one will not brook your pinpricksss anymore!"

Sword in hand, Evan began clawing his way to the surface. He felt Grimyr come up behind him but dared not look back. Above Evan saw Mardi Sinclair holding out a hand for him. He wanted to shout to her to depart but knew that without her aid he would likely never escape.

The moment the knight came within reach, she took hold. Her strength amazed Evan as she pulled him out of the crevice, but he had no time to thank her. Even though they had won his freedom from the mound, Grimyr still sought to take him back . . . and would likely drag Mardi with him.

"Run!" he shouted.

"This way!" she called, heading north.

He followed after her, but as they ran the earth below them shook. Evan took just enough time to peer over his shoulder and saw the ground behind them erupt. Huge paws with talons almost the length of the knight's body burst up through the grass, reaching for either human. Lightning flashed and this time Evan had verification of what he had seen in the mound.

The paws of the behemoth had rotted, scales and bits of flesh hanging loose from skeletal appendages with the stench of death long triumphant.

Although Grimyr clearly had not survived their last encounter so many years before, he, like so much of Evan's past, refused to remain buried.

A hulking form covered by earth and grass rose from the top of the mound. Grimyr, his overall appearance obscured by both his cloak of dirt and the stormy night, hissed. A stream of fire darted not at Evan but at his companion.

The weary knight dove, throwing both himself and Mardi forward. They rolled over the edge of the mound, the unholy flames shooting past Evan's head by a mere few inches.

The pair came to rest at the bottom, the knight's sword falling a foot or two away. Evan heard the familiar snort of his horse and knew that once more he had the creature to thank for his continued existence . . . provided they all escaped.

Helping Mardi to her feet, he pushed her toward the horse. "Mount up! Quickly!"

"But what about you?"

"I'll join you in a moment!" He reached for the sword just as a shape darker than the stormy night stretched over the top of the mound.

"Man Wytherling, there isss no essscape!"

"You said that the last time we met, Grimyr!" Evan readied the weapon. Mardi had nearly mounted; all he required were a few more seconds . . .

"You will be sssaved or elssse! You will ride with usss once more or your bonesss will we have!"

Grimyr reached down, mud and what smelled and felt like bits of old dragonscale peppering the knight. Evan brought his sword up and caught one of the dragon's claws. Again the blade sparked where he struck and this time he had the satisfaction of seeing the tip of one talon severed.

The dragon withdrew his skeletal paw, hissing.

"You are falling to pieces, Grimyr!" the defiant warrior shouted. "Soon they will find you scattered all over the area!"

He heard a great intake of breath. Sheathing the sword, Evan leapt onto his horse just behind Mardi. Seizing the reins, he urged the animal forward.

Fire of no earthly origin scorched the land where the three had been. Evan and Mardi rode, the horse clearly pushing himself to his limit.

"You will not essscape usss, Man Wytherling! Thisss land isss oursss and all within it prepared for the posssession!"

Lupine figures leapt from the woods. Evan pulled the sword free again, slicing at those nearest. He caught one creature across the chest and knew that it would fade into oblivion.

His mount kicked out at a pair of the creatures, then trampled over another. The shadowy horrors tried to drag all three down. Evan used his boot to push one away, then saw Mardi pull out her small dagger. The blade touched one of the more daring horrors and the monster suddenly vanished.

The horse at last fought his way through to a clear path, leaving Evan with no time to wonder about the woman and her blade. Behind them, Grimyr continued to roar, yet strangely the monstrous dragon did not pursue them. His cry dwindled.

Their other pursuers also fell behind and even the dark crows the knight noticed among the trees did not make another foray against them. Evan had the horse bring them toward town on a winding route, the better to give them time to recover from their trials.

Mardi first broke the silence, turning behind her to stare at Evan. This near, she made him feel so very uncomfortable. Her blue eyes, so alive compared to his own, met his gaze. "Are you all right?"

"I should ask the same question of you."

She waved off his remark. "When I came . . . I never dreamt that . . . what was that horror?"

"That was the dragon Grimyr, my lady, a beast long slain."

"Valentin's dragon?"

His eyes widened. He had forgotten for the moment that she knew of Valentin. "Aye, Valentin's pet. It seems I left much undone when I departed this region. First him, now Grimyr. Only the one I truly seek, only Novaris, seems to evade me."

"The dragon . . . Grimyr . . . there was a smell about him, Evan, and I thought . . . what little I could see of him . . . I thought I saw bone . . ."

He could see the revulsion even the memory caused her. "Yes, even more so than Valentin, Grimyr should be dead. It seems his body rots, but not quick enough. There remains some sort of hold the spirit has on it." The knight rubbed his chin. "But he does not leave the vicinity of the mound, which may mean that physically he cannot do so even though his magic stretches beyond Pretor's Hill."

"Beyond the town? What do you mean?"

Evan frowned. "You know that something foul touches this region . . . the magic is spawned by Grimyr. Yet I do not think that the dragon is the guiding force. For that I would choose Valentin."

"But he's trapped below the church!"

"So it would seem, but Valentin is more than a knight. He is Novaris's right hand."

She mulled that over for a minute, giving Evan time to study the dark path ahead of them. Despite the storm, the region seemed otherwise peaceful; perhaps Grimyr had overextended himself. Still, returning to Pretor's Hill would not be so simple a task; the taint already had rooted there.

He doubted if any of the townsfolk had even heard the dragon. Not only had the storm raged loud, but the mound remained some distance away. At best, a few sharp-eared souls likely had taken it for the rumbling of thunder. And if anyone journeyed to the mound come the morrow, Evan fully expected that they would find it undisturbed, no trace of the night's ravages remaining. Grimyr would see to that.

"What did he mean?" Mardi Sinclair suddenly asked, turning once more toward him. His puzzled expression urged her to explain. "The dragon. He said you were to be saved, that you would ride with them once more. Why would he say that, Evan? He made it sound as if you were allies . . ." The gentlewoman faltered. "And Valentin . . . he talked to you as if you'd once been comrades . . ."

So she had noticed. The knight silently cursed. He could try to explain away Grimyr's words but doubted that she would accept a lie.

"Valentin said such, Mardi, because I once indeed knew him as a comrade, even as a close friend." Perhaps she would not ask him to go into further detail.

Such a fragile hope his companion crushed immediately. "You knew Valentin that well?" He felt her draw away ever so slightly from him. "Before he became such a monster, surely!"

"I knew him when I was young, when I had just won my spurs and could claim the rank of knight. He took me on and added to my training."

The ears of the bone-pale steed stiffened. Evan's gaze darted past Mardi, but he neither saw nor sensed anything. Still, he kept the sword ready, just in case Grimyr or Valentin had decided to reach out yet again for him.

"And when he turned to evil and this sorcerer Novaris . . ." Mardi went on, clearly trying to put together a version of his past that would make sense. "You rejected him and turned to Paulo Centuros?"

"I did not meet your famous wizard until the very height of the war," Evan whispered, noting the slowing of the horse's gait.

"When you returned to fight your former friend and his master."

He could evade her no longer. She had to be told the full tale. "Mardi—"

The fluttering of a flock of birds made him pull up on the reins, but the stallion had already chosen to stop on his own. From the branches, several blackbirds cawed viciously. In the dark, a horse snorted, the sound much like a challenge. Evan's own mount snorted in return, turning his baleful gaze to the left. The knight immediately followed suit, knowing that his steed did not react capriciously.

Atop a massive and very familiar spotted stallion sat Lord Steppenwald, cane held in one hand like a riding crop. More shadow than man despite his great size, he tipped his hat at the pair. Evan could barely make out his face, but he did not doubt that the immense figure smiled.

"An interesting night's work," he commended, seemingly unaffected by the storm. "Perhaps I judged too fast, judged too fast! Perhaps you might do as well as Valentin after all . . ."

XV

A DARK AND TERRIBLE TRUTH

Evan had no time for this infernal man, not at this moment. Whatever Steppenwald's role, it did not appear to have anything to do with the machinations of either Valentin or Grimyr. Steppenwald appeared to be interested in an agenda all his own, something the knight had confronted too often in the past. "Aside, sorcerer! We have neither time nor interest in your dabblings!"

"Oh, but you do, but you do . . ." Steppenwald thrust the cane into a loop on the saddle, then held out his hands. In one, a match suddenly blazed. In the other stretched a long wooden pipe that certainly had not been there a moment before. Steppenwald lit the pipe, then took a puff on it. The bowl of the pipe glowed unusually bright, continuing to at least in part illuminate the bearded features of the man. "As much as, if not more than, your dear friend Valentin." He took another puff. "Who no doubt expected you this night to return to the fold of which you've so long been prodigal."

The wind whipped around them but hardly seemed to touch Steppenwald. For a very brief moment, Evan thought he sensed something familiar about the man, something about the signature of his magic. Yet, unless the bearded figure had truly altered his form, the knight doubted that they had ever met.

"I am most curious, most curious, indeed, about you, too, young lady," Steppenwald added, gaze shifting to Mardi Sinclair. "You should be home, safe and bundled in your bed, ever aware of my presence in your life from here on out . . . and yet I perceive that you've rejected my suggestions—"

"Leave her out of this!" snapped Evan. "She's no part to play in any drama, either Valentin's or yours!"

269

"But does she know what part you truly play, knight so errant? Have you told her the truth about the great battle and the role forced upon you?"

Ignoring the tension he felt in the woman riding with him, Evan leaned toward his adversary. "Who are you, king's man? Who is Steppenwald, if that be your name? Do you remember the battle? Did you fight there . . . under another life?"

Yet another puff, which caused the pipe to flare up, revealing the sorcerer's visage in full. Both amusement and irritation worked their way onto Steppenwald's countenance. "You think me Novaris. How flattering . . . and insulting. No, Sir Evan Wytherling, I cannot claim such an event in my short span of years, only knowledge earned at much too harsh a price . . . which brings me back to you."

"And I have said that I will have nothing to do with your dabblings."

"Not even if it brings you to your former master . . . the sorcerer-king Novaris?"

At this, Mardi let out a gasp. Evan swore under his breath, having come so close to telling her himself. Now Lord Steppenwald had revealed his terrible secret to her before he could. Surely the gentlewoman would think Evan a monster as terrible as Valentin or Grimyr.

"Dear me, dear me," the elegantly clad giant muttered, feigning disappointment in the armored figure. "Didn't you know yet, my lady? Your knight in shining armor here has a shadow cast over him, a shadow cast over him. Before he became the protector of the innocent, the judgment of evil, he himself served well the great and glorious Novaris, master sorcerer and monarch of his own realm! Why, your dear paladin even rode beside his true comrade in arms during the earlier battles of that war and it is said that crimson Valentin trusted no other knight more than him, trusted him with his life!" Steppenwald puffed his pipe. "Seems we all make mistakes . . ."

Mardi twisted her head around enough to eye the knight from

under her hood. "Evan?"

"Everything he says rings of truth, Lady Sinclair," the graying knight returned, "but Lord Steppenwald does not know all the facts of the time since I rode with Valentin into battle—"

"Which facts are those, sir knight? That you were captured by the other side, brought in chains to Paulo Centuros, a wizard of great power and questionable judgment, and, against your will, placed under a geas that twisted your very thoughts, condemned you to be not your own man but rather the willing puppet of the wizard? Or perhaps you mean the facts concerning how you returned to your side, led the other knights who followed Valentin, your own comrades, to their deaths—then turned on your best friend yourself?" He shook a finger at Evan. "Most reprehensible behavior for a knight sworn to an oath, Sir Wytherling, most reprehensible behavior."

Evan felt Mardi pull away from him as much as her seating would allow. He knew her well enough at this point to understand that she had from the beginning seen him as some legendary champion from the annals of storytellers; now she knew him instead to be a man with as vile a past as Valentin's who had only joined the cause of justice because a wizard had forced the task upon him.

"But that is neither here nor there," the king's man commented, his tone shifting to one more comradely. "A path you have taken and now that path leads you here . . . and to me. I had no idea, no idea, what to expect when I first came to this region. Research more than anything. A way to rid myself of thoughts beyond my reach. A daring dream, perhaps." He tugged on his beard. "I dream a lot, sir knight, and if you can help me achieve the greatest of those dreams, then perhaps I can help you achieve the peace you seek."

Despite himself, Evan could not help asking, "What do you mean?"

"I watched this night's events, sir! I noted the skills and I noted the luck. I noted how events shaped themselves to open doors for you that should have remained shut. I am a great believer that luck is a very potent form of magic, and you, Evan Wytherling, to have survived what I believe you to have survived since the war, to have even survived the mound, you must be lucky indeed!" He glanced momentarily at Mardi. "Even including the presence of this wild card . . ."

The knight tightened his grip on the sword. "I warned you to leave her out of this."

Steppenwald shrugged, puffing his pipe. "It may be that nothing can leave her out of this, nothing. But if you insist on trying to do that, I'll make my offer to you alone. I have a task for you and in return, I'll show you the peace you surely crave. Agree to serve me, that's all I ask."

"That is all?" Evan frowned at the man's short, cryptic offer. "And what peace do I crave?"

"You desire the truth about Novaris. I can give that to you."

"And why would I trust you to know any truths about him?" He had no intention of accepting such a vaguely worded offer from a sorcerer. Such offers generally demanded even more than a man's soul. Yet, if Steppenwald could give him some clue as to his quarry, it behooved Evan to not turn him away hastily.

Steppenwald lowered the pipe. "Look at me, sir knight. Look at me beyond the physical plane. I allow you to see . . ."

Evan did, utilizing the power of the Sight that Centuros had given him. He stared at the huge figure, seeing not the elegant, bearded aristocrat, but rather the magical force that truly represented the heart and soul of Lord Steppenwald.

And what he saw unnerved him more than anything yet, even Grimyr's unliving menace.

"Do you understand me now, Sir Wytherling?"

Steppenwald had dropped his protective spells just enough for Evan to see the truth. No longer did a man sit atop the Neulander Spotted—a fantastic creature in its own right—but rather a being of flame; dark, violet flame. Short crimson bursts dotted the vaguely humanoid form and occasionally a tiny bolt of blue energy would escape. Of Steppenwald's face, the only features remaining were two blue flickers of fire representing the eyes and a black slit where the mouth had once been.

The magical signatures of sorcerers and wizards infused their entire person and so Evan had in times past seen such forms, the magic wielders as they looked on the higher planes of existence. However, what disturbed him most about this one had little to do with the power Steppenwald clearly commanded so much as from where it had come.

"You are of his blood," he finally murmured. "You are of Novaris . . ."

The signs were all there, plain to see. The coloring of the magical forces, the combinations they made. Even the prickling sensation the knight now experienced . . . all screamed that here appeared one who had the blood of the sorcerer-king in his veins. Here appeared one who represented as much the legacy of Novaris as the evil awash over Pretor's Hill.

Yet there seemed something else familiar about the gargantuan sorcerer, something not at all related to Evan's former master . . .

A flash of lightning caused him to blink and during that blink Steppenwald reverted to normal. Evan tried to regain the image he had seen, but although he could sense much magic around them, the sorcerer looked perfectly mortal, as if one of the unTalented . . . which said much for his abilities.

"So," began the massive figure, puffing again on his pipe. "I've shown you much, so very much. Do you understand now?"

"I understand some," the knight returned, having come to one definite conclusion. "I understand that our goals are the same in some way."

"Then you understand well. And you will take my offer—"

Evan shook his head. "I cannot and will not enter into any offer with you, blood of Novaris! The get of the devil are no better masters than the devil himself!"

Lord Steppenwald lowered his pipe to his side, leaving his

face entirely in darkness. The sudden edge to his voice made Mardi stiffen and Evan better grip his sword. Even the damnable steed tensed, prepared for war. "You are either a fool . . . or the wizard's hold on you is stronger yet! The spells he cast still make you his puppet! Yes, I heard the dragon call to you, heard him call to you!" He rubbed his bearded chin. "You're not ready for me yet; you need to be softened a bit more, better tempered by the hammer . . ."

He began to turn his mount away from them, the last lingering glow from his pipe vanishing. Suddenly the storm, which seemed to have lessened during the time of the encounter, struck the knight and gentlewoman hard. Despite whatever she thought of him, Mardi Sinclair clutched tight to Evan, who held her in one arm as best he could, the reins twisted around his fingers.

"Steppenwald!" he shouted.

The giant turned in the saddle.

"Why not simply tell me what I need to know and let me take my own course? Tell me where Novaris is and I will hunt him; you know that! You achieve your own end that way as well!"

Again the dark edge in the sorcerer's voice. "No . . . I think not. I need more than that."

Lightning flashed again . . . and when it had disappeared, so had Steppenwald and his horse.

Their own horse immediately moved on, seeking now the most immediate route to the town. Neither Evan nor his companion spoke for a time, not until the first glimmers of light from Pretor's Hill could be seen in the distance. Then Evan felt Mardi pull away again, as if seeing her home meant that she no longer had any use for his tainted presence.

"Is it all true?" she finally blurted. "Were you once at Valentin's side? Did you only turn on him because Paulo Centuros forced you to?"

He could not meet her eyes. "Yes, Mardi. Those sins are mine. I served with Valentin through the war . . . willingly. I swore an oath to both him and Novaris and intended to keep true to it."

"And"—she could barely speak—"and the only reason

you've strained so hard to right their wrongs is because Paulo Centuros cast a spell on you?"

Evan wiped rain from his face and forced his gaze to meet hers. He could make out the condemnation in her expression and did not doubt for a moment that he deserved it. Yet, in truth, he could answer her neither as she hoped nor expected. "I do not know."

"What do you mean? Surely you know! How could you not?"

The knight kept his voice calm. "Every day I ask myself the question you asked before; do I serve my conscience or simply the wizard's spell? Would I return to the path that Valentin took or has my time on this endless quest molded a different man? Mardi Sinclair, I have witnessed darkness and light in all its myriad forms these past many decades and learned much concerning the struggles of mortal souls. Yet, for all I feel, for all that I regret, I cannot say in truth what would have happened if Centuros's handiwork had been eradicated by Grimyr's efforts. It may be that I would have fought on until at last the dragon chose to slay me, but it may also be that I would have embraced the presence of a comrade long lost to me, that I would have freed Valentin from his tomb and allowed Novaris's curse to eat away at your land and your people—"

"You wouldn't have!" the soaked woman blurted. "You wouldn't have!"

Her words caused him to smile, however briefly. "You have more faith in me even now than I have had all these years. Believe that if you wish, but I cannot. If I survive this quest to the very end, mayhap I will discover the truth. Once I believed that I would gain release if I succeeded; perhaps I still will." He looked past her. "We are near enough to the town. It would be best if you were not seen in my company, not even by the watch."

Mardi followed his gaze. "It seems so quiet. Surely someone heard the dragon's roar!"

"You do not understand yet the full power of magic when wielded by a master . . . and between them, Valentin and Grimyr have more than enough skill. 'Tis better this way, Mardi. Ignorance protects your townsfolk . . . for now."

"What about Lord Steppenwald?" she asked as she dismounted. Her voice rose in sudden anxiety. "He cast a spell on me in the magistrate's office! I could do nothing! I think I might've remained under his control if not for your horse. I think he broke the spell even though Steppenwald believes I did!"

Glancing down at his mount, who eyed the continuous rain with unconcern, Evan at last shook his head. "The damned beast has no such ability that I know of . . . but, then, he has surprised me often over the years. As for Lord Steppenwald, he has some thought he wishes set in motion, but I believe it only concerns me, not you. Still," Evan added, reaching to his belt, "it might be best if you took this."

He pulled free his dagger, then with his finger drew a symbol Mardi could not identify over the short blade. As he handed the ensorcelled weapon to her, Mardi stared at it as if confronted by the black dragon himself. Evan knew that she had done quite well with her own blade, a puzzle that still intrigued him, but this weapon would serve another purpose. "If you so desire, touch the largest jewel on the hilt with even a single finger and whisper my name. I will know where to find you."

The gentlewoman put it with her own, then looked up at him. "Thank you." After a brief, uncomfortable pause, Mardi suddenly reached forward, putting a hand on his leg. "Evan . . . you must know already . . . that I believe you're not the man who rode with Valentin."

So he had gathered by the simple fact that she had not fled from him at first chance. An emotion that rarely visited him threatened to make the knight utter words he knew he would regret. Mardi Sinclair saw matters too simply. She could not understand the turmoil constantly filling him. He prayed that Mardi would never face the Evan Wytherling who had been a man more foul, in his own way, than Valentin.

"I thank you for your . . . belief, Mardi Sinclair."

She did not notice the catch in his voice. "What do we do next?"

"We sleep. I will see you on the morrow. Go now! When you are safely in the school, I will come around the town and enter near the stables of the good Arno."

He thought she might not listen, but after a moment or two Mardi nodded. Then, reaching into a pouch on her belt, she removed a small book. Shyly, she handed it to a confused Evan. "I—I want you to take this in turn. There's one part in there . . . about the heart . . . that's always encouraged me during turbulent times. The entire book—it's—it's been of special comfort to me and I know that it doesn't mean anything to you, but . . . well, I—"

As much to put an end to his own embarrassment as hers, Evan accepted the book. His eyes widened briefly when he saw who had written it.

Paulo Centuros.

Startled by her choice, he looked up again with the intention of saying something about it. However, before Evan could speak, the gentlewoman gave him a hesitant smile, then rushed off toward her home. Pocketing the book, Evan watched her dwindle into the distance until at last she reached the school. As he promised, the veteran warrior did not move until the gentlewoman had disappeared inside.

Yes, she would be safe for the rest of the night, but he could not yet settle down to sleep. The gauntlet had been thrown down; Evan had to pick it up and respond.

That meant another visit to Valentin.

Mardi had hidden well the tumultuous emotions burdening her since the mound. She had understood far better than Evan had supposed and when Lord Steppenwald had announced the knight's evil past, the gentlewoman had not been nearly so surprised as she had pretended. Grimyr's words, accompanied by earlier suspicions caused by Evan's visit to Valentin, made it all too simple for her to link her companion to the darkness. Mardi had not wanted to do that, but in her heart the evidence had been damning from the beginning.

Her image of him as a tireless paladin had been shattered but not replaced by the unwilling villain forced by others to right his past wrongs. Surely Lord Steppenwald had expected her to see Evan in that way, perhaps with the hope of dividing them, but the young teacher believed that she had already learned more about the knight than either the sorcerer or Evan Wytherling himself understood.

She had seen in Evan's eyes, his tone, and his very posture that he believed himself to be beyond redemption, that behind the spell that made him so dedicated to his quest, the sinister warrior waited to be free in order to wreak havoc in the name of his master. Yet, in her eyes and mind, Mardi felt that he had to be wrong, that the Evan Wytherling who had existed then had given way gradually to one who not only understood the sins he had once committed, but regretted them with each breath.

Mardi had to make him see that, at least in part. Somehow, she felt he would be leaving himself vulnerable to his foes until that time. They had tried once to make him one of theirs again; they would not stop after only one attempt.

Knowing that Evan watched, Mardi entered her home, but she had little thought of sleep. Lighting a single candle, Mardi removed her cloak, then paced the schoolroom. The memories of tonight kept her nerves on edge, her thoughts sharp and quick. Not the reaction the gentlewoman would have expected. Lord Steppenwald alone should have been enough to make her want to hide under the blankets, but instead Mardi felt the need for action, if only in the form of planning.

She had her doubts that Evan planned to return immediately to the inn and wondered if the knight might instead have gone to the church. Mardi supposed she could go there and watch for him, but that would accomplish nothing. Visiting Drulane also appeared a foolish option, for to speak to him was to speak to Steppenwald.

Seating herself at the table from which she taught, Mardi felt slight pain from the two daggers on her belt pressing into her leg near the hip. Removing them and placing her own on the table, Mardi paused to admire the knight's jeweled weapon. The craftsmanship alone gave the knife great value, but as she held it high, Mardi also thought she felt something within, some sort of force.

Magic had always been but a part of legend and myth for her and no one in her family had ever even claimed knowledge of the craft, much less the ability to wield it. Yet, sitting there, the teacher felt certain that what lurked within the blade had to be magic of some sort. It had to be strong for someone with no talent to sense it.

Or did she have talent? Mardi considered events, trying to make sense of them. Twice now she had used her own dagger to ward off, even slay, creatures of darkness. Perhaps she might have understood the death of the shadow wolf, for it had clearly had some substance, but the ghost at the mound . . . how to explain that?

Curious, Mardi Sinclair picked up her own dagger again, trying to compare the magical one with the mundane. Her dagger had been well-enough made but hardly compared to the antique one owned by the knight. On Evan's, the gems had almost appeared to gleam on their own, while on Mardi's the dull, gray cast made it almost invisible in the dim light. How, then, could she have possibly—

The gray dagger tingled.

Mardi nearly dropped it. Where before she had felt nothing akin to magic, now she sensed it almost as strong as in the knight's ancient blade. What happened here?

Magic is of the soul whether dark or light. If one can see the magic in one's own soul, anything can happen . . .

"Anything can happen . . ." Mardi muttered. Paulo Centuros had written something about everything, it seemed, even this.

Perhaps . . . perhaps surrounded by so much magic, whatever its roots or its use, Mardi had been affected. Perhaps she, too, could work some spells . . .

But how did one go about doing that? Did she merely wish something and it happened? Doubtful; otherwise, magic would have been simple enough for anyone to perform. With so many in Pretor's Hill, surely at least one other inhabitant would have revealed such powers.

She started to place her own dagger on the table, thinking to study it more . . . when suddenly the piece dropped out of her hand and stood tip-down before her.

Certain that it had merely embedded itself in the wood, Mardi reached for the hilt, only to see the blade begin to spin. As it did, a dim glow radiated from the weapon, a glow that brightened the faster the dagger turned.

Near her other hand, Evan's elaborate dagger also glowed, but where Mardi's wore about it a faint greenish tinge, this one gleamed golden. Worse, the knight's weapon began slowly edging toward the second piece.

Rising from the table, the gentlewoman stared in wonder at the two daggers, which seemed to be vying for attention. Hers continued to spin and now she noticed that it no longer even touched the wood, but rather floated an inch above.

Something possessed her to try to reach for the hilt again, yet when she tried, the gray dagger pulled away. Frustrated, the teacher sought it again, only to watch as her own knife rose out of reach. A sense of foreboding touched her and she reached for Evan's, which, unlike the first dagger, seemed to welcome her embrace.

The dark, greenish glow had spread now and the dagger floated freely about the center of the schoolroom. So far, it had done nothing more, not made the slightest threat. However, Mardi felt certain that it intended something dire. She had simply sought to experiment with the magic she thought she had; this should not have happened.

Then . . . in the glow beneath the defiant blade, a figure slowly began to take shape. Trembling, Mardi placed a finger on the largest jewel of the dagger and prepared to speak Evan's name.

Someone knocked on the door.

Instantly, the figure and the glow faded. The gray dagger dropped to the floor with a clatter.

The glow around Evan's weapon also faded, but not before the door flung open. The stunned woman, still glancing from blade to blade, did not immediately welcome the newcomer, although she knew it had to be Evan returning. He had proved himself a true paladin once more, coming to her in her moment of need—

"Mistress Sinclair? Mardina! Are you well?"

She held back a gasp, recognizing a voice other than the knight's. Mardi looked up, met a watery but wary pair of eyes.

"Well," began Magistrate Drulane, coughing once. "Seems I've come at an interesting time."

The hour late, Father Gerard had naturally gone to bed. That made Evan Wytherling's task simpler in one respect at least. The good priest no doubt did not even stir when Evan cast the spell over his chambers. Already much drained by his encounter with Grimyr, the knight would not have brooked well any trouble with the balding man.

Once he had made certain that no one else had unexpectedly chosen to visit the church this foul eve, Evan Wytherling went to the task at hand. He drove the sword into the floor with more passion this time, impatient to see Valentin and tell him that his plot had failed.

The crevice opened, its birth as silent as ever. Pulling free the blade, he journeyed down, protective spells ready. Yet, when Evan reached the bottom, he saw no sign of the guardian. The knight lowered his blade to waist level and took a cautious step forward, assuming for the moment that Centuros's creature awaited him around some darkened corner.

Still nothing. Already Evan had nearly made it to Valentin's chamber, where the other knight remained unusually silent. The knight tensed more, wondering if perhaps he would find that chamber empty, Valentin's shackles lying scattered on the floor.

"Looking for something, my dear Evan?" the crimson figure mocked as his counterpart finally peered within. "Or should I say, are you missing something?"

Valentin remained as Evan had last seen him, arms and legs spread wide, broken lance thrust through armor, flesh, bone, and heart. The newcomer said nothing, striding up to his one-time comrade and testing the chains with the tip of his blade. They held strong. The shackles, too, continued to do their task.

"You're unusually quiet, even for you, Evan," Valentin commented, a little more subdued now. "A bit worn-out this night?"

The silver warrior walked behind him. "Not much more than any other night, Valentin."

"Well, you're looking fairly good despite that. The forest air, I imagine." He clattered the chains. "I could do with a little air on occasion, a chance to stretch my legs—"

"From what I have seen, you seem unencumbered enough already. What happened to the guardian, Valentin?"

Although he could not see the imprisoned warrior's expression from where he stood, Evan could imagine it. His former comrade enjoyed any victory, however minute, if only it left his adversaries off balance. "He retired from his post."

Evan slowly completed his circle around the other knight. Valentin gave him a smile and a nod, as if welcoming him back from a long journey. The amber eyes did not blink. This close, Evan could see how little flesh remained under the taut, parchment-colored skin.

"Grimyr failed you."

Now the bearded figure frowned, his expression turning solemn. Still the eyes did not blink. "He did not fail me, my dear friend . . . he failed you."

"The past is behind me."

"Behind you?" A harsh, soulless bark of a laugh escaped Valentin. "Behind you? Evan, you *dwell* in the past! Your entire existence is based on the past! You've hunted shadows since you left this place the first time and you come back hunting those same will-o'-the-wisps with nothing yet to show for it! The past? Evan . . . you *are* the past . . ."

He could say nothing to defend himself from the monstrous words, for here Valentin spoke too true. Evan gripped his sword tight and, before he could stop himself, ran it through the other knight at the waist.

Enhanced by magic even older than Paulo Centuros's, the blade pierced the metal shell as readily as the lance once had, then sank in deep. Valentin grunted and shivered. At last the unyielding amber eyes disappeared behind their lids. Evan could not stop himself until the very hilt of his weapon rattled against his former friend's armor.

Dismayed and disgusted with his impulsive, senseless act, Evan Wytherling quickly pulled the sword free, then staggered back. He stared at the blade, untouched by blood save a few dry black ashes on the edge.

Valentin let loose with a cough, then cleared his throat as if having swallowed something offensive. His eyes flashed open and he took a shallow breath. "I . . . haven't felt that . . . alive since you impaled me, Evan . . ."

"Valentin, I—"

The grotesque figure shook his head. "No, Evan, please don't apologize! It's a different pain than the one I've grown so accustomed to over these many years . . . it'll give me some entertainment for the time remaining to me. Besides, we both knew that your blow would not slay me." His gaze briefly swept over the lance in his chest. "That is left to another device, remember?"

Pulling himself together, Evan recalled the mission that had sent him here. "Valentin, Grimyr failed you and now I know that you are indeed responsible for the evil spreading over this region. I also know that the only way you would have been able to reach out from this place and leave your touch on the townsfolk is if Novaris had aided you in arranging this!"

"And so I demand that you tell me where he is!" the crimson warrior mocked, imitating Evan's voice to near perfection. "You're truly cursed, my friend! Not only are you forced to repeat your mistakes, but even your very words drone on and on with never any variation or new insight to them! When at last the day of reckoning comes, there shall read on your tombstone, HE NEVER LEARNED!"

The temptation to run Valentin through again became a true and urgent one, but Evan would not let his darker desires seize hold again. They reminded him too much that he could be as black as Valentin, if not more so. In a much more controlled tone, he said, "This ends now."

"You cannot stop what is all around you, Evan, what has been built up over the decades slowly and thoroughly. There is only one way in which you might, but you've no stomach for it."

"I could slice your head from your shoulders, just as they did to Haggad."

"And it would be back in its proper place a moment later. You could sever every limb and I would return whole. You know the spellwork of our master; for my loyalty to him he granted me what no other could ever earn."

"And left you then to suffer forever because of the spell that keeps you alive," the silver knight pointed out. Evan touched the lance. "I could remove this and aim more true; that would end your existence, Valentin."

"Then do it!"

Evan sheathed his sword and placed his hands on the broken end of the lance. He started to pull . . . only to release his grip against his own will.

Valentin leaned his head to the side, looking almost wistful. "You always pretended that the choice of leaving me like this belonged to you, comrade of old, when we both know that the fat wizard didn't even trust you under his puppet spell! You can no more remove the lance than I, who am chained, can, Evan, just as you can no more save the people of this realm from the long hand of Novaris . . ."

Standing there, his hands still pained from his attempt, Evan Wytherling nearly fell prey to the futility Valentin preached. Deep down, he had known all along that Centuros had forbidden him the ability to slay the other knight, who might one day prove a valuable tool. Evan quietly cursed the wizard, knowing that the responsibility for what happened in this region of Rundin lay in great part at Centuros's feet. Why had he never prepared for Novaris's treachery? Why leave it all to Evan, who in the end was only a simple warrior despite the tricks he had been given.

"Evan, my friend," Valentin whispered. "Leave this region. Leave Rundin. Novaris commanded me that when you returned . . . and he knew that you would have the wherewithal to do so . . . that I would speed along this work so that you would be trapped with the rest!" As he spoke, the imprisoned warrior nearly looked human again. "I asked him to forgive your transgressions, for they were the wizard's in truth, but he said that you could never be trusted; the touch of Centuros would always be on your soul and he couldn't take that risk."

"So he does live! Where—"

The other knight paid Evan's interruption no mind. "I, who obey him in all, disobeyed him in one thing, my old comrade! He warned me not to try to use the power that he would give me to attempt to break the glamour over you, but with Grimyr's help I endeavored to do just that. We could have ridden together as warriors under his banner once more, Evan; think of it! What battles we would have fought, your sword by mine!" His eyes narrowed and the glimmer of humanity faded away. "But you can't be redeemed and so you must die while all of Rundin eventually learns the folly of its own past arrogance."

The last, cryptic words disturbed Evan enough that for the

time being he put aside any thought about the rest of which Valentin had spoken. " 'All of Rundin'? Do not talk madness!"

"Novaris has a long memory, you know that. You think he would be satisfied with but one tiny town in the midst of nowhere? This taint will spread far and wide, covering all borders of Rundin, Evan. The people of Pretor's Hill—aah, the irony of that name now—will act as its carriers, spreading it willingly among their brethren."

Meeting Valentin's monstrous stare with his own unflinching gaze, Evan Wytherling replied, "I cannot permit that to happen; you know that. I will stop it . . . and you."

"Even when you cannot see what is right before your face, my dear old friend?" The bearded knight sighed, shutting his eyes for a moment. When he opened them again, they seemed to glitter strangely. "I'm sorry, Evan. Sorry for you."

"Valentin—"

"This conversation . . . this charade . . . is at an end, my once comrade. You will not come back here again."

The crimson figure opened his mouth wide . . . and continued to open it wider and wider. As he did, a fearsome wind that dwarfed even that of the storm outside threw Evan Wytherling back. The silver knight struggled to keep his ground, but already he could barely clutch onto one of the walls near the entrance of the chamber.

The wind ceased for a moment as Valentin, his countenance still distorted horribly, paused to speak. "Leave this region, Evan, or you will be laid to waste with the rest!"

Again he exhaled, this time the blast so strong that not even all of Evan's strength could keep the knight in place. The hapless warrior went flying backward through the narrow corridor and up the rock and earth stairs. Even the interior of the church brought no respite, for the howling wind tossed Evan directly toward the outer doors of the building.

Valentin gave him no benefit, those doors remaining shut until the knight's body barreled into them, ripping them open. Still caught up in his flight, Evan shot out into the storm, the wind and rain outside pelting him from what seemed all directions.

He dropped at last onto the center of the street, striking with enough force to leave him momentarily stunned and bereft of breath. As Evan gasped and tried to focus, he heard the doors to the church slam shut and knew even then that no entry would he gain if he tried to return.

The power. He could not have imagined Valentin wielding such power even with his likely link to Grimyr. Valentin drew from a spell far more major, one that surely had been patterned well by the sorcerer-king long ago.

And against such power, what could Evan do? As he rolled slowly over, mud and rain covering him from head to foot, the battered paladin realized that Valentin had only let him live for two reasons, the first being their long-lost friendship, now forever shattered.

The second reason had to be that he felt Evan could do nothing to stop him . . . nothing at all.

XVI

DAGGERS

"Tell me about the dagger, Mardina. No . . . tell me about both of them and what they mean to you."

She held back a shiver as she studied the gnarled man, trying to judge his reason for being here. Had he come of his own choice or did he unwittingly serve Lord Steppenwald? Evan had assumed that the sorcerer would leave them be for the rest of this night, although Mardi had not understood his logic. Now the magistrate's arrival during her sudden encounter with magic made her suspect that Steppenwald might indeed be involved.

"The . . . the grayish dagger is mine, of course, Magistrate. The other belongs to Sir Evan Wytherling, who thought it might be good if I had another weapon about my person. He was simply being protective, I think."

Drulane removed his cloak, shaking it out by the door before hanging it on a peg. He walked over to her fallen blade, then stooped down to pick it up. After a brief study of the item, Drulane looked at her, his expression unreadable. "Where did you get this dagger, Mardina?"

"I bought it here in town . . . in the market."

"Did you . . ." He turned it over, then glanced at Evan's. "Not much to look at compared to this other . . ."

Mardi kept her mouth shut, not knowing what to say. She could not believe that Drulane had simply happened by here. His timing had been too precise.

"You shouldn't be out so late and in such weather, my dear." The aged figure indicated her damp clothes and the puddles of water. "Especially for as long as it seems you were."

"I couldn't sleep."

"Nor could I," Drulane returned with what seemed significance. "I had terrible dreams. I dreamt of ghosts and dragons, knights and sorcerers . . . and I even dreamt of you . . ."

Did he recall their encounter or did Steppenwald hide somewhere without, putting words in his puppet's mouth?

"Tell me, Mardina, what do you know of magic?"

"Magic?" She tried to sound lighthearted. "Only what I've read in stories or heard from my mother when I was young, Magistrate. Children's tales especially deal with such fanciful things—"

"Do not play games with me, Mistress Sinclair."

"I don't really understand what you're talking about, Magistrate, and why, for that matter, it should enable you to come barging into my home!"

"Perhaps I can offer a reason . . ." The gnomish official seized Evan's dagger in his other hand and held it in his open palm for her to see. As the weapon filled her view, the jewels began to glow just as they had earlier.

Mardi gasped, her gaze quickly shifting to her own dagger. However, the blade did not spin nor did it fly up into the air again. She looked back at the first and saw now that it blazed with light . . . not to mention floated just above the magistrate's hand.

"Magic, Mardina. You've seen it before, I'll warrant." He coughed several times. "Pardon. The dampness. The unrelenting and outright unusual dampness. This storm is like none I've ever experienced . . . nor are the dreams I've had."

"What do you want of me? What is the point of all this?"

"I sensed the magic in here, my dear. I sense it everywhere this night, but most of all from here."

"That's absurd!" Without realizing it, the gentlewoman took a step back.

"No more absurd than wandering knights coming in and spending gold and silver two hundred years old. No more absurd than your uncle being killed by wolves who leave no trace. No more absurd than I myself wielding a power that should not be mine."

Thrusting her weapon in his belt, he snatched the elaborate dagger out of the air and tossed it upward. It flew in a precise arc, coming down point-first. Drulane held his hand out, as if he intended to catch the dagger despite the obvious horrific results. Mardi nearly turned away, but morbid fascination kept her watching.

The tip of the dagger came to rest just above his palm, then the weapon flipped over, turning the hilt to the bottom. The dagger did not drop then, but rather Drulane reached up and took hold of it.

"Now then, Mardina. You've seen my magic; now tell me of yours."

She wanted to, yet still she recalled how easily Lord Steppenwald had seized control of him. Words failing her, Mardi could only reply with a shake of her head.

Her lack of an answer, however, evidently told him something, if not what he had sought. The watery eyes narrowed; the lips pursed. Drulane took a step toward her, which Mardi countered with a backward step of her own.

"Mardina . . . are you . . . are you frightened of me?"

He asked with such incredulity that the gentlewoman paused, for the first time thinking that perhaps she spoke with the true Drulane, not one controlled by Steppenwald's strings. The thought made her want to tell him everything, help Drulane realize the pawn that the king's man had made of him. Yet, as the seconds passed by, Mardi could still not bring herself to speak the truth.

"You are fearful of me. I know my advances toward you you've rebuffed and I understand why. I've sided with your uncle many times, much to your anger, but I've never truly been a thing of evil, have I? You look as if I walk the earth as some sort of monster! What do you know, Mardina? Tell me for my sake as well as yours!"

He demanded the truth with such vehemence that the teacher

finally had to say something. "It's not you . . . Magistrate Drulane .
. . it's"—Mardi took a deep breath, expecting the massive figure to
appear at any moment—"it's your master, Lord Steppenwald!"

"My . . . master?" The gnarled man looked at her in outright
astonishment. "I serve under Lord Steppenwald and may, on a rare
occasion, call him by that term because of his rank as king's man
of this region, but he isn't truly my master as you sound to mean
it!"

"You don't even know it!" she burst out. "He comes and you
lose all sense! He commands you to sit; you sit. He commands you
to sleep; you sleep. He commands you to forget his presence now
in Pretor's Hill—"

"Lord Steppenwald is here?"

Emboldened, Mardi Sinclair nodded. "And has been for some
time, Magistrate! The king's man is a sorcerer, a master of dark
magic, and he confronted me with this fact this evening in your
very office . . . before your unblinking eyes!"

"Absurd!" Yet a look passed swiftly across the man's visage,
as if he recalled something that added credence to her claims. "But
that could explain . . . no! Ridiculous!"

Mardi thought rapidly, trying to find more fuel for her
argument. Perhaps if she could convince Drulane of the truth, he
might be able to fight off Steppenwald's influence, thereby
becoming a new ally for her and Evan. One wild notion came to
mind and although she doubted that he would recognize the name,
the teacher at least had to see for herself. "Magistrate, have you
ever heard the name Novaris?"

The watery eyes widened, then peered at her with new
suspicion. "Aye, I have, but I'm surprised that you know it, my
dear. It's one out of an ancient and dark time."

"Yes, he led the legions who tried to conquer Rundin. He was
a sorcerer. If he had not been defeated, our realm would not even
exist now."

"I am impressed by your knowledge, Mardina. So few these
days know, much less also understand, the importance of history."

Now she threw down her ace. "Lord Steppenwald claims to be of his blood."

At first he seemed not to understand. "Claims to be of whose blood? Do you mean . . . surely you jest, Mardina!"

"He said so himself to me this evening and I'll swear that by God and the king if need be!"

"Not necessary. I've known you since you were a child, Mardina. Watched you grow and came to love you as a woman years later. You're stubborn and emotional, but one thing you've never been, despite your tastes for tales of knights and dragons, is either a liar or a madwoman." He seemed to slump a little, perhaps in part due to his confession of love, perhaps also because he realized the truth of her words. "The blood of the sorcerer-king! I cannot believe it . . ."

"He means evil for us all, Magistrate. He wants something of Evan and will take it if he can."

"And that which I've sensed growing about us? That's his doing as well?"

Mardi Sinclair swallowed. "No . . . that comes from another evil."

"Another?" He had accepted her word so far, but now his expression indicated that Drulane could only believe so much. "There is more here than Lord Steppenwald's ambition?"

"There is . . . Valentin."

Evan's dagger seemed to flare briefly at mention of the crimson knight's name, although Drulane did not seem to notice it. He frowned, visibly mulling over her reply, before finally responding, "And who is Valentin?"

So Mardi told him.

She told him about following Evan, discovering the magical cave beneath the church and its terrible inhabitant. When Drulane did not mock her, the gentlewoman went on to speak of the events following, of the attack by the lupine shadows all the way through her rescue of Evan from the mound. Only Evan's own wicked past did she omit, certain in her heart that the man in the tarnished silver armor had changed completely since the terrible war.

Magistrate Drulane had seated himself during her explanation, a shadow growing over his countenance as he heard every fantastic detail. Mardi marveled that he did not simply walk out, and her hope grew. Still, every now and then she found herself glancing at the doorway . . .

When she had finished, the teacher looked at the old man and waited. Either he believed her or she had just guaranteed herself a journey to an asylum.

"We must do something."

At first Mardi did not hear him. "Pardon?"

"We must do something, Mardina!" He rose from his seat, looking, for the moment, hardly like the ill, aged figure she knew. "If you have any doubts as to my belief in your tale, let those doubts die now, my dear. I can't explain why, but what you told me sounds too true, as if I should've known some of it already. It might also help explain a little . . . about this." The magistrate caused Evan's dagger to flare again, then let it die down. "And perhaps why you, too, seem to have been granted such skills."

"I had thought myself alone in that."

"I've been able to cast minor spells for some time now, Mardina, as your noble paladin could also attest."

"But what can we do?" Mardi demanded. "And what can you do about Lord Steppenwald?"

"Lord Steppenwald . . . yes . . . you disturb me greatly with that knowledge. To think that I would be his puppet!" A look of great anger briefly washed over Drulane before he regained control of himself. "I shall deal with that matter, I promise you. Knowing what is being done to me gives me strength. As for the rest"—he fingered Evan's blade—"come see me on the morrow, Mardina. You've given me much to think about and think I will. Tomorrow, we'll have something we can do . . . against both this Valentin and Lord Steppenwald."

He put Evan's dagger back down on the table, mind clearly already at work. Mardi, who had grown up knowing that the magistrate had ever been the true leader of her town, felt less fearful. Drulane would help Evan and her. She had seen him outwit countless rivals over the years, reducing some to ruin. No matter who had run the council, Drulane had run Pretor's Hill.

"I've intruded on you long enough, Mardina," the gnarled man added, giving as deep a bow as he could. He almost reached for her hand but clearly suspected that their alliance did not include such liberties. "Get some rest . . . has the paladin told you of the candles?"

"In each corner. Always lit."

"Do so. I will send Mistress Arden to join you again."

She shook her head, thinking how even the witch woman's presence had not deterred most things. "I'd rather not, Magistrate. I'll—I'll be all right. Please . . ."

Drulane sighed. "Very well. I'll trust to your thinking. Tomorrow, though, we will meet . . . and with your paladin as well, I think."

Donning his cloak, he bid her farewell, then rushed out into the storm. Mardi secured the door behind him, feeling a bit better about events. She felt certain that Drulane would shake off Lord Steppenwald's influence, the magistrate a man of high determination when he put his mind to matters. Evan would be pleased, once Mardi explained everything.

Thinking of the knight, Mardi reached for his dagger, then realized that her own was missing. A quick survey of the room revealed no sign of the weapon.

"Drulane . . ." the gentlewoman whispered. He had secured the weapon on his own person just before his display of magic. The magistrate must have forgotten about it in his haste to leave.

Mardi started for the door, then decided against pursuing the man. Despite the glimpses of magic she had seen, even the startling flight, her dagger still lacked much in comparison to the knight's jeweled blade. Indeed, considering its sudden animation, Mardi was glad to be rid of it, at least for the time being. Tomorrow Drulane would no doubt realize his mistake and return it to her.

Blade in her belt, Mardi headed toward her bedchamber. She feared that she might not be able to sleep despite her exhaustion. Images of the events at the mound still plagued her some, not only the dragon and Steppenwald, but others such as the sinister, decapitated ghost. At least the last one she no longer had to worry about, but the memory lingered, making the shadows in her home ominous.

Thunder rumbled, the storm showing no sign of letting up. The moment she reached her chamber, Mardi sought for tinder. Tonight, she would make certain that every corner had a candle, one that would burn strong and bright until daybreak.

Lightning ripped across the heavens, eradicating for a moment the darkness. Frowning, Mardi checked her candles again.

Maybe it would be best if she let them burn even well beyond daybreak . . .

As the magistrate fought his way through the rain and wind, he contemplated Mardi Sinclair's words. Not for a moment did he doubt that she had spoken honestly with him and that bothered him even more. To think that he had been used by Lord Steppenwald, treated no better than a *dog* by the man! True, the aristocrat appeared to be a sorcerer of some means, but Drulane would not forgive him his trespass; he would see to it that Steppenwald learned the limits of his own power.

He had intended on heading straight to his abode, but something instead caused him to turn toward the church. Drulane had no desire to confront the monster Valentin and for that matter he doubted if he could have even reached the underground prison that Mardi had described. Still, Drulane felt drawn to the building, almost as if the structure itself called to him.

Let not the artisan's mask hide the true face from the light . .
.

The magistrate wiped rain from his eyes. That voice he heard in his head from time to time, the one that Drulane had mentioned to no one, not even the knight, seemed to have become more persistent as events grew direr. It appeared to be trying to guide him, although what it meant now he could not say.

As the church came into view, Drulane saw a murky figure slowly rising from the street. Lightning flashed as the mud-soaked form faced the doors of the holy building. He stumbled about, looking and moving as if he had been thrown bodily to the ground by some great force.

Sir Evan Wytherling. It did not surprise Drulane to find the man about and in the midst of some ominous incident. Had he just arrived at the church . . . or come from it?

Evan seemed to answer that question by dragging himself away from the vicinity of the hallowed building. A horse snorted and out of the mist appeared a larger form, no doubt the paladin's eerie steed.

After his words with the young woman, it made perfect sense to Drulane to approach the knight. He almost called out, but chose not to do so, for fear of drawing attention to both of them.

Drulane picked up his pace. Yes, he had to reach the warrior. At any cost. The knight appeared to be conversing with his mount, not so much of a surprise to Drulane. The creature did not strike him at all as normal. If the horse had spoken back to his master at this very moment, the magistrate would not have been all that startled.

Again he reached up to wipe the rain from his brow, his quarry so very near now.

Something hard rubbed against his forehead as he cleared the water away. Momentarily distracted, Drulane glanced at his hand . . . and found it clutching the gray dagger he had last seen at Mardi's abode.

How it had come to be with him he had no trouble fathoming, but what it did in his hand now caused Drulane to come to a halt. He could not recall drawing it and did not know why he would have done so in the first place. From Evan he expected no evil, only alliance. Yet . . . yet a part of him suddenly filled with the urge to drive the blade into the knight's neck . . .

Frozen in place by wildly conflicting desires, Drulane watched as the mud-soaked paladin mounted. Mind clearly on other concerns, Evan Wytherling did not notice the short figure. He urged his steed on, gaze focused straight ahead.

Drulane stood in the dark, watching the faint forms of rider and mount vanishing into the stormy night. The magistrate barely noticed how soaked he himself had become, thoughts still racing. The urge to kill faded slowly, but not the horrific realization of what he might have done. Over the course of his career as magistrate, Drulane had condemned a few men to death for various heinous crimes, but never had he himself ever personally attempted to slay a soul.

An unsettling vibration from his hand made Drulane look at Mardi's dagger again. A faint, ghastly glow emanated from it, a glow that grew brighter even as he stared.

"What—?" he murmured.

He tried to drop the weapon, but his fingers would not uncurl from the hilt. Drulane attempted to peel them away with his free hand, only to find that he could not even so much as loosen the smallest.

The blade turned toward him.

Swearing, the magistrate began casting a makeshift spell.

Mardi's dagger plunged into his chest.

In all the years of his quest, Evan had never felt so helpless as he did now. Valentin had the power. Valentin had the time. Valentin had the position.

Even what little rest he had garnered since last night had not assuaged Evan Wytherling one bit. He had fallen asleep with visions of the crimson warrior's triumph riding through his head and had awakened with them still rampaging. In addition, Evan noticed that even though darkness had given way to day, one could barely tell the difference. The storm roared unchecked, the clouds and mist made it nearly impossible to see beyond Master Jakes's establishment.

Draping his cloak over his armor, Evan descended from his room. He felt every pair of eyes drawn to him but ignored them, not even acknowledging his dour host. Outside, the knight fared no better; those few he passed always turning to stare, their hostility quite open.

Evan's mind worked as he walked through the rain. He refused to give in to the inevitable. He would continue to do battle against Valentin until one of them finally lay dead . . . and so far Evan had failed to slay his former comrade twice.

Valentin had forbidden him entrance to his underground prison, so for now, at least, Evan could not confront him. Nor did it appear wise to return to the mound just now, ghastly Grimyr having nearly done him in the last time. With both of those options cut off, what part of Novaris's plan remained for the silver knight to attack?

Lightning flashed, illuminating a portion of Pretor's Hill despite the mist. Evan stared blankly at the doomed town, at first seeing it only as his surroundings. Then he paused, taking in what details he could now that the lightning had faded away. The church. A store. The general layout of the streets and buildings . . .

To see the world is a wondrous thing, Paulo Centuros's voice suddenly echoed in Evan's head. *To see the truth of it is divine.*

Something struck the ground near his feet. The knight looked down and saw that somehow Mardi's book had fallen free. It lay open, an odd thing since the tight binding should have forced it to close.

As he bent to retrieve it, lightning flashed yet again. A hint of words revealed themselves in the brief flash.

Evan seized the book and brought it up to read.

The heart is the representational center of one's being,

though physically off center. A pattern of vessels emanates from it, nourishing all in its wake; and a light shines from it, captivating all in its stead. Yet evil lurks, feeding on its light, growing stronger with each beat and corrupting its bearer with darkness. A heart by nature may not always be pure. But virtue will always prevail.

The knight squinted. The words were typical of the wizard, but otherwise meant nothing of significance to—

Without warning, knowledge suddenly flowed through Evan as he realized that the town's layout, which he had already suspected of representing a spell, comprised layers that would suggest a *second,* more heinous spell.

He eyed the book, realizing only then that the words themselves blazed bright. A tremendous truth dawned on him: Mardi carried a book not only written by Paulo Centuros but also ensorcelled by him.

Evan had no chance to consider that astounding fact further, for more knowledge flowed. In the blink of an eye, he also understood that those sensitive to the pattern, the Talented, could wield its magic if able to locate the focus—not the geographic center; rather, wherever the magic drawn in by the spell field fell most into balance. Curiously, the focus itself would be most devoid of power, but by creating a link to it, a sorcerer could channel its powerful energy.

Thus could Valentin bring his master's evil to the people of this region . . . and from there spread it beyond.

Even as the knight digested all this, the book *blackened.* Evan dropped the tome, which continued to blacken and curl, as if on fire. He did not attempt to pick it up; the book had served its purpose. Evan could only imagine the complexity of the spell that had been placed on it so long ago and how the wizard had guaranteed that it would be here when needed. Evan cursed Centuros for this and previous abrupt revelations courtesy of surprising sources during his long quest, revelations that would have been handy to have sooner rather than later. It was often the ways of wizards and sorcerers to hide their secrets until the very end, as if wanting to prove how much they were needed by those serving them . . . even if that got those servants killed first.

He shook off his bitterness and returned to the threat at hand. If Evan could locate that focus, bring such damage to the structure that at even its foundation it did not remain whole, he might disrupt his adversary's spell, salvaging the rest of Pretor's Hill along with its people. That would still leave Valentin and Grimyr to deal with, but both their influence and power would wane the moment he shattered their plot.

But which building? The most logical choice remained the church. Built of good stone, it had lasted longer than most structures here . . . yet that seemed too obvious, not at all like the sorcerer-king. There had to be another possibility, perhaps Magistrate Drulane's home or even Mardi's school, assuming it had been built over another, older structure.

It would make Evan's task much simpler if he could ask anyone about such things, but the hostility he felt from everyone prevented that. The only ones who might be able to answer his questions were Mardi, who he wanted to leave in peace for the moment, or the magistrate himself.

Drulane lived far enough from where Evan presently stood that the knight decided to get his steed. If the gnomish official could not help him, then it would behoove Evan to trace the various streets of Pretor's Hill, searching for a likely choice. Better to do that in the saddle rather than on foot.

No one met him as he entered the stables, but Arno must have heard the knight, for he joined Evan as the latter finished saddling his beast. Even the terrible weather could not dampen the bulky smith's spirits and he seemed especially pleased to see the warrior.

"Master Wytherling, sir! Daring this storm, are you?"

"Yes, I am taking a short ride. I need to go a few places and it will be swifter by horse than by foot."

The large man nodded. "Anywhere in particular, sir? I know the town pretty good. Could be I know better how to get somewhere!"

Evan nearly declined, then paused. How well did Arno truly know Pretor's Hill? "Perhaps you could be of help after all. Tell me, smith, Magistrate Drulane's residence, it is an old building?"

"One of the oldest. The magistrate's family was one of the first here."

"A sturdy and daunting structure, but not as old as the church, is it?"

Arno scratched his bald head, as if trying to keep up with the conversation. "No, you're right, there. The church, she's older yet. Oldest place still standing."

The oldest place still standing. It would have to be the church, then. By necessity, the focus would have to exist first before the rest of the spell field could be created. It was, after all, the foundation of everything cast. Evan barely held his darkening emotions in check. Valentin had sealed off the church to him. Even if Evan tried entering with a group of people during Mass, he doubted that he would get any farther than the front steps before something forced him back.

Valentin and Novaris had planned well . . .

"Of course," began the smith, brightening suddenly, "if you're wondering about the first place built, that'd be the outpost. Pretor's Hill grew up around it, you see."

"The outpost?" The knight seized the straw offered to him. "Where can I find it?"

"Oh, it don't exist no more. When the garrison left, it eventually fell apart."

Again, Evan's hopes sank. The outpost no longer existed; it could hardly be the focus that he sought.

"But it used to stand right here," Arno added, smiling. "Ol' Grandpa, he built this here place right on top of the stone base. Good solid foundation." He pointed at the base of the massive building, indicating a few scant rows of rock coming up to Evan's knee. "No better built smithy and stable in all of southern Rundin!"

A foundation. A foundation that ran, as far as the veteran

warrior could see, all along the base of the building. If it remained unbroken . . .

"A strong foundation for your place of work," Evan calmly replied. "Looks as if you could bring down the entire place and the rock would still remain."

"Aye, that it would. You know, the outpost, it burned to the ground, it did, a terrible fire they say. But this little bit of wall weren't touched, not even scorched. My pa, he said Grandpa wanted to open up one end, but even a good hammer didn't chip off anything . . ."

His words verified all Evan had suspected. The focus had been under his very nose all this time. The key to defeating Valentin lay within his grasp . . . but to do it he would have to destroy Arno's smithy.

A small price to pay, although the man before him would not see it so. Still, destroying the building itself would not suffice; the knight had to see to it that in the process he also destroyed at least a portion of the foundation. With its integrity damaged, the focus would fail and the spellwork would falter.

Mortal means would not raze the stone base, however. For that, only magic would do the trick. Where a smith's hammer had failed, Evan's sword would surely work. The wizard's spells would see to it that even Novaris's work did not survive.

Behind him Evan heard others entering the stables, putting an end to his conversation. No matter, Arno had given him what he needed to know. He would find a way to compensate the genial smith if he could. The pouch from which the knight paid for everything gave him limited amounts each day, but if he kept most of it aside from this day on, he would leave Arno more than enough to rebuild his livelihood.

Evan suddenly noticed that the bulky smith stared past him, clearly surprised by whoever had entered.

Thinking that Steppenwald had dared to enter in the presence of Arno, the veteran warrior immediately turned around. However, instead of the elegantly clad sorcerer, what confronted him were several of Drulane's men, Bulrik at their lead. The venomous looks from each of them, the officer especially, nearly made Evan reach for his sword.

Their bearded leader already had his weapon out, the tip pointed at the knight's throat. "Sir Evan Wytherling, you are under arrest! Keep your hands away from your blade or I'll run you through, make no mistake about it!"

Doing as he had been told, Evan asked, "What charge do you bring before me?"

At this certainly reasonable question, the armed men nearly fell upon him. Bulrik ground his teeth before finally visibly forcing himself to remain calm. "As if you didn't know! Sir Evan Wytherling, you are charged with the attempted murder of the magistrate!" The man paused, then added, "and if you give even the least resistance . . . I'll be more than happy to save the town a trial."

Drulane. Someone had tried to kill Drulane. For what reason and why blame Evan? "How serious is his condition? Will he live?"

"Aye, he'll live, although if it'd been any deeper, we'd be talking about his corpse now!" Bulrik snapped his fingers. The other men began circling the knight. Arno stepped away from Evan, albeit with evident reluctance.

"Then if he will live, he will surely tell you that I was not the one who tried to murder him."

Now the officer laughed harshly. "Listen, you battlefield scavenger! It's the magistrate who's accused you."

XVII

DECEPTION

There stood six men in all around him, including Bulrik and the twins. Each held his weapon as if looking for only the slightest opportunity to use it on the outsider. Evan suspected that he could take the group, but that would serve only to complicate matters further. No, the best way to resolve this would be to see the magistrate, to play Steppenwald's game.

Steppenwald surely had played a part in this preposterous accusation. The sorcerer had not taken Evan's rejection well and so had made other plans for the knight.

If Drulane worked under the gargantuan man's influence, then Evan would make use of one particular trick Paulo Centuros had taught him. He doubted that even Steppenwald's sorcery could stand up to it. Evan did not believe that the king's man truly wanted him dead; Lord Steppenwald likely still thought they could come to an agreement.

Knowing that he took a risk either way, Evan kept his hands out, allowing a somewhat disappointed Bulrik to disarm him. They searched him well, seeming in disbelief that he carried only the sword and no other weapon. Evan gave silent thanks that he had left the dagger with Mardi for her safety; she might need it now more than ever if he could not immediately extricate himself from this predicament.

"What about the horse?" one of the other men asked.

Bulrik started to say something, but Arno cut him off, immediately offering his own services. "There's no better place for it to be and I'll see to it that no one touches the animal without yours or the magistrate's say-so, Bulrik!"

"Sounds good, but we'll need to check the saddle's contents first!"

Under the officer's guidance, they gave the steed a careful search, finding nothing that Evan would not have wanted them to find. Satisfied, Bulrik turned over the reins to the smith, telling him that someone might need to come for the horse at any time on Drulane's orders.

"I'll keep him secure and ready, don't you worry!" Arno replied with a smile. While he seemed to be talking to the bearded man, Evan could not help thinking that the friendly smith actually answered for his benefit. Unlike those now binding the prisoner's wrists together, Arno did not seem to be as determined to believe in the knight's guilt.

They marched Evan out into the storm. Thunder shook Pretor's Hill, sounding much too like the mocking laughter of a dragon.

The mood of his captors had grown even surlier by the time they reached the magistrate's domicile. One of the twins shoved Evan through the door, nearly sending him stumbling to his knees. Bulrik jerked him back up, then pushed him on.

As before, the officer entered first to speak with his superior. As he rejoined his little troop, Evan noticed a strange expression just vanishing from the man's face. Had it been confusion?

"Inside with you!" Bulrik commanded without ceremony.

The accused villain found himself propelled inside. Curiously, none of the guards followed.

"Well, well. Look what we have here . . . the noble knight . . ."

Magistrate Drulane sat behind his massive desk, appearing none the worse for wear. He hardly resembled a man who had just been wounded, supposedly nearly murdered. In fact, despite an even worse paling of complexion, Drulane looked in better fitness than ever. Not only did he not cough, but the eyes no longer watered and the elderly man sat nearly straight, something Evan would not have thought possible without much pain.

Intelligence still radiated from those eyes, but they had also taken on a decidedly malicious look, one that put Evan even more on his guard. This was not the Drulane he had known before.

"Well, my fine friend, you should've ridden off while you had the chance. Now there's nothing for you but to see that you pay for your misdeeds. I'm of a mind to see you hang, maybe slowly. Then again, you won't be of much use like that."

"Drulane, you know that I did not attack you."

The magistrate chuckled. "Now that was a most useless declaration, friend! There's no one here but you and me and those guards outside won't hear anything unless I shout—" He reached down behind the desk and pulled up a dagger that looked much like the one Mardi had owned. "Or you do something stupid."

The dagger stirred up new worries, but not merely for Evan himself. If the blade Drulane held was indeed Mardi's, then the situation was even direr than the knight could have imagined.

"She's quite a pretty piece, that girl," the magistrate remarked in a manner unlike himself and more in tune with the dread thought Evan had concerning the figure before him. "She likes you and I think you're fond of her, eh?"

"Leave her out of this."

Drulane continued to toy with the dagger. He made no attempt to cause it to spin, instead handling the blade more like a seasoned fighter. "She was a part of this before you ever returned here, *boy*. They all were."

Evan stiffened.

Leaning back, Drulane toyed with his shirt. The knight eyed the slit that had been cut into the area of the chest. It was just wide enough to match the dagger.

Holding the weapon in one hand, his host used the fingers of the other to spread the cut wider, revealing the flesh underneath. A savage wound marked the magistrate's chest, a wound still fresh with blood.

A cut that Evan could tell had gone so deep that it should have *killed* Drulane.

306

Evan stared at the figure before him. "*Haggad.*"

Haggad's ghost grinned through Drulane's face, a ghoulish puppet master pulling the strings of a corpse. "In the flesh, boy, if not my own." He pointed the tip of the dagger toward the knight. "An unexpected . . . bonus. That girl has power, though where from, I don't know. Whatever the reason, she used this poor excuse for a warrior's blade and drew me into it."

Evan frowned.

"My sentiments exactly." Haggad chuckled. "Thought I was trapped for all oblivion . . . until I felt this fool near her. Power in him, too, but his mind was more malleable. Wasn't hard to make him take the dagger with him, then turn it on himself when the moment was right." The more the face of Drulane grinned, the more it resembled the Haggad Evan Wytherling knew too well. "He left. I entered."

Steppenwald's continued abuse of Drulane's mind had paved the way for this madness, Evan saw. If not for that, perhaps the magistrate might have been able to withstand the general's manipulation.

"Mind you, this wasn't planned for, but I'm not one to turn down a bit of corporeal activity . . . especially with such an enticing little lady so near."

The knight suddenly leapt forward. However, Haggad proved that none of Drulane's limitations applied to him. He had the dagger up at Evan's throat before the latter's hands could reach it.

"Ah! Some spark in you, after all, boy. Sit!" When Evan had reluctantly complied, the general leaned upon the desk. "Been too long away from the war, you have. That'll cost you. The question is, will it cost *her*?"

"What do you want?"

"Better. You've got something of interest to Valentin and the lizard. My part was simply to float around and obey, pretty galling,

I can tell you, but now I've something to hope for." Haggad chuckled again. "You."

A cold chill ran through Evan. He knew exactly what Novaris's servant desired. A better body than the one Haggad wore now. "Why not simply stab me and do as you did with the magistrate?"

"Now, you know that won't work, boy. You'd be as dead as this shell and wouldn't last more than a few weeks at best! I'm looking for something a bit more long-term, especially with things all coming together at last, thanks to you."

So, it was as Evan had suspected. He was the impetus for this plan to come to fruition. Everything had waited for him to return . . . but why?

"Valentin . . ." Evan murmured. "This is his doing."

"Aye. Novaris had this all planned to come together long before this, but when he found he couldn't free Valentin, he thought the lad would be happy to simply let the chaos rise and remain chained." Haggad came around the desk, the dagger ever pointed at the knight. "We were all good and loyal to His Greatness, but death's got a way of changing someone a bit. Valentin decided he'd like to be free, just as I've recently decided I'd like to feel soft flesh beneath me . . ."

Ignoring his foe's hints at what fate might await Mardi if the knight did not obey, Evan frankly replied, "I have no method by which to free Valentin. He knows that. You should, also."

The ghost smirked. "No . . . you do. The fat wizard just forgot to tell you . . . in case you slipped free of his geas and wanted to rescue your comrade of old."

Gripping the arms of the chair, Evan stared into the eyes that never blinked. He knew Haggad; he knew the general was not lying. *Damn you, Centuros, and the games all you spellcasters play!*

It did not surprise him in the least that the wizard had done such a thing, yet, why give Evan such an ability if he were not to use it? There was only one reason Evan could think of.

Haggad laughed. "He sees the light, the boy does! Aye, the wizard also thought that His Greatness might come back here. It's a game they've played for centuries, those two, each trying to toy with and outwit one another while we all die valiantly around them."

There was more to it than that, Evan knew. Paulo Centuros had read his rival well; Novaris could not help but come back to see if he could make the site of his loss the beginning of his great revenge.

Of course, Novaris was no fool, either . . .

Evan once more silently cursed both spellcasters. Some hint of his anger must have shone through, for Haggad only grinned wider—which made Drulane's much-too-pale face more macabre.

"See, the fat one knew that you might have to free Valentin for one reason or another, but he wanted it on *his* terms . . . as you ought to appreciate. Some circumstance would make you remember when the time was right, some circumstance Paulo Centuros liked, boy. Now, would you be interested in knowing just what?"

It was all Evan could do to keep himself from springing at Haggad again even though that would mean danger, not only to him, but, more importantly, Mardi . . . and Rundin. "Tell me, General, and let's be done with our little chat."

Haggad reached for some of the wine Drulane kept. He poured some for himself and drank before responding. "By His Greatness! Such a taste! Of course, even sludge water would taste sweet after being dead so long!" To the knight, the ghost answered, "It's simple enough—"

A simple answer can often be the most complex one to find . .
.

The wizard's words abruptly echoed in Evan's head. At the same moment, he felt a tingle in his left hand.

The next breath, he gripped his sword.

"Damnation!" Haggad roared. He threw the dagger at Evan. The sword came up of its own volition, deflecting the deadly missile just before it would have struck the knight in the throat.

Haggad gripped the desk and shoved with more might than the body of Drulane indicated. The huge piece of furniture tumbled toward Evan, whose body rolled back off the chair without his commanding it.

Some protective spell that Paulo Centuros had planted in Evan had seized control, an event that the knight had never confronted before . . . at least to his memory. If the wizard had hidden this from him, it was possible he had also made Evan forget past such situations. Evan would have dearly loved to know what the ghost had intended to tell him, but that was a moot point now. Now, his body sought only to put an end to the parasitic spirit.

As the general neared the door, he called out. A guard came barging through. Haggad shoved him toward Evan. When a second man—one of the twins—burst inside, Haggad seized the man's sword.

The twin looked in confusion at the false magistrate—and Haggad ran him through.

The spell still controlled Evan's body. He feared for the innocent guard facing him, certain that the wizard would not be so concerned with the loss of a life where some greater plan was concerned. Yet the knight's sword instead worked to force the guard back, even when it could have gutted him.

But barely had Evan been spared the fear of slaying an innocent, than the man gaped . . . and slumped toward him. Behind the falling figure, a grinning Drulane wiped the blood from the stolen sword.

"You're in a lot of trouble, boy! They're not going to like what you've done here! Killing these brave lads!"

Evan knew better than to argue. Given the magistrate and the stranger, the townsfolk would immediately see the latter as the murderer . . . that despite any evidence to the contrary.

Shouts came from without the chamber. Haggad chuckled, then lunged.

To his surprise and relief, Evan found it was his own reflexes

310

that now responded. With the knight having no choice but to do battle, the spell had faded. Evan felt no gratitude to the wizard for that, aware that his situation had now grown more precarious because of the spell. He had hoped to use the information from Haggad to his advantage, but that hope was no more.

Haggad closed with him. Although the general's blade was not of the quality that Evan's was, Haggad had been a veteran warrior of great skill and the knight quickly found himself backing up. It did not help that Evan still felt in part as if he faced the magistrate, though nothing remained of the unfortunate Drulane save his abused shell.

Bulrik and two other guards charged into the chamber. The surviving twin gazed down at his brother, then roared. He pushed past the other guards, seeing only the man he believed his sibling's killer.

Haggad, intent on Evan, did not see the towering figure come up. Even the presence of the magistrate meant nothing to the distraught twin. With one mighty arm, the giant propelled his master to the wall. Ironically, the act enabled Haggad's blade to briefly get through Evan's guard and cut a shallow slash across his right cheek before the general went flying.

Evan grimaced at the notion of having to confront Bulrik and his men. He glanced past his opponents, but the doorway offered no escape.

The knight slashed at the twin, then lunged for a window.

He went crashing through, glass raining down upon him as he fell in a crouch outside. A few locals gaped at sight of him.

Evan ran.

Bulrik thrust his head through the window. "Stop him! Murderer! Murderer!"

Several of those in the vicinity suddenly began drawing their weapons. Their expressions revealed more than merely determination; they looked eager to take Evan.

He ran toward the stables, whistling at the same time. An anxious moment later, the stallion came charging out of the wooden building. Arno stepped out immediately after, looking much relieved at the sight of the knight. That the horse was still saddled came as no surprise to Evan, who suspected that had Arno even had a chance to remove the saddle, the animal would have prevented it. Both rider and mount had been in such situations often in the past, and the horse—far more than what he appeared—would have suspected that Evan might need to suddenly flee his captors.

Sheathing his sword, Evan leapt atop. The ghostly steed raced on.

A horn sounded from farther within Pretor's Hill. Angry shouts arose everywhere. Evan paid them no mind. He had no choice but to ride.

In the chamber of the magistrate, Bulrik shouted orders, then rushed to the one he believed his master. Haggad allowed the unwary guard captain to help him rise.

"Magistrate! Has he hurt you?"

"I'm fine, boy! Never mind me! Go after that murderer . . . but see that he lives so that we can hang him properly!"

"Yes, Magistrate! Come on, you lot!"

The remaining twin jumped up and raced after Bulrik. For the moment, the false Drulane stood alone save for the bodies of the two men he had slain.

Haggad returned to the sword that he had taken from the dead twin. Hefting it, he eyed the small stain of blood on the tip. Evan's blood.

The general grinned. There had been a reason that he had wiped the blade clean prior to his battle with the knight.

"Should be just enough . . ." he murmured.

Mardi had barely begun her day when she heard the first shouts. Seizing her cloak, she rushed outside to see what was going on.

Two men hurried by. Their faces were filled with anger . . . and something else that the gentlewoman could not identify save that it unnerved her.

"What is it?" Mardi dared call out.

One of the men glared at her but answered, "The stranger's gone and murdered two men and tried to kill the magistrate! We're to bring him back for hanging!"

She could not stifle a look of shock. "He tried to kill Drulane?"

But the men paid her question no mind as they rushed on. As the two vanished from sight, four men on horseback passed the school. Two held torches and all were armed. Their expressions matched those of the pair Mardi had questioned.

Evan couldn't have done this! she insisted to herself. Drulane was one of the few people they both trusted. The knight would have no reason to attack him and certainly would not have killed anyone else.

That armed men continued to pass by indicated that Evan had at least managed to escape. Still, Mardi wondered where he would be able to hide. There was nowhere else around for miles and she knew that he would stay in the vicinity.

Mardi studied the faces of the men who gave pursuit. She saw no mercy anywhere. An obsession filled her fellow townsfolk that went beyond the capturing of a murderer; the people of Pretor's Hill looked eager to spill blood.

Her first desire was to go after Evan and help him, but she saw the folly of that. Mardi had no idea where to find Evan and certainly did not want to accidentally lead some of the hunters after him. Besides, she was aware that the forest was not safe for lone riders . . . and perhaps even search parties.

Drulane. Maybe he can make sense of all this! Surely, he could not be the one accusing Evan. Mardi hastened to the magistrate's building, avoiding the attention of other townsfolk, most of whom seemed to be interested in adding their strength to those already chasing the knight.

There were no guards at the entrance and the door stood ajar. Mardi stepped inside but neither saw nor heard anyone. She almost called out, but something prompted her to silence. With everyone so stirred up, she did not want to cause any unnecessary commotion. It might be that Drulane sat in a chair or lay in his bed recovering from injury.

Mistress Arden! Mardi knew where the other gentlewoman kept her quarters. As the one overseeing the magistrate's home, Mistress Arden had an entire apartment for herself. It was somewhat presumptuous of Mardi to go to her uninvited, but Drulane *had* indicated that Mistress Arden was available to her whenever the younger woman needed help.

Only when she got close to the apartment did Mardi finally call out. She repeated the name twice, but Mistress Arden did not answer.

"Aah, my dear girl . . ."

She gave a start, then whirled to face Drulane. He was clad in a travel cloak and looked as if he had just come back from somewhere. He wore a sword at his side.

The sword drew her attention. It was not sheathed and far too large for someone of the magistrate's general condition to wield. From its size, Mardi would have assumed it more practical for a much larger figure such as one of Bulrik's men.

"Your timing is impeccable," he remarked with a grin.

Mardi shivered. As a woman, she had seen grins like that before and had steered clear of men bearing them. That Drulane now wore such a look bothered her even more, for he had always been most respectful with her.

"Master Drulane! I heard that you'd been attacked . . ." Mardi hoped by turning their encounter to the matter at hand that the magistrate would stop leering at her.

Unfortunately, even though the grin vanished as he replied, his gaze still lingered on her in a way she did not like. "Evan

Wytherling slew two good men and nearly did me in, girl, but I escaped in the end." He extended a hand to her. "Let's continue this down in my chamber—my official chambers—and leave the old lady alone."

Neither his tone nor his language bespoke of the man she had known for most of her life. Mardi hesitated.

Before she realized what was happening, she stepped back from him. Her hand moved as if on its own and seized the door handle to Mistress Arden's chambers.

"Come away from there, girl!"

Mardi threw herself into the room.

Mistress Arden lay sprawled in a chair, blood from a gaping wound in her chest staining her dress. From her startled expression, she had died quickly.

The teacher looked back at the supposed magistrate. "What are you? You're not Drulane—"

"Now, have you forgotten me already, girl?" He held up a dagger . . . her dagger. Blood stained it and when the magistrate opened his shirt a little, she saw the wicked wound that should have killed him.

Now she remembered the tone, the words. What inhabited Drulane's body was something very vile.

The beheaded ghost from the mound.

She had thought that she had gotten rid of him, but instead she had given him the means to wreak worse havoc and claim innocent lives.

"The witch woman, she was too suspicious from the start, but she couldn't figure out why. Would've preferred a little fun first, but time was of the essence." The ghost grinned through Drulane's face. "Course, now that I've taken care of some things, I think you and I can spend a little time together undisturbed after all . . ."

Without a word, Mardi undid the clasp of her cloak. The false Drulane winked. "That's a good girl . . ."

She threw the garment at him.

As it had done with the shadows, it now spread wide. The

cloak enveloped him before he realized what was happening. The false Drulane swore as he futilely slashed at the enshrouding cloak.

Mardi pulled out Evan's dagger, much better designed for a dire moment like this. She prayed that she was right about Drulane. With that wound, he had to be dead for this creature to use his body so.

She lunged at the struggling figure. The ghost had already cut through a part of her cloak. Another moment and he would be free.

Murmuring a prayer for the dead magistrate, the gentlewoman aimed for the chest.

The dagger sank in only a tiny bit. Not enough to kill a foe. Mardi started to panic.

But a glow arose from the blade. Simultaneously, the ghost howled.

The torn cloak went flying away as a blinding light burst from where the false magistrate stood. The possessed corpse fell against a wall.

A shrieking form that vaguely resembled the ghost—but with his head seemingly attached—ripped free from the shell, which slumped on the floor.

"Damned witch!" the specter roared as his form twisted and distorted. "Damned witch—"

A fiery aura surrounded the foul being. It burned away at the ghost's form.

Mardi's attacker gave one last howl . . . and melted to nothing.

She pulled back in shock, nearly dropping Evan's dagger. Glancing from Drulane's body to Mistress Arden's, Mardi knew that she had no choice. It would be impossible to explain this scene, just as it no doubt had been impossible for Evan to do so.

Secreting the dagger in her garments, Mardi rushed out of the building.

Where should I go? She contemplated returning to the school and acting as if nothing had happened, but there was too much chance that someone might have seen her enter the magistrate's place.

Mardi headed toward the stables, where she kept her horse. Much of Pretor's Hill was silent now, but she could still hear activity in the distance. It was as if no other purpose existed for the townsfolk save to find the knight.

The stable doors were open. Mardi quickly but quietly entered.

"Mistress Sinclair?"

Arno stepped from the shadows. He appeared to have been hard at work fixing a harness.

"My—my horse. I need her."

The smith frowned. "Not safe out there, Mistress Sinclair. A lot of hotheads. Good folk not acting like themselves. I don't understand what's going on with this town."

His tone relieved a slight bit of her tension. Mardi had feared that Arno might be like the rest, but he was clearly still Arno. "I know. I still need my horse, though."

"You're going after him. Sir Evan, I mean . . . to help him, not hunt him."

"That's right, Arno."

He set down the harness. "I'll get her ready real quick."

As the smith rushed to the horses, Mardi finally took a breath. She looked around, seeing if there was anything else she might use as an extra weapon.

"Not much, but it serves me well," Arno remarked.

She stirred, discovering that at some point she had drifted off while still on her feet. The smith had her mount ready.

"What was that?"

"This place. It serves me well, like it did my family before me."

Mardi took the reins. "And you've served Pretor's Hill well, too, Arno."

He shrugged. "I try."

She nodded her thanks, then urged her mare on.

The sky continued to darken. Something was stirring and she

felt that it was coming to a head very soon. Mardi did not know why she thought she might be able to find Evan where the townsfolk could not, but she had to try. He was still the town's best hope.

If there still *was* hope.

Arno watched the gentlewoman ride off, the smith more concerned than he had let on. Mistress Sinclair was a good person and one of those whom Arno truly liked. He also liked the knight, even though they had not known one another for very long.

She'll find him, he finally decided. *She'll find him and they'll set the town right, they will.*

He returned to the harness. Hard work always settled Arno's nerves. All these strange goings-on, they were for more clever people like Sir Evan and the teacher.

A brief noise from the quarter where he kept the horses made the smith pause. To his mind, it sounded like one of the remaining animals had gotten out of its stall. Arno had not noticed anything wrong with the other gates, but in all the excitement, he supposed that one of them might have accidentally been loosed by someone who had been too impatient to let the smith get his horse. The initial rush to pursue Sir Evan had meant a number of angry figures in the stables.

Arno ran his establishment with pride, and if even one steed escaped, it would be a blow to his reputation. The smith grabbed a lantern and headed into the darkened area at the end.

A huge figure rose up before him.

"What—?" was all Arno got out before a heavy hoof struck him a glancing but powerful blow to the side of his head.

The smith collapsed, the lantern falling beside him. Fortunately, the glass did not break or else the stables might have gone up with Arno in them.

From his attacker, there was a furious snort. Steppenwald's

Neulander Spotted raced out of the stable.

XVIII

VENGEANCE STIRRING

Evan's mount charged through the forest, leaving behind the other horses. Few creatures could match the beast's speed, at least among those of mortal nature. Yet the knight urged his mount against the horse's full swiftness. He wanted his pursuers to have some glimpse of him . . . at least for a few more moments.

His path took him far west, away from everything. The next nearest town that direction was more than a week from Pretor's Hill. They would assume he had headed that way—at least, that was his hope.

When Evan had estimated that he had gone far enough, he had the damnable steed veer north. The terrain there was far more treacherous for a horse to maneuver than any other direction.

Even the knight's horse had trouble scaling the rough rise. The beast snorted in what seemed determination to show his rider not to underestimate him. The knight rightly held his peace and was rewarded when the horse finally reached the top.

From there, the path evened out. However, Evan chose then to pull on the reins. He waited, watching for the hunters.

They rode by a minute later, not even slowing. To his good fortune, the entire lot vanished to the west.

"Back to town," he told his mount.

The steed gave him a snort that indicated he already knew that, then headed east. Even despite the thick forest, they made good time. Evan sighted the first hints of Pretor's Hill.

But something else caught his attention, something glittering to his left even despite the dimness of the day. Evan considered, then urged the horse toward it.

His eyes widened. The source of the glittering was none other than his own *armor*. It lay jumbled as if hastily dropped.

That this was a trap was the first thing to occur to the knight, yet he could not simply leave his armor. One of his chief reasons for returning to Pretor's Hill had been to retrieve the armor, which had its own special spells imbued in it by the wizard.

"What do you think?" he asked his mount, but the horse chose to make no sound or even movement. The decision was entirely Evan's.

Dismounting, he drew his sword and peered around. Evan neither saw nor sensed any threat, but even the spells of Paulo Centuros could not protect him from everything. The knight would have to take the armor and trust he could face whatever danger surrounded it.

When he came close enough, Evan prodded the breastplate with the tip of his blade. No spell leapt out to ensnare him.

The horse snorted once more.

Evan gave him a glare, then slowly bent down. He picked up the plate.

Still nothing happened. Taking an even greater chance, Evan set aside the sword and sheath and began donning his armor. Even when nothing remained to put on save his helmet, all was calm.

"Mardi's doing? Or some new spell hidden from me by Centuros?" Evan asked his steed as he first hooked on the sheath.

This time, he was rewarded by a shake of the head.

The knight put the helmet on.

As he did, he heard another horse approaching. Someone had not been fooled by his trick.

He quickly mounted, then drew his sword. From what Evan could hear, it sounded as if only one rider approached. A single foe he could take.

A moment later, Mardi rode into view. She looked confused but determined. Brambles dotted her garments and her hair hung loose and in disarray.

"Mardi," Evan called softly, as he removed his helmet.

Her face lit up with relief upon seeing his face. Evan felt an unusual warm flush in his cheeks.

"Evan! Thank God!" She urged her clearly exhausted mare to him. "I was afraid that they might've caught you!"

"I evaded them by taking this path. How did you find me?"

She looked puzzled. "I just . . . I just went where I thought you'd ride."

Evan shook his head in wonderment.

"Evan . . . there's more. That ghost from the forest . . . the one with his head cut off—"

"Haggad?" The knight stiffened. "You know about Drulane?"

"Yes! I went to the magistrate, not realizing then. I found out that he—I found out about how he used my dagger to take Drulane's body!" She was shaking.

Evan suddenly had a strong desire to embrace her, comfort her, but there was no time. "You could not have known that would happen. Haggad will pay for his monstrous crime—"

"It's—he's gone! I used your blade on him this time. I threw my cloak at him like I did in the forest against the shadows; then, while he was tangled in it, I stabbed him with your dagger. Its magic destroyed him, burnt his evil spirit to nothing! If not for that, I'd be dead . . ."

The knight's brow wrinkled. "The dagger has no magic like that. I gave it to you for the reason I mentioned. You should have done as I told you; I would have come immediately."

"In the heat of the moment, I just forgot." Her mind remained on the previous subject of the ghost. "If it's not magical, then . . . how did it happen?"

"There are many questions surrounding Pretor's Hill and a few of them include you, Mardi Sinclair. The only answers I have thus far are—"

A savage howl reverberated through the area. The two looked in the direction of the inhuman cry.

Another howl arose from the south, this one closer.

"Ride!" Evan ordered. "To the northeast!"

Mardi obeyed instantly, her nervous mare suddenly finding the strength to run.

The knight glanced over his shoulder just in time to see several shadows forming among the trees. He shifted his seating and prepared to face them.

A third howl erupted from the direction that he had just sent Mardi.

Swearing, Evan Wytherling turned forward again and kicked the bone-pale steed in the sides. The horse snorted and raced after the teacher.

The howls arose from everywhere. A half-seen form raked at the steed's flank, drawing wicked slashes. Evan's mount snorted again and picked up his pace. The knight slashed at the shadow creature, but missed.

Eyes well suited for the dark, Evan spotted Mardi far ahead. She rode as if all Hell gave chase.

A moment later, it seemed it did. More of the shadow creatures emerged from between the trees.

Evan cut at two that were within range. He chopped off a clawed hand and slashed through a chest, both times watching with satisfaction as the creatures faded. Yet, ahead of him—and between him and Mardi—more came into being.

What is happening here? Evan had not counted on this. So many lost souls . . .

He looked toward Pretor's Hill, but the town was not yet visible. As he chased after Mardi and continued to do battle with the shadows, the knight sought to catch some glimpse.

And then, for just the blink of an eye, the town revealed itself. To most folk, to the unTalented, there would have been nothing to see but a few lights. Even those were gone the next instant.

But Evan had seen what he most feared. To his eyes, to his vision that had been altered by the wizard, Pretor's Hill was aglow in a distinct black and crimson aura.

This game's coming to fruition, to fruition, Steppenwald decided as he entered the church. *Time to give Valentin one last chance to deal . . .*

The sorcerer could not only see the aura now over the town but could *feel* its potency even as he walked among the pews. He cared not a whit what happened to Pretor's Hill nor even Rundin itself, which would surely fall if everything went as Novaris had long planned. Evan Wytherling was fast running out of time himself; the events set in motion with his arrival would soon come to a head.

"Can I be of some service to you— Why it's Lord Steppenwald!"

Father Gerard came from the back doorway leading to his quarters looking quite relieved.

"My greetings, good Father, my greetings."

"Praise be that you are here, my lord! The entire town seems to have gone mad! Perhaps the presence of the king's representative can bring some order back—"

Father Gerard halted as Steppenwald raised the dragon cane. The priest stared at the gleaming, mismatched eyes.

"Do forgive me, Father. I've enjoyed my talks with you in the past, but this is of the utmost importance."

The dragon head hissed.

Father Gerard grabbed at his collar as if it tightened around his throat. He threw his head back as he let out a gurgling sound.

And then . . . the priest froze where he was. However, his skin, his clothing, now all bore a different coloring, a different texture . . . as if Father Gerard were now formed from pearl.

The sorcerer stepped up to the priest. He pressed the tip of his cane against Father Gerard. The tip flared.

The petrified figure toppled to the floor, smashing into countless unidentifiable pieces. Steppenwald made a tsking sound.

The priest no longer a concern to him, Steppenwald tapped the cane on the floor. The moment the steps opened for him, he made his way to Valentin's prison.

"Evan Wytherling would not make such an entrance," the crimson knight called out as Steppenwald reached the bottom. "Therefore, it can only be the fat sorcerer . . ."

"Your jibes are wasted," Steppenwald returned as he entered Valentin's chamber. "And you are wasting your chances, too, wasting them."

Valentin remained motionless. "I've been curious as to exactly what you want from me in return for my . . . release."

Steppenwald leaned close, steeling himself against the crimson knight's deathly visage. "Your loyalty. Your oath of fealty. You and I are bound together in a manner not unlike that which binds you and the dragon buried beyond. That bond is *Novaris*."

The imprisoned warrior slowly grinned. "Aah! I know you for what you are. I guessed it well when last you were here."

"Then you know that besides the power to free you, I also have the power to fulfill my promise in regards to your former master. Give me your solemn oath and we shall bring him down."

"Certainly! I promise!" Valentin gently shook the chains. "Now, if you please . . ."

He earned a look of contempt from the sorcerer. Steppenwald eyed the broken lance. "Play not with me, knight. I can bring relief . . . or pain."

He touched the dragon head to the lance. A faint green glow emanated from the head and spread to the lance.

Valentin let out a cry of agony. Steppenwald immediately removed the cane.

"You will swear loyalty to me in everything that you swore to him and you will include the Throne Oath so that I know that all the others have been sworn true. Otherwise, there is another who can readily fill the same capacity as you and perhaps might be less trouble."

The amber eyes never blinked. It was all Steppenwald could do to keep from looking away. Only by reminding himself just who he was and what advantage he had did he succeed. Valentin was a potent power even chained.

"Even for Novaris, Evan Wytherling would not stoop to sell himself to you, fat man."

"And you?"

Valentin smiled. It was a ghastly display. "Now that you've answered my question, you've nothing more I want."

Taking a step back, Steppenwald eyed the captive with disbelief. "All I heard of you is true! Obsessive in your obedience to him, even at your own cost!" He stamped the cane on the floor, causing angry red sparks that matched his mood. "Very well, very well! Fulfill his vengeance! See Rundin fall! In the end, you'll still be left here, forever the marionette whose strings bind him more than his chains!"

The sorcerer turned from Valentin and headed toward the steps.

Shadows formed there. Shadows with a decidedly lupine cast to them.

Surprised but not dismayed, Steppenwald gestured with the cane. "And begone with you, you pathetic dogs!"

But the shadows only strengthened in both might and number. More to Steppenwald's frustration, they began to move into the chamber, forcing him to retreat.

"You think that you can be Novaris, but you understand him so little," Valentin called from behind him.

Growing angrier, the sorcerer spun back to the prisoner. "Your little game—"

Steppenwald nearly dropped his cane.

The chain holding the knight's left wrist suddenly fell away, clattering against the floor and the wall. Valentin gave Steppenwald a mocking grin and shook his other wrist.

That, too, fell away . . . and for the first time, Steppenwald could see that the bracelet had melted just enough to let the knight free himself. The sorcerer stared in continued disbelief as Valentin likewise shook his remaining chains free, then reached for the broken lance still buried in his chest.

The ancient weapon came loose with a horrific sucking sound. The part that had been embedded in Valentin was crusted over with blackened blood; the sharp tip was still moist.

The wound itself sealed over, the flesh and then the skin becoming whole . . . if not also as pale as death. A breath longer, and even the armor had remade itself. Only then did the knight inhale and exhale greatly, as if taking his first true breath in two centuries.

He finally focused on his visitor. Valentin raised the lance as if to throw it at Steppenwald, then reconsidered. "No. I'll take this with me. It'll make for quite an appropriate gift for another . . ."

"This is . . . impossible . . . impossible," the sorcerer finally managed.

"Had you pressed your case earlier, there would've been a slight chance that I might have weakened," the former prisoner explained, tucking the broken lance in one arm, "but Evan was kind enough to provide me with the key I needed for my personal freedom . . . even if he still doesn't know it."

"But—he would have to give you—" Steppenwald's mind raced madly, his calculations all awry.

Holding up one wrist, Valentin revealed the tiny drops of red liquid still staining his armor and hand. "His blood. That accursed wizard was cunning. With Evan as his slave, there was no chance that my onetime comrade would even donate a drop."

"Then . . . how?"

"You and he can thank the general for that," the crimson knight replied, not bothering to clarify.

"Haggad?" The sorcerer knew of the ghost but had never considered the beheaded officer more than a verbal annoyance.

Valentin gestured to the stairway. Steppenwald followed his hand and discovered that the shadow wolves now clustered in larger numbers. Worse, they seemed quite interested in him.

"I'd love to stay and tell you everything, fat man, but now that I can stretch my legs, I find myself eager to renew old acquaintances . . . and bring Rundin the long-overdue retribution of my lord."

The knight walked through the shadows. Steppenwald tried to follow, only to have the shadows converge on him.

From the steps above, Valentin's voice cheerfully called, "Fret not, my friend . . . I'll give your regards to Novaris once Rundin is no more than a scorched wasteland . . ."

The words were followed by the grating of stone. Valentin had sealed the way behind him, leaving Steppenwald alone with the creatures.

The sorcerer held up the cane. The dragon eyes flared. "Keep away!"

Valentin's beasts continued toward him unhindered. Steppenwald moved farther back, casting a spell at the same time.

Undaunted by Steppenwald's casting, the shadow creatures lunged at the sorcerer.

Valentin glanced at the powdery pile that had once been Father Gerard. Novaris's servant sensed his identity immediately. "Pity. I did enjoy your sermons, misguided as they were."

The crimson knight walked outside. There, Valentin paused and looked up at the darkened sky. He inhaled deeply, then smelled the air.

How sssweet the air mussst be, rumbled a familiar voice in his head. *How sssweet it would be to sssmell it again . . .*

"Calm yourself, my dear friend," Valentin declared to the air. "Soon, we will fly together again . . ."

Thisss will not be over until he isss dealt with . . .

"Evan will be brought back into the fold, rest assured."

And if not . . . ?

Valentin's smile faded. He stared off into distant memory.

"We have a duty to fulfill. That will always come first, will it not, Grimyr?"

The dragon did not reply, save to make a satisfactory grumble. Valentin looked about him, seeing that more of the shadows were gathering near him.

"Aah. Ready to make amends for your failure to your master?" he mocked. When some of the shadows moved as if in anger, the knight added, "Don't worry. Our good comrade Evan will certainly be there. He can also make amends for betraying all of you . . ."

This time, there was much agitation among the creatures. Some looked beyond Pretor's Hill. Valentin peered there as well.

"Aah, yes. I know. Worry not. I promise you that he'll be with us when the time comes. We will all be ready when the time comes . . ."

Valentin began striding through the town, heading toward the forest. Around him, the shadows flowed and mingled, their eagerness growing. Valentin fed off their eagerness and, in turn, felt Grimyr do the same.

How hollow your victory will become, Paulo Centuros! the knight thought, his anticipation growing with each moment. *In the end, the only legacy of the war will be our vengeance upon the fools who followed your lead . . .*

Mardi's mare frothed at the mouth. Her pace flagged. Mardi hated having to push the animal, but she had no other choice. Everywhere she looked, the shadows surged toward her.

But suddenly, out of the shadows burst Evan and his steed. Sword in hand, he cut through shadow after shadow, finally making his way to her.

"Your reins!" he ordered.

She gave them over. Evan pulled the mare close to his horse. The mare was hesitant but finally found the pallid steed more agreeable company than those pursuing them.

Mardi gripped her mount's saddle as they rode, feeling more reassured now with Evan leading the way. She could no longer tell which direction they rode, praying only that it would not lead them to the townsfolk.

"Keep your head low!" Evan shouted.

She ducked as more and more branches rushed close over their heads. As Mardi did that, her gaze returned to some of the shadows giving chase.

For a second, the teacher saw not those shadows, but rather *men*. Soldiers. Armored and armed, they continued their pursuit of the pair. Their faces were drawn, dead, but there burned in them a fury that she knew was focused on Evan.

They regained their shadow forms, and when Mardi turned toward Pretor's Hill, she saw an odd aura over it and the surrounding area.

"What's happening to the town?" she cried out.

The knight's gaze revealed surprise. "You see it?"

"How could I not?"

"Because you are not a wizard or sorcerer . . . but you are clearly something!"

Those words did not encourage the gentlewoman. Mardi already knew that something had happened to her, and she was as afraid of it as she was of the things chasing them.

Evan's steed suddenly reared. A creature that resembled a human only in its most basic shape suddenly stood in their path. It was at least nine feet tall and had a brutish face and form. In one hand, it held a bloody club.

"Through!" Evan commanded his mount.

Mardi thought him insane, especially when the troll—for that was what she finally recognized it to be—raised its weapon. Yet the horse obeyed, charging directly into the monster.

Leaning forward as much as he could, the knight thrust his sword. The point drove through the troll's chest just before the bone-pale steed would have collided with the huge figure.

The troll shrieked and dissipated like mist in the morning sun.

"Another specter!" Evan told her as he sat back. "Have no fear!"

Yet a sense of foreboding made Mardi look back at where the troll had been . . . and there she saw the ghost reform.

"Evan! It's not destroyed!"

He peered at the monster, which had turned to follow them alongside the shadows. "The magic grows stronger! Valentin is unleashing Novaris's vengeance this night!"

"Are you referring to the ghosts?"

"In part . . . but there is surely much more." Evan's expression grew grimmer. "I must find a place to keep you safe! I must return to the mound!"

"I'm going with you!"

"Impossible! The town is—"

The knight abruptly grunted in pain and keeled forward. With twitching hands, he managed to sheathe his sword before he lost it.

Mardi seized both reins. "What is it? What's wrong?"

But the knight could not hear her.

Grimyr's thunderous voice pounded inside Evan's mind. *Man Wytherling! We have not forgotten the price you owe usss!*

The world swirled around Evan. He teetered in the saddle as the force of the dragon's presence made it feel as if the knight's skull were about to explode.

Your comradesss of old demand your penance! They demand your sssacrifice!

The dragon pushed at the final barrier in Evan's mind. Evan felt that barrier begin to give, and the fear of what truly lay behind it made him fight back harder.

Valentin commandsss that you ssserve again! Grimyr went on. *One way or another, thisss will be done!*

The strain grew worse. Evan gasped for breath. His pulse pounded. The knight gritted his teeth and wrapped his hands painfully tight around the reins as he fought to stay conscious. He had no idea what was happening around him, nor whether Mardi was safe.

Mardi. Evan tried to speak her name, hoping it would somehow help drag him back to the real world.

Instead, the frustrating voice of Centuros arose in his head. *Reality and fantasy are two sides of the same coin, interchangeable according to how one flips that coin . . .*

Evan felt consciousness slipping away. With his last thought, he cursed all wizards and sorcerers . . . and especially Paulo Centuros.

"Evan!" Mardi used one hand to push the collapsing knight back in the saddle. At the same time, she tried to see where they were going.

To her surprise and dismay, Pretor's Hill again appeared on the horizon. *But we weren't going that direction! He took us away from that area!*

Evan's mount also appeared to notice this unexpected change in direction and compensated. Mardi watched with relief as the view of Pretor's Hill began to shift to the east.

And then . . . suddenly it was before them, nearer than ever.

The stallion snorted and veered once more.

The town reappeared before the party a moment later, even closer than previous.

Mardi looked to Evan for help, but he was still unconscious. His horse slowed, a sign that he, too, was uncertain as to how to proceed.

The teacher thought hard. Only she could deal with what was happening, yet she was no one. She expected some saying by Paulo Centuros to come forth. This time, though, there were no words.

But there was a feeling.

Mardi pulled out Evan's dagger and held it hilt-up.

"Show us the way," Mardi whispered. She had no idea how to cast a spell, but if some power did lurk within her for whatever reason, then she hoped it—perhaps combined with Evan's own spell—would at least be able to obey a straightforward command.

The jewels of the dagger gleamed in the dark. More than that, they shone a colored light that did not simply spread forth in all directions, but rather *one*.

"That way!" she ordered the two horses.

The ashen steed replied with the sort of snort that she had heard him give to the knight, but the animal followed the glow away from Pretor's Hill. The town gradually faded from view and this time did not abruptly return.

But barely had they begun rushing that direction when Mardi's horse began to flag. The mare simply could not maintain the pace of Evan's unique beast. She tried, but, more and more, it became difficult for Mardi to hold on to the stallion's reins.

Mardi looked around. No sinister apparitions could be found nearby, which both encouraged and concerned her. She debated for a moment longer, then had both horses slow. As soon as the knight's steed was close enough, Mardi climbed from one saddle to the other, sitting herself behind him. With Evan still unconscious, her seating was somewhat precarious, but she was willing to take that chance.

Releasing the mare's reins, Mardi shooed the poor animal off. The horse did not at first want to obey, but exhaustion finally forced her to fall behind. Mardi hoped that being without the teacher would give the mare a chance to survive.

Evan moaned. He raised his head and looked around as if not certain where he was.

"Are you all right?" she finally asked.

He looked over his shoulder. Mardi gasped at a face that was and was not human. Evan's skin had a reptilian hint to it and the eyes burned like fire.

The knight jerked forward. Another groan escaped him. He hissed, then muttered something that she could not make out.

Evan pitched from the saddle.

"No!" Mardi tried to hold on to him, but he was too heavy for her, especially at the awkward angle. Evan toppled, landing hard on his side and then rolling several yards from the path.

His horse needed no urging from Mardi to return to the fallen figure. As soon as they were near, she dismounted and went to Evan's side. In addition to the cut on his cheek—which seemed to have already healed much since last she had looked at it—the veteran fighter now bore a large bruise on the opposite side. Fortunately, it seemed as if his armor, especially his helmet, had saved him from disaster.

"Evan . . ." Mardi leaned close to avoid being overheard. Evan showed no signs of the horrific transformation and Mardi began to wonder if she had imagined that. Still, he had clearly suffered some attack and had evidently fought back.

She repeated his name, but with no better results. Mardi lifted his arms to drag him and discovered just how difficult an armored body could be to move. There was no manner by which she could possibly lift him into the saddle.

The horse snorted quietly in what the gentlewoman somehow recognized as a warning. Raising her head, Mardi heard the clatter of hooves.

It sounded too heavy to be the echoes of ghosts. Mardi assumed it was the mounted party from town. She held still until the clatter began to die away, even though a part of her wanted to call to those she had always considered friends.

When it was silent again, she returned her attention to Evan. He lay as if dead, but she could see that he breathed.

"What's happened to him?"

Dagger in hand, Mardi turned to find Arno peering at the scene. The smith guided two horses, one his own, the other her mare. Arno had a bruise even more spectacular than Evan's across a good part of his head.

The gentlewoman did not answer. She studied the smith carefully. Everything about him indicated that he was who he seemed to be . . . but then, she had thought the same about Drulane.

To the side, the knight's mount snorted quietly again. The animal did not seem at all disturbed by Arno's presence. Indeed, the smith turned at the sound and gently reached a hand to the stallion.

Rather than bite the hand, the horse sniffed the palm, then snorted calmly.

It was a good enough sign of recognition to Mardi. Filled with relief, she jumped up and hugged the astonished smith.

"Thank God! Thank God!"

"Mistress . . . what's going on everywhere? The folks are all acting peculiar! I was kicked by what I think was Lord Steppenwald's Neulander, and then, when I woke up, I had this great urge to go riding out after you. Never thought I'd even find you until I came across your poor girl here."

Mardi petted her horse on the snout, feeling guilty for having abandoned her. "Lord Steppenwald's a sorcerer and a traitor to Rundin—"

"Then, he's gone and done all this?"

"No . . ." She had no idea how to explain. Arno was a good man but a very basic one. How could he understand in mere minutes what it had taken her so much time to accept?

"This is a . . . much older evil than him," came Evan's voice.

The gentlewoman and the smith went to his side. Evan smiled briefly at Mardi, then studied Arno.

"You grew up in the rooms above the stable, did you not?" the knight asked.

"Yes. Like my father before me and his before him . . ."

"The eye of the storm," Evan murmured to himself. "Protected without knowing."

"What do you mean?" Mardi asked.

Evan ignored her question, saying to the smith, "The foundation is the oldest part of the town . . ."

"That's so, Sir Evan."

"I must ask a favor of you, then. I see it now. You must return to town and find a way to break or at least crack a part of the foundation, destroy its completeness."

Arno considered for a moment, then nodded. "If you say it must be done."

His easy agreement surprised Mardi. Evan, however, did not seem so startled. Waving away assistance from either, he rose and then studied Arno close. The smith simply stared back, waiting for the knight to finish.

"Pretor . . ." Evan frowned in thought. "No coincidence. The wizard's doing again, no doubt."

"Pretor?" Mardi repeated in utter confusion.

"The resemblance is there. It had been so long, I'd forgotten how the general looked. Now that I have looked close, there can be no mistake."

Her gaze went to Arno and suddenly she understood. "You mean that he is descended—?"

"The blood of the general flows in this man, yes."

"Me?" Arno flushed. "I'm akin to someone who was supposedly in whatever war was here, but always figured it was just some pikeman, Sir Evan! Not no great general like himself, no sir!"

But Evan was adamant. "It fits Paulo Centuros's tricks. He must have planned this with the general. A guardian who wouldn't even know he was one."

"But . . . can't be true!"

Mardi did not understand, either. "How could Arno be what you say?"

"He of all people proves immune to Novaris's plot. Arno also finds us much easier than he should have, even considering the mare. Nothing here is coincidence."

"General Pretor . . ." the smith muttered. "If you swear it, I'll believe you, Sir Evan, but I don't know nothing about guarding anything . . ."

"But I know the wizard. Do what I ask, but if something else comes to mind—something urgent—follow through with that. Whatever it is, it will be the right thing to do, I believe."

"If you say so." He looked with concern at Mardi. "She coming with me?"

"No," she answered before Evan could.

He did not argue with her, instead saying, "We have little time. Let us be gone."

The smith proved an agile and quick man when motivated. He mounted swiftly, then offered the reins of the mare to Mardi.

Evan shook his head. "My horse will continue to carry us. It will be better that way."

Arno nodded, then rode off with the mare at the side of his own mount. Evan did not even wait for the smith to vanish before mounting up. He then assisted Mardi in sitting behind him.

"I would have you ride in front of me, but in battle that would not be the safest place," he told her.

She nodded understanding. Still, the knight worked to make her seating more secure. As he did, Mardi finally asked, "What happened to you before? What was that change?"

Evan did not look at her as he urged the horse forward. "That was Grimyr. The dragon."

"Evan! What did he try to do?"

"Make me Novaris's servant again, one way or another," the knight said flatly. "He failed in that, though he succeeded in another thing."

"What?"

"Grimyr desires release from the mound. As with Valentin, I am the one who can bring it to him . . . and with this attack, he has convinced me that I must."

XIX

THE DRAGON STIRS

Throughout the forest that had once been a battlefield, the ghosts grew in numbers. Many were without focus, without consciousness, and merely repeated their duties and deaths over and over. Yet more and more began to move with purpose, the shadows of these lucid ghosts appearing briefly in the shapes of both men and wolves. These broke off from the others and began a more methodical trek through the region, their vacant eyes searching hungrily for something.

And separate from even those ghosts moved the original shadows, those that had once been knights serving the sorcerer-king, knights betrayed by Evan Wytherling and cursed by their own lord for such carelessness. Now, they had a chance for redemption, for revenge, and so they acted with intense purpose. They hunted the betrayer . . .

All this Valentin surveyed with growing satisfaction. Helmet in one hand and broken lance in the crook of his other arm, the crimson knight strode among the memories that were quickly becoming things of consciousness, things of retribution.

The beginnings of a new army that would destroy Rundin from within.

Valentin knew of his master's ultimate intentions, but those were matters far off. First, Rundin had to pay the price for listening to Paulo Centuros; and, on a more personal level, Evan Wytherling would pay for being too weak.

My poor Evan . . . I did try to save you! Now, you will have to pay, no matter what.

Grimyr intruded in his thoughts. *Thisss one did warn you.*

Now he will only be trouble.

Evan has played his part. He has only one purpose now, Valentin countered.

Thisss one would be free . . . the dragon reminded Valentin. *How sssoon? How sssoon until Grimyr feelsss the air again?*

Very soon, the knight promised. *Very soon . . .*

The specter of a morag took form a few yards ahead of Valentin. The monstrous warrior from Novaris's army, his bat-wing ears shifting as if to listen, abruptly gazed down at Novaris's lieutenant. The ghost bared his teeth and backed away, moving directly through trees as he sought to avoid Valentin's attention.

Valentin's ghastly grin stretched wider. The specter's acknowledgment of him meant that the spell was growing stronger yet. More and more of the ghosts were crossing from being simply memories held in place by the magic of the great dragon to again becoming things with thoughts, with emotions . . . with hatred for the one who had slain them.

A large party of riders approached. Valentin watched with expectation as they pulled up before him, the newcomers seemingly at ease with the ghosts forming around them.

"He's escaped us," a glaring Daniel Taran informed the knight.

"No. I know exactly where he's going. You've done your part."

As he said this, the faces of Daniel and the others slackened. They simply stared at Valentin, awaiting orders.

Movement from within Pretor's Hill made Novaris's lieutenant turn again. From the various houses and buildings, other expressionless men and women—and even children who could walk—slowly wended their way to him.

"Aah, the core of my army," Valentin jested. "More so than you look, to be sure. After all, through you, the others grow stronger . . ."

He isss nearing . . . Grimyr informed Valentin.

The crimson knight's eyes narrowed. "Well . . . we wouldn't

want to leave our good friend waiting, then, would we?"

He pointed at one of the riders, who dismounted without a word and offered his steed to Valentin. Helmet on, the knight handed the rider the lance, then climbed into the saddle.

Daniel Taran, eyes glazed, handed Valentin his sword. Valentin sheathed it, then took the lance from the other man. Without a word, the crimson knight led the townsfolk toward the mound.

Barely had they departed when Arno entered the area on the edge of town. He had seen his friends and customers moving about as if with no minds of their own and had waited until the sinister figure had led them into the forest. Mardi Sinclair's mare stood tied to a tree just out of town. The smith led his own mount through the empty street toward the stables. He saw no one but could not be certain that there were no stragglers.

Around him, the specters of the past continued to coalesce. They disturbed Arno, but thus far none seemed to notice him. He hoped it would stay that way.

It was with tremendous relief that the smith reached his beloved stables. He loosely tied his horse's reins to a post just inside so as to keep the animal available for a quick escape.

It was a shame to destroy his home, his place of work, but Arno trusted in Sir Evan. If it needed to be done to save Pretor's Hill—and from what he gleaned maybe *all* of Rundin—then he would surely try his best to follow through.

The smith eyed the interior, trying to figure out how best to accomplish his task. In most places, the foundation was covered. He needed—

Movement at the edge of his vision made Arno look that direction.

A pale figure clad in dusty gray armor drove an ax into the smith's head.

Arno let out a gasp . . . then shivered even when the ax continued through him without touching. The ghost swung at him twice more, each strike a fatal blow . . . if either had been solid.

Swallowing hard, Arno stepped back. The specter, a look of rage on its rotting face, vanished.

"Best—best to get started somehow!" the smith muttered, anxiously seeking any other phantasm that might be trying to sneak up on him. The ghost had been too real for his tastes, and he was not all that sure that the next might not be able to follow through better with its attack.

Arno looked at the interior again . . . and finally saw the spot that looked most promising. A long piece of the foundation was visible. It would still require tremendous effort, but then Arno *was* the strongest man in town.

He took hold of the hammer he used for shoeing. A few test blows would show whether it would do the trick. If not, the smith had some other ideas—

A tremor shook the stables.

The smith tumbled to his knees, the hammer dropping. His horse reared, tearing the reins free. The animal turned and raced out of the stables.

"Come back here!" Managing to stand despite the still-quaking earth, Arno ran after his mount.

The horse continued down the street. Arno took a step that direction, then halted when he saw the church aglow from within. The smith hesitated, not certain whether he should check with Father Gerard. He had not seen the priest among the ensorcelled townsfolk.

A figure stepped from the church, but it was not the good father. Arno instinctively stepped back out of view as Lord Steppenwald looked about.

A furious snort made Arno at first think that his mount had returned, but instead it was Steppenwald's Neulander trotting up to the church. The smith put a hand to the bruise on his head, suddenly recalling the last time he had seen the foul beast.

Steppenwald mounted. Only then did Arno realize that the man's path would take him past where the smith stood. Arno pushed himself farther back even as Steppenwald raised his cane and muttered something.

The smith waited for several seconds, but Steppenwald did not ride by. There was, in fact, not even any sound of hoofbeats, as if the Neulander still stood in place. Despite his certainty that it was the wrong thing to do, the smith finally peered around the corner again.

Steppenwald and the horse were gone, gone without having even moved.

Arno swallowed, then immediately turned back to the stables. He had to get to the task at hand. He had the feeling that time was running out faster than he and the others had supposed . . . and that wherever Lord Steppenwald and his horse had disappeared to, it was not going to be to Sir Evan's benefit.

The forest was filled with war.

Evan rode past the ghosts, most of whom were not yet aware of their circumstances. But those warriors that were lucid eyed him with a combination of hatred and fear. By the time the main battle against Novaris all those years ago had reached its culmination, the majority of those still alive had become aware of the traitor in their midst.

From the troll's attack Evan had gleaned that, while they were more resilient, the strengthening specters did not yet have power to injure or slay the living . . . but he suspected that would soon change. Valentin's power was growing stronger. Evan and Mardi had to reach the mound quickly.

Then they would only have to worry about the dragon and Valentin.

Evan felt guilty about taking Mardi along, yet not only was he uncertain as to where he could safely hide her, but he had every suspicion that he would need her inexplicable powers at some point. Besides, the knight doubted that he could have kept her from following him.

The caw of a blackbird was the only warning they received before the air around them filled with carrion crows. The avians swarmed the pair, flinging themselves at riders and mount without concern of sword and teeth. The ghostly steed crushed a pair of birds in his mouth, even as the knight skewered another and then cut two more in twain.

Mardi held Evan's dagger up and sought to stir the light within it as she had against Haggad. The first blackbird to face the light spun in a circle, then collided with an unsuspecting comrade. Mardi held the dagger toward another that approached and saw that the light blinded the creature. She shifted the weapon back and forth, creating chaos among those fiends that attempted to attack her.

Evan cut down another bird. "There is something wrong here! If these creatures still served Valentin and Novaris's cause, then they should *desire* us to reach the mound! Either there is something amiss, or they all serve another . . ."

"Steppenwald?"

"None other! What reason he has to delay us, I do not know. Whatever his purpose, it can bode no good—"

The carrion crows flew off. As they did, Evan spotted another rider ahead, this one no ghost.

"Aah, my good friends!" Steppenwald raised his cane in greeting. The dragon eyes flared. "Here I thought I might not catch you in time, not in time, indeed! Thankfully, my friends were able to slow you a bit . . . and test you again, too." He shrugged slightly. "Admittedly, they weren't too happy about the latter, but, oh well."

"Leave us immediately, sorcerer," Evan warned, "or I will do to you as I did your puppets."

"Now, now! Is that any way to show gratitude—gratitude, I say—for retrieving your armor for you?"

The knight pressed. "What do you want?"

Leaning forward, Steppenwald answered, "An alliance, naturally, an alliance. Together, we can deal with Valentin, then hunt down his master! The power and riches alone should be worth that effort and certainly completing the wizard's quest at last should be of interest to you!"

Evan frowned. "I sense enough about you to understand that such an alliance would serve me as well as joining Novaris himself. Do you think I do not know the blood flowing within your veins, Steppenwald? If Novaris is not your sire, then he is not far removed . . ."

While Mardi gasped at this revelation, Steppenwald simply chuckled. "Very good, very good! You are impressing me! Knowing that, you should appreciate in turn the power I wield!"

"The power you wield is given to you in small amounts by Novaris, who may be blood but sees you only as a slave, I'm certain. Do I impress you with that knowledge, too?"

Much of the sorcerer's good humor fled. "I have served that one much too long! I will have my right, my right! Join with me, Evan Wytherling, and both our desires come true!"

In answer, the knight kicked his horse's flanks. With an eager snort, the bone-pale steed charged.

The Neulander responded with a fierce snort of his own, but Steppenwald gestured with the cane. The mismatched eyes flared.

Sorcerer and mount vanished.

Despite that, Evan slashed at the air near where the two had just been. He turned his mount, then thrust again.

"What are you doing?" Mardi called.

Evan finally stopped his futile attack. "When a spellcaster vanishes, it does not mean that he has always left the vicinity. A casting of concealment takes much less energy than actually moving to another location. I learned that long ago . . . after I lost a comrade due to my ignorance."

She gazed up at him. "You've lost many over the course of this quest, haven't you?"

"I swore to this quest alone, but there were always those who chose to ride with me despite my reluctance. They often had their own reasons. Most I would call friends. Most I also saw perish." He shivered, then stared back at her. "I should not have brought you here. If you die—"

"I choose where I go, not you," the gentlewoman returned defiantly. "Now ride on."

He started to say more, then clamped his mouth shut and nodded. As they moved on, the knight considered the ramifications of what had just happened. Evan had rejected Steppenwald's offer; would that mean he would give it next to Valentin? True, Valentin might see no reason to accept it, either, but neither Evan nor Mardi could be certain of that.

Then, they came upon a region of the forest that made all concern of Steppenwald moot. Evan recognized the rising landscape even in the dark and from the distance.

"The mound . . ." he whispered. "We must beware—"

Welcome, Man Wytherling! And have you brought for thisss one a tasssty morsssel? She looksss delectable!

Evan could not answer, for the sudden force of the dragon's new assault on his mind sent him reeling again. He heard Mardi calling out to him, but she seemed miles away.

Leave my thoughts! he demanded of the leviathan. *You will gain nothing from this intrusion! Nothing!*

The dragon only laughed. Visions flew through Evan's mind. Grimyr again soared above the world, scorching entire lands with his flames. Yet, this time it was not Valentin who rode upon him, but rather *Evan.*

Thisss one will take your mind and if not return you to who you once were, then sssimply keep you from all thought!

The knight groaned as the pressure within his skull multiplied. He fought back as best he could.

Soft fingers against his cheek abruptly brought him some sense of reality. Mardi's voice in his ear cut through the force of Grimyr's mind.

"Evan! You must listen to me! Evan!"

He focused on her voice . . . and suddenly heard yet another with hers.

The strength of two is not merely one doubled . . . it can be a hundredfold greater, if those two are bound by the soul . . .

Evan did not know whether to once again curse the wizard or take heart from those unbidden words. The knight felt Mardi's presence grow. He listened to her, gratefully accepted the touch on his cheek . . .

And Grimyr vanished from his mind.

" . . . the mound!" Mardi cried out. "Watch out for the—"

His vision cleared just in time to see the land rising up in front of them at an impossible angle. Then . . . the world erupted. He and Mardi were tossed into the air as if nothing. His horse let out a sharp cry—a cry of frustration and anger, but never fear—and then all Evan saw was tons of earth falling upon him.

Mardi had scarcely had time to thank God for Evan escaping from what she was sure was the dragon's influence before calamity struck. Unlike the knight, she had been all too aware of how the landscape had suddenly shifted, bringing the two of them and the horse atop the dread mound. Evan had wanted to reach the area, but she was certain he had not wanted to simply charge into the dragon's ghastly lair.

But that no longer mattered. What did was surviving and trying to find Evan. Mardi struck the ground hard and rolled over and over. She attempted to stop more than once, but momentum kept her going.

A tree trunk finally ended her uncontrollable journey. The teacher's shoulder slammed into the wood, causing her to scream. For a few seconds, Mardi had no notion of anything but pain and vertigo.

When she could think again, she tried to push herself to her feet. Her first attempt failed utterly, but at least her breath began to return. She inhaled deeply, ready to try once more.

A tingle coursed through her that had nothing to do with her injury and everything to do with the sudden fear that something dire occurred nearby. Fearing for Evan, she managed to prop herself against the tree, then looked for him.

Instead, what she saw was Valentin.

He was both alluring and monstrous. The knight seemed the master of all he surveyed. He had just dismounted and eyed the ruptured mound with great interest.

It belatedly occurred to her what he held in one arm. The teacher stifled her shock at the sight of the lance, still a wicked weapon despite missing its back half. She did not want to think what Valentin intended for it.

Someone moved behind his horse. Mardi expected either the shadows or more of the ghosts . . . but saw instead something that to her was even more terrifying.

The people of Pretor's Hill followed Valentin as he strode toward the mound. Many of the men carried swords and a few other weapons, while the rest of the townsfolk wielded kitchen knives, pitchforks, pieces of wood . . . anything that could be used to kill. What made the image even more horrific was that even children numbered among Valentin's followers.

The townsfolk moved as if puppets on strings. Valentin gestured and they came to a halt. The crimson knight moved on.

Mardi searched in vain for Evan. She could find neither him nor his horse. She did find the dagger, a small comfort. The teacher managed to push herself to her feet, wondering all the while why Valentin did not see her. Did he know of her presence and merely consider her nothing of consequence?

If the latter was the case, Mardi intended to do the best she could to make Valentin regret that mistaken belief. What the source of her magic was, she still did not understand, but somehow it had to be tied to this dire situation.

She took a step in Valentin's direction, only to have a heavy hand fall upon her shoulder and keep her where she was. Her body no longer responded to her commands.

"Now, now, my dear Mistress Sinclair," Steppenwald murmured in her ear. "I don't think it would be so very good to disturb things at this moment . . ."

Evan gasped for air as he tried to dig himself out from a heavy mass of moist earth. That he was not dead had less to do with luck than it did another's desire to keep him alive . . . for at least a few moments more. He hoped Mardi had fared better, perhaps falling farther from the mound, although he knew she would yet be searching for him.

It was that intention that the knight hoped to use, even if it did mean his eventual sacrifice.

His helmet proved too cumbersome in his limited surroundings. Evan reluctantly tore it off, then renewed his digging. The earth fell around him, forcing him to constantly blink. It filled his nose and mouth despite his best efforts. Just as Evan felt certain he would suffocate, he found a pocket of air. The exhausted knight used what there was to fill his lungs. All the while, Evan felt himself being watched.

The earth began churning and great claws reached for Evan from below. He flung himself back as much as he could, then jabbed with his sword.

Grimyr roared, but from annoyance, not any wound Evan had caused. The great claws tore away at the dirt and rock before the knight and the dragon's shadowy muzzle thrust through. The stench of decay washed over Evan, nearly overwhelming him.

The burning embers that were the behemoth's eyes glared at the puny human. "Man Wytherling!" Grimyr bellowed. "You only delay the inevitable!"

"Better to delay it than simply accept it!" The knight lunged as best he could from his position. The tip of the sword just barely missed the snout.

Laughing, Grimyr continued to tear away at the earth and rock. Evan noted with interest that the dragon did not simply rise above him, which would have left the human no chance. There was a limit to what the fiendish creature could do, at least for now.

"Thisss one will feassst upon you! Thisss one will grow whole again on your blood!" the dragon roared, evidently no longer concerned with Valentin's interest in keeping their former comrade alive.

It was all Evan could do to keep his face from becoming buried while simultaneously fending off the oncoming leviathan. He kicked against the ground beneath him, trying to push backward, but collided with a wall of rock.

"Come, Man Wytherling! At leassst pretend you have a chance! Ssstrike! Ssstrike!"

He ignored Grimyr's goading tone, awaiting his chance. Evan tried not to think about Mardi as he struggled. He had hoped to set her down before reaching the mound, but had again underestimated Valentin's evil and Grimyr's power.

From the earlier revelations given to him by Paulo Centuros's bespelled book, the knight knew from where that power originated. The beast was magical, yes, and, through spellwork that Evan had only just begun to understand, bore a semblance of life even though death had long claimed him. Yet the true driving force that kept Grimyr so animated at this point could only be the same that ultimately enabled his magic to give more substance to the ghostly memories of the battle.

The dragon drew from the very life energies of the people of Pretor's Hill.

His surroundings shook again. Evan managed to get to his knees. Grimyr's ever half-seen visage filled his gaze.

"To dream isss to die, Man Wytherling! If you wish to dream, thisss one will be happy to help you die!"

Grimyr opened his mouth and inhaled.

Evan had no choice. He threw himself forward, the sword held as far ahead as the knight could manage. He aimed for the dragon's gullet.

Grimyr pulled back his head, at the same time canceling the burst of flame. The dragon's left paw swung at Evan. The knight had been expecting such an attack, but it came quicker than even he had calculated. Evan twisted the sword to meet the paw, jamming the blade into what he believed was dried flesh and scale. Sparks of magical energy arose from the wound.

Grimyr let out a furious roar. He withdrew the one paw while at the same time coming around with the other. Evan rolled away, evading the claws, but Grimyr's attack sent rock flying. Much of it pelted the knight. A pair of sharp stones sliced Evan on the hand and the chin.

The dragon inhaled again. The knight had no doubt that this time the flames would come. He held the sword point-up and murmured.

Fire enveloped him as Grimyr unleashed raw fury. From the sword there radiated a light that wrapped around Evan as if an all-encompassing shield. Even then, he felt much of the blistering heat, but it was still better than being burnt to a cinder.

A somewhat startled Grimyr pulled his shadowed face back into the darkness as Evan's desperate feat became clear to him. The knight did not waste the hesitation, instead using the sword to weaken the earthen ceiling above him. Rock and dirt came crashing down between the human and the dragon, and Evan saw a hole leading to the surface.

Sheathing the sword, he pulled himself up just as the dragon's claws tore through the collapsed earth. Evan climbed out of the mound and rolled down the side.

The quaking ceased.

Evan landed in a crouched position. With one smooth movement, he drew his sword and waited.

The mound remained still.

A darkened figure stepped atop the ruined area, then peered down at the knight. In one hand he held a fractured spear.

"Bravo, Evan," Valentin quietly complimented. He took a

step closer and his face became more visible, as did the lance.

Evan said nothing, simply staring back and thinking of his encounter with Haggad.

The crimson figure made a brief, mocking bow. "Yes. Free. Thanks to you and the good general. He came to me in a most unexpected form, a friend of yours, I believe. Offered me the blood in exchange for your body when we were through with your mind. He seemed sure that we would not be able to turn you back."

"He was correct, at least in that."

"And by that statement, I have my answer as to why dear Haggad has gone missing. A shame . . . about you, I mean," the other knight added with a slight frown. "A shame that we have not been able to save you." The ground beneath Evan's feet began to quiver. "And so, since we have what we need from you, the only choice remaining for us is to *kill* you . . ."

With a thundering boom, the mound burst open. The entire region shook. Nearby trees toppled. Dirt and rock flew everywhere, massive chunks larger then men first soaring high, then plummeting everywhere. Evan backed up as the vicious rain poured down on him. Far to the side, the people of Pretor's Hill ignored the potential danger to them, even though several were pelted by clumps and one elderly woman dropped as a rock caved in her skull. The knight cursed such a waste of life, but could do nothing about it.

The eruption threw Valentin into the air, yet he seemed unconcerned. However, barely had he risen up than he landed astride what at first seemed a great serpent made of the very rock and earth around it. The crimson knight grinned and raised the broken lance high as the truth concerning his gigantic mount became obvious.

"I am *free*!" Grimyr roared triumphantly, firing off bursts of flame into the air as he laughed. "I *live* again!"

Evan, now on one knee, stared at the leviathan as Grimyr shook the ground and rock off of him. As he did, his true form became apparent in the flickering light caused by burning treetops and the exhalations of fire he continued to shoot.

Free the dragon might be . . . but *living* he certainly was not.

XX

GHOSTS AND DRAGONS

Arno studied the part of the foundation he had chosen, then swung as hard as he could. Muscles strengthened by a lifetime of shoeing and other arduous tasks imbued the hammer with incredible force as it slammed into the stone.

With an ear-splitting clang, the head struck . . . and then went flying.

Arno spun around to watch the head go crashing into a barrel several yards away. He looked down at the handle, which ended in splinters.

"Not good," the smith muttered. He had promised Sir Evan that he would break the foundation, not his trusted hammer.

Arno quickly retrieved a pick. He did not use it as much as his hammer, but the technique was similar enough. Swing and hit. Swing and hit.

However, this time, Arno first knelt by the area and inspected his target carefully. What he saw there made him frown. This did not remind him of any stone that he had ever seen. True, at first glance it would, but the more the smith studied it, the more he saw that there were no real striations, no true markings one associated with natural stone. It was as if someone had worked to make the substance *appear* like rock.

Despite his trepidation, Arno readied the pick. He tried to choose a spot that looked particularly vulnerable but found none. Shrugging, the smith took a deep breath and swung.

Arno reared the pick back, but halted it in midair, realizing at the last moment that the tool would break as easily as the hammer had. There had to be something better. The smith had some explosive powder, but wondered if he would just end up destroying the stables and leaving the foundation intact. It *had* survived previous damage to the structures built atop it.

Yet, the powder and the pick aside, Arno pondered just *what* could possibly work. He had heard that diamonds were very hard, but other than the jewelry owned by some of the rich folk in town, the smith had no idea where to find any . . . and those little pieces would not serve him. No, Arno needed something larger, and something definitely stronger than his iron and steel tools, that was certain.

He blinked, then stared at the top of the entrance . . . where the supposed dragonscale mounted by his grandfather—in a frame since no nail could supposedly penetrate it—still hung.

In life, Grimyr had been a terrifying sight, a reptilian behemoth that had been the very epitome of doom. Now, the dragon was an even more monstrous, more grotesque horror. Rotting flesh clung to bones that could be seen in many places, and the scale and dried skin appeared to hold together the leviathan's form more than the blackened muscle and sinew that had not yet been eaten away by time. In some places, even the hard scales had broken away, revealing more putrefying flesh and bone.

Evan recalled the dragon's blazing orbs and saw that they were *literally* afire. Some fierce magical inferno burned in each, adding a new dimension of fear to a creature that needed no such enhancement.

"Free!" Grimyr roared again. "Ha, ha! Free!"

The knight touched his still-bleeding chin. Both it and the shallow wound on his hand had been the key to Grimyr's escape. Evan's blood—with the wizard's spell—had enabled the behemoth to do what all his terrible strength and magic could not.

Without warning, the dragon took to the air. Seated where the neck met the shoulders, Valentin waved the lance in encouragement. The pair rose higher and higher, Grimyr soaring even with wings whose membranes were ripped and full of holes. The behemoth let loose with another great blast—

And then it was as if Grimyr hit an invisible wall or perhaps reached the end of some unseen tether. The dragon looked frustrated at first and attempted again to fly higher. He nearly caused Valentin to fall off as once again there proved some impediment that even his incredible strength could not match.

As Evan watched, understanding came not only to him but also the dragon. Evan was not surprised when Grimyr suddenly dove down, soaring directly toward him.

The knight ran. As he did, he heard hoofbeats approaching from the direction opposite where the ensorcelled townsfolk waited. Evan looked.

Three ghostly knights astride ethereal mounts charged him. Their faces were hidden behind visors, but Evan could sense their utter hatred of him. He knew them by the markings on their armor, former comrades among those he had betrayed at the pass. They were no longer condemned to the shadow forms given them as punishment for their failure by Novaris and they wanted Evan's death.

A snort alerted him to another steed, his own at last returning from wherever the mound's eruption had cast him. Evan's mount raced hard, but the knight knew that the vengeful specters would reach him first. He turned back to face them, though their misty lances had several times the stretch of his sword.

Fire engulfed the ghosts. Had the flames been of an ordinary nature, they would have ridden through it untouched, but this was dragon fire. Grimyr's fire. It devoured the phantasms as if they were dried leaves, turning them to nothing in a single blink.

Evan used the moment to grab hold of the saddle as his horse raced up to him. Mounting, the knight readied his sword just as the angry leviathan alighted.

"Man Wytherling!" bellowed the ghastly dragon. So close, the gaping wound in the chest where the lance had slain the creature was still evident, as was the fact that large, glowing maggots moved about in the decaying organs. "What trickery isss thisss of yoursss? What ssspell keepsss me from the ssskies?"

Valentin silenced Grimyr with a pat on the head. To Evan, the other knight shouted, "Another of the wizard's little jests, eh! Your blood was supposed to be enough! That was how it was meant to be!"

"And you *believed* Novaris in this?" Evan retorted. "After all his lies, all his deceptions, to those who had sworn him their blood oaths?"

"That's the wizard's spell speaking," Valentin argued. "And therein lies the crux of the problem, dear Evan! The fat one still hold us all here! You are as much his prisoner as we are!"

Evan said nothing, instead waiting for the dragon's attack.

Valentin's own irritation grew. "You know that to be the truth, Evan! Even with the spell upon you, you should have the will to accept what we say!" He glared. "I give you one last chance! Let Grimyr seek in your mind! Let him find this final damned link in our chains! We will be free! You will be free . . . free after two hundred years of servitude!"

Valentin's words stirred something in the other knight, in great part due to the fact that they were akin to the thoughts Evan had had for many decades. Even Paulo Centuros had likely not expected either the task or Evan to last so long. The knight suspected that, over the many decades, the spell had somewhat changed despite its caster's original intentions. Now, Evan could as much see the wrongness in what the wizard had demanded as he could see the justice in it.

I could let them take it, he found himself thinking for the first time. *I could become myself again . . .*

No fancy phrases from Centuros popped into his mind, nor any sudden urge to cut his own throat rather than let Valentin and the dragon find what they needed. Evan did not know the limits of the wizard's ancient spell, but at the moment it was allowing him to step dangerously close to the precipice.

And then . . . an image, not a voice, touched his thoughts. Not the wizard's, but rather Mardi Sinclair's. He saw only her face, her expression unreadable. There were no words of protest from her, nothing that would keep him from giving in to Grimyr's powerful magic. There were only the emotions—emotions he had thought he would never feel again—that Mardi stirred.

They proved to be more than enough against even the power of a dragon.

"Ask your precious sorcerer-king to help the two of you," Evan at last replied. "From me, you will receive only death."

As he declared this, Evan felt certain that the decision was his, not that of the spell. He had had two hundred years to learn the depths of evil as seen by one who must fight it, and surely that must have had an even greater effect on him than the wizard's magic. He could not still be the man he had been when he had served Novaris. He could *not* be.

Looking truly sad, Valentin sighed. "There is one other way to rip the answer from you, my friend, but it means nothing will remain . . . nothing . . . I'm sorry . . ."

And, with that, Grimyr lunged. Valentin lowered the broken lance and as he aimed it at Evan, the lance reshaped itself. The missing portion regrew, extending the lance's reach as it did. Valentin grimaced, his intention very clear. Whatever friendship had remained between them counted no more.

Evan twisted in the saddle, the long lance just missing him. His horse reared, kicking out at the snout of the dragon. Where the hooves hit, violent sparks of magical energy the color of moonlight burned into the hideous visage of Grimyr.

The decaying leviathan pulled his head back. He opened his toothy maw and exhaled.

Evan brought the sword up again, this time the magical shield encompassing not just him but also his mount. The knight felt sweat suddenly form all over his body as the hellish heat sought to do what the flames could not.

He tugged on the reins, forcing the pallid stallion to retreat.

The horse snorted his disagreement but obeyed.

Valentin laughed harshly, his savage grin almost identical to the inhuman one of his foul companion. "You cannot escape, my dear Evan! At least accept justice delayed, if nothing else!"

The undead dragon rose up. The wind created by the wings buffeted both man and beast. Evan yearned for his visor to obscure some of the refuse caught up in the wind, but he knew it was lost in the earth. He had no choice but to crouch low and try to peer through slitted eyes.

A warning whinny by his horse made Evan glance to the side. There, he saw more ghosts encroaching on him and, worse, the possessed townsfolk. Valentin no longer appeared to have any inclination to keep his vengeance only to himself and Grimyr.

The shadow of a troll swung its translucent club at Evan's side. The knight slid toward the ghost while muttering some of the wizard's words, skewering the troll before it could strike. The phantasm let out a mournful wail and faded to nothing. Unlike the previous troll, this one did not reform.

But dozens of other specters converged upon the pair. Wherever Evan looked, the ghosts of battle now sought his blood. It was not merely to see him dead, either. Evan knew that Grimyr and Valentin would use the magic within him to unbind themselves from this place. If that happened, Rundin would surely fall as both the unliving and the possessed slaughtered any innocents remaining.

Evan had no choice. He jumped down and quickly drew a circle around him and his horse. Silver flames burst wherever the tip of his blade cut. As the knight quickly worked, he pronounced other words given to him by the wizard.

As soon as the silver circle was finished, it *expanded*. The first ghosts to reach it simply faded away. Others began to realize the threat and drifted back. Their gaunt faces radiated rage at being cheated from their vengeance on the living.

The circle continued its expansion, but the greater its diameter, the fainter the glow became. Aware of the limits of the spell, Evan rushed to remount.

Among the circle's limits was keeping back Grimyr's flames. The knight barely pulled back in time as fire cut him off from his horse. The stallion reared, then disappeared behind the fiery wall.

With no other choice, Evan threw himself toward the far edge of the circle. There, ghosts eager for his flesh snatched at him, only to fall prey to the circle's weakening but thus far still-potent force.

From beyond the surge of flame, Evan's mount let out a loud, challenging cry. To Evan's surprise, the damnable steed lunged toward the dragon.

His audacity made Grimyr pull back in surprise. Evan understood immediately what his companion intended and with a silent thanks to the horse, also charged the dragon.

Only a few specters stood between Evan and Grimyr, the dragon's breath an even more dangerous threat to the spirits than the circle. The sword—the jewels in the hilt aglow—made easy work of those that got in the knight's way.

Valentin noticed him as he neared. The crimson knight nodded his admiration of the two-pronged attack, then shouted to the dragon. Evan could not hear him over the roar of fire.

With a low roar, Grimyr forgot the horse. A wave of fetid air enshrouded Evan as the rotting behemoth turned to him. This close, the glowing maggots and other carrion creatures infesting Grimyr became much too apparent. Some were many times the normal size of such vermin. The inherent magic of the dragon, the magic that had enabled Grimyr to keep his bond with Valentin alive these past centuries, had also transformed the worms, flies, and other creatures within.

Grimyr snapped at Evan, but the knight ducked below the dragon's head before the teeth could catch him. The moment he was under the dragon, Evan slashed with his blade. Yet, even then, the ancient dragonscale proved hardy. The sword only scratched it.

The dragon turned in an attempt to snatch up the human. Evan continued to move, seeking any area where putrefaction had left him an opening. Finding one, he leapt up and jammed the tip inside.

Maggots and flies as big as his fist dropped onto the knight as the sword bit deep. Evan swatted away the vicious carrion eaters, aware that as part of Grimyr, their bite could be more than merely poisonous. Generations of living and breeding in the dragon had given them an insidious magic of their own.

Crushing a maggot that sought his face, Evan again forced the sword in. Grimyr's roar took on a pained tone.

The dragon suddenly rose up into the air, nearly taking the knight's blade with him. At the last moment Evan managed to keep his grip strong enough to pull the sword free.

He quickly wiped away the carrion and vermin that rained down upon him, then ran for Grimyr's hind leg. As the dragon continued his ascent, Evan sheathed the sword and jumped. He grabbed hold of the leg, then pulled himself up.

Although Grimyr remained caught between life and death, he still felt pain and other sensations and so it did not surprise Evan when the dragon tried to shake the knight off his leg. Fortunately, there remained many places where the human could keep a strong hold as he wended his way up.

Grimyr evidently realized this also and dropped toward the ground. Evan increased his effort and just barely managed to reach the dragon's back before the collision with the earth would have surely shaken him off regardless of his hold. Even then, he nearly toppled off the savage leviathan.

The point of a sword almost opened up Evan's throat.

"Adaptable to the very end!" Valentin remarked as he withdrew his own blade for another thrust. "Aah, Evan! This brings back such glorious memories! Our crushing of the Namoans in Algemar! The razing of the border forts at the southern tip of Rundin! Do you remember those moments? Do you remember those wondrous triumphs?"

"I recall only the dead and the dying! I dream over and over of the screams of men still alive and lying in the mud, their entrails spilled loose! I remember women and children begging for mercy and receiving none!"

The crimson knight shrugged. "In war, there are no innocents! Their deaths served to fuel the fear and uncertainty of our foes! We grew stronger as their morality made them weaker!"

Evan thrust. Valentin stepped back toward the dragon's shoulder, where the lance lay. He did not seem perturbed by the attack, taking it almost as if the pair were simply practicing. "Ha! Very good, my dear friend!"

"I am not your friend," Evan rasped, trying to drive Valentin farther and farther toward the dragon's head. "Even when I served Novaris, I fought against the senseless violence, the needless deaths!"

"Yes, your nobility was always an amusement! Even brought you to the eye of Lady Cassandra! You remember *her,* do you not, Evan? Do you think she would still find favor with you?"

It had been many, many years since Evan had dared even think of the woman of whom Valentin spoke and even more since the silver knight had uttered her name himself. Memories long buried resurrected themselves with a force comparable to Grimyr's bursting from the mound. Some of those memories were emotionally painful, tearing at Evan as Valentin had surely intended them.

"I remember the name," he quietly answered, punctuating his reply with a series of hard slashes at Valentin's defenses. Novaris's lieutenant now frowned as he concentrated on keeping Evan's sword from penetrating. The two approached the dragon's shoulders. "I remember much more, too."

"So I see." Valentin suddenly countered the attack, putting an end to Evan's advance.

Throughout their duel, Grimyr remained oddly still, a fact that disturbed Evan. While it had aided his efforts against Valentin, Evan feared that it also presaged some trick on his adversary's part.

Eyes narrowing, Evan threw himself into one last lunge. His move caught Valentin off guard.

Evan drove the blade all the way through Valentin, the magic of the sword enabling it to cut through not only the strong armor but the flesh and bone behind. Indeed, Evan did not stop until the tip broke through the back armor and the hilt clanged against the breastplate.

Valentin let out a cry. Dropping his sword, he clutched at the one in his stomach, in the process ripping it free of his foe's grip.

However, Evan paid the loss of his weapon no mind, instead racing past his stricken opponent toward the reshaped lance. Transformed by Valentin's spell and also so linked to the knight by its two centuries buried in his evil heart, Evan felt certain that the weapon had the power to bring down the dragon. He prayed that Grimyr would hold still for just a few seconds longer.

"Shame, shame, Evan," he heard Valentin call from behind him. A scraping sound accompanied his taunt and even as Evan neared the lance he had to look back. There, he saw the other knight pull free the blade. Black ichor dripped over the edge as Valentin turned after his former comrade. "You know that this was a waste of time!"

Turning away from Valentin again, Evan grabbed for the lance.

Grimyr tilted his head as much as he could and snapped at Evan. The yellowed teeth could not quite reach the intended prey, but it was enough to force the knight back a few vital steps.

With a monstrous laugh, the dragon raised a paw to take the lance. "Fool of a manling!"

However, before Grimyr could take the weapon, something caused him to suddenly twist slightly. It was just enough to make the lance slide off his shoulder before the dragon could seize it.

As the weapon vanished from sight, Grimyr glared at something before him that was lost from Evan's view. "Accursssed morsssel! Thisss time you will be crushed!"

Evan could only assume that the damnable steed had renewed his risky attack. Even as Grimyr focused on the horse, Evan twisted around so as to avoid Valentin's strike. The blade came within inches of his head.

"I am truly sorry that it has to end this way!" Valentin shouted. "But if it must, take comfort that it was I who freed you from the wizard's grasp, even if I did have to kill you to do it!"

With a chuckle, Valentin thrust again. Evan threw himself to the side, then made a desperate grab for Valentin's sword arm. He shoved the jeweled sword skyward, then grappled for it.

"Struggle till the end, Evan! It'll avail you not!" his raven-haired foe mocked as their faces nearly touched. "This day has been ordained since you failed to slay us the first time! Look about you! I'll grant you that momentary reprieve from our fight without any subterfuge, just so you can see what I mean! My oath upon it!"

Valentin pulled back a step, maintaining his grip but not fighting to take back the sword from his former comrade. He looked to the side. Evan dared follow his gaze to the land around them.

The forest glowed. The townsfolk stood as if martial guards awaiting their order to attack some unseen enemy.

And ghosts—thousands of *sentient* ghosts—gathered in ever-growing ranks. Humans, trolls, goblins, and more, even creatures that Evan could recall only vaguely—wyverns and other beasts trained to serve the sorcerer-king.

Novaris's army stood fully recreated and ready to resume slaughtering their master's enemies. Paulo Centuros's plots had failed.

Evan had failed.

Mardi Sinclair watched in horror as all of this unfolded—unable to even cry out a warning at the very end. Steppenwald, his hand still on her shoulder, observed the chaos with clinical interest. Around them had gathered several of the lupine shadows, all under the sorcerer's control.

"So," he murmured half to her and half to himself. "Seems to me that Valentin's proved the better of choices, definitely the better of choices. Pity! Almost would have preferred Evan, but the boy's lost out . . ."

Mardi felt tears of frustration dripping down her cheeks as she listened to the sorcerer speak of Evan's doom with such disregard. Every muscle of her being sought to strike at her captor.

The heart is one of the most potent of weapons, able to cast spells any wizard would envy . . .

Another enigmatic saying by Paulo Centuros, and as it coursed through her thoughts, Mardi also felt what seemed a tingle in *her* heart. The gentlewoman focused on that tingling, certain that it meant something.

Her body moved as if of its own accord, first tearing away from Steppenwald's grip and then turning so that she could strike the wizard hard in the chest with her left hand.

Despite his incredible mass, Steppenwald tumbled back. The dragon-head cane fell from his grip and rolled toward Mardi. She seized it up and anxiously faced the rising sorcerer and the shadows.

Steppenwald rose. Replacing his hat, he studied Mardi with a detached look. "Curious. A shame I have no time, no time, to study you further." His hands suddenly glowed an unsettling dark blue. "But you've become much too much an annoyance and I cannot afford that at this time."

Mardi held the cane as she had seen Steppenwald do, but the spellcaster only laughed.

"The only purpose, the *only* purpose, for which that cane will serve *you* is to keep you propped up! You are not of his blood and, therefore, its power will not serve you."

He opened his palms toward her and the dark energy reached out.

Holding the cane out as far as possible, Mardi tried to recreate what she had done with the dagger. Even as she attempted this, the teacher knew her efforts would be futile.

Steppenwald's spell enveloped her.

The mismatched eyes of the dragon head glowed.

The sorcerer's attack reversed.

The last thing that Mardi saw of Steppenwald's face was his utter shock. Eyes wide—eyes matching those of the dragon head— he managed to utter a single word.

"Impossible—"

The spell struck. Mardi watched with astonishment as Steppenwald was flung back over the trees. He let out an angry howl as he vanished from sight.

Howls warned Mardi that the shadows were no longer under Steppenwald's sway. She spun to face them as they attacked, hoping that fortune would remain with her.

The first to be touched by the cane melted into mist, its howl ending in a whimper. The rest paid heed neither to their lost comrade nor to the danger of the cane. By sheer numbers, they sought to overwhelm the gentlewoman.

Mardi swung the cane wherever she could. A murky claw grazed her arm. She thrust there. A shape loomed over her and she thrust Steppenwald's cane toward it. As with the others, it melted away to nothing.

And then . . . Mardi found herself swinging only at the open air. She had destroyed the last of Steppenwald's ensorcelled shadows.

But matters permitted no rest for Mardi. Everywhere, there were ghosts and some of them now suddenly seemed aware of her. Whatever spell Steppenwald had utilized to hide the two of them from the specters' notice had vanished with him.

"Away with you!" she commanded, hoping that words and the glow of the cane would be enough.

They would *not* have sufficed . . . if the cane did not once more react to her as if she were the sorcerer himself. A deep-blue glow emanated from the cane and swept over those shades seeking her death. The menacing ghosts turned without warning and began to assail the others behind them. A macabre, pitched battle took place before her.

Mardi ignored them, instead racing toward where Evan fought Valentin. Grimyr moved about, seeking to either incinerate or devour Evan's mount, depending on where the animal was one moment to the next. Three times, the ghastly dragon exhaled flames—each burst razing those specters nearest rather than the intended target. When the horse risked moving in to kick with hooves that flashed of magic themselves, Grimyr snapped at him, only to find himself with a mouthful of empty air.

That the dragon had not taken to the sky again was clearly due to the two knights in struggle atop his back. Evan and Valentin fought for the former's sword, with no victor in immediate sight. Mardi focused the cane at them, then lowered it for fear of including Evan in whatever spell happened.

Grimyr roared, then exhaled again. Flames illuminated the vicinity . . . and revealed a glittering object to Mardi.

The dragon's constant shifting had left the lance half-buried in the ground below. Mardi was not absolutely certain what she hoped to do with the lengthy weapon, but knew she had to try to retrieve it.

The ghosts scattered ahead of the cane, but Mardi sensed them closing in behind her again. It seemed wherever she looked, the dead were amassing. Worse, none were any longer simply wandering, but instead moved with purpose, with awareness of the world around them.

Mardi pointed the cane at the nearest but could not summon any magic. Inside she felt rising panic, but the ghosts either did not seem to realize her failure or feared the cane for some reason the schoolteacher did not understand.

She was nearly upon the lance. Mardi prayed that the cane would somehow enable her to carry off the weapon . . . or perhaps even *launch* it somehow at Grimyr.

Her body tingled as she touched the lance. It was as if she had become sensitive to all magical energy. Why this had become so, Mardi could not say, though she had suspicions that bordered on the fantastic.

If I can just somehow lift it! If I can—

A pair of strong hands took up the lance from the other end. Mardi looked to the side.

Daniel Taran smiled grimly at her. Only then did Mardi realize that there were others here, as well.

"Valentin will need this," Daniel commented . . . and the smile became one that perfectly mirrored that of Novaris's fiendish lieutenant.

XXI

DRAGON MOUND

Arno tore open the frame around the ancient scale, hoping that he would not again fail Sir Evan. The scale dropped out of the frame before he could prevent it. The piece fell to the floor with a clatter but, despite its age, did not break.

Taking that as a hopeful sign, the smith picked it up and looked for the sharpest edge. He then did his best to mount the scale as he would an ax head . . . though that proved more difficult than he had imagined.

All the while, he heard frightful sounds from the forest beyond, including the roars of a beast that no doubt wore such covering over its flesh. Arno had no idea if this piece somehow belonged to that monster or from another and did not care. All that mattered was that it worked.

As he finished, Arno quickly looked around again. There were no signs of ghosts, but that did not encourage him. Ghosts kept popping up; they did not simply walk in and calmly give notice of their arrival so that mortal folk had time to do something. Arno did not trust that the next specter might not also be a bit more solid, at least when it came to weapons.

The smith returned to the spot that he had chosen. He could not see just what cracking the foundation would do for the knight, but Sir Evan had been adamant about it . . . just as he had been about the notion that Arno was somehow descended from the great General Pretor.

The last sounded too fantastic for the smith to believe, but he did hope that with all the ghosts around that perhaps the shade of the legendary commander might give him some help. True, Pretor had not died in the battle but had instead gone on to lead a long career as an officer and statesman, but Arno hoped that the general's spirit might still be taking *some* interest in the town that bore his name.

With one last glance for ghosts, the burly smith took a deep breath and raised the makeshift ax. Muttering a prayer, he swung hard.

The scale struck the rock with a resounding *boom* that rang in Arno's ears for several seconds afterward. His arms shook as if made of jelly and the ax fell from his twitching grip. His eyes teared up from pain as he clutched his hands together.

Worse, as his vision cleared, he saw no sign of success. The foundation appeared unblemished. In addition, the ax had fallen apart, meaning he would have to try to secure the scale with something even stronger. Unfortunately, Arno had already used the best means he could think of, considering that he knew of nothing that could pierce the scale.

"Could've at least tried to listen," Arno muttered to his supposed ancestor as he bent to retrieve the scale. "Not that much to ask—"

A strange bubbling sound made him freeze. The smith dared look up, but saw no specters. He listened close . . . and realized that the sound was coming from the wall behind him. The wall where he had futilely attacked the foundation.

Only . . . now something was happening where the scale had struck. However, it was not in the least what Arno had expected and certainly nothing he understood, even when staring straight at it.

The scale had evidently made a very fine crack in the stone. Whether that was as much as Sir Evan had desired, Arno did not know. What he did know was that a liquid was suddenly dripping out of the crack, a liquid that the smith, with an occupation that often included injuries, recognized all too well. Recognizing it, though, made Arno feel no better and, in fact, caused him to step back.

Blood was pouring out of the foundation.

"Daniel! You must listen to me!" Mardi looked to the others as they surrounded her. All bore expressions that made them look more like strangers than people whom she had known all her life. "All of you! You must remember who you are!"

"Good soldiers in the service of Sir Valentin!" Daniel retorted as he hefted the lance as if it weighed nothing. "And he in the service of His Greatness, our lord Novaris!"

Several among the others murmured agreement. The teacher looked around, aghast. All of them either believed themselves to be some of the ancient warriors of Novaris's army or were, in fact, truly possessed by those dread spirits.

"She's caused enough trouble," snarled Master Jakes. "Let's be done with the wench!"

"Aye!" agreed Bulrik.

Mardi raised the cane toward Daniel, but felt her heart hesitate to use it on him. It was not out of love, but rather simply because neither he nor the rest could help themselves.

But if she did nothing, they would cut her to ribbons without so much as batting an eye.

Grinning darkly, Daniel stepped back to let the others take her. Mardi prayed for guidance, but this time no voice came.

And then . . . Master Jakes suddenly doubled over. The innkeeper grabbed his head and began to moan. Daniel dropped the lance and did the same. Mardi watched astonished as the rest of the townsfolk fell prey to the same swift and unsettling affliction.

She did not know the cause, but she recognized that this was her only chance. Stuffing the cane under one arm, she grabbed for the lance.

"No!" roared Daniel, trying to stop her despite his obvious agony. A few others joined in his efforts, forcing Mardi away.

Evan's mount came out of nowhere, scattering the townsfolk.

Daniel made a grab for the animal, but the horse snapped at his hand, then kicked out. The young landowner retreated.

The horse turned his baleful eyes to Mardi. Only then did she notice that the steed had the lance under his protection. He stepped back as she approached, enabling her to finally pick up the restored weapon, which proved amazingly light after all.

Barely had she done so when a tremendous tremor rocked both her and the steed. Mardi cried out as the lance fell free, and she tried to go after it, only to have the cane fall between her feet and trip her.

The sky above filled with putrefying dragon. Grimyr used two claws to pluck up the lance. "Fool little morsssel! Did you think it ssso easssy?"

Snatching up the cane, Mardi thrust the head toward the dragon.

There was no visible attack, but Grimyr let out a pained roar and recoiled. The dragon lost hold of the lance. Unfortunately, the weapon went flying far from Mardi, and, worse, she saw that her attack had tossed both Evan and Valentin off the great beast.

Grimyr recovered quickly. The dragon exhaled. Still holding the cane toward the gigantic creature, Mardi flung herself away as flames bathed where she had stood.

She ran as hard as she could. A shadow reared up before her. Evan's mount turned, offering her the saddle. She threw herself atop and the bone-pale steed raced off just as Grimyr scorched the earth there.

Yet, although she was momentarily safe, Mardi knew that something had to be done quickly. She could not see the two knights and feared for Evan. If Valentin slew him, then there would be no one left but her to face both the mad warrior and the undead dragon. Even with Steppenwald's cane, Mardi had no idea what she could do against such odds. Perhaps if she had been a true wizard, she might know all the proper spells that could put an end to the horror before them—

The mind is the master of study, but it is the heart that is the master of learning . . .

Mardi was about to angrily dismiss Paulo Centuros's unwelcome and useless proverb when it was immediately followed by what she initially took as insane ramblings. The words made no sense to her . . . until she concentrated on them. Then, what they meant—and, more importantly, what they could do—became as clear to the teacher as anything she had ever learned.

It was a spell. More to the point . . . it was a spell with which she could use the cane to *vanquish* Valentin and Grimyr.

Neither Evan nor Valentin ceased their struggle even when tossed from Grimyr's back. The two landed hard on the ground, only then becoming separated. Evan's sword bounced away, landing in the ruin of the mound.

Evan jumped to his feet just a moment before Valentin did and rushed after the sword. Behind him, Valentin drew the blade he had received in Pretor's Hill, and though it had been forged by mortal means, it now glowed a deep, disturbing emerald.

Seizing his own sword, Evan turned and blocked Valentin's cut. The two swords clashed again and again.

"Can you feel it, Evan? His power is ascendant! This foul speck of a town, the entire kingdom of Rundin . . . they are his! Glorious, isn't it?"

"A small empire it will be, considering you cannot even leave the vicinity of the mound!"

"A temporary problem, no doubt remedied by using more of your wizard-tainted blood." Valentin lunged.

Evan battled back. If Valentin believed that he could rattle his former comrade, then Evan would play the same game. "Perhaps not so temporary a problem . . . or have you not noticed your puppets?"

He purposely steered their duel so that Valentin saw the townsfolk. Most knelt or lay sprawled, clearly suffering. Evan regretted their torture, but the alternative would have been much worse.

"The spell matrix!" the crimson knight growled. His anger shifted quickly to admiration. "Well done, Evan! That's the comrade in arms I knew!" Valentin laughed heartily.

The laughter did not sit well with Evan. It meant that whatever Arno had accomplished was not sufficient after all. Evan had not expected Novaris's spellwork to be entirely disrupted by the damage to the foundation, but he had believed it would be more troublesome than Valentin's good humor indicated.

"The weakened matrix would have been a worse situation if managed sooner, my friend," the crimson knight explained as he slashed at Evan, "but the spell has spread too far, strengthened too much! Oh, it will delay our lord's vengeance, but only delay it. Soon enough, the matrix will adjust itself and the good townsfolk will return to being both servant and conduit for this realm's destruction!"

With another laugh, Valentin pressed Evan again. The silver knight did not doubt Valentin's assertions. Still, Arno's evident success at least bought Evan some valuable time, though it was a question as to what he could do with it.

"I will remember you to our lord and Lady Cassandra when I see them, Evan! I'm sure that she will at least mourn you . . . if she still recalls your name!"

Evan steeled himself against the jibe and tried not to imagine the face of the woman mentioned. He matched Valentin thrust against thrust, seeking some opening.

Circumstance had other intentions. It was Evan who stepped back and found the footing loose. He slipped and although the misstep was a brief one, it was all Valentin needed.

The tip of the blade caught Evan just at the shoulder where the breastplate and the mail met. Against mortal weapons, the mail would have held, but Valentin channeled the power of Novaris's spell through his sword.

The pain forced a cry from Evan. He managed to deflect

Valentin's thrust, as blood from the wound splattered his cheek.

"It ends now," the bearded knight muttered, all amusement gone from his expression. "I release you, Evan—"

A furious snort presaged sharp hooves striking at Valentin and his sword. Evan's mount kicked away the weapon and nearly did the same with the crimson knight's head. The horse kept between the pair, just as much preventing Evan from reaching Valentin as the other way around.

As he righted himself, Evan's mount made an odd snort. Looking to the beast, Evan saw the horse briefly turn his gaze to the left.

There lay the lance. Evan knew what the horse intended and did not argue. Sheathing the sword, he abandoned the duel to the stallion.

It took a moment for Valentin to see that his adversary had left him. The crimson knight glared at the horse.

"No more of your magic, wizard!" he declared to the emptiness as he faced the furious mount. "And no more of this bloody beast!"

Valentin opened his mouth . . . and kept opening it. His jaw stretched, almost seeming to unhinge.

From the knight's mouth shot a stream of dragon fire.

Evan's horse had no chance to evade it. The magical flames engulfed the rearing stallion. Yet, even ablaze, he kept between Valentin and his rider.

Farther on, Evan heard the horse struggling. He gritted his teeth and did not look back, aware that it would do neither of them any good. The horse intended that he reach the lance. Evan would do that.

Behind him, the stallion made one last kick at Valentin, who continued to breathe fire. The crimson knight fell back as the horse attacked . . . and then Evan's mount turned to ash.

Valentin gasped, the effort taking more out of him than he had supposed. Still fighting for air, he saw Evan nearing the lance. The bearded warrior bared his teeth and looked to Grimyr.

The dragon reacted as if summoned aloud. He quickly bent one wing to the ground so that Valentin could climb atop again.

The female . . . she ran to the north of the mound. . . thisss one tried to sssnatch her, but she carriesss the fat one'sss cane . . .

"And she can . . . wield it?" Valentin found this mildly interesting. "So . . . blood will tell . . ." He waved off any interest in her. "But her blood, diluted as it must be, can only do . . . so much. Forget her! It is Evan we want. He will try for the lance."

Grimyr had already moved to intercept their traitorous comrade. As his rider seated himself and gasped anew for breath, Grimyr prepared to unleash his own blast.

He will not reach it, the rotting leviathan promised, his tone filled with eagerness.

"No! Do not burn him!" Valentin, now more recovered, commanded. "Despite everything, we still need more of his blood! It will be the key to releasing you from the boundaries of the mound!"

With a disappointed growl, Grimyr adjusted his aim. *He may be a bit burnt . . . but he will live long enough . . .*

The dragon breathed—

Words of power echoed through the area. Ghosts held at bay by both fear of the dragon's flames and the magic that Mardi had shown she could wield now fled from the area of the mound as if sensing what was about to happen. Only the ensorcelled townsfolk remained, most of them still stricken by Arno's desperate work for Evan.

Valentin turned in his seat. "What—?"

To the north, Mardi Sinclair directed Steppenwald's cane at the mound. This mismatched dragon-head eyes glared bright. The gentlewoman uttered words that should have held no meaning to her or to any of the unTalented. Yet Valentin and Grimyr could both feel the force behind them.

"Strike her down!" the crimson knight shouted. "Strike her down—"

Mardi finished her casting, then plunged the bottom of the cane into the ground.

Even with his mount's sacrifice, Evan had had his doubts that he would reach the lance. Only Valentin's certainty that Evan's blood—and more than a few drops—would help release the final bonds holding Grimyr to this place had given him any hope.

Like Valentin, Evan heard the voice and the words. He recognized both, though the two should not have had any link. Mardi cast a spell that demanded the knowledge and power of a master wizard. Evan could think of only one such master wizard who would also be audacious enough to make such a long-ranging and outrageous plan.

The blood of Paulo Centuros flowed through Mardi Sinclair, and through that blood, he had ensured some part of him would be there when the sorcerer-king's own plot came to fruition.

Evan had never known the wizard to be one for passions of the flesh. In his dealings with Centuros, he had only seen the war strategist. However, despite the ingenuity of the wizard's plan, Evan did not pause. He hoped Mardi's spell would succeed but could not rely on it until it came to pass.

The wind erupted just as he reached the lance. The knight gripped the weapon tight, fearing that the magical storm would take it.

Grimyr's outraged roar shook the area. Evan braced himself against the wind and watched as the spell took hold.

The ghosts had fled and wise they were to do so. Grimyr— and Valentin astride the dragon's neck—had no such chance. The spell was focused on them and the ruined mound. The decaying behemoth unleashed a burst of fire at Mardi, but the unnatural wind kept the flames from shooting that far.

Valentin gripped the dragon tight. Grimyr tried to fly, but only managed a few yards before the wind pulled him down again. He clawed at the torn earth and snapped at the wind as if he might somehow be able to rip it apart.

Mardi ceased speaking. She stood back in obvious shock at what she had done. The eyes of the dragon-head cane flared so bright that Evan could see them even from where he stood.

Grimyr spun about. Small fragments of the putrefying leviathan crumbled off, but the wind ever kept them orbiting around the struggling beast. The flies and other carrion eaters fared no better.

The windstorm drew tighter still, forcing Grimyr and Valentin above the mound. In the process, it also doused most of the fires created by the dragon. The force of the magical whirlwind was such that even Grimyr could not keep his wings extended. They pressed flat against his massive body.

The ravine below the unholy pair widened more. The wind began to sink in as if drawn there by the inhaling of the ground itself.

With it were drawn the dragon and his rider.

Grimyr struggled. He ripped at the dirt and rock, flinging it everywhere in his desperation. The dragon bellowed his outrage to no avail. His tail sank into the ravine, followed by his hind legs.

The wind rose dramatically. Grimyr let out one last frustrated roar—and was sucked into the gap.

The ravine sealed, the mound reshaping itself.

Silence filled the forest.

She had done it.

Mardi could scarcely believe her eyes. The mound had reverted to its ancient look. Grimyr and Valentin were no more.

She fell to one knee and would have been willing to lie down completely if not for fear of the ghosts, who were slowly returning to the mound. They appeared paler, more transparent, and somewhat unfocused of purpose, but Mardi still did not trust that they were no longer a threat. Behind them, most of the townsfolk were trying to rise now that the tremors created by the mound's astounding reconstruction—and the agony of whatever force had been plaguing them—had ceased.

Taking a deep breath, Mardi used the cane to push herself back to her feet. Questions concerning her lineage stirred, but she shoved them aside. All that mattered to her was Evan—

A hand tried to grab the cane from her. Managing to keep her fingers around it, Mardi whirled, certain that she faced Steppenwald.

Only it was not Steppenwald, but Daniel Taran. At least, it was him in form. The eyes that glared at her were still not those of her former suitor.

Beyond Daniel, three other men from the town, including Bulrik, converged upon her. They, too, had eyes of strangers, murderous warriors.

"Give me—that!" Daniel demanded, using his other hand to shove Mardi back.

She refused to let go. Both Daniel and the other men teetered as they moved, a sign that whatever possessed them no longer maintained a powerful hold. Mardi tried to concentrate, hoping that some other spell would come to her, one that would not do great harm to the innocents. However, the only words that formed in her head were sure to *destroy* the men attacking her.

She heard a harsh *thwack* and one of the men behind Daniel suddenly cried out. Daniel turned, also giving Mardi a glimpse of what was happening.

Evan stood among her attackers. The knight had used the side of the lance to knock senseless the one man and now did the same to Bulrik.

Daniel and the other remaining man abandoned her to take on the knight. Evan threw the lance at his nearest foe, and when the attacker instinctively blocked the oncoming weapon, struck him hard in the jaw.

As the third man fell, Daniel closed with Evan. The landowner grappled with the knight, who clearly did not want to do any more harm to an innocent than Mardi desired. Unfortunately, that gave the possessed Daniel an advantage. Although he no longer had his sword, Mardi's former suitor drew a dagger and tried to drive it into his adversary's throat.

As they battled, Mardi stood frozen. She did not even dare swing the cane at Daniel for fear that doing so would unleash some other terrible spell.

The ground rumbled. Horrified, Mardi looked back at where she had vanquished Valentin and the dragon.

The mound exploded. Those townsfolk who had been rising were again tossed to the ground by the powerful quake.

Mardi, Evan, and Daniel were thrown to the ground. Mardi rolled onto her back and gaped.

Grimyr let out a thundering roar as he rose above the mound. He spread his wings and looked around with vile eagerness.

The burning orbs fixed on her.

"Thisss one will crush you!" he snarled.

The dragon dove at her.

Evan had run as fast as he could with his unwieldy burden the second he had seen the possessed townsfolk going after Mardi. Fortunately, they had moved with less certainty than before, enabling him to catch up.

In another time, another place, Evan would have pushed aside the fact that they were innocents and simply slain them. There was no doubt they would show no mercy to either Mardi or him. However, now he did his best to deal with them while causing minimal harm. Surprise enabled him to knock three unconscious, but the possessed Daniel Taran now struggled close with him and did not reciprocate Evan's compunction concerning injury or

379

death.

The eruption sent both to the ground, where Evan managed to punch the landowner in the stomach. Daniel dropped his dagger. Evan hit his adversary in the face twice before the man could recover, silently apologizing despite their past rivalry. It would have been one thing if Daniel had himself been trying to kill the knight; it was another thing for the specter of some long-dead servant of Novaris to be using him for such a cause.

Evan threw the unconscious man from him, then stared at the horrific tableau. He had hoped and prayed that the spell the wizard had enabled Mardi to cast would seal Valentin and Grimyr in the mound, but deep inside he had doubted it would be sufficient. Novaris's spellwork had for too long saturated this area, tainting the land, the life, and the people, and thus strengthening his two great servants.

He knew what he had to do. Evan grabbed Daniel's dagger, it better suited for the swiftness and precision he needed. The knight held the blade to his wrist—

It was then that Grimyr focused on Mardi.

Evan dropped the dagger. He seized up the lance, certain that he would be too late to save her.

The dragon filled their view as he lunged for Mardi. She held her ground, perhaps aware that there was no point in running, anyway. Unfortunately, that left her in Evan's path.

"Stand away, Mardi!" the knight shouted.

Mardi glanced at him over her shoulder, then threw herself to the side. Yet, as she did, she held up the cane.

The mismatched eyes flared again, growing incredibly bright.

Grimyr faltered as the magical light blinded his infernal eyes. The dragon hissed angrily as he advanced.

Evan reached the spot where Mardi had stood and set the back end of the lance in the ground. He raised the point up, measuring the angle even as Grimyr, still half-blinded, continued his lunge.

The point sank into the cavity in the chest created by the

other lance's thrust two hundred years prior. The strike did not even slow Grimyr, who only then realized that he faced a different prey. The dragon bared his sharp, yellowed teeth. Evan knew that what remained of the first lance was still buried somewhere within the monster, but it was beyond his reach. He would have to rely on the transformed weapon alone.

Astride him, Valentin peered over. Unlike the dragon, the crimson knight saw what Evan did and shouted a warning to his monstrous companion. However, Grimyr, aware that the lance had no effect on him other than to plug the wound, laughed as he snatched at Evan with one paw.

Evan, still bracing the lance, muttered the words given to him by the wizard. They were for the least of spells and more designed to try to protect him in a moment of doom. He relied the most upon his own aim and what Valentin himself had done when refashioning the ancient weapon.

"Rise up, damn you!" Valentin shouted louder. He started to move from his position to escape Grimyr's back, but Evan had already counted on that.

Evan gripped the weapon tighter. He continued to push it through Grimyr's rotting flesh with all the might he could muster.

A horrific scraping accompanied the weapon as it penetrated deeper. At its original angle, the lance would have passed farther into the torso of the beast. Evan, however, continued lifting the lance from the ground. The point rose straight up, heading for an exit spot between the shoulders.

All of this happened in little more than the space of a single heartbeat. Evan cared not a whit about himself, more than willing to pay the sacrifice if it finally ended his quest. He did not even consider whether this was his own original thought or one created by the spell cast upon him so long ago.

But unbidden came another reason that Evan found at least as significant to him in that moment. Saving Mardi.

As Grimyr came down, Evan made one final adjustment to the lance's direction.

The long weapon—made longer yet by Valentin's design—burst out near the base of the neck. Valentin, in trying to escape, had inadvertently moved directly into the path of the lance . . . just as Evan had calculated.

The point pierced his crimson armor at the chest. The force of the strike crushed through muscle and bone. Evan did not aim for the heart; the lance simply took that in with so much else it pierced.

But the heart was *still* what Evan most sought.

Evan muttered a few short words, a spell that could work only in such a situation. It was another simple spell and one that served to bind things. Paulo Centuros had given it to Evan for minor purposes. Now the knight prayed it would work.

Evan had always understood the link between Valentin and Grimyr better than even Centuros. After all, as Valentin's friend and comrade and loyal servant to the sorcerer-king, Evan Wytherling had been witness to it. The reason that Grimyr had existed in a half state between life and death and the crimson knight had not died due to his great wounds had been because their spirits had been so bound to one another that the two could only truly perish if slain *together*. Grimyr had been struck down first and while the magic of the wizard had been powerful, it had not been powerful enough to match Novaris's cunning.

True, Centuros had understood that Valentin lived because of the dragon's magic, but not even he had realized the true depths of his rival's work. Evan, even under the geas, had never been questioned of this and so had not answered.

But Evan had both transfixed through where their hearts had been. The magic that bound them together now acted against them. The deaths that they had cheated, fed by magic, at last took the pair.

Grimyr reared back, large, drying chunks of leathered flesh and moldering scale spilling from him. Valentin struggled to pull himself off the lance, but his own recreation of the weapon had made it stronger and lengthier. Try as he might, the crimson knight could not rise enough.

Sorcerous energy flowed back and forth between dragon and rider. Grimyr swayed, the dragon's roaring becoming hollower in tone.

The leviathan forced his gaze back down at Evan. "Man . . . Wytherling! Grimyr will burn you!"

A vast plume shot toward Evan. The knight had already drawn his sword and again the flames found a barrier. However, Grimyr did not cease his effort, seeking to weaken the magic protecting not only the silver knight but Mardi as well until the heat and flames could break through.

Jaw clenched, Evan ignored the increasing heat. He could not look at Mardi, but prayed that she remained near enough. He could already feel the edges of the barrier breaking down.

The flames abruptly cut off.

Gasping for air, Evan looked up. Grimyr teetered. Much of what remained of him was bone and dried flesh. Evan might have thought him no more save for the burning eyes, eyes that glared in utter hatred for the tiny human.

And then . . . even those fires faded. Only dark pits marked the dragon's eyes.

With what sounded like a fading gasp, Grimyr collapsed.

The dragon did not simply fall. His wings and one forelimb broke off. Scales fluttered free. Bones disconnected.

By the time the huge corpse finished its collapse, what was left of Grimyr lay scattered for quite some distance. Yet, still the long-delayed decay continued, the bones crumbling, the ancient flesh withering away. The carrion eaters were dead as well, their own lives dependent on the magic of their host. The two lances—one unseen for two centuries—clattered to the ground.

But not all was still. There came from the ruins movement, movement with purpose. Despite being barely able to stand, Evan kept his sword ready.

Valentin rose from Grimyr's grave.

The lance no longer pierced him, but the wound remained.

The macabre figure stumbled toward Evan. Valentin's flesh looked like dried parchment and his beard grew more and more white with each passing second.

"Evan . . ." he rasped. "Oh, my foolish friend . . ."

Evan sheathed his sword. "It finally ends, Valentin. May you at last have rest."

The crimson sheen of the other knight's armor faded. Rust formed around the blackened, glistening wound and spread throughout the breastplate and beyond.

"Aah, poor Evan . . ." Valentin managed, his smile more than ever akin to that of a death's-head. Some of the skin near the smile broke away, revealing the bone beneath. "So little do you understand . . ."

Valentin lifted his head to the sky and laughed. The laughter was short-lived. Valentin's voice cut off . . . and his head followed.

As with Grimyr, the crimson knight collapsed into a heap of bones.

"Valentin . . ." Evan knelt by the bones. He tried to pick up the skull, but it broke like soft clay in his hand. The knight peered up at the dragon's skull to see that it had already been reduced to dust.

"I'm sorry . . . Evan," Mardi murmured as she came up next to him. The teacher clutched her shoulder. "I know . . . that you were once friends . . ."

"I swore an oath to ever fight at his side. I broke that oath, but compared to so much I have done, so much he did, that matters little. That friendship, that life, is long past, Mardi." Evan rose unsteadily and looked to her wounded shoulder. "It is one I despise now, though that does not grant me redemption . . ."

"But you're different! Not the same man—"

"I am what Paulo Centuros made me, not what I made myself. I am . . . damned, Mardi Sinclair, and that is all . . . there is to it." He started to weave back and forth, the strain of everything taking its toll. "I am—"

The world spun. Evan's head pounded.

"Evan!" Mardi called from what seemed miles away. He blacked out.

XXII

THE TRAIL

Mardi saw nothing else but Evan. As he slumped, she instinctively dropped Steppenwald's cane and managed to at least keep him from striking his head. With his armor, the knight weighed more than she remembered, yet somehow she found the strength to help him lie down on his back even despite her own injuries. Compared to all Evan had faced, the gentlewoman considered herself very fortunate.

Once she had him settled, Mardi looked to see what else she could do to give him comfort. Curiously, when Mardi inspected the knight, she thought that his bruises appeared lesser than they had been moments before. It was as if Evan were healing before her eyes.

In fact, the cut to his chin *sealed,* then quickly faded. The only remaining indication that not all was right with Evan was that his face was even paler than normal. The teacher put a hand to his forehead and quickly withdrew it. Evan felt as cold as death.

"M-Mardi?"

The voice from behind startled her, the more so because she still associated it with Valentin's evil. Yet, a part of her remembered that the crimson knight was no more and thus the speaker was innocent again.

Daniel stumbled over to her, the landowner rubbing his jaw where Evan had hit him. Two of the other men had also risen, but they also no longer looked nor acted like servants of the sorcerer-king's vengeance. Mardi glanced toward the rest of the townsfolk and saw that more and more of them seemed to be slowly coming out of their trances.

"Mardi—what's going—what happened?"

She did not want to bother with such matters at the moment, her concern for Evan's life more important. Yet, Mardi knew that she had to give him some sort of answer.

"L-lightning . . ."

Mardi let out a grateful gasp. They both looked down at Evan, who had responded. The knight's eyes were open and alert. He was still very pale, yet appeared stronger. "There was . . . a lightning strike. A terrible one. Fear of a forest fire broke out and the good people of Pretor's Hill responded. Under your guidance, they kept the fire from spreading much . . ."

Daniel studied the smoldering trees and the few bits of fire still flickering here and there. His gaze finished on the mound, which still lay torn open after Grimyr's final attempt to escape. "Praise be that no one was there when that struck!"

The knight pushed himself up to a sitting position. He acted much recovered from his brief blackout. "You should help organize the others. There was much smoke toward the end. It nearly overcame all of us—especially those like you, who risked themselves in the worst places."

"Yes . . . yes . . ." Daniel still looked somewhat confused. He eyed Mardi. "I'd better go back and help them again. Will you be coming with?"

"No, Daniel."

The finality in her voice answered more than that seemingly simple question. The young landowner nodded with clear disappointment, but not with any surprise. He remained very subdued, almost as if in another trance. "I understand . . ."

Without another word, Daniel moved on. The other men helped a still-dazed Bulrik stand and followed the younger Taran. As Daniel neared the rest of the townsfolk, he at last grew more animated, immediately giving orders and organizing the others.

"They will not even remember this much when they awaken in the morning," Evan informed her as he stood. "They needed some temporary explanation, though, and this seemed best."

RICHARD A. KNAAK

"Is this Paulo Centuros's doing again?" Mardi no longer admired the wizard as she once had.

"Yes. It was a part of the spell you cast. Centuros is thorough, even when he is not physically present." As he spoke, the knight flexed one arm as if to test it for injury.

"I saw true! You *are* healing."

"Another of his 'gifts'," Evan responded with a grimace. "There is a price to pay for that. You saw only a glimpse of it. The true price is extracted within. I am a warrior, not a wizard. Still, it is a price I am willing to pay this time. The trail is at last warm."

She could not stifle a frown of concern. His last comment was quite clear to her. "You're leaving. Just like that."

Before he could answer, a welcome figure rode up from the direction of Pretor's Hill. Appearing greatly relieved, Arno dismounted and rushed to the pair.

"It's done?" The smith sweated profusely. When the knight nodded, Arno added, "I was so afeared, Sir Evan! I did like you asked, but it turned out different than I expected! First it wouldn't crack, then, when I found a way using the scale my grandpa found, out came *blood*."

Mardi was stunned, but Evan was not at all surprised. "The blood came from Grimyr, I believe, taken by Novaris or a servant soon after his supposed death. It was needed to strengthen the spell matrix. With him now truly dead, you will find it dry and faded . . . and of no more concern."

"Well that's a relief to me, I've got to say! I'm not cut out to be no hero, like Pretor! I'm just a smith . . ."

"More than that . . ." Mardi insisted.

He shook his head vehemently. "No, Mistress Sinclair. You and him, yes. Me . . . just a smith. Nothing else. Please." Arno grimaced as something else came to mind. "Wish I'd been more. Might've saved Father Gerard. Went looking for him after I caught my fool horse, but only found a bunch of ash . . . can't say for certain, but with all this going on . . ."

Evan nodded. "You judge correctly, I suspect. I'm sorry for

388

him. Another victim of Novaris's vengeance."

"Poor Father Gerard . . ." Mardi shook her head. She touched Arno on the forearm. "Praise be that you weren't killed also."

"And you and Sir Evan, mistress." Arno eyed the other townsfolk. "They look like they need a little hand there. That's something I think I can still handle, if you can excuse me . . ."

As Arno walked his horse toward Daniel and the rest, Mardi turned to Evan. "The townsfolk! They can't possibly forget *everything*. I know I won't. What about my uncle and Drulane? The other men who died, like Father Gerard and the guards?"

"They will find explanations for their deaths. A wolf for your uncle and a bandit who perhaps had been up before the magistrate for Drulane and most of the others. Something *sensible* and without magic involved. The wizard was nothing if not thorough when he planned his part in this." The knight's tone was filled with bitterness.

Mardi pretended not to notice it. She could only imagine how many times Evan had witnessed such useless deaths. "Where will you go next?"

"Wallmyre. There are those there who might give Novaris succor, even though the island kingdom was an invaluable ally against him. Do you know anything of the place?"

"Very little. Rundin and Wallmyre have no relations and haven't for as long as I've been alive."

Evan's frown deepened. "No matter. Somewhere along the way I should find out more before I arrive there."

"But your horse! Evan! When you lost him—"

"The wizard accounted for that, too." The dour knight held up his left hand and revealed the dagger that he had given to Mardi . . . the same dagger that the teacher had lost.

"Centuros likes his games," Evan remarked. "His accursed games . . ."

Before she could ask what he meant, Evan brought the blade to his wrist. Mardi tried to knock the blade from his hand, but the knight managed to carve a small slit before she could reach the

389

weapon.

Turning his bleeding forearm down, Evan allowed two drops of blood to fall upon the ground. As it did, he muttered a few unintelligible words.

The dirt sizzled. Evan pulled Mardi away.

Flames the color of the moon burst skyward. Mardi glanced at the townsfolk and did not find it at all surprising that they appeared oblivious to this astounding event.

Then, a sound rose from the supernatural fire, a sound like that of a large animal awakening. A shadow blossomed.

For a brief moment, Mardi saw something that reminded her of the lupine shadows, a thing both human in form and yet something more. Her eyes widened as it looked back at her with eyes that bespoke of another creature.

Then, the shadow reshaped itself, taking on a particularly familiar outline.

The flames gave one last, great burst and then utterly died. In their place, the bone-pale steed, seemingly unaffected by his recent destruction, stared back at Evan and Mardi. The huge stallion was even saddled and packed, and among those items Mardi saw the helm that should have lain lost somewhere in the mound.

Evan momentarily looked shaken up and extremely pale, but the weakness passed again.

"Accursed spellcasters . . ." he muttered. "Accursed demons . . ."

The horse snorted at the knight, as if already impatient to be off. Evan left Mardi and mounted without a word.

She would not accept such a blunt farewell. "Evan! Wait! You may look well on the outside, but I can sense that you need more time to recuperate—"

"There *is* no time. I am not the only one on this quest . . . or have you not paid attention to Steppenwald's cane?"

Not certain what he meant by that, Mardi glanced down at it . . . or where it should have been. "Steppenwald! He—"

"He lives, yes. I knew it even before I saw that the cane had vanished. He is of Novaris's blood . . . and something more. He may be the key to everything."

"He may be your death!" Mardi silently cursed herself for dropping the cane, even though there had been no choice at that moment. "You can't face both of them alone—"

"Arno can help you get back to town," he interjected solemnly, "and your wounds are also already healing. There is nothing more with which you need to concern yourself."

She had not thought about her own injuries, but realized that she had not felt any pain for the last few minutes. Whether that was due to Evan or her link to the wizard was unclear and she cared not a whit at the moment. Evan was her overriding concern. "You don't need to go! There must be someone else . . ."

"There is no one else . . . and if I would ever hope to someday be free, I must find my old master and either kill him or die in the attempt." He looked on ahead. "With Valentin gone, with me gone . . . you will be safe again. I promise that."

"Evan—"

"Farewell, Mardina Sinclair"—Evan cut in again, his face a mask—"and thank you for so much."

"Evan! You can't just leave—"

The knight urged his mount on.

She stood stunned, watching as he rode off without another word and without even looking back. Anger, anxiety, and emotions that she could not yet accept vied for control. She looked at where Daniel, Arno, and the others dealt with the fire whose origins only she and the smith would ever remember.

Mardi came to a decision. Long gone were her romantic visions of a return to the age of chivalry and romance. Those dreams had been replaced with something more significant, a knowledge that there were times when, no matter what the danger, something *had* be done and someone had to take responsibility to do it. Though Evan had been forced to begin his quest, Mardi was certain that, despite his denials, some part of him sought to accomplish it for the right reasons. She knew she could not be mistaken. Not about Evan.

She glanced again at Arno . . . and the horse upon which he had ridden. A fresh, strong horse better suited for long journeys than her own.

Mardi ran toward the smith. As she did, she knew that it was not foolishness that urged her on, though Arno and Evan might have believed so. She knew somehow that the knight would need her if he hoped to succeed against his former master and Steppenwald. Evan could no longer do this alone. He needed not only whatever legacy—and power—she represented, but *her*.

And she needed him as well . . .

The damnable steed trotted along at a pace that irritated Evan Wytherling, not only because the trail was at last a viable one, but also because the knight wanted to be away from Pretor's Hill as swiftly as possible. However, the resurrected steed ignored his commands to increase his speed.

He did not understand why until he heard the hoofbeats behind him, hoofbeats growing louder and louder as the rider caught up.

"Damn you . . ." he quietly growled at the ashen beast.

The horse snorted.

He peered over his shoulder just as Mardi rode up beside him. She smiled briefly, but it was her eyes that spoke most, warning him that nothing could keep her from accompanying him. To those eyes, Evan found he could offer no argument. Indeed, at that moment, his heart pounded with more life than he could ever recall. It was both an uncomfortable, unsettling sensation . . . and a much coveted, welcome one.

"There's a port called Junard northeast of here. It will take about a week to reach it," Mardi finally said, breaking the silence. "I know a merchant there who did business with my uncle. He'll be able to help us secure passage to Wallmyre."

Evan managed to tear his gaze from her and looked ahead. After more than a minute, he nodded. "Junard it is, then."

Mardi smiled again and the two picked up their pace.

Keeping a deliberate distance behind, a brooding Arno—now astride the fine stallion that Daniel Taran would discover missing once the fires were dealt with—followed unnoticed.

END

About the Author

Richard A. Knaak is the *New York Times* and *USA Today* bestselling author of *The Legend of Huma, World of Warcraft: Dawn of the Aspects*, and nearly fifty other novels and numerous short stories, including works in such series as Warcraft, Diablo, Dragonlance, Age of Conan, and his own Dragonrealm saga. He has scripted a number of Warcraft manga with Tokyopop, such as the top-selling Sunwell trilogy, and has also written background material for games. His works have been published worldwide in many languages.

In addition to *Dragon Mound*, his most recent releases include *The Gryphon Mage* for his Legends of the Dragonrealm series. He is presently at work on several other projects, among them *Black City Saint* – the first in a new setting --- a new Pathfinder novel, and *The Horned Blade*, the final volume in his Dragonrealm trilogy, *The Turning War*.

Currently splitting his time between Chicago and Arkansas, he can be reached through his website: www.richardaknaak.com. While he is unable to respond to every e-mail, he does read them. Join his mailing list for e-announcements of upcoming releases and appearances. He is also on Facebook and Twitter.

27877018R00224

Made in the USA
San Bernardino, CA
04 March 2019